THE DESIRE LINE

Jane Cassidy

POOLBEG
CRIMSON

Published 2023 by Crimson
an imprint of Poolbeg Press Ltd.
123 Grange Hill, Baldoyle,
Dublin 13, Ireland
Email: poolbeg@poolbeg.com

ISBN 978-1-78199 -693-5

www.poolbeg.com

About the Author

A native of Mourne in Co. Down, Jane Cassidy now lives in Belfast. After graduating from Queen's University, Belfast, with a degree in English and French, and a post-grad in Education, she spent her twenties as a professional folk singer and has released 5 albums. Performing brought her into the world of the media where she freelanced as a presenter and researcher before joining the staff of BBC Northern Ireland where she produced and edited educational content. Now retired from her role in the BBC, Jane combines performing her beloved folk music with writing. This is her first novel though she has had 6 radio plays broadcast by BBC Radio 4 and has dramatised the Maeve Binchy novel *Firefly Summer* in 6 episodes for BBC Radio 4.

Acknowledgements

Heartfelt thanks to Paula Campbell at Poolbeg for believing in me and for her support throughout the whole process of bringing my first novel to print. Thanks also to my editor Gaye Shortland for her expert editing skills and astute insights.

Thanks to my husband Maurice whose steadfast love and support is the bedrock of my life. To my daughter Anna, my sister Moya and my daughter-in-law Maura, thank you for reading my early drafts and giving me much-needed feedback and encouragement. To my son Cormac for being the best son a parent could wish for. Thanks also to my great friend and fellow writer Marie Leprêtre who has been a loyal and enthusiastic cheerleader for my literary aspirations.

I am extremely grateful to Louise Phillips, Kate McCabe and Paul Brady for their generous endorsements. I was lucky enough to receive some expert mentoring from Louise Phillips, courtesy of Arts Council NI, which helped me greatly and which I followed up by attending one of her excellent writing courses. Thanks also to Damian Smyth of Arts Council NI who encouraged my writing.

Finally, thanks to my mum Joan who passed away in April 2023 at the age of 98 years, for passing on her love of literature to me and for feeding my reading habit when I was growing up.

Dedication

For my husband Maurice

Friday 24th October

Chapter 1

When Jeremiah McCabe walked into the clinic that day, he found Nora sitting in one of the grey, plastic chairs facing the door, deep in conversation with a woman who registered his arrival before his wife did. He immediately assumed the woman was a new psychiatrist he hadn't met and gave her only a cursory glance, his attention focused on his beloved Nora who to his relief was smiling. Her short, white hair had been trimmed and he was encouraged to see her wearing make-up, even if the crimson lipstick she'd chosen made her skin look unnaturally pale. She'd lost weight during the weeks in hospital – probably due to the absence of alcohol in her diet, he thought ruefully. Nora was small and fine-boned but what had made her exquisite in her twenties, now, thirty years later, rendered her terrifyingly fragile.

She jumped up, grabbed the lapels of his jacket, pulled him down towards her and kissed him lightly on the lips, then laughed into his face while using the pad of her thumb to wipe a smear of crimson from his mouth.

"Helena, this is my husband Jer," she said, turning to her companion.

When Helena stood up, he found himself eye to eye with her. There was a penetration to this woman's gaze that gave him a sudden glimpse of himself as she saw him – a man on the wrong side of middle age, a compact body with a softness around the abdomen, hair like an animal-pelt under moonlight, but eyes that were all human.

A classic belle-laide, which he'd always thought of as female beauty tending towards the masculine. Those strong features would be a gift to a portrait painter if they weren't betrayed by an air of uncertainty. Helena gave him a tentative smile then looked away, gathering her long hair over one shoulder in a gesture which might have been seductive if it hadn't been so self-conscious. She seemed surprised by him, making him wonder how Nora might describe her husband to a stranger. "Hopeless" was her favourite epithet when she was teasing him, to which she sometimes added "hapless and helpless" when in an expansive mood.

He looked at Nora who was busy putting on her coat. He nodded in satisfaction, for his wife seemed to be in a good place and if this woman Helena was the doctor he had to thank for that, he was keen not to be misrepresented.

He and Helena shook hands.

"I've promised Helena a lift," Nora announced, passing him a holdall.

He was momentarily taken aback. "Of course. You're more than welcome," he said quickly, wondering if he was wrong about Helena being a medic. She didn't appear to have any luggage so had to be a member of staff.

Outside, the autumn wind encircled them, and he couldn't help noticing the statuesque Helena was underdressed for the elements

2

in layers of pale linen which she made no attempt to control as they flapped and billowed around her. Her only defence against the gusts of rain was a silky, grey cardigan which hung from her long arms like gossamer and a long pale-green skirt which flapped in the wind. She slipped a cloth drawstring bag from her shoulder, hugged it close to her chest and climbed into the back seat of the car.

Nora sat in the front beside him and immediately began struggling to raise the seat.

"For God's sake, Jer, who've you had in this car?" she sighed. "Why can't people leave well enough alone?" She turned and gave Helena a fierce smile. "He works with all these peculiar media types."

The clinic lay on the outskirts of Belfast City and had once been a minor stately home with an extensive demesne which had now been lopped to a few acres. Some of the original copper beeches had survived and still guarded the curved drive. He turned on the wipers to clear his windscreen of the wet, tawny leaves left plastered on it by the wind. Reaching the gates, he asked Helena where she wanted to be dropped off.

"She lives in Islandmagee," supplied Nora before Helena had time to answer.

His heart plummeted. Islandmagee was half an hour in the wrong direction, and he realised there was no way he'd be able to get to his production office by lunchtime. He felt his stress levels beginning to rise, painfully reminded that life with Nora was never simple.

"You work at the clinic then, do you, Helena?"

"Gosh no, I'm – "

"No, no!" Nora interrupted. "Helena was a patient like me, but she's much better now, aren't you, darling?"

"I think so," she said, sounding uncertain.

He had a sudden fear their backseat passenger might be fleeing the clinic without the knowledge of her physicians, aided and abetted by Nora, who'd done the same herself on more than one occasion. Nora had a generous soul and a penchant for adopting strays, making him hope that Helena was a casual acquaintance rather than a project.

"You'll have to direct me, Helena," he said, careful to keep his voice neutral.

Nora turned and smiled in the general direction of the backseat. "I'm sure you can't wait to get back to your studio!"

He looked in the rear-view mirror and caught a startled look from Helena. "You're an artist?" he said, grateful for some clue about her background. "Are you a painter or . . . ?"

"A painter."

"I wish you'd seen her wonderful sketching in our art sessions, Jer. She should've been giving the class."

He glanced in the mirror again and saw with approval that Helena's face relaxed when she looked at Nora. His wife tended to wear out friendships quickly and he was glad she'd found a kindred spirit, adding a silent prayer she was no more than that.

Nora chattered on gaily while Helena said very little.

They left the motorway where normal life hummed and hurried, and began weaving their way towards the coast. It was years since he'd been in Islandmagee and when they entered the narrow peninsula it felt like going back in time.

"How long have you lived here?" he asked.

"Oh, not very long," she said, her voice trailing off.

Nora put her hand on his arm, and he understood that he shouldn't press Helena for any more information. He followed the undulating road, running up the centre of the peninsula, imagining it as the skeleton of a giant, fossilised creature which had once taken refuge at the margin of land and sea and expired there – knots of petrified spine pushing up from under the black, tarred surface of the road. Cloud shadows flitted across the fields, evidence of a battle going on between fire and water high above. Rain fell suddenly out of a cold sky and hammered on the roof of the car, water flowing over the road like mercury and gurgling in the drains and ditches. A ragged tear in the clouds widened and the sun's eagle eye locked onto them, moving across the glittering landscape. He tilted the visor against the sun-dazzle and hugged his side of the road to let a tractor towing a trailer of wild-eyed sheep blunder past.

They could now see all the way to the port of Larne with the deeper blue of the sea challenging the rip in the sky. Helena had said very little during the drive but now she leaned forward and offered detailed directions. He felt her warm breath on his ear each time she spoke, guiding him through a maze of narrowing roads, until she urged him to slow down and execute an acute right turn into a lane, its centre tufted with grass. Navigating the rough surface, he swerved in a vain attempt to avoid a large puddle, making the car lurch.

"Sorry, I shouldn't have dragged you up here," she said, sounding embarrassed.

"It's an adventure, isn't it, Jer?" Nora assured her brightly. Without waiting for him to agree, she swept on, "I'm ready for an adventure. It was so dull in there."

He wondered if Nora was on the way up or on the way down. Either way, all would soon be revealed, he thought with a twinge of resentment, which made him press too hard on the accelerator, making the engine growl in protest and the wheels spin and slither.

Nora gave a little scream. "*Jer, take it easy!*"

"Sorry," he said more gruffly than he intended.

He crawled up the lane between overgrown hedges which brushed the sides of the car, curious about how Helena would have got herself home without Nora's intervention. The car crested a rise and he jumped on the brake, skidding down a steep slope and coming to a halt inches away from a metal gate which barred their way.

"What on earth?" Helena gasped. "Who put this here?"

Jer and Nora turned to see her staring at the gate with a horrified expression.

"Wasn't it here when you last – ?" Nora began.

"There was never a gate here!"

They sat in silence studying the obstacle, which was the kind of galvanised, metal, field-gate common to the Ulster countryside. It doesn't look new, he was thinking. He noted that the tall hedges on either side of the lane ended at the gate, which was slung from two, thick, wooden posts. Fencing stretched away from each upright, obviously delineating a boundary. On the far side of the gate lay a sea of mud and he could see no clear sign of a continuation of the lane.

"Who owns the land?" he asked, keen to break the silence.

Helena was taking fast, shallow breaths. "I don't know."

He leaned his elbow on the window frame and rubbed his hand across his mouth. What had Nora landed him with? This woman was obviously not fit to be discharged on her own. He heard the car door open behind him.

"*Helena, wait!*" Nora shouted, scrambling out of the car after her friend.

Helena stumbled to the gate and shook the large padlock

securing it. Mercifully the rain had ceased, but a spiteful gust of wind lifted her hair which was coiled over her shoulder and splayed it across her back. She hoisted up her skirt and started climbing over the gate. He got out of the car, and joined Nora, both watching in dismay as Helena hurried away from them.

"She's not well, Nora," he whispered, putting an arm around her shoulders.

He cursed himself inwardly for agreeing to give Helena a lift but reasoned that it would have upset Nora if he'd refused. She'd have probably done something daft like call a taxi to take Helena and herself to Islandmagee. At least he was here.

"She must have mistaken the lane. Maybe her medication's making her confused," he suggested gently.

"We need to help her, Jer, but I can't go in there – my boots would get ruined."

He looked down at her suede boots and grinned at her. "Listen, you stay in the car and keep warm, and I'll go and get her."

"What would I do without you?"

"Ruin your boots?" he retorted, earning a playful punch on the arm.

Nora got back into the car and, as he closed the door safely on her, he looked up to see a front of pewter-coloured cloud advancing from the west, trailing a curtain of paler grey which he knew was heavy rain. How long till it reached them, he wondered.

Helena had now disappeared. Grasping the cold bars of the gate, he was assailed by a childhood memory of being warned about catching lockjaw from old gates. He climbed awkwardly over the barrier and felt his shoes sink into the glar of cow-manure and muddy water on the other side. He gave Nora a reassuring wave then tramped in the direction Helena had taken. Was there a track? He found it hard to tell, since the land was churned up by the cattle grazing nearby, a few of which eyed him suspiciously. He walked up an incline to a ridge from where he was able to survey the hillside beyond.

From where he stood, the land sloped away to a small, wooded area which lay between him and what he guessed were sea-cliffs. He caught sight of a flutter of pale cloth between the trees and set off in that direction. Passing through the copse, he saw that it had probably lain undisturbed for centuries. The trees were gnarled and stunted by the salty, onshore wind and the large, glacial boulders were velveted with moss. The branches were almost bare, with only a few flame-coloured leaves still clinging to the lower limbs. He stopped for a moment to catch his breath and looked over his shoulder, uneasy at leaving Nora alone, then plunged on, emerging from the trees to see Helena some distance away, sitting in a crumpled heap on the muddy ground. He straightened his shoulders and approached her.

"I know you'll think I'm mad, but our house was here," she said hoarsely, making a sweeping gesture. "Everything's gone!" Her face was chalky-white and her eyes wide with shock.

Baffled, he scanned the empty space, seeing no sign of a house. He squatted beside her. "Helena, is it possible we've – taken the wrong turning?"

He watched doubt flood her face. She closed her eyes for a moment and took a deep breath, letting it out in a shuddering sigh. He stood up to ease his aching thighs and stretched out his hand which she grasped to pull herself up, then neglected to relinquish. She looked around frantically, as if trying to get her bearings. The area where they were standing was bordered on three sides by trees and brambles, and on the other gave way to a meadow which ran down to a wide bank of gorse. Beyond that were cliffs and the sea. A wonderful site for a house, he thought, gently pulling his hand away, causing Helena to sway and almost fall.

She took a few unsteady steps away from him, the wind tugging at her clothes, hair blowing around her head. Suddenly she howled like an animal in pain and started to sob. He felt a surge of panic. How was he ever to get this distraught woman back to the car without help? He considered ringing an ambulance but what could he possibly say to summon medics to this isolated spot? He needed to get a grip.

She sank down on her hunkers, careless of her pale skirt, and dug her fingers into the mud as if she might be able to unearth the house she had expected to find there.

Was it possible there'd been a house in this place? He thought of the old folksong 'The May Morning Dew' and the line about the singer's childhood home being but a stone on a stone. Here there wasn't even a stone on a stone, just mud, grass and a bitter wind. At that moment the sun seemed to lose patience with them and closed its eye, stealing all colour from the scene.

He felt a spit sting his face. He glanced up at the leaden sky and back at Helena who had risen and was using the hem of her skirt to wipe the dirt off something she'd found in the mud which she now held out to him. He kept his hands in his pockets and noted that she seemed disappointed that he was unwilling to take the object from her. To placate her, he frowned in concentration and bent down, pretending to puzzle over what appeared to be a fragment of blue-and-yellow pottery.

"It's from one of my Italian bowls." She stroked its muddy

surface with her index finger. He straightened up and the incredulity she saw in his face made the light in hers flicker and die. "I know it must be hard to believe," she said despairingly, "but our house was here. I can see you don't believe me." Her voice broke.

"I'm just worried about Nora," he said, relieved to see that this registered with her.

She nodded, letting him take her arm and shepherd her back towards the trees. Before they reached them, she broke away from him and made off to the right and he realised she was intent on skirting around the wood. Reluctantly he followed through long, wet grass. She stopped, turned and looked back, her eyes ranging to and fro.

"The house was there," she said. "I sat at this very spot and painted it many times. Can't you see the way the trees sheltered it? I know the shape of every one of those branches."

He looked back and saw that the trees did seem to be leaning towards the empty space but thought it might have more to do with the prevailing wind than any human intervention. He had a strong visual imagination but was wary of the power of suggestion.

Strands of hair were blowing across Helena's face and her teeth were bared. She returned his stare and he shivered, seeing madness there as well as grief.

The heavens opened and the rain finally drove her back to the car. By the time they reached the gate, they were both soaked through, as was Nora, who was standing waiting for them, with a pinched, frightened face. He was tempted to drive straight to the clinic to hand Helena back but, since they were all cold and wet, he gave in to Nora's entreaties to go home and they drove to Belfast through veils of rain, the car steamy with the smell of mud and smothered hysteria.

Chapter 2

Jer put the key into the lock of his front door and was suddenly glad he and Nora weren't on their own. The last time he'd brought her home from the clinic, he'd rushed into his study to take a call and emerged later to find her sitting on the bottom stair, still wearing her coat.

"What do I usually do?" she'd asked him.

Today she was fully in charge and had reverted to her mothering role, shooing Helena upstairs for a hot bath. He'd remembered to leave the central heating on, and the house was comfortingly warm. It was a typical Belfast Edwardian red-brick house, with a large garden, which he and Nora had bought for a song during the Northern Ireland Troubles. After a flurry of improvements when they moved in, their baby Liam's death had brought an end to any interest either of them had in décor, and the increasingly cluttered rooms were now soiled and faded.

He went into his study and closed the door, determined to ring the clinic without delay. A faint smell of whiskey lingered in the air from an empty, cut-glass tumbler he'd been using the evening before. It was balanced precariously on top of a pile of books beside a worn, brown-leather armchair in the bay window, his favourite perch. He sat down at his antique roll-top desk which was flanked by floor-to-ceiling bookcases stuffed with books. An old, upright piano filled the wall behind him, and any remaining wall-space was covered in paintings and an assortment of stringed instruments.

He asked to speak to Nora's consultant, the only senior member of staff he knew, and was told she was unavailable. After some persuasion he was put through to a nurse and described what had happened with Helena.

"Can I bring her back to the ward this afternoon?"

"I'm sorry, Mr. McCabe. Once a patient has been discharged, she'd need to be referred by her GP. If the situation is an emergency, you should take her to your nearest A&E."

He was disconcerted. It seemed that Helena was now his responsibility. He thought quickly before the nurse rang off.

"Would you mind giving me her address? I'm hoping there's a postcode I could check to make sure she took us to the right place."

"I'm sorry. We can't give out information like that."

"I see – thanks," he said through gritted teeth.

He rotated his chair in frustration and stared out the bay window at the rain which was fairly pelting down. He could hear Nora's voice upstairs, talking in the higher register he associated with the early years of their family life, when she had excelled at jollying their children Eimear and Rory to bed.

He saw there were a couple of missed calls from the office. There had been a time, not so long ago when his first call would have been to his co-director Stella, but these days he was more inclined to ring his young producer Rosie, reluctant to betray his domestic challenges to the former. Leaning back in the chair, he gazed at the ceiling, tracking the tell-tale creaking as Nora and Helena moved around the master bedroom.

He called Rosie.

"Jer, where've you been? Stella has been doing her nut. You've a meeting or something."

He suppressed a groan. "I've been looking for a house in Islandmagee."

"You and Nora are splitting up?"

"What? No, of course not." What on earth had Stella been saying, let alone thinking? "Rosie, do you think it's possible for a house to be cleared off the face of the earth while the owner is away?"

"Seriously? Suppose depends how long they were away."

"I'm not sure, a couple of months maybe."

"Theoretically possible then. So this house you went hunting for eluded you?"

Rosie was in her early twenties and did a great line in mild exasperation when conversing with anyone over thirty. He enjoyed her irreverence.

"It was the strangest thing. We got to the place, and the person we were with recognised the lane and the trees, but where she expected the house to be was a big empty space."

"Wow! That's weird." She paused. "Was she having you on?"

"Possibly, but she was very convincing."

"Well, if there had been a house, surely there'd be rubble or signs of a garden or something? What about foundations, wouldn't they still be there, even if it'd been demolished?"

"Good point. There was a muddy area, but that could be due to the cattle."

"This is a farm?"

"Not sure who owns the beasts, but I don't think my friend does."

"Are you sure you were in the right place? One Ulster hillside looks much like another."

"I know, that's my worry, but she's an artist and she recognised the shape of the trees around the site. She's painted them many times apparently."

"Then all you have to do is find one of her paintings of the house."

"Ah, but her studio was in the house that's disappeared."

"Blimey, where do you find them?"

He was tempted to say "in the asylum", but restrained himself.

"Has she sold any paintings or exhibited anywhere?"

"Must find out."

"Maybe there's something online. There'd be records of houses for rates, electricity and stuff. Did you ask any locals?"

"No, didn't get a chance. Look, thanks – all great ideas. How did the shoot go?"

His small team were currently working on a quirky TV series for the BBC, producing amusing shorts showing people behaving antisocially.

"Really well! We were cursing the rain, but it made it more poignant! There's nothing sadder than watching a person in a wheelchair in the rain, struggling to get back to their car, only to find some shithead has parked too close to it and they can't get in."

"Can't wait to see the footage."

"We're in the Sugarhouse drying out."

"So I can hear," he said, smiling.

"Come and join us."

"Would love to, but I need to sort things out here."

"With the homeless artist?"

He ended the call, trying not to imagine how she would report this call to her young sidekicks, Hugh and Amy, never mind Stella.

He opened his study door to see Nora and Helena coming down the stairs, the latter now dressed in a grey tracksuit of his, which looked better on her than it ever had on him. Her hair was wet, and she'd scraped it away from her face into a tight bun. Without its softening effect, her face looked older and more angular. He decided she must be around forty. The muscles around her eyes were tensed.

"Helena, do you know your postcode by any chance?" he said, causing her to stand stock-still in the hall, looking panicked. "It's okay," he said quickly, putting his hands on her upper arms, "it was just a thought."

"We can talk about all that later," said Nora breezily, steering Helena towards the kitchen.

He noticed Helena's cloth bag on the hallstand and on an impulse took it with him into his study and closed the door. He needed to find out more about her, fast. Feeling guilty for what he was about to do, he granted himself absolution, citing his concern for Nora's welfare to the Almighty, then unceremoniously upended the contents of the shoulder-bag onto his desk. He looked doubtfully at what appeared to be Helena's only worldly possessions.

There was a pack of medication, a green silk scarf, a purple hairbrush and a collection of pencils, all of which he quickly chucked back in the bag. A silver earring in the shape of a seahorse caught his eye, and he held it up to the light before squirreling it away in the depths of the bag, along with the fragment of blue-and-yellow pottery she'd found earlier. There were umpteen tissues, which he gathered and stuffed back in. He examined a bunch of keys attached to an enamel keyring, which included two Yale keys, which might belong to a front and back door, a larger iron key, and a car-key. Helena had a car! A slim, embroidered wallet yielded thirty pounds in notes, a few coins, a book of stamps and a debit card. He examined the card, pleased to find one detail. Her full name was Ms. Helena Santoro.

Nora called him from the kitchen, and he slipped the wallet back into the bag, opened the door and responded, buying himself another minute. He picked up a squat candle and a posy of what looked like dried herbs and replaced them in the bag. The last item was a brown envelope, which he guessed was her discharge letter. Mercifully it wasn't sealed, but he resisted reading anything other than her address: *Carraig na Rón, Mullaghboy, Islandmagee.* There was no house number or postcode.

Nora called him again and he replaced the bag on the hallstand before joining the two women in the kitchen where Helena was seated at the long, battered pine table staring out at the rain.

Nora carried bowls of steaming tomato soup to the table.

"These are the Breton bowls I told you about, Helena. I've given you Eimear's. You see each one has a different name."

He watched their guest glance down at the pretty bowl and felt sorry for her. The last thing the unfortunate woman needed was Nora's brittle gaiety.

"I hope you're feeling a bit better now," he said to her quietly.

She looked at him gratefully and nodded. "You're both very kind."

"Thanks for the soup, Nora – we all need warming up," he said, spreading a thick layer of butter on a chunk of bread. "I'd love to see some of your paintings, Helena."

"She had an exhibition in the Cathedral Quarter recently," Nora said proudly, as if Helena were her child.

"I was part of an exhibition of paintings by an Artist Collective based there."

"Would any of your paintings of the house have been exhibited or sold?" he said.

There was an awkward silence and she set down her spoon.

"Helena thinks you don't believe there was a house there," Nora said reproachfully.

He looked down at the surface of his soup, where a crumb from Nora's mouth had landed.

"I'm just worried we were in the wrong place."

"I'm sorry to have got you involved in all this," Helena said, her voice shaking.

"Don't mind him. It's his job that makes him question everything. He's Doubting Thomas personified." Nora stroked her friend's arm.

"It's not fair to be imposing on you but I don't really have any friends here." She sounded on the verge of tears.

Nora gave him a meaningful look. "She only came to Northern Ireland a few months ago."

"And where were you before that?"

"*Jer!*" Nora snapped. "Can't you just eat your bloody soup and stop asking questions for five minutes?"

He stirred his soup, imagining a thin trail of saliva mixed into it.

"I was living in Skye for a couple of years before I came here in April," Helena offered, looking embarrassed. "That's where I met Malachy."

Jer chewed on a mouthful of bread and hoped said Malachy might be a partner who would turn up and claim her shortly.

Nora read his thoughts. "Malachy passed away recently."

He swallowed his bread with difficulty. "I'm very sorry to hear that, Helena."

"Nora, I don't know that for sure," Helena said.

Jer looked from one woman to the other, baffled.

His mobile rang in his pocket, and he escaped back to his study with relief.

Returning to the kitchen later, he found Nora sitting at the table, waiting for him.

"I told her to have a lie-down. The woman's exhausted."

"Nora —"

"I know what you're going to say. This is the opposite of what I need when I'm just out of hospital."

Disarmed by her self-awareness, he sat down facing her.

She leaned towards him and whispered, "In a way I'd love to drive back to the clinic and leave her to her own devices, but I know I'd be haunted by her if I did."

He frowned.

"No – *haunted* is the wrong word," she went on. "I'd be worried about her. She's a lovely person, Jer. You'll like her when you get to know her."

His heart sank. He was obviously fated to become better acquainted with Helena. He took a deep breath, "You're not —"

"No, don't be silly." She looked away, embarrassed.

They sat in silence for a moment, avoiding each other's eyes, Jer struggling to master his emotions. He felt stung by the injustice of

Nora characterising his fears as silly when she'd once left him for a woman and carried on a short-lived, lesbian affair which had devastated him. The fallout from her sexual experiment was still a pollutant in their lives, not least because it had precipitated an affair between him and Stella, something he now deeply regretted.

Determined not to have a row on her first evening home, he muttered, "Okay, what do you actually know about her?"

"She's been through an awful lot, Jer. It's only a couple of months since she was found unconscious on a beach and her partner had disappeared."

He sat back. "How come she was unconscious? Did he attack her and then take off?"

Nora shrugged and shook her head. "She says he'd never have hurt her but it sounds as if the police think he tried to kill her and then took his own life. Presumably by drowning."

"*Wow!*" said Jer.

"But she won't hear a bad word spoken about him. She says he'd never have committed suicide. He was a wild swimmer though."

"Sorry? A wild swimmer?"

"Apparently he liked to go swimming in open water, in wild places."

"What then? She thinks he went for a swim and drowned by accident?"

"*Em*, well, no. Apparently he never went swimming on his own and it seems the beach was dangerous. He was part of some swimming club and they always swim in a group."

"What does she say happened? "

"That's the thing, Jer. She can't remember. The police came and questioned her but I think the doctor called a halt because she was so traumatised. Maybe they'll want to question her again now she's been discharged."

"His body hasn't been found?"

"No. Maybe if it's washed up somewhere she'll be able to accept that he's dead because at the moment she doesn't."

"Where does she think he is if he's not out there in the sea?"

Nora shrugged and looked out the window. He reached across the table and put his hand over hers, making her turn back to him.

"I've tried to comfort her and befriend her, Jer, but now this business with the house . . . she thinks she's bewitched."

He lifted his hands in mock revolt. "Nora, her mind has been unhinged by whatever has happened. I'm sure we'll discover where she was living in due course. She must've taken us to the wrong place today for I couldn't see any sign there'd ever been a house there."

"But she found a piece of her Italian bowl. She showed it to me."

"She could've picked up anything and claimed that, or even had it in her pocket all along."

"But why would she do such a thing?" She chewed her thumbnail.

"To convince us. To get our sympathy. You mustn't take on the burden of her confusion, love. We'll run her back to the clinic tomorrow. I don't care what they say, they can't discharge someone who's homeless. The social workers will find out where she lives or, if she has nowhere to go, they'll sort out accommodation for her."

"But she'll be completely alone, Jer. What would've become of me if I'd been alone when Liam died?"

His throat constricted and he realised with a pang that this was the first time in several years that Nora had been able to utter Liam's name. Helena's grief had opened something up in her. Whether for better or worse only time would tell.

"I want her to stay here until she's stronger. You'll be able to find out what happened to her home, won't you? She couldn't wait to get back to it. All her memories of Malachy are there, and her paintings. Could you imagine if you came back one day, and this house was gone?"

He had a flashback to the day at work when he'd got the call about the accident. The bricks and mortar of their house might still have been intact, but they'd lost their baby boy, and family life had never been the same again.

"Okay, love, I'll do my best to help but you need to let me ask her some questions. I promise I'll be gentle."

"I feel very protective of her."

"And I feel very protective of you. If this starts to make you ill again . . ."

"Even if it does, it's something I need to do."

Chapter 3

When Jer and Stella had set up Indigo Productions, they'd rented the second floor of a dilapidated, former linen warehouse in a shabby, neglected corner of Belfast's city centre. With the advent of peace on the city streets and a certain level of prosperity, the city council had seen fit to dignify the area with the title Belfast's Cathedral Quarter, in deference to nearby Saint Anne's. The christening seemed to have bestowed, not so much a state of grace as a state of trendiness on this, the oldest part of the city, and it was now buzzing with new pubs and restaurants.

Climbing the steep, concrete stairs to his office that afternoon, Jer remembered the feeling of creative freedom he and Stella had shared when they set up production here, looping transparent bunting from one iron pillar to another in protest against Belfast's political forest of flags. He pushed open the door and glanced around the room, to see his four members of staff were present. The office was furnished with castoffs, and there were always more desks than people at Indigo Productions, an imbalance he kept meaning to rectify by getting rid of some desks.

He heard the rhythmical clatter of an invisible loom and registered that today's office soundscape was a weaving-shed. In the early days, he'd suggested using his library of sound-effects tapes to create a different atmosphere each day in their silent office. Stella had embraced the notion with alacrity and, a decade later was still dedicated to it while he would gladly have let it slide.

On one side of the room, Rosie was holding sway over Hugh and Amy, and she acknowledged his arrival with an airy wave and a marginal reduction in the volume of her voice. The three of them were not long out of academia and keen to forge careers in the media. Of the three, Rosie was the dominant personality. Noisy and colourful, she brought an energy to Indigo which Jer found stimulating. She was larger than life in every way with a wide face, big eyes and full lips, though any pretensions she might have had to beauty were compromised by a prominent, square jaw. In contrast, Amy's face was pretty in a symmetrical way, her tidy features framed by long, dark, straight hair which was cleanly parted from the centre of her smooth forehead. She was a reserved girl who was too shy to promote her physical assets while Rosie made the most of hers, monopolising any available male attention. He wondered occasionally if either of the girls was sexually involved with Hugh. He glanced over at the young man who was short and overweight, with statement glasses that overwhelmed his fleshy face, and decided once again that it was unlikely.

The only other human being in the office had been on the planet almost as long as he had. Stella looked at him over the rim of her glasses and then took them off. These days they were attached to her by a gold lamé cord, so she could let them lie on her bosom instead of jamming them into her abundant, curly hair the way she used to do. He missed Stella's hair. It had made him happy to look at it of a morning. She still had hair, but her mass of black curls was now salt and pepper, and short. He couldn't help feeling she'd cut it to punish him for wasting the prime of her life. In the absence of hair, she'd taken to wearing dangly earrings, which he thought looked incongruous with the chunky knits her mother provided to ward off the office draughts.

Rosie gave him a wry smile. "Any luck finding that missing house?"

He immediately wished he hadn't confided in her. He frowned and turned away.

"Harry's pulled a fast one again," Stella said quickly.

Harry was a former protégé of Jer's who now ran his own production company round the corner from Indigo and seemed intent on besting Jer at every opportunity.

"What's he done now?"

"Poached the crew we'd booked for next week."

"Hang on, if we had them booked – "

"Harry gazumped us and I hadn't the heart to hold them to their booking with us."

"What's he offered them?"

"I don't know but more, obviously." She sighed. "Do you think I should've played hard-ball?"

"No, of course not, Stell." She looked down and he immediately regretted using the more intimate nickname. "Is anyone else available?"

"I'll ring round."

"Thanks. We'll live to fight another day."

"Lose another day, you mean." She put her glasses on again, ending the interchange.

Rosie, Amy and Hugh had scattered to their computers like birds settling on a wire. They often chose to work standing at their screens, having inveigled Jer into investing in adjustable stands. All Jer could think of was an amusement arcade. He threaded his way to his own desk and sat down, kneading his temples against the throb of electronic music from their side of the office which was doing battle with the creak of the loom and thwack of the shuttle. Eyeing the layers of neglected paperwork currently obscuring his lovely mahogany desk, he decided it was high time to impose some order on the chaos. He pulled a pile of unopened mail towards him, hoping it might be quickly disposed of to create a little space for thinking. He urgently needed to generate more zany ideas for the *Thoughtless* TV series which was paying all their salaries, all too aware that the humour he'd injected into the early episodes was increasingly lacking and the whole project was curdling into something lumpy and sour.

The first two envelopes he tore open were bills, which depressed him and made him wish he'd tackled his emails first. He was tempted to make a cup of coffee, but powered on through the pile, launching several items of junk mail in the direction of the bin.

He was feeling more productive by the time he unsealed a small, padded envelope and applied pressure to the side-seams to open it. He peered inside but could see no paper contents reflecting the light so poked three fingers into the opening, immediately withdrawing them. He took a clean sheet of paper from the printer and slid the contents of the envelope onto the virgin page. It was a thin plait of auburn hair, about four inches long and tied at one end with a brown, rubber band. His breath caught in his chest and bile scalded his throat.

He looked over at Rosie who was talking animatedly on her mobile and, no doubt sensing he was about to summon her, she turned her back on him. At that moment Stella emerged from their little kitchen carrying a mug and met his eye with a mixture of guilt and half-hearted defiance, both aware that in the past she wouldn't have dreamt of making a cup of coffee without including him. She set the mug down on her desk with an unsteady hand, spilling some coffee in the process. He looked back towards Rosie, Hugh and Amy who were preparing to go out on a shoot and imagined their collective gasps if he drew attention to the plait. One of them would be sure to take a photo and share it with the world on social media.

The idea of taking a photo was a useful one. He set the envelope, address side up, beside the sheet of paper and took a couple of shots with his mobile, then slid the plait back into the envelope and put it in his jacket pocket.

He felt like bolting from the office but forced himself to pause long enough to wish the team well with the afternoon's endeavour, which involved filming dog-walkers collecting the faeces of their pets in the requisite, black, plastic bags and depositing them in the gutter or in an adjacent hedge. On his way out he heard Rosie caution the other two that if they couldn't make it, they'd have to fake it.

At the bottom of the concrete stairs, which Rosie had painted in multicoloured stripes, he stopped in the doorway to light up. Raindrops were staining the cobbles of Sugarhouse Lane and he wished he'd brought his Barbour but couldn't face running the gauntlet of the office again to fetch it. He sucked in a lungful of acrid smoke and rang Trix Maidstone.

"TV Commissioning," came the clipped voice of Trix's personal assistant.

"Hi, Carol, it's Jer McCabe here. I need to speak to Trix."

"She's in a meeting and can't possibly be disturbed."

"This is urgent."

"If you'd like to tell me what's so urgent, I can maybe go and whisper in her ear."

Lifting the cigarette to his lips he crushed it slightly with his fingers, such was his irritation at her withering tone. "What time will she be out of the meeting?"

"Hard to say. You know how it goes. She's back-to-back all day."

"Has Trix changed her . . . hair at all recently?"

"I beg your pardon?"

"I mean her hairstyle. Has she changed it recently?"

"What? No . . . I mean, what are you talking about?"

He breathed out.

"There's a slot at eight thirty on Monday morning, but that's the soonest I can fit you in."

"I'll text her."

"She doesn't –"

He rang off, his heart thumping with annoyance. He put the cigarette between his lips and texted: **Threat against u in post. C u Deane's 10 mins.**

Discarding the remains of his cigarette, he set off at a brisk pace through the narrow streets, assailed by the smell of beer from the doorways of yuppie pubs and restaurants. When he and Stella had set up shop here, rents had been at rock-bottom but now that it was considered cool, rents were rising, and he knew it was only a matter of time before Indigo would be forced to relocate to somewhere cheaper and duller.

He walked quickly, his stress levels rising the nearer he got to the BBC. How would Trix react to this personal threat? She might want to contact the police but, then again, he knew he wasn't the only journalist who had an uneasy relationship with the local cops. Stop catastrophising, Jer, he castigated himself, suspecting she'd probably just shrug it off and toss the envelope to BBC Security. A commissioning editor like her must have to deal with a lot of heavy stuff, he reasoned, particularly since her latest boss was a blow-in from London, who understood nothing of the vagaries of life in Northern Ireland and cared less. He folded his lapels across his chest, in a vain attempt to protect himself from the rain. His *Thoughtless* series had been the subject of a steady flow of complaints from BBC viewers for weeks now, but there was something so visceral about human hair that it might call into question the wisdom of continuing to broadcast it.

He entered the warmth of Deane's café with relief. He bought an Americano and sat far away from the windows with his back to the wall. He checked his phone. No response yet from Trix. Maybe she wouldn't show. He sat sipping the bitter coffee, his energy draining away. Why had he chosen to meet her in Deane's, the place where, years before, he'd been given the news that his BBC career was over? He remembered the cowardice of his boss Simon, who'd seated them both on high stools by the window, presumably making it less likely that Jer would weep or punch him. It had been five o'clock and every BBC staffer who passed by had looked in their direction. He'd been treated to a glass of wine, as if it would console him for the havoc being wreaked on his life and career. Younger than Jer, and a bluffer who'd been promoted far beyond his capabilities, Simon had trailed his anglicised Ulster accent and dubious reputation home to Belfast and proceeded to demonstrate his operational talents by getting rid of the most creative people in his immediate vicinity.

Simon's disembodied, false smile floated like a reflection in the café window, making Jer wince, remembering his own reaction which had been hurt and sadness rather than anger. He'd forgiven the younger man in that moment. He'd even embraced him, for God's sake. In the months and years that followed, he'd discovered that forgiveness is not a finite act, but a tide that ebbs and flows. It was cold comfort that the brave Simon managed to thoroughly disgrace himself and get bucked out of the BBC within the year, but too late for Jer, who had already been exiled to the insecure world of independent production, with only Stella for company.

Trix materialised at the counter. She ordered a double expresso, before slipping her skeletal body into the seat opposite him, her eyes bright and hard, her lips pursed. She was wearing high-heeled, black boots and a short, black trench coat which she didn't bother to unbutton, signalling her intention to keep the meeting short.

"This better be good!" she said by way of greeting.

He masked his nervous swallow by groping in his pocket for the envelope.

Her eyes narrowed and she reached out to take it, but he pulled it back.

"Hang on a second. Don't touch it, Trix. The police may need to get DNA from it."

He went to the counter and returned with a plate.

"God, it's not a finger or something, is it?" She leaned back in her chair in disgust, looking round to see if they were being observed.

He carefully slid the hair out of the envelope onto the plate.

Trix's hand went to her mouth as she stared at the lock of hair. She bent her head, letting her hand creep around the back of her neck. She wore her hair very short but sported a little plait at the nape of her neck which he imagined she saw as representing the more creative side of her nature which she otherwise kept firmly in check.

"So it's not yours."

She shook her head. "It's sick," she muttered, covering the trembling of her mouth with the back of her fingers. "Is there a message with it?"

"No, nothing."

"I assume it's another protest vote against *Thoughtless*?"

"Well, that's what connects us," he said. "Your or something very like your little plait is sent to my office – "

"Addressed to you?"

He handed her the envelope which she scanned, turned over and returned without comment.

"Has the BBC had any more complaints?" he asked.

"Lots." She shrugged. "We always knew it would be controversial. You can't produce something this edgy without getting a lot of conflicting reactions."

Jer's series was a satirical response to the BBC's worthy, long-running *Thoughtful* series which trumpeted good works. After a few months, Indigo's irreverent romp had become a bit of a cult online with younger people but was attracting increasingly virulent protests from Northern Ireland's religious right.

His shoulders sagged, recognising a form of words she'd honed and polished for the boardroom. He knew she was proud of the originality of the series, but recently he sensed she was using it as a weapon in one of her professional vendettas.

"What's Cliff's take on it?" Cliff was Trix's current boss who'd been parachuted in from BBC London over her head.

"He hates it with a passion." She gave a sly smile. "He has all the local God-freaks baying for his blood. His London coffee-shop formation didn't prepare him for dealing with Ulster fundamentalist Christians in full cry."

He could hear the reverberation of her treacherous conversations with fellow execs and almost felt sorry for Cliff. "Will he axe it?"

"If he does, it'll make him look like a complete wimp."

He took a slug of coffee, feeling like a small mammal living in the T. Rex enclosure.

"We can't let ourselves be derailed by a silly stunt like this. There's no message, so no actual threat. You should grow a little plait in solidarity with me, don't you think?" She gave a dry laugh.

"That might take a while."

"We're going to see out the year, Jer, come hell or high water."

This was good news for Indigo, and he tried to dwell on the positive and ignore the hollow feeling in his stomach.

"What are you going to do with it?" she asked, pushing the plate away with distaste.

"Me? I thought you'd want to show it to Security or something?"

"You should take it to the police." She lifted her expresso and took a sip.

He looked at the offending plait and saw that some of the strands were beginning to unravel at the untied end. "They'd haul me in for questioning. Don't you think it'd be better coming from you?"

There was a moan under the table and she fished her mobile from her pocket and spooled through numerous messages.

"It's obviously a threat against you," he insisted.

"It was sent to *your* office," she said, without taking her eyes off the phone. "I'll certainly mention it to the Security guys . . . and Policy. You're delivering another ten eps at the end of the month, aren't you? All on schedule, I hope?"

"Pretty much."

"Pretty much?" She picked up his phrase like a barrister preparing to entrap a defendant.

"We're on schedule."

"That's what I like to hear."

She drained her cup and left without another word, the plait lying on the plate like a rejected love token, her own plait snug at the nape of her neck. He stared after her. She'd already forgotten him, hurrying to her next meeting, her next issue. What had he expected her to do – take this horrible article off his hands and get the lumbering BBC machine to creak into action to protect them both? He should have known better. He was on his own, prey to all the crazies, while she was safe behind her castle walls.

Chapter 4

Jer knew he should head home to Nora and their strange houseguest but kept putting off the evil hour, working late into the evening. In the end it was after ten by the time he got home and walked into a silent house. They must both be in bed, he thought, relieved to be spared an evening of futile conjecture about the fate of Helena's partner Malachy and the mysterious house. He poured himself a glass of wine, went to his study and sat down at his computer.

A little rationality and the internet should do the trick, he decided, googling the address he'd found in Helena's bag. He was rewarded with an offer to translate *Carraig na Rón*, which he discovered meant "*Seal Rock*". The other links were to tourist websites featuring Islandmagee. If the house was a figment of Helena's imagination, was it possible this man Malachy might also be imaginary, the product of a troubled mind? A few seconds later, he felt ashamed of his doubts, when an online search brought up the story.

. The man's full name was Malachy Murtagh, and he had been declared missing, presumed drowned, after his jacket had been found on rocks at Cladrach Beach on the North Coast back in August, with what the police had decided was a suicide note in the pocket. Jer wondered why Nora hadn't mentioned the suicide note. Perhaps Helena hadn't told her. The report went on to say that a woman believed to be the missing man's partner had been found unconscious on the same beach, hidden under seaweed, although her name was withheld. The story was accompanied by a picture of a curved shore of black stones. It looked an unlikely spot to go swimming. There was also a photo of Malachy with a group of grinning people in wetsuits on a wide, sandy beach in bright sunshine. He was a tanned, handsome man who looked a fit sixty, with a generous beard and a head of long, wavy, grey hair. Jer had a sudden image of a body sheathed in a black wetsuit, being nosed by seals. He shook his head, trying to banish the image, thinking that if Malachy had taken his own life, he wouldn't have been wearing a wetsuit. Had he, in fact, swum out to sea fully clothed as only his jacket was found? Either way, shouldn't his body have washed up somewhere by now? How far out might a strong swimmer have swum before succumbing to cold and fatigue? Perhaps the body would never be found. He tried to imagine striking out into the open sea. There would have been a point of no return when Malachy Murtagh knew he hadn't the strength to get back to shore. It seemed an agonising way for a swimmer to end his life.

Resuming his search, he found that Malachy's presence on social media seemed to be limited to a wild-swimming group and their Saturday meet-ups. The most recent post announced a rendezvous at ten the following morning at Tyrella Beach in County Down. He scrolled down the group's Facebook page in the hope of finding a photo of the Islandmagee house. There was a shot of a sunrise, with the little Isle of Muck lying off the end of Islandmagee in the background. Could the picture have been taken near the spot Helena had directed them to?

He did a search for the Artist Collective she'd mentioned and found the page was hosted by someone called Derek Galvin. It took him a while to find any mention of Helena Santoro but eventually he spotted her name listed in a recent exhibition. He clicked on the link, hoping to see a painting of the missing house but instead his screen was filled with the torso of a naked man.

A creak on the stairs interrupted his thoughts and he opened the study door to find Helena standing in the hall, dressed in her own clothes, her cloth bag over her shoulder.

"Do you need something, Helena?" he asked, feeling self-conscious about what he'd just been doing. Rosie had told him it was called "creeping" and he did feel a creep for failing to believe that Helena's grief was genuine.

She gave a sad smile and shook her head. "You and Nora have been very kind, but I really should leave now. All this – me being here isn't fair to you both."

He was disarmed. He didn't want this stranger in his home but, now that she was offering to take herself off, he felt responsible for her.

"But have you anywhere to go?"

"I'll be fine. You need to concentrate on looking after Nora and keeping her well. Say goodbye to her for me. Thank you for everything."

He stood chewing his lip and watched the inner glass door swing closed behind her. She struggled with the heavy front door and had just managed to wrench it open when he joined her in the porch.

A chill wind encircled them, as if the darkness outside was intent on invading the house.

"Nora will be terribly upset if you go like this," he said, worried about Nora's reaction next morning when she found her friend had left during the night.

Her face crumpled. "I don't want to cause a fuss."

"You're more than welcome to stay a few days. I can make some time tomorrow afternoon to drive you back to Islandmagee to make enquiries."

"Enquiries?"

"About the house. Helena, please come back inside before Nora wakes up."

She stepped back into the hall, allowing him to close the front door, then followed him into his study. She stared at the image on his screen.

"It's called *Skyclad*."

"Sorry?"

"The drawing. It means naked."

He glanced at his screen and blushed. "I was trying to find a picture of your house, but I could search in a different way if I knew your postcode."

There was a beat of silence between them.

"We hate all that stuff," she murmured.

"Bureaucracy?"

"Malachy refuses to use the postcode. There's probably lots of mail we never get. He says it's killing the old townland names."

"He's right about that. Does he own the house?"

She frowned. "Yes, at least I presume so. I don't think I ever asked him."

He licked his lips and tried again. "How long did you live there?"

"I've only been there since April, but he had it before I met him. We love it." Her face fell. "I can't believe it's gone."

Afraid she was about to weep, he went on briskly, "I still think the most likely explanation is that we were in the wrong place. I mean, you've been through something traumatic. It's not surprising you're still disorientated. Sit down here with me and we'll try and find it on Google." He pulled over a chair and Helena sat shoulder to shoulder with him, her eyes fixed on the computer screen. "That main road we drove along is Middle Road, isn't it?"

"Yes, that's right." A note of optimism had entered her voice.

He could smell Nora's fruity shampoo off her hair.

She crossed her legs under the long skirt and clasped slender hands around a knee.

"Okay, I've put in a search for Middle Road, Islandmagee. It's a long road." He clicked on Street View.

"Oh my, that's – how clever!" she exclaimed.

"Are we near your laneway?"

"*Em*, no. It's off the Mullaghboy Road which is further on."

He navigated another half mile or so while she leaned towards the screen, fascinated by the virtual journey along the familiar road.

"It was obviously filmed on a beautiful day!" she said, smiling. "I recognise that house on the left, and there's the cottage I've been longing to paint. Turn right there!"

He slowed their progress along the narrow road and, after what he judged to be another quarter of a mile, she said, "Our lane should be round the next bend."

He inched forward until they could see the entrance to a lane, which looked very much like the one they'd taken.

"*That's it!*" she declared in triumph. "Can you go up the lane?"

"I'm afraid not." He circled the location, the foliage of the hedges expanding and contracting with the movement of the cursor.

"There's our post box!"

He steadied the image and moved closer to the post box. It was in the form of a little thatched cottage and appeared to be attached to a wooden post.

"Very cute. I didn't spot that this morning," he said, making a mental note.

"Malachy made it." She leaned back in her chair. "I dreamt about the house when I was asleep just now. It was on fire, and I knew Malachy was inside. I kept trying to get to him, but there were brambles everywhere that kept growing, blocking my way."

"You said you'd painted the house and the trees around it many times. Are any of those paintings online?"

She shook her head. "There is – was a series of them I was preparing for an exhibition. The theme was 'Hearth and Home'. There were exteriors and interiors, but all the paintings were in my studio."

"Maybe you sent photos of the paintings to the gallery via email?"

He saw hope dawn on her face, and she nodded slowly.

"Malachy took a photo of one of the finished canvases to send to the gallery."

"Can we access your email account so I can have a look?"

Her face fell. "He sent them from his email account. He looks after all that," and she bit her lip to stop the tears which were threatening.

Not for the first time Jer wondered at how many women were

willing to put their lives completely in the hands of their male partner. It seemed that Helena had nothing from her previous life but some keys and a piece of broken pottery.

"You found something earlier, in the mud," he said, keen to focus on something tangible.

She looked momentarily at a loss then made a dive for her bag and rummaged in it feverishly, finally drawing out the piece of pottery.

He cleared his throat. "You said it was from one of your Italian bowls."

"Yes, I had three of them on the kitchen windowsill. "*Sfusato Amalfitano*, the Amalfi Lemon. I love the lemon and blue together."

"You speak Italian?"

She hesitated. "It's a very long time since I've been in Italy and I'm very rusty."

"But your name is . . . ?" He trailed off, remembering that he only knew her name because he'd secretly searched her bag.

"Santoro, yes. My grandfather came to Scotland after the war." She turned to face him. "How does a bowl on my windowsill come to be broken and ploughed into the mud?" She brought the fragment to her lips.

Afraid she was going to break down, he said quickly, "Do you think you could draw a sketch of the house for me?"

She sat up straight. "Yes, of course."

He lifted some sheets of printer-paper and handed them to her. "Do you need a pen or – "

"No, no, I have pencils here." She picked up her bag and put the piece of pottery into it. "I'll use the kitchen table, if that's alright." She left the room with a reassuring sense of purpose.

He sat staring at the blurred foliage on his computer screen for a few more moments. What was that weird term she'd used? Skyclad, that was it. He typed it into Google and found, as expected, that it meant naked, but its usage intrigued him since it was associated with modern pagan ritual.

Feeling dog-tired, he turned off his computer and tried to obliterate all thought by listening to an album of pipe-band music on his headphones. He woke forty-five minutes later with a start when the final note dropped him into a silence that left his ears ringing. He lifted off the headphones and listened. The house was quiet save for the tick of the cooling radiators. Heading for the kitchen patio for a final cigarette before bed, he saw the sheets of paper he'd given Helena neatly stacked on the table. The top sheet was blank, save for a few smudged fingerprints. He lifted it to reveal a page covered in an intricate weave of grey brambles. He leaned over the drawing, searching in vain for the straight lines of a building behind the tangle of branches. The remaining sheets of paper were blank. He placed both hands on the table and let his head hang for a moment. Time to take matters into his own hands.

Saturday 25th October

Chapter 5

Assailed by constant headaches from clenching her teeth, Nora had taken to wearing a mouth-guard at night and her sibilant breathing woke Jer early. Getting out of bed, he took care not to disturb her, gathered an armful of clothes and headed for the bathroom. Fifteen minutes later he slipped out of the house without breakfast. He knew she wouldn't surface till eleven and he was determined to find out more about their houseguest before any more time elapsed.

Outside the sky was clear and there was a touch of frost in the air. The leaves on the ancient vine clinging to their rickety pergola were stained with red as if they had each been dipped in blood. He always felt a little sorry for the vine which had outlived the graceful conservatory where it had started life a century earlier. The conservatory was long gone by the time he and Nora had bought the house in the 1980s, but the old vine refused to die, yielding up fists of tiny, bitter grapes each autumn.

It was Saturday and driving across the quiet city he felt a lightness of spirit. Saturdays always made him feel young again – everything was still to play for on a Saturday. It was the day he and his brother Samuel used to get their pocket money. He smiled to himself, remembering how they'd make a dash to the corner shop for sweets and a comic. Being the eldest, Samuel always got to read the comic first. He resolved to ring him and ask his advice. If this house had an existence somewhere other than in Helena's imagination, Samuel would know how to find it.

He crossed the city in no time and had travelled twenty miles south of Belfast before hunger demanded a pitstop in the village of Clough for coffee and a croissant, and diesel for his ageing Volvo. The sun was beginning to establish its presence and he stood for a moment in the forecourt of the service station sipping his coffee, admiring Slieve Donard which was presiding over the landscape like a benign godhead.

Back on the road, he turned east towards the coast, following signs for Tyrella, intent on seeking out Malachy's swimming friends. It was nearly half past nine and he put his foot down, keen to talk to the swimmers before they disappeared into the sea.

There was already a scattering of cars at the beach carpark when he arrived, and he spotted a straggle of people in wetsuits heading for the beach. Grabbing his camera-bag from the boot, he jogged after them until soft sand slowed him down. The sea's breath came to him as a sweet scent, the gentle swell releasing with a sigh at the water's edge. He longed to get his camera out to capture the curve of flesh-coloured sand being caressed by the sparkling water but hurried after the swimmers who were busy dumping their gear in a pile further along the strand. Half a dozen of them were dressed in wetsuits and two men were fully clothed, one of whom was holding an exuberant Labrador on a short leash.

He brandished a smile and called out, "Morning!" as he approached the group. "I'm Jer McCabe, an independent filmmaker. I'm working up a proposal for the BBC for a documentary about wild swimming." He paused for breath. "I was wondering if you'd let me do a little filming of you doing your thing?"

"Who's it for again?"

He met the gaze of the alpha male who'd spoken. "BBC. At this stage it's only a proposal, of course. But a proposal is always more persuasive when you can provide some footage." He made a face, afraid he was being anything but persuasive.

"What do you think, guys?" said the alpha. "It would be great to get a higher profile for wild swimming, wouldn't it?"

This was greeted with a general murmur of assent.

"As long as you don't show our wobbly bits when we're dressing," laughed an older, apple-cheeked woman.

"No problem, wouldn't dream of it," he assured her.

"Don't worry, Babs, we'll defend your honour," said one of the men stoutly.

"Would any of you be up for doing a wee interview with me before you take the plunge?"

"Sure, okay," declared the alpha before anyone else had the chance to volunteer. "I'm Paul, by the way. But can you be quick? We want to have our swim before the tide turns."

Jer got his camera up and running while Paul posed with his back to the sea, hands on hips. Jer caught a few wry smiles being exchanged between the others.

"Paul, tell me what's to like about wild swimming?"

"What's to like?" Paul expanded his chest. "What's not to like, you mean?"

Jer nodded and raised his eyebrows encouragingly.

"It's the best thing in the world – that feeling of being totally immersed in the element. I think I must have been a seal in a previous incarnation, because I feel most at home in the sea."

"How far would you usually swim?"

"Oh well," he smiled in a self-satisfied way, "sometimes miles, but the challenge of the swim is more about dealing with the conditions than the actual distance. We could all swim for miles in a swimming pool but, out here, it depends on the temperature of the water, how rough it is, tide, currents, the wind." He turned for affirmation from the group who, at that moment resembled a small colony of penguins.

"I know you're all keen to get into the water, but one last question. Have you ever come close to drowning?"

Paul frowned and raised his right hand to indicate the interview was at an end. He shook his head disparagingly and turned his back on the camera, rubbing his hands together.

"Let's do this!" he proclaimed.

Undaunted, Jer hoisted the camera onto his shoulder and followed the group to the water's edge, getting down on one knee to get a shot across the surface of the sea, feeling the damp penetrate his jeans. The swimmers waded out several yards until the water reached their hips, then started swimming east, parallel to the shore in the direction of Saint John's Point. Before long they'd separated into two groups, the leaders striking out strongly using the crawl and the slower group employing breaststroke, each swimmer towing a fluorescent orange float. He tracked them to the limit of his zoom, did a few panning shots of the beach and the sweep of the Mourne Mountains then switched off the camera.

He wished he'd asked Paul how long their swim would last.

Surely they couldn't stay in longer than half an hour? It was October, after all. The two clothed members of the group had headed off along the beach with the Golden Labrador racing ahead. There was nothing for it but to await their return.

His left knee was feeling uncomfortably chilled as he retreated to the sand dunes for a pee. Then he settled himself in a sheltered spot and lit a cigarette, thinking about Malachy and realising that this group of friends had to have been questioned by the police about his disappearance.

His mobile vibrated against his thigh, and he was surprised to see it was Rosie calling.

"Can't believe you're conscious this early of a Saturday morning," he began.

"You know those clips someone put up on YouTube?" she said breathlessly.

"Hugh put up."

"Yeah, but if anyone asks, some anonymous fan put up," she said firmly.

"Okay," he said slowly. "Have there been more complaints?"

"No – one of the clips has gone viral."

"That's a good thing?"

"It's certainly a good thing. Last week our most popular clip – you know, the one about the dog turds – had a hundred and twelve views. Now it has half a million."

"You mean our wee clip has been watched by half a million people in a week?"

"More like a couple of days. And the other clips are lifting too."

He had a mental image of a twister, plucking objects from the earth and whirling them away into a dark, debris-filled cloud. "Why now? That clip's been up there for a couple of months."

"I don't know. It can just take one of those American influencers, sitting in his smelly bedroom, to pick up something funny and share it, and it goes viral."

"You mean the clip is circulating in America?"

"Definitely the States, judging by some of the chatter on Twitter. But it's global, Jer."

"It's on Twitter?"

"Of course it is. That's where it's being shared. You really need to get your head around this stuff!"

"And do people like it? Do they find it funny, or do we now have a global army of do-gooders baying for our blood?"

She sighed. "Jesus, you're a real killjoy. Don't you realise how big this is? We'll be flavour of the month with the Beeb! It's bound to be driving traffic to their website. Their hits must be through the roof!"

"Hope so," he said, doubtfully.

"Where are you? I can hear a dog."

The dog-walkers were returning, and the Labrador had spotted him and was bounding in his direction, barking madly.

"I'm out for a walk."

"I don't believe it, and you've acquired a dog?"

"No, it's somebody else's bloody hound and it's eyeing me up for breakfast, so I'd better go." He ended the call, trying to ward off the wet, slobbering Labrador which was determined to lick his face.

"Down, Goldie, down! Sorry, sorry," apologised its owner, a short, ruddy-faced, bald man in his sixties. He clipped on the dog's leash and dragged him off Jer. "He's a big baby. I'm Ed, Babs' husband."

"Glad to meet you, Ed."

"This is Leo," he said, indicating his young companion.

"Another wild-swimming widower?" said Jer, grinning.

The two men stared at him.

"Sorry, I just meant, you know, golf widows and all that." He clenched his teeth in embarrassment.

Ed's face relaxed. "That's me, certainly, but Leo here's a swimmer."

Leo looked of an age to be Ed's grandson. Small and compact, his face was lean and tanned. He was wearing a black, woolly hat pulled down over his ears and a fashionable black anorak and jeans. He looked cold despite the warm clothes.

"I'm going to take a leak," Leo said, walking away.

"Sorry, have I upset him?"

Ed sat down heavily beside Jer and put his arm round the Labrador. "We lost one of the swimming group recently."

"Oh no! Did he – drown?" When Ed didn't answer, Jer pressed on. "He did, didn't he? I'm so sorry. No wonder your friend Paul didn't like my question. Leo's obviously very cut up about it. Were they partners?"

"What? Lord no, nothing like that," Ed sounded scandalised and made a move to get up.

"What happened?" Jer said quickly. "It wasn't during one of their regular swims, was it?"

Ed slumped back onto the sand, gathering the dog into his arms once more. He shook his head and muttered. "No, no, he was on his own. We're all still shell-shocked."

Jer nodded. Keen to keep the man talking, he said, "What was he like?"

"I didn't know him all that well, to be honest. Quiet type," he said, caressing his dog.

"You know, I think I read something about it online. Wasn't his wife found on the same beach?"

"He wasn't married."

"Maybe she was his partner then?"

Ed shifted uncomfortably. "I wouldn't know about that."

"I suppose you all were questioned by the police?"

"Paul was, I think. As I say, I hardly knew the man myself. Listen, Mr. . . ."

"Jer."

"I think we need to respect the man's privacy."

"Sometimes it's good to talk about these things. Leo's obviously finding it hard to deal with."

Ed looked over his shoulder anxiously but there was no sign of the young man. "He refuses to go into the water now. The body hasn't been found, you see, and he's afraid of coming across it out there. I've told him over and over that's not going to happen, but the idea's really taken a hold on him."

"Poor fella. Maybe they'll find the body soon and that'll bring some closure."

Ed bowed his head.

"You don't think that's likely?" He examined the other man's profile.

Ed raised his head, turned to meet Jer's eye fleetingly, then stared out to sea.

"Don't bodies usually get washed up somewhere?" Jer pressed him.

Ed shook his head wearily. "I've no idea. I can't bear to think about it."

"I'm sure you're gutted."

Ed's shoulders sagged. "To tell you the truth, I can't think straight since it happened. If I could just get a good night's sleep, it might clear my head. Goldie here is the only one that keeps me sane." He hugged his dog.

"How's your wife dealing with it?"

"Babs is very religious. That's her rock."

"*Look, they're coming back!*" Leo called out from behind them.

"Please don't say anything to him," Ed muttered.

Jer held up his hands and Ed struggled to his feet. Leo joined him and the two of them stood close together, watching the black heads and bright floats moving slowly towards them, parallel to the beach.

"They've made good time," said Ed, with a clearly forced heartiness.

"Perfect conditions," agreed Leo – a little wistfully, Jer thought.

"Let's go down and meet Mammy, will we?" Ed said softly to his dog, which was pulling on its lead.

Jer laughed. "You could go kitesurfing with that animal!"

He watched Ed stumble across the sand, pulled towards the water's edge by the excited Labrador. He looked up at Leo.

"Have you ever tried it, kitesurfing?"

The younger man squatted beside him. "Yeah, have done. It's magic."

"No wind today, I suppose?"

"It's a good beach for it, though, especially when it's empty like this."

"Would you do it on your own? I'm sure you can end up in deep water very quickly?"

"Always best to do these things with a buddy."

"I'm sorry about your friend Malachy."

Leo stood up and gazed seaward.

"Did you know him well?" Jer asked.

"I knew his partner better."

"Helena?"

Leo turned and stared down at Jer. "You know her?"

"I met her yesterday."

"She's still here then?" He was obviously startled.

"Yes. You know she's been in a psychiatric ward?"

He frowned in confusion and shook his head, without taking his eyes off Jer.

"The thing is, yesterday she asked me and my wife to give her a lift home to Islandmagee, but when we got there the house was gone."

"How do you mean?" said the young man, sounding winded.

"Helena directed us up a lane to a muddy field, but there was no sign of a house ever having been there."

Leo licked his lips and took a step back, then turned and walked quickly away.

"*Did Malachy have a house in Islandmagee, Leo?*" Jer shouted after him, getting to his feet. He turned to pick up his camera-bag and straightening up came face to face with Paul.

The cold of the sea was coming off the wetsuit and he was breathing heavily. His face was purple and contorted with anger.

"What the hell are you doing?" he growled.

Jer's instinct was to step away from the man, who was towering over him, but he managed to stand his ground and speak calmly. "I'm trying to help Helena."

"You know Helena?"

"She's just been discharged from hospital and is staying with me and my wife."

Unappeased, Paul leaned into his face. "Who the hell are you?"

"I told you. I'm Jer McCabe, an independent filmmaker."

"And you're what – making a film about poor Malachy?" Paul recoiled in disgust. "With friends like you, Helena doesn't need enemies!"

"Does she have enemies?"

"How the hell would I know?"

"Did Malachy?"

Paul stalled and rocked back on his heels. "I think it's time you fucked on out of here!"

Ed and the rest of the swimmers were approaching, and Paul turned and shouted. "*This guy's a reporter wanting information about Malachy!*"

Babs reached them first, her cheeks pink with exertion and her plump, pleasant face tense with concern. She was followed close behind by her husband and his dog.

Before Jer could defend himself, Paul rounded on him again.

"What have you been saying to Leo?"

"Go after Leo and make sure he's okay," said Babs in a commanding tone to her husband who hurried off. She peered at Jer. "What do you want?"

"Look, Babs, I met Helena for the first time yesterday and she's in trouble."

"How do you mean? She's in hospital, isn't she?"

"You knew about that?"

Paul answered for her. "We all knew that Helena was – wasn't well."

"Why didn't you say you knew her at the start?" said Babs, looking troubled.

He licked his lips in embarrassment. "I'm sorry, I – "

"I think you should leave now," she said coldly.

"I will but, please, can you just answer one question? Did Malachy and Helena have a house in Islandmagee?"

Paul leaned towards him again. "The lady told you to fuck off!"

"Okay, okay," he said, lifting his camera-bag. Why hadn't he just been honest with them at the outset? He was definitely losing his touch.

When he was at a safe distance from Paul, he turned and called out to the group who had gathered around Babs and were watching him. *"Jer McCabe, Indigo Productions! If any of you want to help Helena, please get in touch!"*

Paul took a step in his direction, and Jer walked away as quickly as the soft sand would allow.

When he was driving out of the car park, annoyed with himself for mishandling the situation, he saw Leo standing beside a black Mini, staring after him.

Chapter 6

Jer was back on the main road heading towards Ballinahinch before he noticed the black Mini, one car behind. This one had a red roof. Had Leo's Mini a red roof? Even if it was Leo, the guy probably lived in the city and was simply heading home. He sought distraction by filling the car with a blast of bagpipe music and tried to forget about the black car. Entering the town of Ballinahinch, the Saturday morning traffic slowed to a crawl, and he wound down his window to get some air. A couple of passers-by stared at the car, startled by the skirl of the pipes. One gave him the thumbs-up and he grinned in response. He liked the idea of his car being a music-box on wheels.

At the roundabout in the middle of the town, the car directly behind peeled off and the black Mini was now sitting on his bumper. He looked in the rear-view mirror and saw Leo looking back at him. The woolly cap was gone, revealing a head of cropped, bleached hair. He turned off the music and gripped the steering-wheel. He's counting on me leading him to Helena, Jer decided, feeling queasy at the thought. What was it Leo had said when she'd been mentioned? 'She's still here?' He'd sounded shocked. Don't be getting paranoid, Jer, he counselled himself. Young Leo may just be heading to the city. If he's still breathing down your neck when you're nearing the office, time to start worrying.

It took him a further tense forty minutes to reach the city centre and Leo was still visible behind him, though there were now a couple of cars between them. Determined not to lead him home to Helena, Jer headed for his usual parking spot in a social-housing development where he paid one of the residents a stipend to let him park outside her house. He cruised past the City Hall, and at the bottom of Chichester Street he turned left on amber, leaving the Mini to be netted by the lights. He accelerated away from the lights but was forced to come to a shuddering halt at the next junction, not daring to go through a red light. On the move once more, he couldn't see any sign of the black Mini and made a quick left turn into the little cul-de-sac but was exasperated to find a people-carrier parked in his spot.

Although it was now approaching midday, Aggie, the lady of the house, was standing in her dressing gown at her front door, sharing a fag with a neighbour. He hailed her and pointed at the offending car. Aggie took the fag from her mouth and cradled the elbow of her smoking arm in her left hand.

"*You know you have to pay more if you want Saturdays as well!*"

He blew out his cheeks. He'd forgotten it was Saturday. He gave her a conciliatory wave and scanned the cul-de-sac, relieved the Mini was nowhere to be seen. He executed an awkward three-point turn to extricate himself from the narrow street, then he drove to a nearby multi-storey carpark, checking his rear-view mirror every couple of minutes. He seemed to have finally shaken off his pursuer.

Walking to the office, his mobile rang.

"Jer, at last! Why don't you answer your phone?"

"Carol?" He juked into a doorway to escape the street-noise.

"I don't know what class of a row you've caused, but you've already ruined my weekend."

He waited.

"Are you still there?"

"Yes, I'm here. Does Trix want to talk to me?"

"*Duh!*"

"Right." He took a deep breath. "Where and when?"

"Right now, in the Beeb!"

"Fine, I'm on my way."

"How long will you be?"

"Ten minutes. Is that – ?" but she'd gone. He expelled a breath.

He didn't have to fret long in BBC Reception, before a tight-lipped Carol arrived to escort him to the sixth floor. He stalled when he realised she was heading for the office of the Head of TV rather than Trix Maidstone's next door.

"What's going on?"

"You've landed yourself in deep doo-doo!"

She knocked the door and waited while he broke into a sweat. What could Cliff want with him? He'd met the man fleetingly a couple of times at commissioning events and tried to remember what he knew of him. Rumour had it Cliff had been banished to the BBC Gulag that was Northern Ireland, for insulting an unnamed British National Treasure by email. Prematurely wizened from a TV career measured out in cigarettes, Cliff was looking sixty in the eye and staring the wrong way down the barrel of his media career. His irascibility was matched only by his arrogance. Was Cliff about to axe the *Thoughtless* series? The commission had been Jer's reward from Trix for helping to see off her previous boss. She'd spent a triumphant year acting as Head of TV only to be passed over for promotion when the job was finally advertised – a disappointment which had soured her already brittle personality.

At a guttural sound from inside the room, Carol opened the door and ushered him inside. He felt like a piece of meat being tossed into the lion enclosure. The Head of TV was staring out the window, a mobile phone clamped to his ear, making grunting sounds. Trix was seated at a large meeting table and acknowledged his entrance with a narrow look. He looked meaningfully at her, hoping to get some indication of where he should sit, but she'd already turned away and was staring at Cliff's back with a look of dull hatred. He sat down on the same side of the table as her, leaving a buffer of an empty chair between them. Cliff ended his call, put the phone in his trouser pocket and continued to stare out the window. Jer began to wonder if he knew he was in the room, and nervously cleared his throat, to be rewarded by a gleam in Trix's eye and the slightest shrug of her shoulders.

Finally, Cliff turned round, leaned back against the windowsill and folded his arms.

"Are you two having an affair or what?"

Trix's mouth dropped open and she laughed. "Are we *what?*" she said, challenging him to repeat the question.

It occurred to Jer that she might be taping the meeting, a thought Cliff might also have had since he declined the opportunity to repeat the provocation.

"You heard that, Jer?" she said. "This is sexual harassment!"

Jer suddenly felt as if he and Trix were sitting at the table naked. "For the record, we're not in a sexual relationship," he said, trying to keep his voice level.

"Well, what kind of relationship are you in?" snarled Cliff, striding to the table like a tennis player moving to the net. He leaned his fists on it and stared at each of them in turn.

"Text-book alpha-male, isn't it! said Trix, "*Ooh*, I'm scared!"

"*What's it going to take then – somebody knocking you off your fucking bike?*" he shouted.

"Was that you?" she gasped.

"Was what me?" he said, straightening up.

"A big, black car nearly ran me off the road this morning at the Arches."

"Deliberately?"

"I don't know." She looked disconcerted.

"This is a whole other ballgame," he said, with a note of satisfaction. "Online trolls are one thing, but someone trying to run you over represents a direct threat to your life."

"No-one tried to run me over. I was just . . ."

Cliff pulled out a chair opposite Jer and sprawled in it. "I take it you're aware that Donald Trump and the Archbishop of Canterbury have tweeted about your squalid little series?"

"*What?* You're kidding?"

"I wish I was."

"What on earth did they say?"

"Oh, well, Trump thinks you're destroying the Free World. The Archbishop was rather more measured."

Jer laughed in disbelief.

"The First Minister has now weighed in," muttered Trix, staring at her phone. "He says the BBC is bringing Northern Ireland into disrepute!"

"As if that were even possible! Let me see," said Cliff, taking the phone out of her hand. He glared at it, rolled his eyes, and handed it back. "London are going to go ballistic!" he said under his breath.

"Oh dear!" she said, turning down the corners of her mouth in mock derision.

"I think they'll want to pull the series," said Cliff, standing up.

"The BBC can't be seen to give in to political pressure." She stared at her boss.

Cliff began pacing. "A physical threat to a member of staff changes everything." He paused and announced, "I would be failing in my duty of care to you both if I didn't act on the threats we've had!" He nodded to himself as if pleased with the line which he would undoubtedly use in his next call with London.

"This person who tried to run you over," said Jer quietly. "It could it be the same one who sent the plait?"

Cliff rounded on him. "What plait?"

Jer looked at Trix for help, but she averted her head. "I got it in the post yesterday morning," he said, taking the envelope out of his inside pocket and sliding it across the table to Cliff who dumped the contents onto the table and gave a dry laugh.

"Turn around, Trix!"

"It isn't mine," she said through gritted teeth.

He stared down at the little plait which looked as if it had once graced the head of a doll. "You knew about this and failed to tell me or Security?" he said ominously.

Jer wondered if he should try to cover for her, but experience told him to keep his head low.

"There's no message with it so it can't really be interpreted as a threat," she said.

"It's just a bloody TV series. It's not worth dying for!" Cliff sighed.

"I don't feel my life is at risk," she said archly.

"Famous last words! Anything else like this arrived through the post?"

"No, but we had a slogan painted on our front door: '*God died for our sins.*'"

He nodded. "How many more episodes before Christmas?"

"Ten," she said quickly.

"Great! Ten more opportunities for the leader of the free world and the Head of the Church of England to be offended." He looked at Jer. "Then we let it die a natural death."

"Oh, for God's sake!" Trix leaned forward, "So you're going to let politicians, not to mention the Ulster evangelicals dictate what does or doesn't get broadcast in Northern Ireland? What a pity you weren't here during the Troubles – you could have made cowardly decisions like this on a daily basis!"

"You're no-one to talk – you're a post-conflict babe."

Jer's mobile chose that moment to come to life, startling Trix and Cliff with its bagpipe squeal. He groped in his pocket and was about to silence it when he saw it was Nora. "Sorry, I'll have to take this," he said, rising, relieved at being able to escape.

"Jer, where the hell are you? You promised to take me and Helena to Islandmagee today."

"And I intend to." He looked over his shoulder, then dropped his voice. "Donald Trump has been tweeting about my series so I'm at the Beeb being lightly grilled. I'll be home in an hour. Promise."

"*Ha, ha!* You better be," she said and rang off.

Had she even registered Donald Trump's name, he wondered?

Of course, she might have thought he was joking. He straightened his shoulders and re-entered the office where the two execs were still sparring.

"I expressly told you to commission on a quarterly basis. If you've commissioned a whole year, you've seriously overreached," Cliff was saying.

"*It's been commissioned on a quarterly basis as per your instructions, sir!*" she hissed.

"Then how has the BBC committed itself to a year?"

"Because you announced it in your press release the week you arrived." She bared her teeth in triumph. She had him on the ropes.

Jer watched the calculation going on behind Cliff's eyes.

"As I already told you, a threat to the life of one of my staff trumps any concerns I might have about my own credibility or BBC editorial independence. I don't want your blood, or indeed your hair on my hands. These will be the last ten episodes we'll be broadcasting of *Thoughtless*, Jer. I think you know it's already run out of rope."

He rang Rosie on the way back to his car.

"*You've heard?*" she shouted at him before he got a word out.

"Donald Trump, the Archbishop of Canterbury and the First and Deputy First Minister!" he muttered.

"I know, isn't it hilarious!"

"Hilarious wouldn't be the first word that comes to mind!"

"Come on, did you ever think a series you made might be top of the news agenda in the US?"

"For all the wrong reasons! I feel a bit nauseous, to be honest."

"I suppose the Beeb are doing their nut?"

"Yip. I've just come from a spirited meeting with Cliff and Trix."

"Oh my God, Cliff has weighed in. Is he going to pull it?"

"I'm afraid its days are numbered – he's saying that the eps we're working on will be our last."

"*Mmm*, okay."

"You don't sound too upset?"

"*Wey hey, bring it on!* Stuff I directed is being watched by people all over the world. Do you want me to meet you in the office?"

"To do what?"

"I don't know. Surely we need to get our ducks in a row before the press come looking for a comment. Maybe we should write a press release?"

"The BBC machine is cranking up to deal with this. They certainly won't welcome us chipping in."

"Are we a flipping independent company or are we not? We've every right to comment on our own series."

"Of course we have, but I honestly think we shouldn't get involved in all the chatter. We made the ball, let the rest of the world play with it if they want to."

"Yeah, suppose that's cool." She sounded unconvinced.

No sooner had he ended the call than he regretted not issuing a clear instruction to her and the team to refrain from tweeting about *Thoughtless*, but he had no idea how to control what was happening. They would just have to try and ride the wave and hope it didn't break over their little company and sweep it away. Malachy invaded his thoughts again, this time as a body caught in a fishing-net, being dragged along the seabed. Jer decided he needed distraction and the search for Helena's elusive house suddenly seemed very appealing.

Chapter 7

Jer suspected Nora was already tiring of their guest, when she insisted Helena sit in the front with him that afternoon on the drive to Islandmagee. Helena was wearing the grey tracksuit again and a black anorak of his which had seen better days. He drove for a few miles along the shores of Belfast Lough, trying to decide how he should broach the subject of Leo. He had no idea how Helena might react if he confessed he'd taken it upon himself to go to Tyrella that morning to find Malachy's swimming friends, but he had to tell her – how else was he to find out why Leo had followed him?

"I was looking at some photos of wild swimmers on Facebook," he began. "They posted a lovely shot of Tyrella Beach."

Helena seemed miles away and he wondered if she'd heard him.

"Tyrella is beautiful," she murmured then.

"Do you swim yourself, Helena?" he enquired gently, hoping Nora wouldn't veto the conversation.

"Yes, but it has to be Mediterranean temperatures to tempt me."

"You'd need to be hardy to get into the Irish Sea in October," he said and immediately wished it unsaid, thinking of Malachy.

She was silent for a few moments then blurted out, "I'm sorry about the drawing. I tried to start again but – "

"Not to worry. There's a lot going on in your head just now."

"You must think I'm losing it!"

He shifted his hands on the steering-wheel. "I think you're grieving, and it'll take time for things to become clearer."

"I have this overwhelming feeling that Malachy is there at home, waiting for me."

"I used to feel that about Liam," Nora said suddenly from the back seat.

Her voice sounded calm, but Jer held his breath.

"Every time we went somewhere, I'd get upset and have to rush home," she said. "I was convinced he was there, alone in the house, needing me."

Jer blinked away a blur of tears, remembering the family outings fractured by Nora's panic and compulsion to run for home, and their children's distress and frustration.

Helena looked back at her.

"It was prams too," Nora said. "If I saw a pram in the street, I'd have to look and see if Liam was inside."

He winced at the memory of how Eimear and Rory had eventually refused to go out with their mum, terrified by the scenes she caused at the school gate or in the street.

"But you got over it, didn't you?" said Helena anxiously. "You don't do that now?"

"God no, I don't do that now, do I, Jer?"

"No, no. It . . . diminished over time," he said, unwilling to bring up the other, equally distressing behaviours which had replaced it.

Helena stared straight ahead, and he stole a glance at her profile.

"I need to get a grip, don't I?" she whispered.

"Tell me about your house," he suggested, hoping to change the subject. "Is it a bungalow, two-storey or what?"

She drew in a breath and began speaking in a deliberate way. "It's an old cottage with a couple of rooms in the roof-space."

"What kind of roof does it have?"

She turned to him questioningly.

"I mean, has it a thatched roof, or maybe slates or tiles?"

"Oh right – slates, those thick grey slates."

"Good, an old house obviously, so probably built of stone."

"I'm not sure."

"Maybe it's rendered. Is it painted white?"

"No, a lovely olive green. Malachy likes it to blend into the landscape."

"Right, this is all really helpful. And your studio, is it in the main part of the house or built on?"

"It's a sort of garden room, with a glass gable looking out over the sea. It's a most wonderful place to paint."

"Sounds like it," he said. "Did many people come to the house – postman, bin-man?"

"The post box was at the end of the lane, as you know, and the bin-lorry can't manage the lane, so Malachy deals with the rubbish himself."

He noted her use of the present tense in relation to Malachy. "Helena, we really need a plan B this time. If you lead us to the same lane, the gate and the empty field, we need to decide what to do next."

She turned her face away.

"Don't be so negative, Jer," said Nora from the back. "I'm sure Helena will take us to the right place this time."

"He's right, Nora," Helena said sadly. "I've thought of nothing else since yesterday and at this point I'm not sure of anything."

"Do you drive?" he asked her.

"Yes, yes, of course."

"And should your car be at the house?"

She put her fingers to her lips, seemingly unable to answer.

"When did you last see it?" Nora said, leaning forward and putting a hand on her friend's shoulder. "I'm always leaving mine at the Golf Club then thinking it's been stolen."

"The last time it was the day Malachy disappeared," she said slowly. "I drove back to the house and there was no sign of him. He'd left the spade sticking in the earth where he'd been working, but he was nowhere to be seen."

Jer glanced at her, wondering if her memory was returning. "Was anyone else around?"

"No, only me, though I did feel a presence."

"You felt Malachy's presence?" said Nora eagerly.

"No, I felt the presence of evil."

Jer imagined a detective taking her statement and dismissing her as a head-case. "You told the police all this?"

She looked at him in dismay and shook her head. "They tried to question me in the hospital but I couldn't remember anything clearly and the doctor made them stop. I was getting so upset."

"You poor love," said Nora.

"What can you remember now?" Jer asked hopefully.

"I saw the spade stuck in the earth in Malachy's herb garden but . . ."

Jer could see her chest rising and falling and knew her heart-rate had speeded up.

"The next thing I remember is coming round, lying on the beach." Then she added in a whisper, "I was so cold."

"So you were on that beach with Malachy," he said. "Have you any memory of what happened?"

"Stop badgering her, Jer!"

"I'm just trying to piece together what happened," he said in frustration.

"Nora, it's important I try to remember," Helena said.

They drove on in silence for a few minutes.

When he thought Nora had tuned out, he spoke to Helena in a low voice. "The news report online said you were found unconscious. Did the police have anything to say about that? I mean, had you been attacked or drugged?"

"Sorry, yes, they did say they thought I had been attacked – because I had a wound on my head." She pushed her fingers into the back of her hair, obviously searching for a scar. "They said I couldn't have been in the water long or I would've drowned."

"Hang on, were you found in the water or –"

"I remember now! The police said someone found me on the beach and rang them."

"Right, so you weren't found in the water?"

"No, but, you see, I was soaking wet."

"Do you remember how you got injured?"

"No," she said sadly.

"Have the police any theory about it?"

"They think it was Malachy but he would *never* have hurt me and left me there like that," she said passionately. "He's the kindest of men."

"Maybe you injured your head in the sea?" suggested Jer.

When she didn't answer, he glanced at her and realised she was weeping.

"For heaven's sake, Jer, don't!" Nora scolded him. "Poor Helena doesn't know. She was unconscious."

"Sorry, I'm just trying – "

"I know," Helena said. "I wish I – "

"Here, sweetheart," said Nora, handing her a tissue. "Please don't cry. The truth will out, you'll see."

It won't if you stymie every attempt I make to question her, Jer thought, irritated, but said nothing.

When they reached Islandmagee, he resolved not to pre-empt any of Helena's directions. He kept his speed steady, hoping she'd indicate a different route along the peninsula from the day before, but her directions, when they came, were unequivocal, leading them inexorably to the mouth of the same lane. With a growing sense of dread, he pulled up short of the opening and looked around.

"Where's the post box?"

She got out of the car and walked over to a wooden fencepost, her face drawn. He left the engine idling and joined her.

"It was here. You can see the marks where it was screwed on." She probed symmetrical, rusty indentations in the wood with her fingers.

He examined it and confirmed that there had been an object attached to the fencepost. The car engine shuddered into silence.

"Someone is trying to erase all trace of Malachy," she said.

"Have you found it?" Nora called through the car window and Helena went over to her.

He took a photo of the fencepost before following her.

"It was definitely there," Helena was saying.

"You can see the marks where it was screwed on – someone has removed it," he agreed, feeling like a witness for the defence.

"My God, show me!" said Nora, slipping out of the back seat. He left them to it and leaned his back against the car. What if Helena was telling the truth and there had been a house, Malachy's house, at the end of this lane and someone had wiped it off the face of the earth? He tried to imagine lorry-loads of rubble rumbling down the narrow lane. Surely that couldn't have been accomplished without someone noticing. Plan B had to be asking the neighbours if they'd seen anything. He looked up and down the road for signs of habitation. That was when he noticed the telegraph poles. Shouldn't there be poles and wires carrying power to the house?

"Helena," he asked, "was the house connected to the grid?"

"What – sorry?"

"There are no telegraph poles going up this lane."

"Malachy's passionate about the health of the planet. He had solar panels on the roof and a small wind turbine. He did have a generator as a back-up, but he prided himself on using it as little as possible."

"He sounds like a fantastic guy," said Nora. "Helena's sure this is the right place, Jer, so the house is not going to be there."

He was surprised and encouraged by Nora's clarity of thought, used to the medically induced miasma in which she normally existed.

"What do you want to do, Helena?" he said, mollified, thinking that Helena's presence might be good for Nora after all.

Nora answered for her. "Since we've come this far, I think it would be good for Helena to settle this in her own mind."

"I'd like to go up there one more time, just to be sure this isn't some kind of bad dream – if you don't mind, Jer?"

"No problem."

They climbed back in the car, and he proceeded carefully up the lane, remembering to slow down before the top of the rise. This time, he pulled up well short of the gate.

"Would it be alright if I filmed this, Helena?"

"You're not going to make some weird documentary out of Helena's troubles, are you?" sighed Nora.

"I gather evidence, Nora. It's what I do, and the only way I know how to help," he said, trying to keep his temper.

"It's fine, Nora. I think it would be good to have a record – "

"You don't know what he's like! Everything that happens becomes cannon fodder for his films."

"You're an artist!" Helena looked at him with approval. She shrugged. "I use everything and everybody too, in my art."

It occurred to him that he and Nora were being used right now. To cover his discomfort, he got out of the car and fetched his camera from the boot. He filmed Helena and Nora climbing over the gate, then followed them. The two women walked along a little track through the grass and disappeared into the trees. He turned off the camera and hurried on, catching up with them on the far side of the wood. He started filming again, following Helena's progress as she walked down the slope then squatted and dug her fingers into the mud. His filming was interrupted when Nora grabbed his arm and pressed herself close to his body. He realised she was upset.

"I don't like it here. There's something horrible about this place."

He moved the camera to his other hand and put his arm around her, while they watched Helena, who had risen and was now revolving slowly. She raised her arms to the sky and threw back her head.

"What's she doing?" whispered Nora.

"It looks like some sort of ritual. Is she religious?"

"I don't know. I caught her mumbling sometimes and sort of humming, but there's a lot of that in there." Nora looked up at him and gave a half-hearted grin.

He hugged her closer. "Your friend Helena is not a well woman."

"I know. What on earth are we going to do with her?"

Helena was now feeling for each step with her feet like a blind person, her arms outstretched. He lifted the camera again.

"Are her eyes closed? She's going to fall into those bushes," hissed Nora.

He thrust the camera into her hands and ran but was too late to prevent Helena stumbling into a patch of briars where she sprawled among the thorns, thrashing with her arms and legs, and lifting her head like a swimmer struggling in a choppy sea.

"Keep still and I'll get you out!"

He waded into the thicket, feeling thorns tear at his skin through his trousers. He grabbed her hand and pulled her onto her feet. A spur had caught in her hair, and she clawed it away, leaving a bloody trail across her cheek. By the time he got them both out of the brambles, his trousers were torn in a couple of places, and she looked as if she'd been attacked by a wild cat.

"Have you ever heard the old saying, 'You look as if you've been pulled through a hedge backwards'?" he said.

She started to laugh – laughter that had turned to tears by the time Nora joined them. Nora handed Jer the camera without a word and put her arms around Helena. Embarrassed, he looked away, and suddenly could see the position the house must have occupied. As Helena had said, the very trees themselves seemed to be pointing to what was absent – the small stone house they had sheltered and moaned over through a couple of centuries of stormy nights. Realising the camera was still running, he took a panning shot of the area before switching it off.

"Come on, let's get you back to the car and clean up those scratches," Nora was saying.

"I feel his spirit here, Nora," Helena sobbed. "He's not lost in the sea, he's right here," she gasped, looking around, as if Malachy might magically appear. "There's blood on your shoulder, Nora." She brushed her fingers across her own face and stared at the traces of blood on her fingertips. "I've stained your lovely coat."

Nora glanced at the smear of blood on her shoulder of her pale-blue coat with revulsion.

"I have wipes in the car," Jer said quickly. "We can remove all traces of our swim in the brambles." He tried to steer them back towards the gate, but Helena stood her ground.

"Be honest with me, Jer, you don't believe there was ever a house here." She looked him in the eye.

He was tempted to placate her but sensed she would know he was lying. "You've created the house so strongly in my imagination, it would be easy to believe it was here, but I need evidence to be convinced."

She reached into the pocket of the black anorak and pulled out two objects and held them on the palm of her hand for his inspection. One was a small piece of crumpled metal which had once been a bird.

"This was part of a wind-chime that hung in the window of my studio." The other object appeared to be a chunk of plaster. "I told you the house was painted olive green." She turned it over so he could see that one side was green. She looked into his face, searching for belief but was disappointed. She put the objects back in her pocket.

"What I don't get is how you used to drive up here. I mean the lane peters out back there."

She looked around then pointed. "The track used to curve around the side of the trees and enter the gate over there."

"There was a gate then?" said Nora.

"A lovely wooden gate and a stone wall."

She has a vivid imagination, Jer was thinking. He had to give her that.

"Can we walk that way? There must be something left," she said desperately, striding ahead, followed reluctantly by Jer and Nora.

When they caught up with her, she was staring at several cattle which had taken up residence in a muddy area between the wood and a thick hedge.

"The lane ran along here."

"Was it tarmacked?" He looked doubtfully at the depth of the mud ploughed up by the cattle.

"No, it was just rough gravel."

They gave the cattle a wide berth and continued up the slope, skirting the hedge. Helena kept turning to her left, measuring the distance between where they were walking and the trees.

"It should be here," she muttered to herself.

Nearing the gate where the car was parked, she suddenly veered off to her left, walking quickly back up the hill.

"Oh Jesus, we'll never get home," panted Nora.

"*It's here! I knew it must be!*"

Jer and Nora joined her, scanning the immediate area to see what had occasioned her burst of joy but could see nothing but mud and clumps of grass.

"Whoever covered up all traces of the house missed this!" she said. "Do you see the wee path here? When we were out walking, we'd take a short-cut to the house this way."

"You'd go through the trees?" Jer said.

"Yes," she agreed, encouraged. "Our feet made this little trail." She hunkered down and laid her palm on the narrow trail which looked like a sheep track, only there were no sheep around.

"It's a desire line," he said.

She looked up at him questioningly.

"It's a term used by architects and planners to describe a route people insist on taking, ignoring a designated path." He shrugged. "Human beings can't resist a shortcut."

"A desire line," she repeated and nodded.

At that moment he believed her – believed there had been a lane, a garden and a house. She sensed the change in him.

"I'm not losing my mind," she said softly.

He scanned the countryside around them. "Where's your nearest neighbour?"

Chapter 8

Helena directed him to turn right on exiting the lane, and a hundred yards further on, right again into a private road. A tarmacked surface and neatly clipped hedges announced a well-tended property. Unlike the site of Malachy's missing house, this homestead was tucked into the lee of the hill, sheltered from the prevailing wind, with no sea views to render it attractive to the holiday-home buyer. The farmhouse itself stood at the heart of a clachan of small, stone buildings, testament to a working farm which had supported multiple generations.

"Have you met the family?" he asked her.

"When I first arrived, I walked over the hill to say hello but the only person I met was Samuel Ewart, who was working out in the fields. He was adamant his mother and sister wouldn't welcome a visitor."

"You've never seen the mother and sister?" said Nora in surprise.

"I did catch a glimpse of them in the back seat of their car one Sunday morning. They were wearing hats. I presumed they were off to church."

Jer nosed his car into the farmyard and parked beside an ancient, green Morris Minor. Before he'd even cut the engine, two sheepdogs charged them, barking madly.

"Jesus!" said Nora. "There's no way I'm getting out while those two beasts are on the loose."

"How are you with dogs, Helena?" Jer asked.

"Fine."

"Why don't you stay in the car, love? This shouldn't take long. I'll leave the radio on to distract you from the Hounds of the Baskervilles."

The moment he stepped out of the car, one of the dogs sprang at him, pinning him against the door while the other snarled menacingly at his feet but when Helena joined him they quietened. She squatted down and stretched out her hand. One of the dogs sniffed her palm and then allowed her to fondle its ears, while the second lay down on its belly, thumping its tail on the ground.

Jer brushed the muddy trace of the dog's paws off his thighs and clicked the car-door shut.

When Helena looked ready to rise, he helped her up, meeting her glance with a smile.

"You're a dog-whisperer?"

"Hardly."

All the tension had gone from her face, and he saw the woman she had been before Malachy's disappearance.

The front door opened, and a woman's head and shoulders appeared.

"Don't mind them dogs. They won't ate you."

When she showed the whole of herself, they saw a stout woman in her sixties, dressed in layers of clothing, rounded off with a faded, floral apron, on which she was wiping her hands. She was wearing man-sized Wellingtons. He walked over and stuck out his hand.

"Mrs. Ewart, I'm Jer McCabe and this is my friend Helena."

"Miss, and I know who she is." She ignored the proffered hand and squinted past him at Helena and then at the car.

"That's my wife Nora," he said helpfully. "She's not good around dogs."

Miss Ewart snorted.

"It's good to meet you at last," said Helena. "We've been neighbours for the last few months."

Miss Ewart merely raised her eyebrows and looked from one of them to the other.

"We just want to ask you a couple of questions," Jer said pleasantly.

"Who is it, Lizzie?" came a querulous, female voice from the depths of the house.

"Come on in," said Lizzie Ewart, looking suddenly flustered.

Jer and Helena exchanged a glance as they were led along a dark, narrow hall into a kitchen. With only one small window, the room was gloomy, and it took them a moment to realise there was an old woman sitting in the shadowy corner beside the range. She was dressed completely in black and wore small, round, dark glasses. There was a sour odour in the room that made Jer want to bolt back outside.

"Mother's blind," whispered Lizzie Ewart.

"But I'm not hard of hearing!"

"Indeed and you're not, Mother. This is a neighbour woman, Helena, and – " She looked heavenward for inspiration.

"Jer McCabe."

"Now there's a grand old Scottish name," announced the matriarch. "And Jer – would that be short for Jeremiah?"

"It would indeed," he said proudly, thinking they might have stumbled on some common ground.

"A fine biblical name!" said Mrs. Ewart. "Now your name, dear – Helen was my grandmother's name. Have you a family name to go along with that?"

"Santoro."

This was greeted by a charged silence.

"A papish name if ever I heard one!" The old woman leaned forward, her head cocked.

Helena glanced at Jer and frowned. "It's Italian. It means Feast of All Saints."

"Aye, papish!" declared the crone triumphantly. A black shadow detached itself from her lap and leapt at Helena. It was a large, black cat which circled her then rubbed its body along her ankle.

"Cat-whisperer too?" he said under his breath.

"I'll thank you not to whisper in my kitchen," said the old woman.

"Mrs. Ewart, you've probably lived here all your life – "

"All of my lives," she corrected him darkly.

"What about a nice cup of tea?" suggested Lizzie Ewart.

"There'll be no tea drunk in this house till we know what these folk are lookin' for."

Jer cleared his throat. "You'll both be familiar with the house where my friend Helena and her partner Malachy have been living?"

"Malachy!" The old woman spat out the name. "That's a Fenian name, and you say he was her partner, not her husband?"

He wondered fleetingly if it would be better for Helena to be living in sin with a Catholic than to have actually married one, according to this woman's narrow moral code.

"The love of my life," said Helena in a tight voice.

"The devil cloaks sin in many's the fine word and that surely is the finest of them all," said Mrs. Ewart, as if addressing an unseen congregation.

"I think we should go," said Helena.

Jer put up a hand to stop her. "Mrs. Ewart, would you be familiar with the house, Carraig na Rón, over the hill there?"

"There's no places with Fenian names like that around here," said Lizzie Ewart, her cheeks flushing with annoyance.

Helena looked at Jer, shook her head, and headed for the door. He took a last look around the ancient kitchen and wished he could have filmed the encounter.

"Thank you for your time, Mrs. Ewart."

"My time? My time comes at a heavy price, Mr. McCabe!"

The woman should be on a pulpit somewhere, he thought, following Helena along the hall and out the front door, where he had to shade his eyes against the glare.

They climbed back into the car without a word, and he swept out of the farmyard, with the dogs snapping at his tyres.

"How did you get on?" said Nora.

"How did you know the house was called Carraig na Rón?" Helena's voice was tense.

He swallowed. "You must have mentioned it yesterday."

"Did I?"

He felt ashamed of adding to her self-doubt.

"That old woman is a witch!" she said through clenched teeth.

"We might've got something from the daughter if the mother

hadn't been there," he said, glad to change the subject.

"No, I don't think so. The mother is in her head and always will be, even when the old hag finally dies."

"What on earth went on in there?" said Nora, leaning forward.

He slowed in preparation for turning out onto the main road and without warning a burly man in his sixties appeared at his window. The man leaned his arm on the roof of the car and bent down to stare in at them. Jer wound down the window and was immediately assailed by the smell of sweat from the man's armpit.

"I told her before," he said, indicating Helena with his head. "My mother and sister don't like visitors."

"You must be Samuel Ewart?"

"And you are?"

"Jer McCabe."

"Well now, Mr. McCabe, what business did you have with the women of the house?"

The man's tone was affable, and Jer decided to cut to the chase. "You'd be familiar with the house over the hill there, Samuel, where my friend Helena's been living up to recently."

"I wouldn't say that."

"Why not?"

Ewart stared into the distance. "We were never let near thon place. Me mother always said it was cursed."

"What on earth do you mean?" Nora leaned forward, trying to see his face.

"I dunno the whole story of it, but they say the young one who cast them spells was reared there. It's not a place I would ever want to lay my head. Are you looking to sell the land, now he's – gone?"

This last question was directed at Helena who got out and faced him across the roof of the car. "His name is Malachy. Malachy Murtagh, and he's – his body has not been found."

"He's out there beyond in the sea, isn't he? Youse'll have a hard job finding him out there."

Jer wished he could get out of the car to be some support to Helena, but Ewart's bulky body was now full square against his door.

"Was it you who demolished the house?" she said in a choked voice.

"I told you I wouldn't go near thon place for love nor money."

"Did you see who did?" said Jer. "They must have made quite a racket."

"*Hear no evil, speak no evil.*"

"Then you're not your mother's son," said Helena bitterly.

"Them's women's ways and you're one of them." He leaned down and spoke conspiratorially to Jer. "You'd best be taking your womenfolk away out of here – but if your one there has the selling of the land, I'll give her a fair price." He straightened up, slapped the roof of the car as if it was a recalcitrant cow and disappeared through a gap in the hedge.

When Helena had regained her seat, Jer turned for home, feeling they'd raised more questions than they had answered.

"The neighbours from hell," said Nora sagely from the back seat. "I'm glad I didn't go into the house."

"Some of Ulster's finest there," he agreed.

"Did you find out anything useful?"

"From the mother and sister? Not really, apart from the fact that they're bigots and prudes. We got more information from Samuel than the two women put together. Interesting that he wants to buy the land, Helena."

"What? Oh yes," she murmured.

"He did imply that there was a house, didn't he?" he said, replaying Ewart's words in his head.

"He said they weren't allowed near the place when they were children," said Nora.

"What did he mean about a young one being reared there?" He searched his memory for Ewart's exact words.

"The young one who cast the spells was reared there," said Helena.

"Spells?" Jer said.

"Have you not heard of the Islandmagee Witches?"

"Wasn't it a dreadful witch trial like the Salem Witches thing?" said Nora.

"Some local women were accused of bewitching a girl called Mary Dunbar."

"Yes, I know the house where it all happened is still around here somewhere," Jer said. "A thought struck him. "It wasn't your house, was it?"

"No, no, that's Knowehead House. I can show it to you if you want. "

"But was this Mary Dunbar reared in your house?" Nora asked her.

"It was the servant, Margaret Spears, who was reared here. I only found out about the story when I told Malachy I thought our house was haunted. You see, Margaret Spears claimed she saw a ghostly young boy haunting Knowehead House."

"But that was all rubbish, Helena," he said. "I remember now – it was the servant who dreamed up the whole thing with Mary Dunbar. Adolescent attention-seeking, I would say."

"With horrible consequences," said Nora.

"I thought it was an old wives' tale, until I realised there was a presence around our house."

Nora gave her shoulders a shake. "How did you go on living there?"

"Because Malachy was there with me, Nora."

"Did you ever see the ghost?" said Nora, sounding scared but intrigued.

"A few times I thought I saw someone moving through the trees. I stopped mentioning it to Malachy because it annoyed him. He'd lived there for several years before he met me and had never had any sightings."

"Maybe you brought your wee ghost with you?" said Nora.

Jer thought of the baby ghost at Nora's side night and day.

On the way back to Belfast, they stopped at an Indian restaurant for a meal and Helena insisted on paying – but when she attempted to use her debit card, it was refused. To cover her dismay Jer quickly did the needful and they left.

On the outskirts of the city, she asked him to pull into a garage forecourt where she spent some minutes at the cash dispenser. When she got back into the car, she was ashen-faced.

"My account's empty!"

Sunday 26th October

Chapter 9

Jer slept badly that Saturday night, troubled by dreams of brambles growing up from the depths of the sea. When the central heating clicked on at seven-thirty, warming the chill air of the bedroom, he finally fell into a deep sleep. Nora woke him at eleven with a cup of coffee. She was dressed in golfing clothes.

"Sorry I had to wake you, but I've been invited out to play a few holes, and I didn't want to leave Helena on her own."

"Okay, that's great," he said, trying to unglue his eyes and struggle to a semi-recumbent position. He was pleased that she felt up to some exercise but uneasy at being left to babysit their guest. "How is she this morning?"

Nora sat on the side of the bed beside him. "Very low, Jer."

He winced. "Do you think she might do anything . . ."

"You mean, take her own life?" She chewed the skin around a nail which was already bitten to the quick. "What do *you* think?"

He took a sip of the coffee. It was lukewarm.

"I should never have landed you with this." Her spine sagged.

He reached out and rubbed her back. "Listen, love, it's not your fault. You offered her a lift home, which was kind. How could you possibly have known she'd no home to go to?"

"I thought about it a lot last night – what it would be like if I came out of hospital and you were missing and our house gone."

And your account was empty, he thought. "I'm sure the neighbours would notice," he said, making her laugh. "Seriously, love, you have me, Eimear and Rory and a big network of family and friends. This could never happen to you."

"I know, I'm very lucky to have you all." Her eyes filled up.

"So that's why I'm getting my coffee in bed?"

"Don't push your luck, McCabe!"

"Go out and play a lovely, relaxing round of golf and I'll look after Helena. The good thing about modern technology is that everybody leaves a digital footprint. I'm going to try and track down some of her artist friends."

"That's a good idea. I'd better go."

Five minutes later the front door slammed, and he was acutely aware of being alone in the house with Helena. He threw the duvet off his naked body, got up and searched a pile of clothes on the chair for his bathrobe. He caught sight of himself in the full-length mirror and tightened the belt, then padded downstairs, feeling like a visitor in his own home. He half expected to find her sitting at the kitchen table, but the room was empty. He stood at the sink listening. There was an oppressive silence in the house, accentuated by a distant church bell. He filled the kettle and headed for the living room, where he found her sitting on the sofa, wearing a faded, pink dressing gown of Eimear's. Her feet were bare, emphasising her vulnerability. She was bent over, staring into a mug, her face obscured by a curtain of hair, which seemed to him to have become greyer overnight. She raised her head slightly to acknowledge his presence, apparently unable to lift her eyes to meet his.

"Did you manage to get some sleep?" he asked her.

"She's won, hasn't she?"

He was perplexed. "Who's won, Helena?"

"Margaret Speers. She's taken my whole life."

He struggled to place the name. Then it came to him. She was still thinking about the story of the Islandmagee Witches.

"Margaret Speers died hundreds of years ago."

She lifted her head and looked at him in despair. "I had over three hundred thousand pounds in my account. How could it all be gone? I was very muddled last night, but I've thought about it since. You see, I sold my house in Edinburgh before I moved here, and that money was sitting in my account. Malachy kept telling me I should invest it, but I'm hopeless about that sort of thing."

He sat down on the sofa beside her and adjusted his bathrobe to hide his nakedness. "Helena, it's possible that someone means you harm, but I don't believe a ghost is going to steal money from a bank account."

"You sound just like Malachy."

At that moment, he fervently wished the said Malachy was still around. Then again, what if it was Malachy who had cleaned out her account and done a runner? He shivered. "Follow the money, isn't that what they say?" he suggested half-heartedly.

"I know you think the house in Islandmagee is a figment of my imagination, but there must be a way I can prove money has been stolen from my account."

"I'm sure there is."

"Should we ring the police?"

He nodded slowly. "We probably will in due course but, if it's okay with you, I'd like to get my brother Samuel's advice first. He's a barrister."

"Whatever you think is best. Thank you."

"Samuel is a churchgoer, so I can't ring him till later. Would you like to use the shower while I get a bite of breakfast?" he said, standing up.

"Thanks." She pushed herself out of the chair like a ninety-year-old, and he stood back to let her pass through the door before him, but she stopped in front of him. "I feel as if I'm falling, Jer, falling through empty space."

He grasped her arms, enveloped by the smell of her warm flesh. "We're here, Helena. Nora and I are here, and we're going to help you get your life back." He felt her breath on his face as her body relaxed. He was tempted to fold her in his arms, but released his grip, allowing her to continue out of the living room.

He followed her into the hall and watched her climb the stairs as if her feet were made of stone.

He made himself a slice of toast and mug of coffee, carried them into his study and fired up his computer. How was he going to start rebuilding her life when he still knew so little about her and what had happened to cause her breakdown? She was like the survivor of a natural disaster – left with only the clothes she stood up in and the few items in her handbag.

Her art was the way she interacted with the world, so he typed in 'Artist Collective, Cathedral Quarter, Belfast', and scrolled through their Facebook posts covering the last few months.

He was about to abandon his search when he came upon a series of photos which seemed to have been taken in the evening, around a fire. Helena was one of a group of people holding hands in a circle. She was smiling across the fire towards a male figure who had his back to the camera. A couple of the photos had been taken further away from the fire and he could see the silhouette of a hillside and the sea mirroring a clear, twilight sky. There was no sign of a house in the background. Before exiting, he sent a message to someone called Derek Galvin who managed the page, introducing himself as a friend of Helena's, giving his mobile number and asking the Collective to get in touch.

It was now after twelve and he thought it safe to ring Samuel.

"McCabe."

Jer straightened his spine as soon as he heard his brother's voice. Samuel was a workaholic who rarely let down his professional guard – a consequence of being one of Belfast's most successful barristers.

"Sorry to bother you on a Sunday, Samuel."

"How's Nora? Has she been discharged?"

"Yes, and she's doing really well."

"Good, that's the main thing."

"This is not about Nora or, at least, not directly." He paused, but Samuel knew better than to step into a silence. "The thing is – Nora's brought a friend home with her from hospital."

"You're kidding! Female?"

"They're just friends," he said hastily. A conversation with his elder brother was never comfortable.

"You mean you now have two female psychiatric patients in the house?"

He swallowed, imagining the way Samuel would report this conversation to his wife Myra, who had scant affection and even less respect for her brother-in-law. "If you want to put it that way, yes."

"Be careful, Jer. If she's a vulnerable person, she could be on your hands for the duration."

"Right, well ..." He got up and closed the door of his study. "She asked Nora for a lift home when they were both discharged, which I duly provided, only when we got to the place she directed us to, there was no house."

Samuel burst out laughing, making him hold the phone away from his ear and grit his teeth. "What are you like? You're a total sucker for a hard-luck story!"

Jer sighed. "She's here for Nora's sake, Samuel. Nora's in a really good place and I don't want to upset her."

"Okay, okay, so why are you ringing me?"

"There's a bit of a mystery around Helena."

"You don't say!"

"Please, just bear with me. Her partner Malachy Murtagh went missing recently, presumed drowned, which is why she ended up in hospital. You maybe saw something about it online,"

"Rings a bell. She was found left for dead on the beach, right?"

"You got it in one. I'm guessing she had some kind of breakdown in the aftermath of it all. But while she's been in hospital, the house she lived in with him has disappeared off the face of the earth, and her bank account has been cleaned out."

"Well, let's forget about the fantasy house for a start. Sounds to me like the boyfriend tried to do away with her and then went AWOL with her money."

"That thought has crossed my mind."

"Or she's just spinning you a yarn."

Jer cleared his throat. "She doesn't come across like that."

"Maybe she's a very good liar."

"She put on quite a performance on the hillside where she expected her home to be."

"That must have been weird."

"Very weird!"

"What does she look like?"

"Tall, very striking, long hair. She's an artist."

"My, my, just what you need in your life."

Jer closed his eyes. "Seriously, I'm thinking of ringing the police but – "

"No, don't do that till we've had a chat. Bring her over here after lunch and I'll see what I make of her."

It was two o'clock by the time they left the house, and he was glad to see their guest had dressed in her own clothes. He realised Nora must have washed the skirt which had been stained with mud. He was keen for Samuel to see Helena in her own bohemian gear rather than his old tracksuit. She'd washed her hair and coiled it over one shoulder the way she had the day she'd left hospital.

The Sunday traffic was light and, fifteen minutes later, they were driving up the Lisburn Road. Samuel and Myra lived between the Malone and Lisburn Roads in one of the poshest parts of Belfast and he always felt a little overawed by their avenue, where the houses were tall and the trees taller. Today he saw that the leaves had already turned and were like tiny flames flickering against the red-bricked walls. He made a silent entreaty to the gods that his sister-in-law would be out, quailing at the thought of Helena, in her vulnerable state, being exposed to Myra's caustic tongue. He decided to warn Helena about Myra as they pulled into Samuel's drive.

"Listen, Samuel's wife can be a bit off-putting, but don't let her get to you. Her heart's in the right place. Hopefully she won't be around."

He might as well have saved his breath, since it was Myra herself who answered the door, looking resplendent in her Sunday best, a coppery silk dress which accentuated the bronze highlights in her beautifully coiffed hair. Her make-up was impeccable as usual, and the mulberry lipstick, outlining her full lips, made her teeth look startlingly white when she greeted them with her social smile.

"You must be Helena," she said, gesturing for them both to enter.

Turning after she had closed the door, Myra took in Helena from head to toe. She gave Jer a perfunctory peck near, rather than on his cheek, and offered Helena her hand to shake. It was then, standing in the russet glow of the leaded lights, that he realised Myra and Helena were very alike and he could see Myra was also struck by the resemblance. With her statuesque build, it was rare that Myra got to look another woman in the eye but, as she held Helena's hand, their faces were close, and Myra was spellbound.

"Have we met before?" she said, disconcerted.

He was fascinated – rather than feeling intimidated by Myra, it seemed that Helena was the dominant spirit here. Samuel might be the terror of the Belfast courts but, in this palatial house, it was Myra who normally ruled supreme.

Helena's face had come back to life, and he saw she had an ageless quality – her skin sculpted over high cheekbones and a smooth forehead defined by a widow's peak and dark eyebrows. He had never admired Myra's looks, chilled by her distain, but looking at her now next to Helena, he had to acknowledge that his sister-in-law was also a strikingly handsome woman.

"You could be sisters!"

It was Samuel who'd spoken, riveted by this doppelganger of his wife. Samuel had married above himself in terms of height but what he lacked in altitude he more than made up for in attitude.

"It's uncanny, isn't it?" said Myra.

Helena broke the spell and turned to greet Samuel.

"Thank you so much for letting us interrupt your Sunday."

Jer audibly let out a breath.

"Come into my study, Helena," said Samuel in his sonorous voice.

"No, no, come into the drawing-room," countered Myra. "I understand you're an artist and there's a painting I want to show you."

Myra put her arm around Helena's shoulders and ushered her into the drawing room, a space Jer hadn't been invited to enter since the death of his mother some years before. This was Myra's holy of holies, and he wondered if Helena had any sense of the compliment that had just been bestowed. The room's décor wouldn't have looked out of place in a stately home, even if the scale was limited by the dimensions of the room. The soft furnishings were upholstered in blue velvet, giving the room a regal feel. The mantelpiece was black marble, and the brass fender and fire irons shone like gold. The blue-and-gold theme was picked up in the embossed wallpaper, creating the effect of an underwater cavern worthy of Neptune. Myra led Helena to the far end of the room, where the entire wall was dedicated to the display of a painting. She flicked switches as she passed, illuminating the painting, and drawing all eyes towards its subject – a tall, slender woman dressed in a dark-blue cloak.

"Oh my, you have a Lavery! It's Hazel Lavery herself, isn't it?" Helena turned to Myra with shining eyes.

"You could feed a small country with what it cost," muttered Samuel, who had positioned himself in the traditional male spot, standing with his back to the fireplace.

"Don't mind my husband, Helena, he's a philistine!"

Samuel pursed his lips.

Jer looked at the velvet-covered furniture, wondering if it was permissible to sit down. He joined Samuel at the fireplace.

"It was painted by a man, of course," Samuel said confidentially to Jer. "Sir John Lavery, from Belfast."

"Is it too early for a wee dram of that Laphroig you're partial to?" Jer whispered to him.

"Not too early at all. Capital idea."

Samuel disappeared and Jer decided to risk life and limb by sitting in an armchair which commanded a view of the whole room.

Myra and Helena were still admiring the painting, Myra with her arm around Helena's shoulders and talking in an excited undertone into her ear, while Lady Lavery looked on with an air of faint derision. He wondered if Sir John's American, socialite wife would've been disappointed to know her portrait was presiding over a middle-class drawing room, rather than the great hall of some aristocrat's pile.

Samuel returned with two cut-glass tumblers, each holding a generous measure of whiskey. He paused for a moment to observe the female tête-à-tête at the other end of the room, before turning his back on the women and sitting down on the other side of the fireplace opposite his brother.

"You didn't tell me your Indigo Productions was going to feature on the lunch-time news!"

Jer's hand stalled in the act of lifting the glass of whiskey to his lips.

"They showed a clip of your wee woman Rosie talking her cotton socks off in one of those Sunday morning discussion programmes.

"*What!*"

"You didn't know?"

Jer reached into his pocket for his phone, only to remember he'd left it by the side of the bed. "She's probably been ringing me. With all this, I've been a bit distracted. What was she saying?"

"She was attempting to dignify your nasty little series as a public service. I gather a leading churchman made reference to it in a tweet."

"Apparently." Jer swallowed some whiskey and felt it curdling his breakfast.

"The BBC are obviously going ballistic," said Samuel, enjoying his brother's discomfort.

"So far, so predictable." Jer took another swig. There was a burst of female laughter from behind him and Samuel half turned his head.

"Nora met her ladyship in hospital, you say?"

"Yes, she's smitten."

"Ah!" Samuel raised his eyebrows. "And where's Nora today?"

"Playing golf."

"Not quite so smitten then?"

The females finally left Lady Lavery to her own devices and Samuel watched Myra settle Helena on the sofa.

"Can I make you coffee, Helena? It seems these two have already made free with the whiskey decanter, unless you . . ." Myra's expression made it clear to her guest that she thought whiskey inappropriate at this time of the day.

Helena picked up the cue. "Coffee would be lovely, Myra, thank you."

Helena gave a wide smile, surprising Jer who realised it was the first time he'd seen her display this level of charm.

Samuel waited until his wife was out of the room before addressing Helena. "Jer tells me your bank account has been cleaned out. Who do you think might have taken the money?"

"I've no idea," she said, gazing at him earnestly.

"Could it be connected to the disappearance of your partner?"

She shifted uncomfortably and looked from one brother to the other. "Are you suggesting Malachy might have taken it?" She closed her eyes and shook her head slowly from side to side. "Malachy would never do something like that. He's not remotely interested in money."

"You believe he's still alive?" said Samuel.

She opened her eyes and met his penetrating stare. "I just know he'd never have gone off like this without a word."

"People can do all sorts of things when they're under stress," said Samuel evenly.

The two men watched a tear slip over the rim of one of her eyes and run down her cheek.

"Had he money worries?"

"No, I don't think so." She frowned in concentration.

"And your relationship? Was he the jealous type?" asked Samuel.

She brushed the errant tear away with her knuckles. "No, not at all. I wasn't being unfaithful, if that's what you think."

Jer thought of young Leo.

"You sound unsure," said Samuel, looking pained.

At that moment, Myra re-entered the room, carrying a large tray, laden with a silver coffee pot and blue china cups and saucers, dainty enough for a toy tea set.

"Has he been grilling you, Helena?" she said, looking daggers at her husband. "Occupational hazard."

"No, it's fine. I'm very grateful for his help." Helena gave a watery smile. "I only wish my head was clearer."

"We're not in court now, Samuel," Myra warned her husband.

Oh, but we are, thought Jer, trying to keep his hand steady as Myra handed him a tiny cup and saucer. He didn't want the coffee but knew better than to protest. It was bitter and scalded his lips when he took a sip.

"Helena was talking about her partner Malachy's state of mind before he went missing," said Samuel, trying to take up the thread of his questioning.

"It must be agonising not knowing what's happened to him," said Myra, sitting down beside Helena, making Jer realise that Samuel and Myra had both read up on Malachy's case online.

Samuel crossed his legs abruptly, irritated. "Can you think back to the last time you saw him?"

Jer watched Helena search her memory. Her face suddenly cleared.

"I was heading off somewhere and went over to say goodbye. He was digging in the herb garden. He tried to put his arms around me, but I wouldn't let him." Her face clouded over, and her eyes welled up. "His hands were covered in soil so I wouldn't let him touch me."

"Did you have a row?" Myra asked her.

Samuel lifted his chin in annoyance at her intervention.

Helena shook her head doubtfully. "No, there was no row. We were fine. Malachy was smiling at me and wanting to kiss me. He wouldn't have done that if he'd been upset, would he?"

Jer's spirits sank, newly aware of how suggestible Helena was. She didn't seem to have any reliable memories of the hours and days leading up to Malachy's disappearance, and her own hospitalisation. Samuel had relaxed back into his armchair and Jer sensed his brother had decided it was pointless to question her further.

"If we could just find out who took the money from her account, it would give us a lead," said Jer.

"Can you do that for her, Samuel?" said Myra in a tone that brooked no refusal.

"Of course. You'll just need to appoint me as your legal representative, Helena. I'll get a form for you to sign."

Myra took Helena's hand. "I understand your house and all your things have disappeared too."

"You must think me mad!"

"No, I don't. You've been through something very traumatic, and the detail will only come back a little at a time, when you're ready to receive it."

"You think so?" Helena pressed her fingers to her lips in a vain attempt to stop the tears which were now running down her face.

"Come with me." Myra led the weeping Helena from the room.

When Jer and Helena got home a couple of hours later, Nora was curled up on the sofa in her dressing gown, exhausted and in a foul humour.

"I played appallingly badly! I just can't believe I've slipped back so much. I'm convinced it's that bloody medication they have me on."

"Please don't stop taking your meds, Nora," Jer said wearily.

"What's all this?" she said, when he deposited two bulging plastic bags beside the sofa.

"Myra's been kind enough to give me some of her old clothes," said Helena.

Nora glanced at the bags and curled her lip. "Myra doesn't have any old clothes, and she doesn't do kind. She'll just be trying to annoy me by giving you all that stuff."

"They're the same size, Nora," Jer shrugged, "so it makes sense. Helena needs some warmer clothes."

"Are you really the same size as Myra?" Nora frowned in displeasure as if she'd just discovered a serious fault in her friend.

Jer announced that he had to take a run into the office and made himself scarce, only pausing to find his mobile in the bedroom. He was tempted to charge it but decided to wait until he got to the office to do it, reluctant to witness Helena's transformation into Myra.

Chapter 10

The Sunday afternoon jazz session was in full swing when Jer walked past the Sugarhouse Bar on his way to the office. He was sorely tempted to go in and dive into a pint but knew that would be madness. Normally he took a circuitous route to his office to avoid the premises of a rival production company owned by a former friend, but today was Sunday and he was confident there'd be no-one working in Harry's offices. The street was quiet, and he couldn't resist cupping his hands to peer through the tinted glass. He registered the number of sleek desks in the open-plan office, knowing they'd all be occupied come Monday morning. He puzzled over some dark shapes at the back of the room, recoiling when he realised a face was staring back at him. He hurried on, hoping he hadn't been recognised.

His own shabby office was empty and silent. He missed Stella. In the past, she'd have dropped everything to meet him there at a moment of crisis for the company like this one. He plugged in his mobile to charge and made himself a mug of coffee. The arrival of texts and notifications of missed calls made his phone chirp and burble on the floor like a grounded bird. Most media folk were addicted to the unrelenting stream of communication, but he hated it, especially when his company was attracting negative attention. Not for the first time, he reflected that he was in the wrong business.

He turned to his computer, giving himself and the phone time to gather more energy, before attempting to return calls. Four hundred and fifty-two unread emails clamoured for his attention. How is that possible, he thought, trying to remember when he'd last checked his inbox. His heart was beating uncomfortably fast, and he felt a prickle of sweat above his eyebrows. He minimised his emails, wishing he could do the same with a few issues in his life, and sat down on the floor to accommodate the short flex of the phone-charger. It was only when he leaned back against the wall and stretched out his legs that he realised he'd left his coffee-mug on the desk and felt like Alice in Wonderland, unable to reach the table-top. Most of the missed calls seemed to be from Rosie. There was one from Stella, two from Trix and a couple from unknown numbers. He needed to get up to speed before ringing Trix, so he tried Rosie, only to be informed that her phone was currently switched off. Had she turned it off before going on TV and forgotten to switch it on again, he wondered? Unlikely. He checked his texts and was surprised to find none from her. She usually followed up a non-response from him with a snappy text.

There was one from Trix which he opened with trepidation: **Cliff furious ring me asap.**

The text was already three hours old, and his stomach churned. Maybe Stella would know what was going on. She picked up immediately.

"Hi, Stella, you were ringing me earlier?" He heard a man's voice in the background, followed by a burst of laughter.

"Just a minute."

The voices receded.

"Sorry to interrupt your Sunday afternoon."

"What on earth is going on, Jer? Carol was ringing me looking for you," she said in a hushed voice.

"I'm sorry. I was out and forgot to take my phone. I'm playing catch-up."

She gave a short, mirthless laugh. "Don't tell me, Nora trouble?"

He gritted his teeth and tried to keep his irritation in check. "Apparently Rosie was on TV this morning talking about Indigo."

There was a pause. "I wouldn't know. I was at church."

"Donald Trump has mentioned our series in a tweet, and not in a good way. And the Archbishop of Canterbury and the First Minister have also got in on the act."

"So I gather!"

"Rosie and Co put some clips up online."

"Those have been up for months, Jer. I bet Trix is in meltdown!"

"Not so much her as Cliff."

"That doesn't bode well!"

"I know, I need to talk to Rosie before I do anything else."

"Don't tell me wee Rosie's gone dark on you?"

There was a beat of silence between them.

"Sorry to take you away from your friends. See you tomorrow," he said, ending the call.

He was shaken by her coldness and sat with the phone in his hands, remembering the times they'd made love here in the office. Was she jealous of Rosie? Surely she didn't think he was romantically involved with a girl younger than his own daughter? He decided to ring Hugh, who'd posted the clips in the first place.

"Hi, Hugh, I'm just catching up with all this. Can you fill me in?"

"You haven't spoken to Rosie?" He sounded incredulous.

"No. I tried her a couple of times, but her phone's switched off."

"Well, that's probably because she's in the air."

"On air?"

"No, in the air."

"You mean she's on a flight?"

"Look, I don't want to speak out of turn here, Jer."

"There's no question of speaking out of turn – we're a team. Rosie's been trying to reach me all morning, but my phone was out of juice. Where's she going – London?"

"No, New York." Hugh sounded embarrassed. "She's been invited over to give some interviews, I think."

He felt breathless. "I see."

"What about tomorrow's shoot – do we go ahead without her?"

Jer closed his eyes. "What's the set-up?"

"Teens behaving badly on buses."

"Right. Best go ahead."

"Will you be directing?"

He sighed. "Sure, send me the schedule."

Afterwards he sat nursing his mobile, thinking about his last conversation with Rosie. She must've decided to take matters into her own hands. He was dismayed but tried to rationalise his feeling of betrayal. How could he blame her when he'd failed to take ownership of the situation? She'd told him the online clip had gone viral and his reaction had been to go dark on her. Not my finest hour, he thought. He knew it was a cop-out to covet large audiences for his programmes while shrinking from the public controversy his irreverent content provoked. His immediate problem was how to present Rosie's behaviour to Trix who would accuse him of letting the tail wag the dog which was, of course, exactly what was happening. He could throw Rosie to the wolves and admit she'd gone rogue but that could damage her career and he was loath to do that. She reminded him of his younger self, always charging ahead with little thought for the consequences. What was needed was a clear, written instruction to her. He texted her: **Don't give any more interviews until we've spoken!**

Feeling he'd clawed back some semblance of control, he felt empowered enough to ring Trix.

"Where've you been, the dark side of the moon?" she said.

"Sorry."

"This has gone nuclear – you do realise that?"

"Define nuclear."

"Worst nightmare and then some. I can't believe you let that infant go on TV to represent your company!"

"She's twenty-two."

"Oh well, that's fine then."

"She's impulsive, I know, but it's great to have that youthful enthusiasm on the team."

"She gave that interview off her own bat?" she guessed.

He hesitated. "I'm not saying that."

"Ah, what then? You sanctioned it?"

His stomach sank. "Is Cliff going to axe the series?"

"Cliff's in London, no doubt bad-mouthing me, and arguing for the swift demise of *Thoughtless*."

"He didn't waste much time getting his ass over there," he said miserably.

"He was already there. He doesn't spend a second longer in Belfast than he has to. He must be costing them a fortune in airfares, never mind hotel bills. He stays in the Culloden, you know!"

Jer didn't care about the internal BBC politics at play here. All he could think about was the ramifications for Indigo if the series was pulled. "Do you want us to cancel tomorrow's shoot?" he asked dejectedly.

There was a pause while she reflected. "Could be seen as pandering to our critics. No, go ahead with whatever you've planned. At least it'll keep Minnie Mouth busy."

Trix had already given Rosie a derisive nickname, making him wonder what she called him behind his back.

He decided it would be best to level with her. "Rosie is on her way to Amerikay."

"*What?*" Trix sounded gobsmacked. She wasn't often caught unawares, and she didn't like it. Her voice was steely. "You need to stop her giving any more interviews, Jer. You tell her from me that her fledgling media career will be over before it's started if she shoots her mouth off on some American chat-show and brings the BBC into disrepute."

"Why don't you tell her that yourself, Trix?" he said hopefully, "It would have a lot more weight coming from you."

"It would be completely inappropriate for me to go over your head, and discipline one of your people."

The old Pontius Pilate act, he thought.

"You're such a wuss, Jer! You need to manage your own team and, if I may say so, manage your PR better."

He'd never been called a wuss before. He made a mental note to act a bit tougher around Trix and almost immediately decided he wouldn't be able to pull it off. He tried to focus on the matter in hand. "Have the BBC put out a statement yet?"

"It's being carved into a tablet of stone as we speak. Oh, and we'll need you to give a comment on behalf of Indigo Productions. News may send a camera crew round to do a quick interview with you for the evening news."

He groaned.

Trix was unmoved by his discomfort. "Well, it's either that or they'll take a clip from Rosie's spiel this morning, and you might want to avoid that."

"Is the interview up online yet?"

"You mean you haven't even seen it?"

"Trix, if I'd known it was happening, it wouldn't have happened, if you know what I mean."

"So, she didn't have your agreement to do that interview?"

He sighed, feeling cornered. "No, she didn't."

"Good to know." Her voice had a self-satisfied tone now she'd scored a point. "Right, have to go. Draft a statement and send it to me asap."

His buttocks were numb from sitting on the floor but before he could summon the energy to get up, a text from Hugh informed him that their dog-turd clip had now got over a million views. That clip is funny, he thought. It was one he'd directed. He cast his mind back to his original proposal for the series. He'd set out to show human beings acting thoughtlessly, but presented with humour, rather than in a preachy way. Were they now guilty of seeming to advocate vile behaviour? The God Squad obviously thought so. He should've kept a tighter editorial rein, and not handed over those recent episodes to Rosie.

He got up stiffly and sat at his desk, found Rosie's interview online, lit a cigarette and watched her betray them all, on live TV. What stayed with him wasn't the content of what she said, which was naïve and ill-advised, but the way she began every sentence with "I". He tried to convince himself that she was being careful not to drop him in it, but finally had to accept that she was taking credit for everything – for the *Thoughtless* idea itself and the direction of every clip. His throat ached. Anger would come later, for now he felt only disappointment. His mobile rang and he dived to the floor to whip it off the charger.

"Rosie?"

"Is that Mr. McCabe of Indigo Productions?"

He took a breath, assuming it was a journalist looking for a quote. "Yes, this is Jer McCabe."

"It's Babs here."

"Babs?" He searched his memory. Did he know a Babs?

"We met yesterday at the beach."

"Babs, yes, sorry, I have a work thing going on at the moment. Thanks for getting in touch." He conjured up an image of the motherly woman with rosy cheeks.

She cleared her throat. "I was thinking of Helena. How is she?"

"Well, she's okay, Babs, but still very sad and traumatised by what she's been through."

"I'm sure she is, poor thing. Is she staying with you?"

"Yes, she and my wife Nora have become good friends."

"I see. How did your wife and Helena come to know each other, if you don't mind me asking?"

He did mind and felt a little disconcerted by the question.

Before he could think of a response, she went on, "Maybe I

could call and see her? Where is it you live, Mr. McCabe?"

"Please call me Jer. It would be great for her to see a friend. By the way, did you ever visit Helena and Malachy at their house in Islandmagee?" There was a silence. "Hello, Babs, are you still there?"

"You broke up for a moment there," she said. "No, I wasn't ever at their home. I only really knew Malachy from the swimming group."

"Of course. You must all be very shocked by his . . . disappearance."

"Sorry? His disappearance?" she said politely.

Jer felt suddenly unsure of his ground. "You'll have to help me here, Babs. I really don't know what happened."

"I thought perhaps . . ."

"That Helena had told us? No, no – she's still very traumatised and, you know, one doesn't like to ask about something so painful."

"Ah, I see."

"You knew Malachy well, Babs. What do you think happened?"

There was a long pause. "Poor, poor Malachy. I'm afraid it does appear that he has taken his own life. There was a suicide note after all."

"You don't sound surprised?"

Babs cleared some phlegm from her throat and he felt a heel for pressing her for detail.

"Did he suffer from depression?" he asked.

"Oh yes. Swimming was his way of dealing with it." She gave a deep sigh. "I hope he found peace out there – in the deep."

"Did the police tell you what he said in the note? I mean why . . ."

He could hear Babs breathing on the other end of the line.

When she spoke, her voice was very soft and he wondered if she was crying. "No."

"I'm sorry, Babs. You must all be very upset about what's happened."

"We are. He and Helena have been in my prayers."

"Before I let you go, can I ask you about that young fella Leo? Was he a particular friend of Malachy's?"

"What makes you say that?" The warmth had departed from her voice.

"It's just – Leo followed me from the beach yesterday. What's the story with him?"

The line went dead and, when he checked his phone, he found the number had been withheld.

Monday 27ᵗʰ October

Chapter 11

The beginning of another working week and Jer was woken early by the musical drone of his mobile. He checked the time and did a second take. It was only six-thirty, not a time he normally rose to face the day. Nora and Helena had already been asleep when he'd got home the evening before and he hadn't had a chance to talk to either of them about what Babs had said on the phone. Lying there, he began to wonder about the suicide note. Helena had to know about it and indeed have been shown it by the police while she was in hospital. Was she simply in denial about what Malachy had done? Jer was about to turn over and go back to sleep when he remembered that, because of Rosie being AWOL, he was due to go out filming. He groaned and Nora turned over furiously, pulling the lion's share of the duvet with her.

He slid his legs out of the bed and sat shivering, scanning his messages with a sinking heart – still nothing from Rosie. She would have to leave Indigo, for he couldn't see how their working relationship would ever recover from her betrayal of him and the team.

He grabbed a pile of clothes, tip-toed past the room where

Helena was sleeping and entered an icy bathroom. The central heating wasn't timed to kick in for another hour and the air in the house was cold as a tomb. Downstairs he couldn't face any breakfast and set off for work on an empty stomach, sucking his first cigarette of the day. It was still dark outside and heavy rain during the night had left the streets awash. The dawn, when it came, was a meagre affair.

On his journey into town, he spotted a large puddle on the Antrim Road, where pedestrians were getting soaked by passing traffic and made a mental note to return to do some filming before the morning was out. He smoked a second cigarette in the dank doorway of the office, before heading upstairs to find Hugh and Amy getting ready for the shoot. To his consternation there was no sign of Stella. Evidently, she no longer showed up when there was an early shoot. Maybe it was also time for her to leave Indigo, he thought, feeling irritated and depressed. Hugh and Amy eyed him uneasily and he wished he had dedicated more time to nurturing his working relationship with them over recent months instead of leaving them to be bossed around by Rosie.

He greeted them with gusto, but they remained self-conscious with him, and Rosie wasn't mentioned. Amy informed him that they were booked to meet the camera crew at eight, leaving no time for a warming coffee. He tried to ignore his growling stomach, resolving to identify a source of coffee before too much more of the day had unfolded.

In the event, he became totally absorbed in his craft, picking lots of low-hanging fruit during the rush hour, as the downpour brought out the worst in the morning commuters. They caught some teenagers in grammar-school uniforms crowding an elderly man out of a bus-shelter, while the same jostling crowd laughed and pushed a couple of younger kids off the kerb into the path of a bus. He directed the crew to film a succession of pedestrians being soaked by cars, which appeared to accelerate towards the giant puddle on the Antrim Road.

Once the rush hour had subsided, they boarded a bus and filmed Hugh's muddy feet up on a seat, and the back of Amy's head while she inflicted a tinny version of what she was listening to on her headphones on the unfortunate older lady beside her. They got shots of fingers secreting well-chewed gum in unlikely places, and an empty Coke can rolling around on the stairs of a double-decker, under the feet of hapless passengers. All in all a good morning's work, during which they all laughed a great deal, despite the rain.

At eleven, he treated the crew to coffee and a bacon soda farl in the Central Bus Station café. The soundman Billy was the same age as Hugh and Amy and they sat at one of the tiny metal tables while he occupied another with Dave, the cameraman, who was an old friend, swapping stories of their glory-days in the BBC.

At a moment when the younger generation were intent on their phones, Dave spoke conspiratorially to him.

"Who are you putting your money on?"

"Sorry?"

"Trix and your man Cliff! I'd put my money on him. He's bound to be well in with London."

Jer screwed up his nose. "I thought he'd blotted his copybook big-time over there. He wouldn't be here otherwise."

"Bet you a tenner she bites the dust this time."

"And I bet you twenty she ends up Head of TV," he countered, grinning.

"Nah, she'd have got it last time round if they wanted her in that job."

"Double jeopardy!" He became aware that Hugh and Amy were staring at something on Hugh's phone.

Hugh glanced guiltily in his direction.

"What is it?" Jer asked apprehensively.

"Rosie's going on some chat show in New York today! Bitch!" said Amy, handing Hugh's phone to him.

He read the text: **On Your USA this AM wish me luck don't tell J.** He started typing a response.

"Hey, that's my phone!" said Hugh. "You can't – "

"Sorry, Hugh, I have to. She isn't answering my texts or calls."

J here. You do not have my permission to give any interviews in connection with the *Thoughtless* series or Indigo. Ring me ASAP Jer.

He waited until he was sure the message had been sent before handing the phone back to Hugh, who began feverishly typing a text.

Amy was staring at Jer.

"So, you didn't give her permission to go to the States?"

He shook his head.

"Do you know she's taking credit for the whole bloody series?"

He was taken aback by her vehemence, having assumed that Rosie, Hugh and Amy were pals. The jealousy and resentment he saw in Amy's young face worried him.

"She's taking the wave," Hugh said, looking dejected.

Dave had been listening with interest to this team conversation. "Well, I hope for her sake she's good on a surf-board, for she could be in for a rough ride." He got up and held out his hand. "A pleasure as always, Jer."

"You too, Dave. Thanks. Cheers, Billy."

The cameraman bent down and whispered in his ear. "Good riddance to that wee bitch Rosie! She can't direct to save her life."

Back at the office, Stella responded to his greeting by announcing that his brother Samuel had been trying to reach him. He checked his phone, which he'd silenced during the filming, and sure enough there were a couple of missed calls from him.

"Trouble at home?" Stella said, in the derisive tone she used every time she drew attention to his ongoing domestic dramas.

"No, actually, trouble at mill," he said, stung.

She sat up. "You mean here?"

"Rosie's in New York and probably on live breakfast TV at this very moment, saying God knows what."

"Did you tell her she could go?"

"Of course I didn't."

"What possessed her to do that?"

He sighed. "I guess she got fed up waiting for me to jump on the bandwagon and jumped on herself."

Stella shook her head. "It's like something you'd have done when you were younger," she said wearily.

"What are we going to do with her?"

"What can we do? Sounds like she's taken matters into her own hands."

"You don't seem too bothered about it?" he said irritably.

"We can sack her if you want, I don't mind, but I suspect she has plans of her own anyway."

He was baffled. "Has she said anything to you?"

"No, no," she said airily.

He suddenly suspected that Stella was using Rosie's defection as a veiled reference to her own intentions. He wished she'd simply say what was on her mind but shied away from asking her outright, feeling he hadn't the bandwidth to cope with any more complications in his life.

"Best do nothing then, is that what you think?"

Stella gave a dry laugh. "Jer, it won't make a blind bit of difference what I think – you'll always take the line of least resistance."

She headed for her desk, leaving him feeling wounded to the core. *Is she implying that my staying with Nora is the line of least resistance*, he wondered.

He went out into the stairwell to ring Samuel.

"Come round to my office. I have some information on the witch!" Samuel announced by way of greeting.

"The witch?"

"Helena's a white witch! Didn't you know? Just one of the fascinating facts she shared with Myra in our bedroom."

Jer attempted to smoke a cigarette to calm his nerves while he walked the few blocks to Samuel's chambers, which were located in a tall, sandstone building near the courthouse. Helena a witch! That would certainly explain her strange, ritualistic behaviour in Islandmagee. Did Nora know her new friend practised witchcraft? His blood ran cold at the thought of her being encouraged to dabble in the occult.

There was a tang of the sea in the air as he neared the river, and he took a last couple of drags before tossing away his cigarette and stepping inside.

The old building had been beautifully restored, and even boasted the original iron-grilled lift. Pulling open the double gate, the smell of warm oil and dust transported him back to childhood and the afternoons he used to spend with his mother in Belfast's Olde Country Tea House. He caught sight of his distorted reflection in the polished-brass control panel and pushed his fingers through his hair. In the lift, his mother would invariably wipe his nose and attempt to smooth his shock of hair, before bustling into the warm fug of the Tea House, where his granny and aunts would be waiting. Where had Samuel been on those treasured afternoons? Four years older, he'd probably preferred the football pitch, while Jer had never tired of those feasts of ham sandwiches and sticky buns, and the comforting family narratives shared by his favourite females.

The lift jolted to a halt at the third floor, and he knocked deferentially on the carved door, where Samuel's name was emblazoned on a brass plate, before entering. The secretary looked up and smiled, holding his gaze a fraction longer than was seemly.

"Go on in, Jer," she breathed at him.

She was a platinum blonde, on the wrong side of fifty with an eye for the male of the species. Did Samuel have a thing with this one, he wondered for the umpteenth time. No, Myra would hang, draw and quarter him if he strayed.

Samuel glanced up at his brother and back at his screen without a word while Jer wandered over to the window, from where he could see the oily water of the Lagan. He thought back to other times he'd been here, when this very window had been sealed with a thick layer of plastic, to reduce the risk of injury from flying glass in the event of an explosion. During the decades of the Troubles, Samuel had lived with the daily threat of attack, due to his diligent defence of violent clients on both sides of the Northern Ireland divide. The new era of peace and relative political stability should have been a time for him to reap the benefits of those difficult years, but Samuel never seemed to be comfortable in his own skin.

"You didn't know she was a witch?" he said now, without taking his eyes off his screen.

Jer went over and sat down facing him across the imposing desk. "That fact had escaped me."

"Apparently she's a practitioner of the Wiccan religion or so I gather from a birdie in the good old PSNI."

"What in the name of God is Wiccan?"

Samuel raised his eyebrows. "God has nothing to do with it! It's pagan."

"*Wow, okay!* Is Myra somewhat disenchanted with our guest then?"

"On the contrary, she's fascinated," said Samuel with a hint of weariness.

"Blimey! She doesn't dabble herself, does she?"

Samuel gave his younger brother a venomous look.

Jer grinned. "What are we thinking? One of Helena's witchy friends has cast a spell and made Malachy's house vanish into thin air?"

"You're in a very flippant mood today. Maybe we should do this another time?"

"Sorry. It's just our own junior witch Rosie has gone off to the States to shoot her mouth off on live TV."

Samuel snorted. "Do I take it she's done this without your permission?"

"Yip."

"You should sack her before she embroils your company in a lawsuit."

"Won't I lose any control over her if I do that?"

"It doesn't sound like you have any control as it is."

Jer sighed. "I don't want to seem vindictive."

Samuel rolled his eyes. "We looked into Helena's account and there was three hundred and fifteen thousand pounds in it, before it was cleaned out and closed at the beginning of August."

"Who on earth keeps that kind of money in a current account?" said Jer. "Do we know who cleaned it out?"

"No, but it had to be someone with access to her account number and password. We've requested details of the account it was transferred to, and initial indications point to an account in Italy."

"Maybe good old Malachy has done a runner to Italy with her money? She did tell me that he did all the online stuff for her. Do we know the date the money was taken?"

"That's where it gets interesting. It was the day Malachy went missing, presumed drowned," Samuel said, leaning back in his chair.

Jer whistled.

"I had an off-the-record chat with the PSNI about the case. They had been treating it as an attempted murder-suicide, but now, with this money issue, they're looking at it afresh."

"I take it they've checked if he's left the country."

"There's no evidence he has."

"He could've simply crossed the border?"

"The Garda have been alerted down South and will shout if he's spotted or tries to leave the jurisdiction by air or sea. If he's alive, he's probably still here."

"Have the police spoken to the person who found her?"

"Yes, it's a . . . Mr. Flynn," said Samuel, consulting his notes. "Apparently he took his dog for a walk early in the morning and the dog found her buried under the seaweed."

"Buried? That's a bit weird."

"Only a bit?" said Samuel sarcastically.

"Have the police ruled out this man Flynn as a person of interest?"

"Yeah. He checks out."

"Lucky he had a dog with him or she could have been lying there a long time," said Jer, trying to imagine what it would have been like for Helena to regain consciousness buried under a pile of seaweed. "So the question is, did someone cover her in seaweed or was she washed ashore with the stuff?"

"Well, if she'd been washed up she'd be dead, wouldn't she – drowned?"

"It looks like Malachy thought he'd killed her and hid her under the seaweed to make his getaway."

"But not in his car which was left at the beach with traces of her blood on the back seat."

"Ah, right." Jer's heart sank. Poor Helena was going to have to accept that the man she loved and trusted had tried to kill her.

Samuel looked at his watch. "The police are looking into his background to see if he had any money problems."

"None of this explains the mystery surrounding the house."

"You don't honestly believe that tale about the house, do you?" Samuel looked contemptuously at his brother. "She's delusional."

"Did you ask the police about it?"

"I did not! I don't want them to think I've lost my marbles."

"But where were they living if not there? She gave an address in that area in Islandmagee when she was admitted to hospital."

"She really has bewitched you, hasn't she?"

"For heaven's sake, Samuel!"

"Well, she's certainly managed to charm Myra."

"What do you mean?"

"Myra's round at your house right now."

Chapter 12

Jer headed for the riverbank, where a breeze was agitating the surface of the water. He lit a cigarette and leaned on the balustrade, reflecting on the cold-blooded nature of Malachy's act. Yet Helena was adamant that he was a kind man and incapable of such cruelty.

If this had been a murder attempt, she'd survived it. He shivered. What if Malachy was still around? He rang Nora.

"Where are you?" she said accusingly before he had time to speak.

"I've just had a chat with Samuel." He realised she was in a car. "You're not driving, are you?"

"Myra's driving us to Cladrach Beach."

"*What?*" He swallowed.

"We think it might help Helena to visit the beach where it all happened."

"Help her how?"

"We can chat later, have to go."

He set off at a brisk pace back to the office. He would spin a few plates then head for Cladrach Beach, wherever it was. Nora had sounded fine, but he was uneasy.

Turning into Sugarhouse Lane, he saw Amy cornered by several people at the door of his building. The flash of a camera made him break into a run.

"*Hey, what the hell's going on?*"

The journalists immediately turned their attention on him, a much more interesting target than his scared junior. There were two photographers and three reporters.

"Ah, Jer McCabe himself!" declared one of them, a middle-aged female with a head of frizzy hair. She squared up to him, the others seemingly content to let her lead the chase.

He nodded to Amy to make herself scarce.

The woman became aware that one of their prey was escaping and turned towards the door which slammed in her face. She rounded on him. "Would you like to comment on accusations that you're inciting people to behave anti-socially?"

A camera flashed, making him flinch. "In my experience, people don't need any encouragement to do that! Now will you please go away! And if I find you've been harassing my staff I'll be making a complaint."

"A complaint, how are you!" she trumpeted. "You can broadcast your nasty little series under the cover of free speech, but you're not prepared to account for the vile stuff you're peddling as entertainment, paid for by the licence fee!"

"If you don't stand aside and let me into my office, I'll have to ring the police."

"You heard that, Mick?" she threw over her shoulder to one of the other reporters. "He threatened me with the police. So much for free speech! You can dish it out, but you can't take it, McCabe!"

He knew if he attempted to push past them, a photo of the tussle would end up on the front page of the *Belfast Chronicle*. On an impulse, he turned and walked back the way he'd come. This took them by surprise, and he heard muttering behind him.

"*Off home early are you, Jer? Nice for some!*" one of the males shouted after him.

He refused to be provoked and continued up the entry.

"*Running home to hold your poor, wee, weirdy wife's hand!*" shouted the female reporter.

He stopped dead in his tracks and felt like running back down the narrow street to put his hands around the woman's neck. Instead, he turned and walked slowly back towards them. She looked disconcerted at his expression – but her surprise was quickly replaced by calculation. She knew she'd landed a punch and identified his weak spot.

His anger was growing, and he brandished his mobile, the only weapon he had.

"Would you like to say that again on camera?" he challenged her.

Her face was stony. The photographers advanced on him, cameras flashing repeatedly, momentarily blinding him.

"Is this *Thoughtless* series some kind of revenge on society for the loss of your baby son?" she said.

He glared in her direction. "*Have you any children?*" he shouted and immediately wished it unsaid.

She looked triumphant. "This isn't about me. It's about you preaching selfishness as a life-choice."

"When did Belfast become a humour-free zone?" he flung at her. "No, don't answer that!" He was suddenly overtaken by a feeling of disgust with the world and turned away. Why had he even tried to defend himself? He should know by now that the press would twist whatever he said or did or failed to do.

"*Coward!*" she shouted at his retreating back.

When he turned the corner, he rang Stella to warn her and the others that the front door of the building was still being staked out, and he'd had to abort his attempt to get into the office.

"You're leaving us to our fate then, are you?" she said bitterly.

He lowered his phone and took a breath. He knew he was stressed and was afraid of saying something irrevocable. When he put the phone back to his ear, she'd rung off.

It was four o'clock by the time he left the city's tangled web behind with relief and headed north up the motorway. He'd been shaken by his brush with the press but told himself he shouldn't be surprised that the reporter had brought up Liam's death. Everything was on record, yet the thought of the press conflating his family's tragedy with his silly *Thoughtless* series made him feel sick. It was bound to impact badly on Nora, if the papers carried the old photo of Liam's pram, crushed and splintered on the footpath. He reflected that Liam would be twenty-two now if he'd lived and wondered who this second son of his might have been. Would he have wanted to make films like his dad and been part of Indigo? A car came up fast behind him, forcing him back into the left lane. Had he been hogging the fast lane? He tried to clear his head of disturbing thoughts and concentrate on his driving.

It was going to take him over an hour to get to Cladrach Beach and Nora and the others would probably be heading for home before he even got there. He put his foot down and pulled out to overtake a couple of lorries, feeling a gust of wind buffet the car. He felt a spurt of anger towards his sister-in-law for coming up with the crazy idea of visiting an isolated beach in this weather, never mind taking two vulnerable women to the site of a possible murder-suicide. He decided to ring Nora once he exited the motorway.

His phone came to life on the seat beside him and the whine of his bagpipe ringtone taunted him for the next thirty seconds while he fought the urge to answer it. After a few seconds' silence, it rang again. Maybe Nora was in trouble.

He lifted the phone and struggled to answer the call with his left hand, swerving to the right.

"Jer, it's me," Nora said, her voice hoarse.

"Are you okay?" he asked anxiously, watching a white car gaining ground on him fast in the rear-view mirror, wondering if it could be a police car. "I'm on the motorway so may have to end this call in a hurry."

"I wish I hadn't come here. It's a horrible place."

"Tell Myra to take you home. She shouldn't have taken you there."

"She didn't want me to come. I've only myself to blame."

"Is Myra there? Can I speak to her?" he said.

"No, they're down on the beach somewhere. I watched for a while, but I got too cold so I came back to the car."

"Hang on a minute." He put his phone down on the passenger seat as the white car overtook him. He let out a breath. It wasn't a police car. He realised he'd let his speed drop and put his foot down again and lifted his phone. "Nora?"

"Yes, I'm here." She seemed to be outside now, because the roar of the wind was cutting through her words.

"Why don't you stay in the car and keep warm, love?"

"What if they don't come back, Jer? It's getting dark."

"I'm on my way and anyway I'm sure they'll be back soon. Get into the car and turn on the radio."

"I can see them now, away along the beach."

"What are they doing?"

"God knows!"

"Nora, I need to exit the motorway. Hang on a sec."

He left the motorway and picked up the phone again only to find that she'd rung off. He cursed and looked for somewhere to pull in. He spotted a gateway, wide enough to allow him to sidle in. Leaving the engine running, he called her back, but her phone was unavailable.

"Stop trying to call me," he muttered. He waited for a minute, hoping his phone would ring, and tried her again, with the same result. Now he was wasting time. He gave it one last try, then texted her: **Sit tight am on my way C u 30 – 40 min.**

Light was draining from the day and he couldn't bear the idea of Nora sitting alone and frightened in the gathering dusk in that cursed place. He concentrated hard on his driving, eating up the miles as the daylight faded.

His phone rang and he picked it up.

"Nora?"

"Mr. Jer McCabe?" said a male voice.

Thinking it was a reporter who'd got hold of his private number, he was about to ring off when the caller announced himself.

"This is Detective Inspector Wright."

There was a roar of blood in Jer's ears and time seemed to stop. A car passed him at speed on the narrow road. He knew he should find somewhere to pull in, but nowhere presented itself, and he was loath to waste more time getting to Nora.

"We've met before, Mr. McCabe. I'm sure you remember?"

"How could I forget? What can I do for you, Detective?" His jaw was rigid.

"Inspector," clarified Wright.

"You've been promoted. Congratulations!"

"Good things come to those of us who wait."

Jer had embarrassed this man in the past by being innocent of the crime for which Wright had pursued him. Jer had been working on a documentary about people-trafficking and had found himself in the frame for the murder of a young woman.

"Are you driving, Mr. McCabe?"

"Yes."

"I take it you're using a hands-free device?"

"Of course," he said and immediately wished it unsaid. There was one lie already. It would be easy for Wright to check his car. He should have ended the call already.

"And where are we off to this evening, McCabe?"

"Much as I'd enjoy a little chat with you, Inspector, would you like to tell me why you've contacted me?" he said, trying to sound unfazed.

"It's come to our attention that you have a woman called Helena Santoro staying with you."

"Yes, my brother Samuel has been in touch with you about it."

"We'd like to talk to Ms Santoro, and you and your wife as soon as possible."

"Why do you need to talk to me and my wife? We're simply putting Helena up for a few days. I presume you're aware she's just been discharged from hospital."

"We are aware of that. I understand your wife was a patient in the same psychiatric ward?"

Jer frowned. He didn't want Nora implicated in all this. Maybe he should pretend he was losing the signal and end the call.

"Were you close to Malachy Murtagh, Mr. McCabe?"

"What? I never met him in my life. Look, Wright, don't try to rope me into this. Nora and I are the Good Samaritans here."

"And what's your wife's connection with Helena Santoro?"

"She has no connection with her. She simply befriended her in hospital and offered her a lift home."

"We'll be calling at your house first thing tomorrow morning, Mr. McCabe, and we would like you and your wife to be present."

"No, I have to get to work. I'm filming."

"Ah yes, your current series has become quite controversial."

"Is that now a crime?"

"If you aren't available to be questioned at home tomorrow morning, what's the earliest you can attend Musgrave Park to be interviewed?"

His blood ran cold. It was at Musgrave Park Police Station that he'd been interrogated by Wright about the murder of a young woman. He still had nightmares about being in the holding cell, contemplating the potential ruin of his life.

"I'll try and rearrange my schedule and be at home in the morning."

"That would be best," said Wright in a self-satisfied tone. "We'll be there at nine."

Jer cursed and threw the mobile into the seat beside him. He was now on the Antrim coast road and the fitful beam from

Maidens lighthouse kept drawing his eyes seaward. Sky and sea had become one in the murk. The tide was full, and the wind was whipping flecks of spray across the road, smearing his windscreen. Time for this glowering, restless sea to give Malachy Murtagh up if he was out there.

Chapter 13

Night had overtaken him by the time his GPS brought him to the entrance of a sandy track leading to Cladrach Beach. He followed the narrow trail, wondering if there would be anywhere to park when he got to the end of it, concerned for his ageing suspension. He rounded a tight bend and spotted Myra's car lit up like a lantern. There was no carpark and she'd left her car on a stretch of grass. He drew up alongside and saw that the internal light was on because the passenger door was wide open.

He switched off his engine and climbed out into the cold night air, aware of the roar of the sea close by. He investigated Myra's car and found it empty. He realised Nora was on the beach and said a silent prayer she was with Myra and Helena and not alone out there in the dark. He closed the door of the car, plunging himself into darkness. Waiting for his eyes to adjust, he listened but could discern no human voices amidst the tumult of air and water. He called Nora's name but the wind whipped it away. He tried ringing her again with no success. Using his phone as a torch, he headed towards the sound of the sea through low sand-dunes fringed with marram-grass.

The wind attacked him as soon as he left the comparative shelter of the dunes and he wished he'd brought his coat but was too anxious about Nora to go back for it. He stumbled over a bank of large, round stones which shifted and rolled under his feet.

Without warning, a small figure rose before him and a pale face stared into the beam of light, eyes wide with shock. He wrapped his arms around Nora, holding her close to his body, and felt her heart beating furiously. He loosened his embrace and moved her back a little to look at her face, the light from his phone casting strange shadows across her features.

"Nora, love, what are you doing out here? You should've stayed in the car."

He moved the beam to catch her eyes and realised with dismay she was staring into the light, seemingly unable to speak. He led her away from the crash and hiss of the surf, out of the wind and made her comfortable in the back seat of his car, covering her with his coat. He turned on the engine to get the heating working again and left the radio and interior light on.

"I'm just going to find Myra and Helena. I'll be back in a jiffy," he reassured her, but got no reply.

Afraid of draining the battery of his mobile, he used the meagre spill of light from his car to find the path back to the beach. The sky was clearing, and he could now make out the lights of Rathlin Island across the channel. He made his way through piles of rotting seaweed to the water's edge where choppy waves were clawing at the shingle. The wind seemed to be getting stronger and shredding the clouds above him. The rising moon juked from cloud to cloud, ringing each in an ochre bruise. His eyes were used to the dark now and the faint illumination of the moon was giving form to shapes around him, allowing him to see that he was near one end of the beach. He activated the thin beam of his phone and swept the black, striated surface of rocks, which gleamed wet with spray. He presumed this was where the police had found Malachy's jacket with the suicide note. The light from his mobile was growing weaker so he switched it off again and stood in the darkness to orientate himself.

A flicker of light at the other end of the beach caught his eye. He squeezed his eyes closed for an instant then tried to refocus. There were three, no, four pinpricks of light now. He started walking towards the lights. A wave crashed beside him, sucking away the pebbles beneath his feet and filling his shoes with water, making him scramble away from the waterline. More lights appeared and he began to pant as he trudged through the loose stones, trying to keep clear of the surf which licked at his feet. Closer now, he could see that the lights formed a circle and were flickering. He moved forward more carefully, trying to make sense of the shadows which flitted inside the circle.

There was a moan which seemed to be coming from the sea itself. A second voice echoed the first, moaning and sobbing. The sounds coalesced into a name which the wind whirled away into the darkness. *Malachy.* If his spirit was near, he could hardly resist this powerful supplication.

He halted twenty yards from the circle of lights, which he could now see were candles in jam-jars. Helena and Myra had loosened their hair and were dressed in pale flowing clothing which reflected the light. They were circling inside the ring of candles, chanting Malachy's name. He wondered what Samuel would think if he could see his sensible wife at this moment.

Intrigued by the beauty and strangeness of the scene, he pulled out his mobile and started videoing what was happening. A gust of wind blew out several candles, provoking a howl of anguish. The two figures became one, their arms wrapped around each other and stood swaying in the centre of the circle, hair blowing wildly around their heads. He edged closer to get a better view. The wind eddied and suddenly parted the veil of hair to reveal Helena and Myra kissing each other hungrily. They sank to the ground, their bodies entwined, writhing unnervingly close to the lighted candles. He stopped filming and put the phone back in his pocket, knowing he could never show this footage to his brother. He backed away, not wanting them to know he'd witnessed their moment of abandon but managed to set off a mini-avalanche of stones, lost his footing and fell heavily.

Helena screamed Malachy's name and, when he struggled to his feet, he saw Myra was staring in his direction like a hunted animal, though he didn't think she could actually see him beyond the pool of candlelight. The moon appeared from behind a rag of cloud, lighting a glittering path across the sea and Helena suddenly took flight towards it. She was in the water before either Jer or Myra had time to stop her. Then she was gone. He was the one who reacted first, tearing off his jacket and flinging it aside, before wading into the freezing, black water. He tried to keep his eye on the place he'd seen her slip under. Her head resurfaced a few yards further out and he lunged towards her. Calling out to her, he tried to grab her hand, but the shelf of shingle under his feet fell away and he went under. It was the sudden change of sound as much as the cold that shocked him. He was caught in the giant pulse of the ocean, drumming in the icy darkness.

When he broke the surface again, the moon was hidden and he struggled to find his bearings, turning until he could see the circle of lights on the beach which now seemed very far away. He knew he should be panicking but a strange detachment had overtaken him. The stabs of pain from the glacial water were easing and his limbs felt heavy. He could no longer see Helena and he tried to swim back towards the lights but didn't seem to be making any progress. A pair of cold hands gripped his head like a vice and rolled him onto his back. He flailed feebly, throwing his arms wide and looking up into the night sky. A film of water passed over his face, making him cough and splutter. He could feel a body kicking out strongly below his and the sensation of being pulled through the water.

Then there were two voices and long wet hair covered his face.

"I've found him, Myra! I've found him!"

The two women dragged him out of the sea onto the stones where he rolled over and retched, struggling onto his hands and knees, coughing seawater from his lungs.

"It's okay, my love, you're safe now!" Helena was saying over and over.

He pushed himself onto his knees and saw Myra coming towards him, holding one of the lighted candles in its jar. Lit from below by the flickering candle, her face looked demonic. She leaned over and held the candle near his face, her hands trembling.

"Jer, what the fuck?"

She backed away, leaving him in the dark with Helena who touched his face with icy hands as if trying to read it by feel like a blind woman.

"Helena, it's me, Jer," he whispered.

"I know it's you," she whispered back.

He was shuddering with cold. "We need to go back to the car and get warm," he said through chattering teeth.

"Your skin is so cold," she said, holding his face between her hands.

She leaned in and kissed him on the mouth with bloodless lips. Myra loomed over them, and he felt her long hair sting his eye as she pulled Helena away from him.

He heaved himself up, shaking with cold as the wind circled him. He stumbled across the shingle and found his jacket, which he put on over his wet shirt, though it did little to halt his plummeting body temperature.

Myra led Helena away from him along the beach. He picked up one of the jam-jars with its lighted candle and followed them. He could hear Helena weeping and Myra's voice, low and tense, hurrying her along the water's edge.

He reached the cars in time to see her push Helena into the front seat of her car and slam the door. He blew out the candle he was holding and threw the jam-jar away before climbing into his own car. He turned to check on Nora who was still curled up in the foetal position on the back seat with her eyes open. The car was mercifully warm. With a roar of her engine, Myra reversed up the track and was gone, carrying Helena away with her into the night.

"It's okay, Nora. We're going home now," he said breathlessly, his voice shaking.

He turned the heating up full but realised he'd catch his death sitting in wet clothes all the way home. Reluctantly he opened the door of the car and stepped out to strip off his clothes which he pitched into the foot-well of the passenger seat. He got back into the driver's seat, closed the door, and let the hot air from the car-heater warm his body. He was shivering less violently now, and leaned back and closed his eyes, shaking his head slowly from side to side at the absurdity of his situation. He wondered fleetingly about the tiny flames they had abandoned on the beach. How long would they resist the wind and spray, beckoning to the ocean of ghosts? He imagined Malachy emerging from the dark water, drawn by the empty circle of light.

He shouted with shock when the passenger door was suddenly wrenched open, and cupped his hands protectively over his genitals. It was Helena, who climbed into the seat beside him, accompanied by a current of icy air. She pulled the door closed and turned to him, tears streaming down her face.

"Jesus, Helena, you scared me half to death!" His heart was pounding.

"I'm sorry," she murmured then gasped when she realised he was naked. She smiled at him through her tears, then burst out laughing. "You've got no clothes on!"

Perplexed, he watched her laugh, a smile creeping onto his face despite himself. He glanced down at his clothes which were in a sodden heap under her feet then reached back and lifted his coat from Nora's prone body. Helena's eyes followed his hand, and she stopped laughing and stared at Nora, as if she'd never set eyes on her before. He struggled awkwardly into his coat, unwilling to step outside into the cold wind, even for a moment. He wished the coat was longer, but at least it covered his torso.

"Has Myra gone?"

She nodded. "I made her let me out. I wanted to be with you."

Unsure what to make of this declaration, he turned to check on Nora whose eyes were now closed.

"I wish you hadn't left Nora on her own," he said reproachfully, relenting a bit when he saw Helena's stricken expression. Her face was deathly pale and her lips purple with cold. He felt he should offer her his dry coat but that would mean putting his sodden underwear back on. "Do you want to take off your wet things?" he suggested half-heartedly.

"No, I'm fine," she said, wrapping her arms around her body.

He fought exhaustion all the way home and wished Helena would talk to him, but she seemed to have fallen asleep, despite her wet clothes. He kept the heater on full the whole way and the heat, combined with its drone, threatened to lull him into unconsciousness. He put off thinking about the ramifications of what he'd witnessed, intent on getting the two sleeping women to a place of safety.

When they reached home, Helena helped him get Nora out of the car and into the house. Upstairs, she headed for the bathroom while he put Nora to bed and tried to persuade her to take her medication. She was like a sullen child now, refusing to swallow anything. She turned her back on him and disappeared under the duvet. He took off his coat, threw on some clothes and went downstairs, where there was no sign of Helena. She must have gone to bed, he thought. He made himself a hot whiskey and brought it up to the spare room, unable to face climbing into bed with Nora.

Despite his exhaustion, sleep didn't come easily and when it did it was troubled and feverish. He dreamt he was in the sea again in the dark, trying to find Nora, who was being pulled away from him by a powerful undertow. He became aware of the presence of an unknown woman near him. He was desperate to reach Nora, but this other woman kept stopping him, running her hands across his naked body, fondling him, arousing him. Then he was lying on the beach entwined with this stranger, surrounded by flickering lights. Strong hands were pinning down his upper arms and cold lips kissed his closed eyelids, forcing his head back. He tried to open his eyes but that seemed impossible, and he was finding it hard to breathe. A wave of desire lifted him, arching his back and covering his body in a film of cold sweat. His hands were lifted onto the splayed thighs astride him. He groaned as he was mounted, moving his hands along the thighs till he could feel hipbones grinding on his pelvis, carrying him away into orgasm. There was hair in his mouth and hoarse breathing near his face, mingling with his own moans of desire.

Nora's voice came from somewhere, a long way off, sounding frightened, calling his name.

Tuesday 28th October

Chapter 14

A long peal of the doorbell woke him in the morning. He turned to check he was alone in the spare bed, sending a shooting pain up the back of his head. His mouth was dry and his throat ached, as if he had been drinking the night before, although he'd only had the one hot whiskey. He wondered if he was sickening for the flu. Someone used the front-door knocker with considerable force and the sound of metal hammered on metal vibrated through the house and seemed to penetrate his skull. He swung his legs out of the bed and attempted to stand up, but his head swam and he felt nauseous. He sat back down, head in hands, pressing his fingertips into tender eye-sockets. He heard the front door open and a male voice, followed by a cry from Nora which propelled him to his feet. He dressed hurriedly in a track-suit and stumbled down the stairs.

Through the frosted glass of the inside hall door, he could see the dark shape of a tall man framed by the front door which lay open. He pulled open the inner door to find Nora on her knees sobbing, with Detective Inspector Wright standing at the front door and a uniformed, female officer behind him. He knew it was the police uniform that had upset her.

"Something awful's happened, I know it!" she sobbed.

"Nora, love, there's nothing wrong." He put a hand up to signal to the police officers to wait while he helped Nora to her feet and led her into the living room. "They're here to talk to Helena." He got her to sit on the sofa, then turned to find Wright and his sidekick had followed them into the room. "Excuse me but no-one invited you in!"

"Just wanted to see if I could help with your wife," said Wright undaunted, looking curiously at Nora, who stared up at him with terrified eyes.

A stab of pain shot up the back of Jer's head, causing him to close his eyes and sway. Nora moaned and broke down again, weeping as if her heart would break.

Eyeing him unsympathetically, Jer saw that the detective had put on weight since they'd last encountered each other and now seemed to loom large in this suburban living room. He had a bullet-shaped head with gunmetal grey hair, cut to within an inch of its life.

The female officer was half her colleague's size, and her dyed-blonde hair was mousey at the roots and restrained in a short ponytail. She took it upon herself to perch on the edge of the sofa and put her arm around Nora.

"I'm afraid we're going to have to do this some other time," said Jer. "You've upset my wife."

"If you remember, we're here by prior appointment. Perhaps you omitted to tell your wife to expect us. Is Helena Santoro here?"

"*Em*, I think so. I haven't seen her yet this morning." He looked anxiously at Nora. Her sobs had now subsided, and she let her head fall back on the cushions and closed her eyes, taking quick, shallow breaths. "Nora, let me take you upstairs to bed," he said, keen to get her away from the police officers.

"I don't want to go back into hospital!" There was a thread of hysteria in her voice which he didn't like.

"I don't want you to either, love," he said soothingly. "The police are here to see Helena about the money that's missing from her account. It's nothing to do with us."

"But I know him," she said, pointing at Wright. "I've seen him before."

Jer made a grimace and tried to think how to edit his next sentence. His efforts to avoid anything which might upset Nora had a way of stymying a lot of their attempts at communication. This morning he was too tired to think of a comforting lie.

"He's Detective Wright, the one who – "

"*Who's out to get you!*" She glared at the detective who raised his eyebrows. "He accused you of murdering some girl!" She looked manic.

"He's just doing his job," said Jer lamely. "Have you seen Helena this morning?"

"No!" she snapped. "I hope she went home with Myra!"

He knelt in front of her. "Do you want her to leave, Nora?"

She stuck out her chin. "We can't just chuck her out if she has nowhere to go." She looked up at Wright. "Her house has disappeared, you see."

Wright's eyes widened, and he glanced at the female officer.

"She must still be asleep," said Jer, getting up wearily. "I'll go and wake her. Maybe you can find her missing partner and house," he said to Wright grimly. "We don't seem to be getting very far."

When he got to the top of the stairs he turned and was annoyed to see Wright following him.

"Which room is she in?" the policeman asked.

"Will you please go back downstairs and wait in the living room instead of wandering around my house uninvited!" Jer said forcefully.

He waited until Wright had retreated to the bottom of the stairs before knocking on the door of Helena's bedroom. "Helena, the police are here to talk to you!" He leaned his head towards the door and listened. There was no sound from inside. He knocked again, more firmly this time, and called her, trying to stop a note of irritation entering his tone. *"Helena, please wake up, the police need to talk to you!"* He put one hand on each side of the doorframe, and stepped back, letting his aching head hang down. Had she come into his bed during the night and had sex with him? He lifted his head and was assailed by a wave of nausea. He grasped the door handle and entered the room.

Inside, the curtains were closed, and his eyes were drawn to a lighted candle, which he recognised as the one he'd found in her bag. It was now almost burned away, the flame guttering in the draught from the open door. There was a strange, bitter smell in the air, which he struggled to place. He stared at the bed where she was lying naked on top of the duvet with her eyes closed. Her hands were clasped across her abdomen, holding the stem of an oval hand-mirror of Eimear's. He approached the bed and realised he was walking over discarded clothes which felt damp under the soles of his bare feet. He bent over to look down at her body and his own eyes, dark with desire, stared back at him from the mirror, giving him the peculiar impression that he was looking out from inside her womb. Was she breathing? He tried to focus on her chest but her nut-brown nipples distracted him.

"Is she dead?"

It was Wright who'd spoken. Jer turned to look at the policeman, too shocked to respond. Wright walked briskly to the bed, reached past him and lifted Helena's wrist to feel for a pulse. She gasped, like someone coming up for air, and her eyes snapped open.

"*Matthews, get in here!*" barked the detective.

The young policewoman entered the room a few seconds later and recoiled at the sight of the naked woman.

"Find something for her to put on!" Wright commanded.

Helena started panting, her eyes darting from one man to the other.

"Take it easy, Helena," said Jer, his voice faltering. "This is Detective Wright who's here to talk to you about your missing money."

She struggled to rise, and the two men took her arms and helped her sit up and swing her legs over the edge of the bed.

Jer felt deeply uncomfortable handling the naked Helena in this way. He met Wright's eyes, seeing no similar unease in the policeman's expression.

"I think we should leave the room now, Wright, don't you?"

"After you," said the detective with the ghost of a smile.

They left Matthews to help Helena into some clothes while Wright followed him downstairs. Jer asked him to wait in the living room. He went into the kitchen to make a pot of coffee, glad of a moment to gather his wits.

Approaching the living room with mugs of coffee on a tray ten minutes later, he was concerned to hear Nora's voice, gabbling in a high-pitched, urgent tone. He was reduced to kicking the closed door to attract attention.

"Come in and join the party," smirked Wright, opening the door wide. "We've been hearing all about last night's fun."

Nora was curled up on one of the two sofas in the room, looking bemused to hear her account of their visit to Cladrach Beach described as fun. Matthews was sitting beside her.

Now fully dressed in Myra's castoff peach-coloured cashmere sweater and black slacks, Helena was sitting bolt upright on the other sofa. All that's missing is the string of pearls, Jer thought. Her anxious face had relaxed into a smile when he'd entered the room, a transformation not lost on Wright, he noticed.

He set the tray down on the coffee table and invited all present to help themselves to a mug of coffee, unwilling to go on playing housemaid. He wondered what Nora had been saying.

Wright had seated himself in Jer's favourite armchair, forcing him to sit on the two-seater sofa beside Helena who smiled at him and slipped her arm under his.

At a nod from Wright, Constable Matthews passed her superior a mug of coffee and it was then that Jer noticed the recording device on the table.

"You're recording this?"

"Just for note-taking purposes," said Wright. "Have you any objection?"

He was tempted to fetch a recording device of his own but decided it might be unwise to appear defensive. None of this had anything to do with him. He shrugged.

"And what was Mrs. Myra McCabe doing while you and your friend here frolicked in the waves?" Wright asked Helena.

Jer felt cold all over. Wright now knew about Myra's involvement and would enjoy gossiping about it in judicial circles and embarrassing Samuel.

"Just a minute," he said. "I thought you were here to investigate the disappearance of money from her account?"

"Oh, we are, Jer, but we – "

"I would prefer to be addressed as Mr. McCabe."

"Of course. No offence intended."

"None taken," he said evenly, mindful that every word was being taped.

"Have you any idea why such a large sum might've been withdrawn from your account, Miss Santoro?"

"No."

"Could you tell me who has access to your account?"

"How do you mean?"

"Whoever accessed it must have your account details and password. Did you give that information to anyone?"

"Only to Malachy." Her face fell, the realisation dawning. "Malachy would never do such a thing. I would trust him with my life."

She put her hand on Jer's knee and he shifted uncomfortably in his seat, moving his leg away from her hand.

"The money was taken from your account the day your partner went missing," said Wright. "Perhaps you can shed some light on all this, Mr. McCabe?"

"What, me? No, of course I can't. I only met Helena for the first time a few days ago when my wife offered her a lift home from the hospital."

"And you brought her here to your home, despite the fact that she was a complete stranger?"

Jer looked desperately at Nora, dismayed to see her glaring at him.

"You never told me you knew Helena!" she said.

"Nora, what are you saying? I didn't know Helena before you introduced her to me at the hospital!"

The house-phone chose that moment to ring, and Jer excused himself with relief and went to answer it in his study.

"Jer?"

"Hugh! What time is it?"

"We've been waiting for you for almost an hour now."

"Shit, I'm –" He didn't know what to say. He could hear birds singing and guessed that Hugh had stepped out of the sports centre to ring him. "I'm really sorry. I have a situation here at home. The police are here."

"What? Oh my God! Have you been threatened?"

"It's nothing to do with *Thoughtless*. It's a long story which I promise I'll share with you when I can."

"Are you coming to the shoot?"

"I'm not sure I'll be able to make it. Who's on camera?"

"Esler."

Jer's heart sank.

"We have him booked till one," said Hugh miserably.

"Would you mind making a start? You know what we were planning to do."

"Shit, Jer. He'll never take direction from me."

"Give him the phone and I'll talk to him." He waited, listening to the change in the acoustics when Hugh went inside.

"Jer? Slept in again, have we?"

"Hi, Johnny. Apologies for this. Beyond my control, I'm afraid. We have all the permissions sorted there in the Sports Centre, so I don't want to waste the moment. Hugh has a list of the shots we need so I'd greatly appreciate it if you could work with him in the meantime, and I'll be there as soon as I can get away here."

"Where's here?"

Jer closed his eyes in irritation. There was a knock and Matthews stuck her head around the door.

"Inspector Wright would like to speak to you, Mr. McCabe."

"I'll be right there."

"Wright?" said Johnny. "Well, well, who's he saying you murdered this time?"

"For Christ's sake, Johnny, give me a break."

"Hard to resist. You're very accident prone."

"Tell me about it! Johnny, get something decent on tape for me down there and I'll be eternally grateful."

"Consider it done, but you owe me a pint and the back-story."

"Thanks, you're a mate."

He ended the call and stood with the phone in his hand, resisting the impulse to fire it across the room. He felt as if he'd lost control over his life. The news that the police were at his house would be round the tightly knit Belfast media world by lunchtime.

Re-entering the living room, he wondered what had been said in his absence. To his surprise Nora and Helena were nowhere to be seen and Wright was standing with his back to the door, staring out the bay window. He noted the recording device was still on the coffee table.

Wright turned to face him. "Mr. McCabe, did you take three hundred and fifteen thousand pounds from Helena Santoro's account?"

He stalled in shock. "No, of course I didn't. I wouldn't have the first idea how to steal money from somebody else's account even if I had a mind to. I don't even do online banking."

"When I asked Ms. Santoro just now if she thought you might have taken her money, she said if you had you must have had a good reason. Why would she say such a thing, Mr. Mc Cabe, if you and she didn't have a relationship stretching back some time?"

Jer glanced towards the door and lowered his voice. "The woman is delusional. I've been trying to get a coherent account of what happened to her for the past few days and I'm none the wiser."

Wright rolled his eyes by way of response.

"For God's sake, man, the woman is a psychiatric case!" Jer fought to control his temper. "For the record, can I reiterate that my wife met Helena Santoro recently while they were both patients in hospital. I met Helena for the first time on Friday, when my wife asked me to give her a lift home."

"A lift home to here?"

"No! Helena told us she lived in Islandmagee, so I drove there and – "

"Was your wife with you?"

"Yes, of course."

"If you drove Ms. Santoro home to Islandmagee, how did she end up here?"

Jer felt a measure of relief at finally being able to tell someone in officialdom about his predicament. "Helena directed us to a lane, but there was no house at the end of it."

Wright frowned and shook his head. "You really can spin a fine yarn!"

Jer sat down on the sofa, feeling exhausted.

The detective's face darkened. "I'd like to take your computer and mobile phone to be analysed."

"No, you bloody well won't – I need them for my work!"

"It'd be preferable if you handed them over voluntarily, but I can get a warrant easily enough."

"Well, then, that's what you're going to have to do. In the meantime, I'm not prepared to answer any more questions without my legal counsel present."

Wright leaned over and lifted the recording device, switched it off and slipped it into his pocket. "Ah yes – big brother. It's always so much more fun with Samuel in the game. And this time we'll get to play with his wife too. Happy days!"

Wright walked out of the room, leaving Jer feeling ill with apprehension. He heard voices in the kitchen and then the front door slam. He looked towards the window to see Wright and Matthews pass by. The female officer shot him a parting look of disgust.

He found Nora in the kitchen, washing up the coffee mugs.

"What on earth was said when I was out of the room?" he asked.

She stopped for a moment without looking at him then continued rinsing the mugs, setting each one carefully on the draining board.

"Please, Nora, that detective now thinks I stole Helena's money and may have something to do with her partner's disappearance."

She reached past him for the towel and stood looking at him curiously while she dried her hands. "Is it Jer talking to me or Malachy?" she said in a timorous whisper.

His mouth fell open in dismay. He took a step towards his wife, but she backed away. "Nora, it's me, Jer, for God's sake!"

"I'm glad Malachy's spirit entered you and not Myra," she said, smiling at him strangely.

"What are you talking about? Nora, I'm completely in the dark here."

"Helena needed one of us to be the receptor for Malachy's spirit. I wanted to do it for her but, in the end, it was too dark and cold, and I was scared."

"Oh my God, you didn't actually agree to that?"

"She was so desperate. When I couldn't face it, Myra stepped in. I knew she would – she's such a bitch."

"You're telling me Helena was attempting to conjure up Malachy's spirit and – " At this point, words failed him.

"And ask him to enter Myra, yes."

Jer felt a chill move across his back.

"But you got in the way, and Malachy's spirit has entered you."

He rocked back on his heels, put his hand up and pressed his forehead. "Nora, this is all mumbo-jumbo. You mustn't believe this stuff!"

She looked hurt. "But you do believe in an afterlife? You believe Liam's little spirit is still here with us? I've always known he's somewhere near us, just out of sight."

He gazed at his wife in dismay. He couldn't tell her he believed their baby son lived only in their memories and the few photos they'd taken of him before his life had been extinguished. "Have you taken your medication?"

She shook her head defiantly. "Medication isn't always the answer," she said, her voice tight.

"I'm sorry, love, I didn't mean …" he said, holding out his arms, but she dodged away from him.

"Don't fight it, Jer. Malachy won't do you any harm if you accept him," she said, backing out of the room.

Chapter 15

Jer took a quick shower and put on some clean clothes, trying to regain some control over his own body if nothing else. He left the house and jumped in his car, desperate to put some distance between himself and the two women currently under his roof, both of whom seemed to be laying claim to him. Was this what it was like to have two wives? His affair with Stella had never felt claustrophobic the way this did. He grudgingly admitted to himself that he was disappointed that Nora was happy to share him with Helena – payback for having to share him with Stella, he thought ruefully. But then, he'd never have been unfaithful if Nora hadn't gone off the deep end after Eimear and Rory had left home in quick succession, and declared herself a lesbian, albeit for only a few months.

No-one would have blamed him if he'd divorced her back then and he'd been working up to it when she came home, lost and broken, and he'd taken her back. Hardly in a position to complain that there were now three people in their marriage, she'd adamantly refused to acknowledge Stella's role in his life. His affair had eventually petered out, although Stella had clung to the belief that he would divorce Nora sooner or later, an expectation she now seemed to have finally relinquished.

So Nora was ready to share him with this stranger. He was exasperated with his wife and sickened by the possibility that Helena had had sex with him while he slept, yet acutely aware that, if it had been a vivid dream, it had been generated by his own desire. At least he was now sure there was no sexual attraction between Helena and Nora. Myra was a different story, judging by her reaction when she'd first met Helena, and the scene he'd witnessed on the beach. Then again, it was possible she had been playing the part of Malachy.

Despite her struggle with mental illness, he knew Nora had a highly competitive personality and was becoming jealous of the developing relationship between Helena and Myra. What had she said? 'I'm glad he entered you, not Myra.' Her rivalry with Myra was such that she was unwilling to share Helena with her, even if it meant the haunting of her husband by a dead man. His headache was getting worse and he squeezed his eyes shut for a moment, trying to banish an arc of splintered light at the periphery of his vision.

He pulled up at a newsagent's in search of painkillers and a bottle of water. Standing at the counter, the front page of a newspaper caught his eye. '**THE FUTURE'S ROSIE!**' read the headline and it was accompanied by a photo of none other than Rosie herself. He added the newspaper to his purchases and headed back to the car.

"Young Rosie White, a producer with the troubled Indigo Productions, has just landed a plum job in New York. It's an ill wind and all that . . ."

He threw the newspaper aside and fumbled with the pack of tablets, swallowing two with a slug of water. "Nice one, Rosie," he muttered. "Not even a phone call."

A bus bore down on him from behind, forcing him to pull away from the kerb. His priority should be to ring Samuel. If Wright was intent on pinning something criminal on him, he needed Samuel's expert legal advice and protection.

He parked in his space outside Aggie's house and phoned his brother.

"Jer, what the hell?"

"Samuel, I need to talk to you, I – "

"Who is this infernal woman you've brought into our lives?" When he failed to respond, Samuel swept on. "She has Myra bewitched!"

He felt sad for his brother – his sister-in-law wasn't bewitched, she was in love. "I trust she got home safely last night?" he said sheepishly.

"No bloody thanks to you. What the hell went on at that beach?"

"I only arrived towards the end of proceedings."

"Proceedings? You make it sound like a courtroom drama!"

He took a deep breath. "Helena was carrying out some sort of . . . ritual."

"You mean spell?"

"Well, yes, I suppose I do."

"And Myra was party to all this?"

"Yes, she was, Samuel." A silence hummed between them. "Is she okay?"

"She's many things, but okay wouldn't be one of them."

"Nora's not great either."

"I hate to state the obvious, but you need to get that woman Helena back to the clinic right now."

"Believe me, there's nothing I'd like more, but there's been a complication."

"When is there ever not a complication in your life?"

"Detective Wright paid us a visit this morning."

"Wright is on the case?" Samuel sounded thrown.

"Because of the money missing from Helena's account, they're taking a fresh look at Malachy's disappearance."

"I know."

He waited, giving Samuel time to calculate and was surprised and deflated when his brother returned to events at Cladrach the evening before.

"I need you to tell me exactly what went on last night."

He felt conflicted. "What has Myra said?" he began cautiously.

"That Helena ran into the sea, and you went in after her."

"Guilty as charged. But, to be honest, she saved my life rather than the other way round. I think my body went into shock because of the cold, and she got me back to the shore."

"And where was Myra while all this was going on?"

"She was on the beach. She helped Helena drag me out of the sea."

"I take it Helena was trying to do away with herself?" said Samuel flatly.

"Gosh, no, I don't think she was trying to take her own life. You see, she was trying to summon Malachy's spirit and she ran into the sea to find him."

"Oh, boy! She must've been disappointed when she only found you!"

"Here's the thing …" Jer paused, finding it hard to believe he was saying this. "She seems to believe that Malachy's spirit has entered me."

Samuel gave a shout of derisive laughter.

"Just be thankful Malachy's spirit hasn't taken up residence in Myra!" Jer snapped. "That's what was supposed to happen."

Samuel fell silent, making Jer regret what he'd said. He needed to be more careful.

"Apparently the original plan was for Nora to be the receptor for Malachy's spirit."

"Oh my God!"

"I know. But it was dark and cold on the beach –"

"And Nora got scared," finished Samuel.

"Who wouldn't?"

"Myra obviously."

"Helena must have talked her into it."

"Then you arrive, playing the hero and Malachy's spirit ends up in you." Samuel started to laugh again. "So how does it feel having the ghost or, sorry, the spirit of Malachy in your – head?"

"Like a hangover," he said, grinning despite himself. "The only problem is Helena kept relating to me oddly in front of Wright, who's now convinced we're in a relationship."

"Are you?"

"No, we bloody aren't!"

"I get it. He's putting you in the frame for getting rid of Helena's partner so you can have your wicked way with the willowy Helena?"

"He wants to take my phone and computer."

"*Mm*, he probably can make a case to do that."

"I told him I wouldn't answer any more questions without you present."

"Hang on, I can't represent you in this. There's a conflict of interest."

Jer experienced a falling sensation. "Christ, Samuel, I need you." He thought quickly. "Wright knows Myra's involved," he added desperately.

"What did you say about her?"

"I didn't say anything, but Helena and Nora obviously did when I was out of the room."

"You left those two alone with him?"

"I had a phone call from work I had to take."

At that moment Aggie's front door opened and the woman herself emerged, enveloped in her oversized, cerise dressing gown, the inevitable fag in hand. She advanced on his car. He lowered the window.

"Why the fuck are you sitting there staring at my house?"

"Morning, Aggie, sorry, my head's away with it. I'm just talking to my brother."

"I don't care if you're talking to Elvis *fucking* Presley, you're not doing it in my front garden!"

"No problem. Didn't mean to disturb you."

"And you can tell that friend of yours to piss off too!"

"What friend?"

"The young fella in the Mini who keeps nosing round here. Is he your boyfriend or what?"

"No, he is not!"

"I can get the lads to see him off if you want, for a price."

"No, no, Aggie, please don't do that!"

She looked disappointed. "I need something for all this – disturbance."

He searched his pockets. The only note he had was a twenty. He handed it out the window reluctantly.

"You have a nice day now, Jer, and mind yourself," she said ominously.

He lifted his phone again and saw it was dead.

On his way to the office, he remembered he should have headed straight to the sports centre where the crew was filming. He stopped in the middle of the street and groaned. It was now a quarter to twelve and even if he made a superhuman effort to get there, he'd be too late to be of any use.

He climbed the stairs to the office, hopeful of an hour's respite before Hugh and Amy would return, and was embarrassed to find Amy there alone, slumped in a chair, her feet up on a desk. She stared at him, then turned back to her laptop which was balanced precariously on her thighs. He could hear the tinny beat of rock music from the headphones she chose not to remove. He mouthed a greeting and headed for his own desk where he plugged his phone in to charge.

He quickly came to the conclusion that he'd never be able to concentrate on what he had to do with her simmering on the other side of the room, so made two mugs of coffee and went and stood in front of her. He set the mug of coffee down beside her and waited, sipping his coffee till she finally boiled over, tore off the headphones and shouted at him.

"*Everything's gone to shit! Rosie's done a runner and you've really upset Hugh! You know what a bully Esler is! He gave Hugh such a hard time this morning!*" She looked at him accusingly. "Where were you anyway?" she added, her vehemence losing momentum.

He set down his mug, pulled over a chair and sat down facing her. "I'm really sorry about this morning, Amy." He looked into her young face, trying to decide how much of his middle-aged angst to share with her. "Maybe Hugh told you – the police turned up at my house this morning."

Her eyes slid away. "Yeah. He said."

Jer wondered if she thought it was a lie. "A friend of my wife is staying with us, and we've discovered that her savings account was cleaned out while she was in hospital." He had her attention now.

"Is this the artist whose house has vanished?"

He nodded. "Rosie told you about that?"

Amy looked uneasy. "Maybe she wasn't supposed to?"

"It's fine, Amy."

"You're saying her house is gone and now her money's been stolen? That's horrendous!"

"My brother Samuel contacted the police and they arrived at my house this morning, first thing." He was relieved to see he'd succeeded in distracting her from her bad humour. "It's a bit complicated. This friend, she lost her partner recently."

"You mean he died?"

"Yeah, well, he's missing – he left a suicide note on a beach."

"Blimey. He drowned himself?"

"That's what the police were thinking but now that my friend's money is missing, they're beginning to wonder if the partner has taken it and disappeared." He didn't choose to mention that they had all but accused him.

She looked at him apologetically. "And you and your wife are looking after her."

"Nora has really taken to her and wants to help. They met in hospital, you see." He saw by her expression she already knew about Nora's mental illness and felt a wave of resentment against Stella who had to be the person who'd shared that information with their young team.

Amy gave him a sheepish look. "You have your hands full! Stella says you attract trouble."

"Where is she today anyway?" he said, frowning.

"She went out to buy her wedding dress."

The hand holding his coffee mug stalled on the way to his mouth and he stared at Amy, whose face mirrored the shock in his.

"You didn't know," she said, looking appalled. "I'm so sorry, Jer, I should have . . ." Her voice died and she took a swallow of her coffee to hide her dismay.

"Who's she marrying?" he said, trying and failing to keep his voice steady.

"Some guy from her church. I think it all happened quite fast."

He nodded and stood up.

"Is there anything I can do for you?" she said, her eyes moist.

He thought for a moment, "You know what started this whole thing off? When I went to collect Nora from hospital, she asked me to give Helena a lift home. I presumed it was into Belfast and was pretty pissed off to find I had to drive all the way to Islandmagee."

"Where's that?"

"It one of our best-kept secrets – a beautiful, wee peninsula between Belfast and Larne. She directed us to a lane, but when we got to the end of it, there was no house."

"Wrong lane?"

"That's what I thought. We brought her home to Belfast that evening because she was distraught. We had another go the next day, with the same result – she took us to the same empty hillside."

"Maybe the house is just a figment of her imagination?"

"Possibly, but when I was standing there in that empty space, I believed her. I could see the house."

"The power of suggestion!"

"You're probably right. I just haven't had time to delve into it properly and prove whether it existed or not."

"You want me to?"

"Could you bear to? It would be such a relief to have something firm to go on."

"I'll give it a try. Have you got an address?"

"It's pretty rudimentary, I'm afraid – there's no postcode. Carraig na Rón, Mullaghboy, Islandmagee." He scribbled the address down on a Post-it note. "And the guy who owned it was Malachy Murtagh."

"The missing partner!"

"You got it."

He left her to it and walked back to his desk, his head bent. He took up his usual position, checking his messages, while his phone was charging. There were several voicemails from various press-outlets wanting an interview which he quickly deleted. The final message was from someone called Derek. Did he know a Derek? This one was blessed with a plummy English accent. The content of the message made him scramble to his feet, grab his coat and head for the door.

"Jer, hang on! I have a map of Islandmagee up here. Can you show me the route you took?"

He peered at the screen, located Middle Road and followed the twists and turns they'd made, which he'd tried to memorise. He touched the screen to show Amy where the house should be, and the map quivered and slipped away.

"Sorry, always forget these things are touchscreen."

Amy got the map back and zoomed in on the spot he'd indicated.

"That's the best I can do," he said.

"Okay. Did she describe the house?"

"She said it was a one-storey building with a converted roof-space and a glass gable. It had a slate roof and, oh yes, it's rendered and painted olive green."

"Great, all very specific. I can see why you believed her."

"There were other things too. You know the way people always planted trees around their cottages for shelter? Well, the trees there seemed to be pointing to the missing house."

"Right, so a circle of trees?"

"Not quite a circle – and there's a big area of brambles between it and the cliffs. Look, thanks for doing this, Amy. I can't tell you what a weight it's taking off my mind."

"No probs. You heading out?

"Yeah, I've just had a message from someone who knows Helena."

Chapter 16

Jer stood in the doorway of the building to light a cigarette, drawing the smoke into his lungs and holding it there till his head swam. He closed his eyes. When he opened them, he was crying. So, this was it – Stella was getting married. He knew he'd no right to feel aggrieved that she hadn't told him, but he was hurt all the same. It was so sudden. He hadn't even been introduced to her fiancé, for God's sake. He felt it was his fault that she was marrying in haste and couldn't bear the idea that she might be making a mistake. Then there was Indigo – would it be possible to go on working alongside her if she was married to someone else?

He wiped his face on his sleeve, hoping she wouldn't come upon him now and see his distress, afraid that she'd be gratified to know how much he still cared about her. There might be a tearful reconciliation and things would go on as before, only now she would have a wedding dress. He dropped the remains of his cigarette, extinguished it underfoot and stepped out of the doorway at the very moment a black van reversed at speed up the lane, its mirror missing him by a hair's breadth. His heart thumped violently in his chest, and he fell back into the aperture, flinging his arms wide to steady himself. A tremor ran through him from head to foot, reliving the moment the car had hit Liam's pram, tearing it from Nora's hands. People are terrifyingly fragile, he thought, trembling. When the shock subsided, he was filled with a wave of resentment against Stella. If she's doing this to force me to choose between her and Nora, he thought, she needs to understand that I could never leave Nora alone in the dark.

He was preparing to exit the doorway, more cautiously this time, when he came face to face with Stella who looked taken aback at his expression. He glanced down and saw no shopping bag.

"No luck?" he said coldly, making her frown with incomprehension. "Amy said you'd gone shopping."

"You look terrible!"

"Thanks," he said wryly, a flicker of irritation in his stomach.

There was a pregnant pause, then she moved past him towards the door, and he made no move to stop her.

In his phone message, Derek Galvin had said he was part of the Artist Collective with Helena and was responding to Jer's Facebook message. He suggested meeting in the Black Box Café on nearby Hill Street where he added, unnecessarily in Jer's view, he spent most mornings. Approaching the building, Jer's eye was drawn to the black-and-white mural gracing its gable. The painting depicted three men, with a slain deer at their feet. One of the figures was seated, watching the other two sword-fighting. The face of the older swordsman had a sly look as he lunged at his combatant, who was immortalised parrying the thrust, looking shocked by his brush with death.

The hallway of the Black Box was a kaleidoscope of posters and fliers announcing local arts events. Inside the café there was a scattering of people, and he scanned the room for the owner of the effeminate voice on the voicemail. The voice hailed him from behind and he turned to see a bearded bear of a man taking up most of a faded, chintz sofa set against the back wall of the room.

"Derek? Please don't get up. Can I get you another coffee?" he said by way of greeting.

"A large Americano, thanks," Derek said, the high register of his voice jarring with his outward appearance.

Jer ordered the coffees at the counter then went over and sat down facing Derek, who'd settled back into the sofa. Jer suspected he spent a great deal of time in its embrace.

"Thanks very much for getting in touch," he began. "You've got some information about Helena?"

"And how is the lovely Helena?" Derek said dramatically. "I was devastated to hear about Malachy's death."

Jer sensed this was a lonely man whose currency was attention. Any information he had about Helena wouldn't be given up without an investment of Jer's time.

"Did you know she'd been in hospital?" he asked.

Derek cocked his head. "No, I didn't. I thought she'd gone away, back wherever she came from."

"No, she's still around."

"Is she okay?"

"She was discharged a couple of days ago and is staying with me and my wife."

Their coffees arrived and Derek rocked himself forward to reach a large paw for his mug of black coffee.

"Did you know Malachy?" Jer asked when the waitress had left them alone again.

Derek pursed his lips. "I never had the pleasure, though she talked about him a lot. Seemed nuts about the guy."

"What about their house in Islandmagee? Were you ever there?"

Derek rested his mug on the curve of his stomach, sighed and shook his head. "She only ever invited the ladies." His lip quivered, and he stroked his beard nervously, as if reassuring himself it was still there.

"So, she definitely lived in Islandmagee?" Jer said, desperate for a shred of corroboration of Helena's story.

"Well, somewhere up the coast there. As I say, I was never invited to one of her evenings."

"Her evenings?"

"She's into spiritualism and that sort of thing. Apparently, you have to be a maiden, mother or crone, and I don't qualify," said Derek sulkily. "She likes to celebrate the Sabbats. I'd love to do that. I think I'd be great at that."

"Sabbats?"

"There's eight of them, you know – Winter Solstice, Spring Equinox, Beltaine etcetera. She had one of her nights for the Summer Solstice in June. That's when the God and Goddess are at the height of their powers," he declared, his eyes gleaming.

"I might've seen some of that on Facebook," said Jer, thinking back to the photos of the circle of people around a bonfire.

"Yeah, someone posted pics. It looked like a great party." The corners of Derek's mouth went down, and he took refuge in his coffee mug.

"And there were no men there?"

"Maybe Malachy was allowed to be there. I wasn't invited

anyway. It was creepy how he took his life on the next Sabbat –
Lammas, the first of August."

Jer looked into his own mug of opaque, black liquid and set it
down on the rickety coffee table between them. He wanted to ask
Derek to put him in touch with some of the female members of
the Artist Collective but was afraid of alienating him.

"What's Helena like as an artist? Is she any good?"

"Ah, well now," Derek lifted his chin, obviously delighted to have
his opinion sought, "she has a modicum of talent but …" he shook
his head sagely, "she doesn't seem able to take flight. There's some
obstacle to her fulfilling her artistic potential. She's good at bringing
others along though. I think that's her real talent, though one
daren't hazard such an opinion."

"Really, that's interesting. Who was she teaching?"

"Not teaching in the formal sense, more mentoring, I suppose."

"Was she mentoring some of her female friends?"

"Oh, none of them would take instruction from anybody," he
said vehemently.

Jer gritted his teeth. "So, who then?"

"That was what I wanted to talk to you about. I've been
wondering if I should tell someone, but now Malachy's dead, it
doesn't really matter anymore – it's too late."

Jer felt exasperated but made an effort to conceal it. "Derek,
you're being very cryptic. Come on, do tell!" he said mischievously
and gave a little shake of his shoulders.

"You're making fun of me!" Derek's face darkened.

"God no, I'm not, I'm just – baffled by Helena. I'm afraid she's
bewitched my wife, who's very vulnerable. They met in hospital,"
he said quickly.

"*Ooo*, dear, you should really get your lovely lady away from Helena asap! I mean Helena is wonderful, but she does rather draw people in."

"I'm beginning to realise that." Jer took a mouthful of sour, tepid coffee and tried again. "You know it's possible Malachy is still alive. His body has never turned up."

"Really?"

"There's a line of thought that he may have done a runner with Helena's money and faked his own suicide." He watched Derek's jaw fall open. "If Malachy walked through that door right now, what would you tell him, Derek?"

Derek licked his lips and glanced fearfully towards the door. "If Malachy was here now, I wouldn't dare tell him what I know."

"Why? Would it make him angry?"

"It might make him take his own life."

Jer felt dizzy. They seemed to be going around in circles. "Derek, I think you really need to share this information with me. It's obviously troubling you."

Derek's eyes welled up. "You're right. It's been bothering me ever since I heard about Malachy."

Jer waited.

"Helena had taken a young man under her wing. Now *he* has talent, prodigious talent, but I think his parents are dead set against him pursuing art as a career. Helena was the first person to really encourage him."

"Okay, and you thought what – it might make Malachy jealous?"

Derek sighed and looked at the ceiling. "I don't like to repeat gossip, but rumour has it they were having a rip-roaring affair. I mean, I couldn't blame her. Leo's beautiful!"

"Did you say Leo?"

"You know him? I only wish he'd come to me. I'd have mentored him, encouraged him. He's a young Leonardo."

"I think I have met him. He's into swimming?"

"Is he? I didn't know that." Derek looked distracted, presumably by the thought of Leo in swimming trunks.

Jer remembered Leo's shock when Helena had been mentioned. He now understood why the young man had tailed him from Tyrella, perhaps hoping Jer would lead him to her. "Derek, you said this was all gossip and rumour. Have you any proof that Helena and Leo were having an affair?"

Derek set down his mug and lifted his mobile while Jer watched him uneasily, dreading what he was he about to see. After some poking and scrolling, he nodded and turned the screen towards Jer, revealing a life-drawing of a naked Helena, with a Mona Lisa smile hovering about her lips. "Leo drew this. Isn't it incredible?"

Helena was sitting cross-legged, looking directly at the artist. Jer tried not to let his eyes linger on her pudenda which was as hairless as a pre-pubescent girl's.

"He's definitely very talented, but it doesn't prove they're lovers."

Derek looked offended and slapped the mobile onto the table, face down.

"Do you know how I can contact Leo?"

"I don't have a number for him," Derek said huffily.

"Do you know his surname by any chance?"

"Oh yes, it's Greatrex! He's studying architecture at Queen's, you know. You might be able to track him down that way."

"Thank you, Derek, that's very helpful."

"If you find Leo, will you tell him I'd love to mount an

exhibition of his work, when he's ready to exhibit," he said wistfully.

Jer nodded and got up to leave.

"And do tell dear Helena I was asking for her. You might like to suggest me as a guest at her next Sabbat. She must be planning something special for Samhain. It's the most important Sabbat, of course, when night dominates day, and the veil between the spiritual and the material world is at its thinnest. I was reading about it online." Derek's his eyes were round with excitement.

Jer made a mental note that if he had anything to do with it, Helena would no longer be staying with him and Nora by Halloween.

Determined to avoid the office while Stella was likely to be there, he headed for Queen's University in search of Leo. He parked in Cromwell Road where, as a student, he'd shared a mice-infested flat with three friends. Walking towards the university campus, the sun came out and transported him back to his nineteen-year-old self. A female student was walking ahead of him, the sunlight setting her long, red hair aflame. She reminded him of Nora, as she had been when they first met.

Alerted in some instinctive, animal way that someone was staring at her, the girl, looked over her shoulder at him and quickened her step. Chastened, he looked away.

He'd first laid eyes on Nora during Freshers' Week and longed to ask her out but had been paralysed with terror. The opportunity to speak to her came when she and her friend sat down beside him on a bench in the Botanic Gardens, one unseasonably warm day in October. Studiously ignoring him, she'd kept up a highly indignant narrative about how she'd just been turned down for the Queen's netball team on the grounds of being too short. He'd stolen a glance at her profile. He could still remember the way she kept curling a long lock of hair around her ear, only for it to cascade forward each time she gesticulated to emphasise what she was saying. He smiled to himself, remembering the sheer joie-de-vivre she exuded.

"I told her I'd take ten shots at the goal and asked her how many I needed to score for her to let me be the team shooter. She looked really annoyed but said seven out of ten would clinch it."

"So how many did you get, Nora?" asked her friend breathlessly.

"Nine!" came the triumphant reply.

"Great. I suppose you're now on the team?" her friend said, nodding.

"No, I am not. I told her to stuff her bloody team!"

Nora hadn't played netball from that day to this. His nostalgic mood gave way to something darker, reflecting on his wife's tendency to be her own worst enemy.

He headed for the University Administration Building, concocting a story in his head, in case he should need one, to explain his interest in Leo Greatrex.

In the event, he'd no trouble ascertaining that Leo was no longer a student at the university. The clerk couldn't tell him why Leo had left, nor was she able to give out his address or phone number, but Jer got the impression that his defection was pretty recent. On his way back to the car, he remembered the desolation on Leo's face that day at Tyrella. Maybe he'd suffered an emotional breakdown like Helena? Jer decided he needed to get home and ask Helena some searching questions about her relationship with young Leo.

His mobile rang and when he saw it was Stella he rejected the call and put it back in his pocket.

On the drive home, his headache crept back, and he resolved to take more painkillers when he got to the house. He now identified his headache with Malachy's ghost. He'd have to be on his guard with Helena and Nora if they were still treating him oddly. Maybe he could use Helena's delusion that he was Malachy to get her to open up to him but, for that, he needed Nora to be offside. What would Malachy say to Helena if he was here now? If he'd suspected Helena was having an affair with Leo, surely he'd have been deeply jealous.

Jer gasped, shocked by the blare of a horn. Had he dropped off and swerved? In that split second of semi-consciousness, he'd glimpsed tumbling soil and heard the rasp of a spade on stone.

"Get a grip, McCabe! You're feverish from last night's antics on that bloody beach," he admonished himself.

He drove home on edge, the pain in his head spreading across the top of his skull.

Chapter 17

The house was quiet as the grave when he got home in the early afternoon. He tip-toed to the kitchen to swallow a couple of tablets, wincing when he threw back his head.

Turning from the sink, he saw Helena standing a few feet away, looking at him with concern.

"Are you alright?" she said softly.

"Just a headache after our shenanigans on the beach last night."

Her face fell.

"Where's Nora?" he said, more abruptly than he intended.

"I suggested she lie down."

"We need to talk, Helena."

She sat down at the kitchen table with her back to the wall and watched him carry his glass of water over to the table and sit down facing her. There were shadows under her eyes, but he was newly struck by her beauty. She was gazing at him with an expectant look, her lips slightly apart and he reminded himself that she might still be labouring under the misapprehension that Malachy's spirit was currently residing in his reluctant body.

"I met Derek this morning," he said as an opener.

"Derek?" She looked puzzled.

"Of the Cathedral Quarter Artist Collective."

"Ah." Her face cleared. "How did you find him?"

"On Facebook and we had a cosy little chat in the Black Box Café."

"I meant, how is he?"

"Fine, asking after you and Leo."

She went very still.

"I don't want to upset you, Helena, but I feel I have to ask this. Were you and Leo having an affair?"

She gave him a disappointed look. "Why do people have to make things so ugly?"

"I'll take that as a yes."

Now she was stung. "You're very quick to judge. You should know, when it comes to human relationships, it isn't always possible to answer every question with a simple yes or no."

"Okay, avoiding black and white, let's take a wander in the grey. Tell me what Leo means to you."

She looked away from him towards the window and her face relaxed. "When I think of my time with Leo, it's filled with light." She smiled. "He reminds me of myself when I was young, desperate to be an artist and live in the world of artists."

"I take it you were encouraging him to become an artist."

"I'm not sure it's about becoming. He already is an artist – he just needs to be true to himself."

"Not always clear how to do that though, is it?"

"I know. I probably wasn't much help."

"On the contrary, Derek said mentoring is your true talent."

She looked surprised by the compliment. "Leo told me his

parents are dead set against him being an artist. He's studying architecture and feels he owes it to them, to his mum especially, to see that through."

He hesitated, unsure if he should tell her Leo had abandoned his studies. "Have you met his parents?"

"No, he keeps his artistic life secret from them, which is so sad. I kept telling him I was sure they'd understand once they knew how passionate he is about art."

"And is he passionate about you too, Helena?"

After a pause, she said, "Passion is a wonderful and dangerous thing, you know that."

He shifted uncomfortably in his seat. Even if he'd only dreamt about having sex with this woman, any interaction with her was bound to be coloured by his desire. His head throbbed and he suddenly became aware of another presence in the room, as if Malachy was standing at his shoulder. He massaged his temples.

"I've just been to Queen's University and discovered that Leo Greatrex is no longer a student there."

She stared at him, looking worried. "I wonder if that means he's left home," she said, biting her lower lip.

"If he has, where would he go?"

She shook her head. "I've no idea. His parents must be in meltdown."

"That sounds a bit dramatic. Surely they'd get over it, once it's a fait accompli?"

"I got the impression his mum's quite religious and thinks artists lead debauched lives."

"Well, now you know he's left his course, are you going to contact him?"

"I don't know how to, Jer. It was always Leo who sought me out."

"Where did he seek you out?"

She gave a little shrug. "At the Artist Collective and in Islandmagee."

"He came to the house?"

"A few times during the summer."

"And when did he start coming?"

She frowned in concentration. "After the Summer Solstice."

"Was he there at Lammas when Malachy disappeared, and someone tried to kill you?"

She turned pale. "What are you suggesting? Leo would never harm me or Malachy."

He leaned across the table. "Helena, you were found on that beach with a head-wound."

She recoiled.

"Don't retreat into the grey again. Malachy's jacket was found on the rocks there. Do you remember going to that beach with him?"

She put both hands over her mouth and nostrils and breathed in noisily through her fingers. Jer was afraid he'd gone too far. She'd just been discharged from a psychiatric ward, after all. He'd no business putting her under pressure like this. She lowered her arms and spread her hands flat on the table as if trying to keep her balance.

"Neither Malachy nor Leo would ever harm me."

"But if Malachy thought he was losing you to Leo, could that have made him desperate enough to take his own life?"

She shook her head. "We both believe death doesn't free us from anything unresolved. We just return again and again to confront the same problem, the same grief, until we learn how to live with it."

"He believed in reincarnation?"

She looked searchingly at him.

"Help me here, Helena. If Malachy is dead, according to your beliefs, he'd be in line for reincarnation, rather than taking up residence in another person?"

"If he lost his life violently, his spirit might remain close for a time, and enter another living creature."

Jer pinched the bridge of his nose. "I presume the police showed you Malachy's suicide note. What did it say?"

Helena looked away and he could see she was searching her memory. "They did show me something when they talked to me in the hospital. It was nonsense."

"How can you be so sure?"

"It talked about God. Malachy doesn't believe in God."

"You're suggesting someone else wrote that note and left it with his jacket."

"Leo wouldn't be capable of such evil."

The doorbell chimed and he rose, glad of the interruption. His relief was short-lived when he opened the door to Myra, who swept past without speaking.

"Helena's in the kitchen," he said to her back.

Myra closed the kitchen door firmly behind her while he went in search of Nora.

He found her propped up on pillows on their bed, the duvet littered with family photo-albums.

"Was that Myra?" she asked warily.

"Yes. They're in the kitchen. How are you feeling?"

"I'm okay. Just thinking about the night I had Liam. Do you remember?"

He sat on the bed beside her and took her hand. "Nora, love, don't you think it would be better –"

"I know, I know. I shouldn't dwell on it all. But this is a happy memory. Helena and I were talking about being in labour and I was showing her pictures of Eimear, Rory and Liam when they were babies."

"Helena had a baby?"

"Yes. It was something we talked about a lot in hospital. Like me, she's never got over losing her baby."

For the first time he understood why they'd bonded. "Was this recently?"

"God no, it was years ago. She was just a teenager, poor thing. Her daughter was stillborn. Isn't that awful?"

"It is. And she's never had any more children?"

"Apparently not. You see, she has much more in common with me than Myra. Myra's never even been pregnant."

He bowed his head. "That's a loss of a different sort, don't you think?" he said gently. She looked away. "And the father of her baby, did Helena say who he was?"

"No, she said it happened when she was very young." Nora dropped her voice. "She had an affair with an older, married man. I got the impression she's ashamed of it all, so I didn't pry."

A floorboard creaked outside on the landing and he went and opened the bedroom door to find Helena there.

"Sorry, is Nora asleep?" she whispered.

"No, no, she's not," he said self-consciously, hoping he and Nora hadn't been overheard.

"May I speak to her?"

"Of course."

He opened the door wide to let her enter, feeling uncomfortable at the sight of her in his and Nora's bedroom. She went straight over to the bed and sat in the spot he'd just vacated.

"Myra wants to see where my house was," she said. "Would you like to come with us?"

He was tempted to intervene but knew if he tried to veto the expedition, Nora would be all the more determined to go.

"I don't think I could face going back there, Helena. I hope you don't mind. Are you sure you want to go back there yourself? It'll upset you."

He breathed out, glad Nora had opted out.

"I still can't believe the house is gone. It's only by going back there, over and over again that I can begin to come to terms with it."

"I know. You better go then. You only have a couple of hours before it'll get dark."

Helena leaned over and kissed her. "You get some rest and I'll see you later."

He folded his arms, and watched Helena leave the room without meeting his eye.

"Do you think – " Nora began, but he put his finger on his lips and raised his eyebrows.

He stood in the bay window looking out into the garden, until he heard the front door slam, then he lifted the photo-albums onto the floor and lay down beside her.

"Do you think they'll be casting some kind of a spell out there?" she breathed.

"Don't you just know they will?" he said, closing his eyes.

He was woken from a doze sometime later by a hammering at the front door. It felt like *Groundhog Day*.

Nora was still beside him. She grabbed his sleeve. "*It's the police again!*"

"I'm sure it isn't. You stay put and I'll see who it is."

His head swam when he stood up. The hammering came again, accompanied by the chime of the doorbell. Muttering darkly, he hurried downstairs in his socks to find Wright on his doorstep, flanked by Constable Matthews. Wright waved a piece of paper in his face.

"What's this?" Jer squared his shoulders.

"It's a warrant authorising me to seize your personal computer and mobile phone."

"For God's sake! You're barking up the wrong tree as usual! You can just wait here on the doorstep while I ring Samuel."

"No, this order gives us the right to enter your home and seize the aforementioned items," Wright said, walking into the house, closely followed by Matthews, who shot Jer another dirty look which he was beginning to realise was her trademark.

He closed the front door and went to his jacket which was hanging on the newel post at the bottom of the stairs to get his phone. He was typing in his password when Wright plucked the phone out of his hand and pocketed it.

"You can't do that!"

"I can, McCabe, and I have. Sign this receipt for one computer and one mobile phone and write down your password for each."

He took the document into the living room, put it on the coffee table and attempted to read it. Constable Matthews handed him a pen and he scribbled his signature.

"I'm not giving you my bloody passwords."

"Up to you, sir," she said coolly, "only we'll have to keep your equipment longer if we have no passwords."

"How long can you keep them for? I have a company to run."

"Up to ten days initially," said Wright.

"*Ten days. Jesus.*"

Wright and Matthews headed for the door, Wright carrying the laptop.

"Okay, okay, I'll give you the passwords."

Matthews handed him the document.

"How long with the passwords?" he said, scribbling them down.

Matthews took possession of the document. "Oh, anything between five to ten days."

"Why the hell are you torturing me?" he said, standing up. "All I've been doing is trying to help my wife's friend. It's Leo Greatrex you should be going after."

Wright turned to look at him. "Leo who?"

He licked his lips uneasily, afraid he was about to incriminate an innocent young man. "Greatrex."

"And why didn't you mention him this morning when we questioned you?"

"Because this morning I didn't know he had anything to do with it."

"And what has he to do with it?"

He wished Samuel was there. "It's been suggested to me that he was having an affair with Helena."

Wright raised his eyebrows. "And how did you come by this information?"

"I met a guy called Derek Galvin who runs an Artist Collective in the Cathedral Quarter. He said it may be just gossip, but they certainly are very close."

"And where can I contact this Leo Greatrex?"

"I don't know. Apparently he was studying architecture at Queen's up till recently, but has left."

"Left Queen's or the country?"

"Left Queen's."

"Do you have an address for him?"

"No, I don't."

Wright put the laptop down on the sofa, took out a notebook and scribbled something in it.

"I'd like to speak to Helena Santoro again."

"She's not here."

"Oh? Where is she?"

"She's gone to Islandmagee."

"Ah, the mystery of the disappearing house," said Wright, glancing at Matthews.

"That's the one," Jer said bleakly.

"And how is she travelling to Islandmagee? Is she with your wife?"

"No, my wife's upstairs in bed. Helena's with my sister-in-law."

"Mrs. Samuel McCabe, if I'm not mistaken." Wright smirked.

A thought occurred to Jer. "Did you guys go looking for Malachy Murtagh's laptop and phone when you found Helena half-dead on the beach and his suicide note?"

Wright's eyes narrowed.

"Wouldn't that be routine in a case like this? Surely you searched his house?"

"The house was searched, sir," piped up Matthews, addressing Wright who silenced her with a look.

"You were there, Constable, inside that house?" Jer asked eagerly.

"Look, McCabe," said Wright, "that woman Santoro isn't the full shilling. She led you to an empty field so you would take pity on her and take her home. Seems to have worked a treat."

"Can't you just send someone back to the house you searched to confirm it's still there?" Jer asked him, in desperation.

"Tell me this, how do you know it was a laptop?" said Wright, putting his face close to Jer's.

"What? I don't know. You've just taken *my* laptop so . . . Look, I've got nothing to do with this. Did you find a laptop? Did he write the suicide note?"

"How do you know about that?"

Jer swallowed, trying to remember how he knew about the suicide note. Had Samuel found out from someone in the PSNI off the record? Afraid of making trouble for his brother, he said, "Helena mentioned it, but she thinks it's nonsense. Apparently it mentions God and Malachy didn't believe in God."

"You've discussed his religious beliefs with him then, have you?"

"For heaven's sake, I've told you already, I never met the man. Was Helena's money transferred using that laptop?"

Wright remained inscrutable.

"It was, wasn't it? Think about it, Wright. Why would he transfer money then take his own life? He has to have done a runner or there's someone else involved here. Are you actively looking for Malachy? I mean not just a body but . . ."

Wright closed his eyes in irritation. "There's no trace of him."

Chapter 18

Jer felt deaf, dumb and blind without his mobile and computer, and was reduced to ringing Directory Enquiries on the landline to get Samuel's office number.

"Is Myra in your house?" Samuel fired at him as soon as he answered.

"She was only here long enough to pick up Helena."

"Where are they going this time?" Samuel's tone was leaden.

"Myra offered to take her to Islandmagee to see where her house – "

"The non-existent house! Why in God's name did you let her go, Jer?"

"Myra isn't even acknowledging my presence on the planet. She's certainly not going to take orders from me, no more than she does from you." He could hear Samuel breathing heavily. "Sorry, I shouldn't have said that."

When Samuel spoke, his voice sounded uncharacteristically vulnerable. "I've always loved that about her – that she's her own woman."

"How are you doing, Samuel?"

"This is a difficult thing for me to ask but – are Myra and Helena lovers?"

Jer felt a tightness across his chest, remembering the footage on his phone of Myra and Helena kissing and that the phone was now in the hands of Detective Wright who'd relish the chance to hurt and embarrass Samuel. He felt powerless to protect his brother.

"What makes you think they might be?" he said lamely.

"I wish to God you'd never brought that infernal woman into our lives!"

He decided the best thing for Samuel would be to get him refocused on the case. "Look, I need your help to protect Myra."

"You think she's in danger?"

"Wright has just been here and seized my mobile and laptop."

"And what's that got to do with her?"

"Last night I filmed something at the beach she wouldn't want to be seen."

There was silence on the other end of the phone.

"Are you still there?" Jer said.

"What have you done?"

"It's not the end of the world if it gets out there – it's just that I know Myra wouldn't want that . . ." He trailed off, afraid he was gabbling.

"You stood there and filmed whatever it was they were doing instead of stopping them?"

"It was harmless enough really. They had a ring of candles and were . . ."

"What? What the fuck were they doing?"

"Casting a spell, I think. I just know it's not the sort of thing Myra would – "

"You're damn right. That witch Helena has some weird influence over her. Why the hell didn't you delete the footage?"

"With all that's going on I forgot about it. When Helena went running into the sea, it all got pretty crazy. Anyway, I thought you were going to stop him seizing my stuff?"

"Why can't you just be honest? You knew you should delete that footage but no doubt you're keeping it for some shite little documentary you'll make about witches."

He felt the truth of his brother's accusation like a punch to the stomach. "Samuel, please, the best way to forestall Wright doing anything with it is to solve this case before he does."

"I don't respond well to blackmail!"

"I'm not blackmailing you. Jesus, I'm not that Machiavellian!"

"How true. You're just a complete idiot!"

"That I'll admit to. Listen, earlier today I met a guy called Derek who runs an Artist Collective. He knows Helena and, according to him, she was having an affair with this young fella Leo."

"The one who followed you from Tyrella?"

Jer was newly impressed by his brother's ability to recall detail. "Wow, I wish I had a brain like yours!"

"No, you really don't," Samuel sounded mollified. "And have you tackled her about him?"

"Yes, I did, just now," he said, feeling that, at last, he'd something positive to report.

"And?"

"Well," he hesitated, trying to remember exactly what she'd said on the subject, "she refused to be drawn."

"Why am I not surprised?"

"But that's revealing in itself surely," Jer insisted. "She certainly didn't deny it. She said it wasn't something that you could give a black or white answer to."

"Ha! Yeah, right, like being a little bit pregnant. Actually, I think it is something that you can give a definitive answer to."

"What are we saying? That Helena was having it off with this young buck?"

"Or she wants us to think she was."

"Now you've lost me," Jer said. "Why on earth would she want to throw sand in our eyes? We're trying to help her!"

"To throw the blame for Malachy's disappearance onto somebody else."

"You think she's done away with Malachy herself?"

"It has to be one possibility."

Jer's head began to swim. "But why would she draw all this attention to the missing house when everyone seemed to have accepted Malachy drowned himself and would never be found." Normally he could depend on his older brother to be logical and objective, but he began to fear Samuel's conflict of interest was interfering with his reasoning powers.

"We need to find this guy Leo and hear what he has to say. He hasn't shown up at your house yet?"

Jer was relieved – Samuel's brain was still functioning. "Funny you should say that. He's been seen hanging around the wee cul-de-sac where I park."

"He'll get himself kneecapped if he's not careful."

"I went to Queen's to try and find him, but he's no longer a student there."

"Now that's interesting. Hope he hasn't left the country. What's his surname?"

"Greatrex."

"Unusual name – shouldn't be hard to track him down. I'll see what I can do at this end."

"That would be great, thanks."

"This isn't for you, pinhead, it's for Myra. Make sure and text me when she gets back!"

"I can't text, I haven't – "

"Of course – Wright! I've a good mind to text a few red herrings to your phone, to put him in a tailspin," and Samuel was gone.

Jer rang his office on the landline, to warn them not to text or leave any messages on his mobile. It was Amy who answered.

"You got my text?"

"I'm afraid not, Amy, the police have taken my mobile. What did it say?"

"Just ring me asap. What's going on?"

"Please don't worry, it's just a particular detective who's got it in for me and my brother, and he's playing silly buggers with us."

"Can he get away with that?"

"What did you want to tell me?"

"Stella remembered an old BBC series – you know, the one where a helicopter flew all over Northern Ireland. *Sky-High*. I got them to send me over the footage of Islandmagee. I was just about to have a look to see if I can spot Helena's house."

"Brilliant. Aren't you great!"

"It was Stella really."

"I'll be there in half an hour."

Jer left Nora dozing and drove into town, with a stop-off to buy himself a pay-as-you-go mobile. He got to the office in time to meet

Stella coming down the stairs, carrying two large carrier-bags. She avoided making eye-contact with him.

"Stella?"

She stopped halfway down and swayed slightly, shifting one of the bags to her right hand, so she could grasp the handrail.

"Thanks for coming up with the *Sky-High* series. That was a brainwave."

"Why didn't you ask for my help, Jer?"

He looked up at her from a couple of steps below. "I should've. I just thought you wouldn't want to help with anything that concerns Nora."

"Whatever affects you affects Indigo, so of course I'll help."

He nodded. "That's good to know. I'd begun to think your heart wasn't in it anymore." He glanced at the carrier-bags.

"I've invested a lot of years of my life in this company."

He was hurt by the bitterness of her tone. "I know that."

At that moment, the timed light clicked off, leaving them both illumined by the crepuscular glimmer from the grimy stairwell window. She seemed to be waiting for him to say something further, but he moved up the stairs past her.

Amy was alone in the office, chatting on her phone when he walked in. He mimed drinking from a cup and got an enthusiastic nod. She'd wound up her conversation by the time he joined her with two mugs of coffee.

"Thanks for getting this together so quickly – you're a star!" He sat down beside her.

"It's Stella you need to thank. She pulled in a favour from one of her old BBC pals to get this couriered over. Didn't you see her on the stairs?"

"I did, yes." He took a sip of coffee. "Did she get the dress?"

Amy gave a ghost of a nod and screwed up her face in sympathy. "It's a beautiful, pale-pink suit. Really pricey one from House of Frazer."

"Okay, too much information."

"Sorry."

They sat in an uncomfortable silence for a few moments.

"So, the police have your phone. That's crap!"

"I bought a cheapy to tide me over. Would you mind putting in the numbers of the team. You'd do it much quicker than me."

"Sure."

"Is the footage of Islandmagee just the broadcast programme?"

"No, it's the off-cuts and other stuff as well."

"All the library footage they have of Islandmagee? Well done, Stella," he said, chastened.

While Amy fiddled with his phone, he opened the video file. In the first sequence, the helicopter swooped low over Carrickfergus Castle and followed the coast northwards. He recognised the terrace of colourful houses along the seafront at Whitehead and the lighthouse gleaming white in the sunshine. They were following the coast of Islandmagee now. The cliffs of the Gobbins stood sentinel in an emerald sea, their caves and indentations like the cloven hooves of an ancient beast. He spotted the pig-shaped Isle of Muck, Portmuck Harbour and the horseshoe of golden sand at Brown's Bay. Then, abruptly, the peninsula was behind them, and the camera was over the sea, zooming in on the Larne-Stranraer ferry far below. He was frustrated to find the next piece of film continued northwards past the town of Larne and Carnfunnock Country Park. He played several more clips but, again and again, the helicopter swung away towards the sea at the moment he willed it to cross the centre of the peninsula.

He clicked on one of the last clips. The eye of the camera was moving over the sea towards the wall of brown rock that is the Gobbins when it swooped up and across the top of the cliffs, travelling fast over small green fields and patches of yellow gorse. He caught a glimpse of a couple of buildings, but a flash of sunlight reflected from the ground created a lens flare, hazing the image, and the helicopter swung north-west towards Larne Bay. He replayed the footage, pausing it just before the glare washed out the image.

He was so intent on what he was doing, he hardly registered Amy's farewell as she slipped out of the office.

He watched the piece of video repeatedly, pausing it at different intervals and peering at the shapes of fields, hedges and trees, trying to make sense of the patterns being revealed. He didn't notice the door of the office opening but became aware of someone standing behind him, breathing heavily. He swung round to see a small, plump woman dressed in a black, quilted anorak, staring at the computer screen.

She looked familiar, but it wasn't until she spoke that he recognised Babs, one of the wild swimmers.

"Where is that?" she asked, taking a step nearer and leaning over, squinting.

He stood up and turned his back on the screen to hide it. "It's Babs, isn't it?"

She straightened up and lifted her chin to look at him. "What did you say to the police about my son?" Her voice was thick with emotion.

"Your son?" He shook his head, confused.

"The police just called at my house looking for my Leo. They said you accused him of being involved in Malachy's disappearance."

"Leo? You're – right, sorry, I didn't make the connection."

"But you managed to make some false connection between him and – and that woman."

"Can we sit down and talk about this, Babs? You're obviously upset."

She turned her face away from him, struggling to control her emotions.

"Please, sit down over here and I'll make us both a cup of tea," he said, indicating the circle of chairs at the far end of the room.

She walked stiffly over to the corner and sat down on the edge of one of the old armchairs. She put her hands between her knees and rocked herself backwards and forwards.

"Would you like tea or coffee?"

"No, I just want to know where Leo is," she said, her voice shaking.

He sat down facing her and leaned back, trying and failing to look relaxed. "I've only met your son Leo once, and that was last Saturday at Tyrella. I've no idea where he is."

"You told the police he's no longer a student at Queen's. How could you possibly know that, when I don't?"

He cleared his throat. What had that bastard Wright been saying? She was glaring at him now.

"*Did that bitch Helena tell you?*" The sudden snarl of aggression from this motherly woman shocked him.

"No, Helena doesn't know where he is, because I asked her."

"And you think she'll tell you the truth?"

"I wanted to speak to Leo myself, so I went looking for him at Queen's. The admin people there told me he's no longer a student at the university."

Babs' face crumpled and a nerve twitched in her eyelid. "You told the police she and Leo were lovers. It had to be her who told you that!"

"No, no, she didn't, Babs. It was someone else entirely, and he said it was probably just gossip."

"Please be honest with me, Mr. McCabe – has my son been to see her since she's been staying with you?" Babs had removed her hands from between her knees and clasped them, as if in prayer. The aggression had gone, and all he could see now was a mother, desperately worried about her child.

"Please, call me Jer, and I promise you, Babs, Leo has not been to see Helena while she's been staying with us."

He saw some of the tension leave her body. She looked haggard.

"Have you any idea where Leo might be?" he said. "I mean, has he uni friends he might be staying with?"

"He lives at home with me and his dad so, hopefully, sooner or later he'll come home."

"I'm sure he will. When did you last see him?"

"This morning. He left for uni as usual at eight-thirty," she said sadly.

"Then there's every reason to suppose he'll come home for his tea as usual."

She shook her head. "Ed rang him while the police were there. He had no choice. They asked him to."

"And?" he prompted.

"He begged him to come home – that the police were there and wanted to ask him about his relationship with Helena."

"And what did he say?"

Her lips trembled. "He said he's never coming home again."

The pain evident on Babs' face made his heart quail.

"It's all that woman's fault. Why did she have to come into our lives? Leo was happy and doing so well. Now he's thrown everything away – everything I've done for him – the life I created for him."

"Don't you think you should be at home, Babs?" he said gently. "Despite what he said, he may well come home to you and, if he does, it would be important to be there for him."

"Ed's there. But I don't think he'll come home to me. He'll go looking for *her*," she said bitterly. She looked at him imploringly. "Will you ring me if he turns up at your house?"

"Of course," he said, not at all sure that he would do anything of the sort. Leo was an adult after all. He lifted a notepad and pen. "Give me your number."

She took the pad from him, wrote down a number and handed it back.

"Babs Cromey," he said slowly, reading her scrawl. "Not Greatrex?"

"Greatrex is my maiden name."

"So, Ed isn't – "

"Ed is Leo's adoptive dad and a wonderful dad he is," she said passionately. "He loves Leo just as much as if he was his own son."

He nodded, observing her closely.

"You need to get that woman out of your house, Mr. McCabe. She's evil. Aren't you worried about your poor wife? I understand she's a very vulnerable person."

"Who told you that?"

She put her hands on the arms of the chair and pushed herself to her feet. "It's only a matter of time till she offs herself." Seeing his horrified reaction, she added, "I mean *her*, not your wife." She leaned towards him. "But then again, suicide can be contagious."

Chapter 19

He got a couple of carry-out pizzas on his way home that evening, but when he turned into the driveway, he could see Nora, Helena and Myra already eating at the kitchen table. Alerted by his headlights, they looked out of the window, and he was struck by how easily they could be observed by anyone hiding in the garden. Nora made no move to open the patio door, and he had to plod around to the front door to let himself in. He'd brought home a laptop from the office and deposited it in his study before carrying the pizza boxes into the kitchen.

"Oh, you've got pizza!" said Nora, looking surprised. "Helena's made a wonderful fish stew and there's plenty left."

He thought of Samuel sitting across town in an empty house, and felt like driving straight over there with the redundant pizzas. He set the boxes down on the worktop and lifted the lid of the casserole to inspect its contents. An aroma of smoked fish dominated, but he spotted a few mussels lurking in the glutinous mixture and replaced the lid.

"Sorry, Helena, but I'm not keen on mussels. I'll stick to my customary carb-fest if you don't mind. Anybody want a slice of pizza for dessert?" he said, earning a snort from Myra. He lifted a slice of pizza and stood eating it, watching the three women. "How did you get on in Islandmagee?"

Myra stared across the table at Helena, refusing to meet his eye.

"It was very good of Myra to take me," said Helena, smiling pleasantly in his direction.

"And?" he said, taking an enormous bite of pizza.

"We weren't expecting to find anything," snapped Myra. "Helena has accepted that her house is gone."

He held up the crust of his pizza slice like a finger and bit off the top. To his satisfaction, Myra turned her face away in disgust.

"One of my team has sourced aerial footage of Islandmagee," he said casually, putting the other half of the crust into his mouth and crunching it.

"What?" whispered Helena.

"*Wow*, does it show the house?" Nora's eyes lit up.

"Most of the clips are of the coastline, but there's one sequence where the helicopter flies across the peninsula. I really need you to view it with me, Helena, to be sure, but I think it might show your house."

"Oh my God, that's amazing, isn't it, Helena?" said Nora, as if he'd just scored a winning goal.

Myra put a long, manicured thumbnail between her teeth and bit into it.

Helena's eyes welled up.

"If it's there, it's just a glimpse," he said quickly.

Myra sniffed derisively.

"Can we look now?" said Helena, starting to rise from the table.

"OK, but I need another slice of pizza to revive my drooping spirit."

"That's one of Malachy's favourite sayings!" She smiled at him while a single tear bloomed at the rim of her eye and ran down her cheek.

He tore off another slice of pizza, took a large bite and exited the kitchen, holding it aloft, closely followed by the three women.

It was Myra who set up the laptop he'd brought from the office while he finished off his pizza slice and wiped his oily hands.

He sat down with Helena behind him, located the clip and clicked play.

Helena gasped and knelt beside him, one hand on the edge of the desk and the other on his arm. "Can you play it again?"

"Sure. Unfortunately, there's lens-flare at twelve seconds in, which spoils the shot."

"*Then why did you get her hopes up?*" hissed Myra.

"The hexagon of light," breathed Helena. "I think I know what that is."

He turned to look questioningly at her, their faces close.

"Can you slow it down?" she said eagerly.

"I can go through it frame by frame."

She nodded and turned back to the screen.

They followed the camera's halting progress towards the cliffs.

"Stop! Do you see that patch of gorse there on the cliff-edge? I know that place. That's where Malachy and I often go to watch the sunset. Move it on."

Helena's hand felt heavy on his arm as he negotiated the mouse from frame to frame.

"*There!*" she shouted. "Those buildings on the right have to be

Ewart's farm! The roof of their barn is a rusty, red colour."

The clachan of houses was out of focus, but he could see the smudge of red among the greys.

"And there's our house," she whispered, staring at the screen, her face radiant.

Myra moved closer to his other side and Nora put her arms around his neck and rested her chin on the top of his head. Helena pointed to an indistinct grey rectangle on the left of the screen.

"Can't you move on one more frame to get a clearer image?" Myra said impatiently.

He could smell her fishy breath. He moved on a frame and the screen was filled with light. "Christ, that's not much use!" she declared, straightening up.

"Nora, love, I can't breathe," he implored.

She planted a kiss on the top of his head and released him.

"You see?" Helena said.

He looked up at her.

"That's the sunlight reflecting off the glass gable of my studio."

"Of course!" he said, a shiver running down his spine like a fingernail.

"It did exist! I'm not losing my mind," she said, starting to weep with relief.

"We have to tell the police!" said Nora. "Now we have proof, they'll have to investigate."

He thought of Wright's cynicism and hostility. "We need to ring Samuel," he said, pulling out his mobile, then remembered he hadn't Samuel's number listed on it. "Myra, I don't have his number on this phone, can you ring him and ask him to come over?"

"Is that really necessary?" she said and a hush fell over the room.

"The police won't listen to me, but they'll have to listen to him," he insisted.

She gave the barest nod and left the room, closing the door behind her.

Helena sank back on her heels and hugged herself. "There is a terrible power at work here – the power of three."

He pushed his chair back from the desk and away from her. What was she talking about? Surely, she didn't mean herself, Myra and Nora?

"Tell him about that," said Nora. "It's called the Law of Return, isn't it?" She knelt on the floor beside Helena.

Helena looked up at him. "I believe whatever energy any of us puts out into the world, whether positive or negative, will be returned to us threefold."

He frowned, trying to digest this. "You think Malachy had made an enemy or done something terrible?"

"No, no, none of this is Malachy's fault. It's me. I did something shameful years ago. I've been waiting for the third death. I knew it had to come, but I fooled myself into thinking that some other – difficulties in my life had atoned for my wickedness."

"The other deaths?" he said. "Who were they?"

"My baby Isabella and my father."

"Gosh, what happened to your father, Helena?" asked Nora, looking scared.

"He got sick, so sick."

"Couldn't that just have been in the natural order of things?" Jer suggested, trying to hide his impatience.

"And you think Malachy is the third?" said Nora.

"I don't know." Helena took Nora's hands. "If he is, it's my fault.

I should never have let him fall in love with me. Anyone who gets close to me suffers."

Jer felt a flash of anger. "What about Nora?" he said accusingly.

Shocked, Helena released her hands.

"Jer, don't!" said Nora, putting an arm around Helena's shoulders. "What harm can come to me that hasn't already been done? I live every day in the presence of death. What do you think we did to deserve losing Liam?"

"*Nora, no!*" he cried out. "We did nothing! That was – that was just a dreadful, chance thing, an accident. Helena, you've got to stop this, for Nora's sake, if not for your own. I accept that there's cause and effect – that our actions and sometimes failure to act can have consequences, but there's no preordained formula governing all this. Each of us has the power and the responsibility to shape our own lives. Sometimes, terrible things happen to the best and most innocent of people. I mean, how could your baby Isabella or our wee Liam deserve to die?"

She hung her head, like someone trying to gather the courage to leap across a great chasm. "You sound just like Malachy," she said, smiling sadly. "He'd managed to convince me that my sin had been expiated and no more harm would flow from it."

"He was right."

"*Then where is he?*" she wailed. "*Where's Malachy?*"

He had a sudden need to get away from her. He got up, went to the window and stood looking out into the darkness. Why did he find it hard to keep a clear head in her presence, he wondered. When he turned round, he saw that Helena and Nora were locked in an embrace. He swallowed, remembering Babs Cromey's exhortation to get Helena away from his wife.

"While we're talking sins, Helena," he said, "don't you think it's more likely Malachy's wish to leave this world has more to do with a recent sin of yours?"

"Jer! What are you talking about?" cried Nora, hugging Helena closer.

Helena looked bewildered.

"Didn't she tell you, Nora, about her affair with a fella young enough to be her son? Poor old Malachy must have been gutted."

Myra chose that moment to enter the room and she looked from him to Helena.

"Go on, Helena, tell them about Leo!" he growled.

"There's nothing sexual between me and Leo," she said, trying to disentangle herself from Nora.

"You didn't seem at all sure of that the last time we talked," he said, unappeased.

"I was confused," she said in a pleading tone. "Don't you understand how much medication muddies your thinking?"

"I do, Helena, don't you worry!" declared Nora.

"I stopped taking my medication a couple of days ago and things are becoming much clearer," she said, earning an enthusiastic nod from Nora.

"Please don't follow her example, Nora!" he said despairingly.

"It's awful living in a perpetual fog, Jer," she cried. "Just, sometimes, you long to see things clearly."

"Seeing is one thing, but feeling is something else entirely, and I don't want you crushed by grief again."

They'd forgotten Myra, who was still standing at the door, staring at Helena. "Who's Leo?" she asked, her face dark with jealousy.

"Leave her alone, Myra," said Nora.

"It's okay." Helena sounded exhausted. She got to her feet like an old woman, stepped around Nora who was still crouched on the floor and approached Myra. "Leo is a young artist I've been mentoring, but there's nothing sexual going on between us."

"Just some nude life-drawing sessions," he said, unwilling to let her off the hook.

She reacted as if he'd given her an electric shock.

She turned and stared at him. "What did you say?"

"Derek showed me a drawing Leo did of you. Very – revealing!"

"Jer, what's got into you?" said Nora sharply. "It's not like you to be unkind!"

"I'm just sick of being spun a yarn. I asked you about Leo last night, Helena, and you were very evasive and left me thinking you were lovers."

She took a step towards him. "I'm sorry, I didn't mean to be evasive. Now that I've got those chemicals out of my system, my memory is coming back. You see, when I was in hospital, I had strange dreams and thoughts, where people and events were jumbled and would come back to me in fragments."

"I wonder if his mother would see it that way? She came to my office this afternoon, worried sick about him."

She shook her head in confusion, and he decided not to mention that he'd told the police about Leo.

He looked at Myra. "Did you get hold of Samuel?"

"No, he's not at home and his mobile's switched off."

He gave his sister-in-law a searching look – Samuel never switched off his phone.

Myra moved close to Helena and cupped her hands around the latter's face. "He doesn't believe a word you say, Helena. Come away with me and I'll look after you."

Helena gazed sadly at Myra, then took the other woman's hands and brought them to her lips. "Dearest Myra, thank you for everything, but I want to stay here with Jer and Nora."

Myra looked as if she'd been slapped in the face. She backed away from Helena and fled.

Wednesday 29th October

Chapter 20

How was he going to get Helena out of his house, out of their lives? He lay listening to the moan of the wind and the spatter of rain on the window. Nora was curled up on the far side of the bed, deeply asleep. He'd have to be vigilant with her, convinced she'd follow Helena's example and stop taking her medication. He wondered how late she and Helena had stayed up talking the previous evening. He'd eventually left them to it and gone to bed, emotionally exhausted by Helena's struggle with guilt and Nora's retelling of stories from their past. Helena seemed to think the blurred, snatched image in the video was enough to prove she'd been telling the truth about Malachy's house and its disappearance but now, in the cold light of dawn, he was once again assailed by doubt.

On a purely practical level, it raised the question of where Helena was to go. He reflected that he wasn't the only one who wanted her to move on, remembering Babs' visit to his office the evening before. He understood the woman was distraught about her son but that didn't excuse the viciousness of her comment about Helena offing herself. Maybe Helena's instinct was right and she herself was the target of some undefined malevolence and not Malachy. The evening before he'd been frustrated by her insistence that everything was related to her own shameful behaviour, presumably the affair she'd had as a teenager which resulted in a pregnancy, but could she be right? What if the father of her stillborn child was somewhere in the shadows, exacting a terrible revenge? After so many years, it seemed unlikely.

He fought the urge to turn over and fall into a doze and decided to face the day – after all, he had a company to run. He lifted his phone to check the time. It showed 07:20 and he resolved to get up and out of the house before Nora and Helena stirred, hoping to avoid any further agonised conversations.

Downstairs in the kitchen, Helena's cauldron of fishy stew had been forgotten on top of the cooker and announced its presence as soon as he opened the door. He finished the remains of his pizza for breakfast, washed down with a glass of milk. In his haste to get out of the house, he hadn't showered or shaved, and grimaced at his grizzled reflection in the hall mirror on his way out.

He planned to put in a concentrated day of filming and editing, determined to distract himself from all thoughts of death and witchcraft. Pleased that for once he'd managed to beat the school traffic by getting out of the house before eight o'clock, he turned on the radio news.

"*The BBC is coming under increasing pressure to axe the popular, satirical TV show Thoughtless, produced by local company Indigo.*"

He jumped on the brakes to avoid rear-ending the car in front, such was his shock at hearing his own company cited as the top story.

"*Many commentators are voicing concerns about the negative, societal impact of the content,*" the announcer continued. "*The*

President of the United States and the Archbishop of Canterbury have both criticised the series in online comments. There followed two condemnatory tweets from the First and Deputy First Ministers of Northern Ireland, decrying the misuse of the BBC licence-fee." Well, at least I've united them on something, he thought, but had an overwhelming urge to visit the toilet. *"Reporters were waiting to speak to Mr. Clifford Finnlater, Head of Television for BBC Northern Ireland, when he arrived in Belfast on an early-morning flight from London."*

The sounds of the arrival hall at Belfast City Airport filled the car and he imagined Cliff steeling himself to meet the pack of journalists staking the place out. There was a babel of voices firing off questions, then one authoritative male voice dipped below the rest and there was a hush.

"Mr. Finnlater, can you comment on accusations that this series is bringing Northern Ireland into disrepute?"

"Well, the bar is set very low there, so no, I don't think it's an issue," snarled the Head of TV.

Jer gasped. Steady, Cliff, now's the time to stop digging and start running!

There was a momentary lull as the journalists realised the import of the exec's words, then they went in for the kill.

"Can you explain exactly what you meant by your last remark, Mr. Finnlater?"

"It's satire. Do you think Jonathan Swift was actually exhorting you to eat your own children? Northern Ireland seems to be an irony-free zone!"

Jer groaned. Had Cliff learned nothing during his time in Belfast? The locals routinely tore each other to shreds but God help any outsider who had the temerity to deride or patronise the good people of Northern Ireland, particularly an Englishman. He doubted if Cliff would survive the day.

A horn blared behind him. He gripped the steering-wheel, and let off the brake, edging forward. Why on earth hadn't the stupid man just stonewalled them with a 'no comment'? He imagined Trix's glee. Mind you, he reflected, this time she might well have overplayed her hand. He chewed his lip and glanced at the drivers in the nearby cars, wondering if they were also listening to the report. Something must have happened to bring the whole controversy to a boil. She'd probably left umpteen messages on his phone, but why hadn't she rung the office? Maybe something had happened overnight? That suggested the trigger had been pulled on the other side of the Atlantic. It had to be either Trump or Rosie. He gave a despairing laugh. How he wished he had his own phone! Damn Wright and his persecution campaign.

'THOUGHTLESS & GODLESS' He stood staring at the headline. He'd juked into a little newsagent's to buy cigarettes. The *Belfast Chronicle* featured a photo of him and the crew filming passers-by being soaked by drivers speeding through puddles. The worst of it was, he was foregrounded, laughing his head off.

Oh my God, he mouthed, lifting a copy of the paper. Maybe he'd have to emigrate. His previous, prize-winning documentaries had cast him as a local hero, but now he was being called a pariah. Stella was going to find all this horribly embarrassing. Hadn't Amy said she'd met her fiancé through the church?

The air in the office was so cold he could see his breath and he struggled to remember how to activate the heating, normally Stella's responsibility. He went into the galley kitchen to make himself a coffee.

"*No milk!*" he groaned, cursing himself for forgetting to buy some at the newsagent's. He emerged into the silent office, and set his mug of black instant coffee beside a large pile of post. Didn't Stella normally open most of the mail? Perhaps she was operating a work-to-rule? He knew he was being unfair and resolved to put her current distraction down to her impending wedding? Waiting for the computer to come to its senses, he lifted a padded envelope uneasily and squeezed it. There seemed to be more bulk inside than a lock of hair. He opened it and carefully drew out a plastic bag and immediately dropped it on the desk. In spite of the sealed bag, he caught a whiff of faeces. Holding his breath, he leaned closer and confirmed that there were pins and feathers mixed through the brown mess. He ran to the kitchen and threw up into the sink.

When he felt composed enough to return to his desk, he found several furious emails from Trix, commanding him to contact her. He martialled his energy and wrote a grovelling reply, explaining how his phone and laptop had been seized by the police. It was now eight-thirty, and he decided to try ringing her at the BBC, half hoping she wouldn't be there. To his dismay, he was immediately put through to her office.

"Morning, Carol."

"Jer! We were about to send out a search party for you." She sounded at the end of her tether.

Not for the first time, he felt deeply glad he was no longer a cog in the BBC's staff machine.

"Long story and circumstances beyond my control."

"Sure, Jer, isn't it always?" she said, her voice dripping with sarcasm.

He wondered that she felt empowered to speak to an independent producer in such a tone. Was the woman about to lose her job and had nothing left to lose?

"I imagine things are pretty torrid in there?"

"I think you better come and join the party. Trix wanted to see you asap yesterday so asap is right now."

"Okay, Carol, I get the message."

"Well, that makes a change. How soon can you be here?"

"Fifteen minutes too long for you?"

"Make it ten."

He put the plastic bag and its loathsome contents back in the padded envelope and got rid of it in a litterbin on his way to Ormeau Avenue, determined not to be spooked by the thought of witchcraft. Unlike his last visit, his appearance in the BBC foyer this morning attracted some curious stares.

Well, at least now they know who I am, he thought, nostalgic for his erstwhile invisibility. Carol appeared, her face pinched. He began to wonder if Trix herself was going to get the old heave-ho and Carol was afraid of being consigned to the outer darkness along with her boss.

"Difficult day all round," he ventured.

She stared at him. "What are you like? You haven't even bothered to shave."

He swallowed and rubbed his chin.

She set off at a crisp pace into the bowels of the building, Jer following, his heart growing heavier with every step. Exiting the lift on the sacred sixth floor, he saw Trix standing reading a broadsheet.

"'*Thoughtless and Godless*'," she said, setting it down on top of a pile of newspapers.

He shrugged. She appeared preternaturally calm and glanced in the direction of the Nation Head's office, where tightly drawn blinds shrouded the room.

He followed her into her office.

"Where the fuck were you yesterday?" she said. "You went to ground on me."

"The police have seized my phone and laptop."

She looked at him, concerned. "On what grounds?"

"Nothing to do with this."

She blew out her cheeks in relief. "For heaven's sake, what else are you involved in? Is it another production?"

"No, it's a domestic matter."

"You must be a suspect in a crime?"

"Not exactly."

"You need to tell me *exactly* what's going on. I can't risk being blindsided in the middle of all this."

He took a deep breath. "While she was in hospital, my wife befriended a woman who's now staying with us. This friend recently lost her partner in suspicious circumstances, and someone cleared out her account while she was in hospital."

"Wow, your personal life is never boring, I'll say that for you." She moved away from him, sat on the edge of her desk, and gave him a penetrating look.

He stuck his hands into his trouser pockets to hide his agitation.

"I thought you were going to say it had something to do with Stella. Rumour has it she's getting married."

"So I believe."

She rocked back and folded her arms. "Is Indigo Productions in a state of crisis?"

"No more than usual."

She gave a pained smile. "But the police? You haven't explained why they felt moved to take your phone and laptop."

He licked his lips. "The detective in charge of the investigation has an axe to grind with me and suspects I'm implicated in the case."

She laughed. "I see, so this little BBC crisis is just a side-show compared to your domestic drama?"

"I use one as a distraction from the other. Keeps me really well balanced," he said, raising his eyebrows in a show of nonchalance.

He became aware of raised voices in the adjoining room.

"What's going on? I heard Cliff's faux pas on the radio driving in. I couldn't believe he could be such a twat."

She lowered the corners of her mouth in an inverted smile, inclining her head towards the voices in the room behind her. Feeling exposed in the middle of the room, he moved to the window and looked out. Belfast was hunched under a pall of moisture, and the reassuring arms of the hills had disappeared behind the mist, leaving the city alone in the murk. He turned and met her curious gaze.

"Who's next door?" he said.

"The usual suspects."

"Do you think Cliff's on his way out?"

"I don't see how he can stay in Northern Ireland after what he said."

"I presume they'll find him something in London?"

She smirked. "London only ever sends us their damaged goods, and they sure as hell don't take them back when they balls-up here."

He frowned, trying to recall the London luminaries he'd known. He couldn't remember clearly what had happened to any of them, and wished he'd paid more attention. Stella would remember. He wondered if she was getting married today. He hoped not. It would be a rotten day to get married. His thoughts were interrupted by Trix's sudden move to her desk-chair.

"Jer, sit down there. I think they're winding up next door."

He sat on the chair across the desk from her, beginning to think she'd cast him as a supporting player in a scene she was determined to direct. A door was slammed nearby, making the glass walls of the room tremble.

"I got another horrible thing in the post this morning."

She stared at him, distracted. "Not another plait?"

"No – faeces mixed with pins and feathers."

Her face was displaying disgust when Cliff entered the room. His was contorted with anger. Ignoring Jer, he strode over to her desk. She half rose and to his surprise, Jer saw she was afraid, making him wonder if she'd summoned him for physical as well as moral support.

"Be very careful, Cliff, I'm recording this," she said.

Jer wondered if she was bluffing. Whether she was or not, it had the desired effect, and Cliff bridled in mid-charge. He leaned his fists on her desk and gave her a look of complete contempt. Jer's mouth was dry. He tried to calculate how long it would take the security guys at the front door to get up here, if Cliff decided to go for her skinny neck.

"You may have won the battle, but don't think for one minute you've won the war." Cliff's voice was hoarse with emotion. "There'll be a reckoning to be paid for what you've done here. *You mark my words.*"

Jer watched her eyes twitching as she mentally reviewed the

moves she'd made, and their possible consequences. Was there something she'd overlooked? Cliff was a man of passion and emotion, easy to wrong-foot as it turned out, while her killer weapon was her sangfroid.

Cliff straightened up, turned and looked at Jer, "*And your bloody series is axed!*" he snarled as a parting shot, before turning his back on them and stomping out of the room.

Jer held tightly to the arms of his chair, as if attempting to steady a rocking boat while Trix lowered herself back into her chair, still on alert.

"What happens – " he began, interrupted by a chirp from her desk phone.

She lowered her eyes, lifted the receiver and listened. "Of course, I'll be right in." She rose and lifted her chin.

"Should I – " he said, longing to make himself scarce.

"Stick around, this shouldn't take long."

He paced the empty office for what seemed like an age before deciding to nip up one floor to the canteen to get a coffee. On his way he passed Carol's desk where he saw her deep in a whispered conversation with Cliff. The intensity of the look that passed between them made him wonder if they were lovers. It might explain her behaviour earlier. She must know that Cliff would now disappear back to London and never be heard of in Belfast again. But had she been feeding Cliff information about Trix's wheeling and dealing all along? He found it hard to believe that Trix would've failed to notice her assistant's partiality to the Head of Television. Same lady didn't usually miss a trick.

He wondered how she was getting on in the Nation Head's

office. She lived dangerously, making enemies as she advanced. He knew she was determined to become Head of Television, but it was possible she would be passed over again. Either way, it looked likely that Indigo Productions would be caught in the crossfire. His head ached and, in his agitated state, he'd climbed the stairs too quickly. He paused on a landing to get his breath back and looked out the window towards the old Gasworks building, remembering how he'd watched a partial eclipse of the sun from this very spot a few years back.

The canteen was quiet at this hour, and he was heading for the coffee machine when a familiar voice hailed him from across the room.

"Well, well, Jer, what has you up and at it so early this morning?"

It was Harry, his professional nemesis. He wondered if it was merely a coincidence that Harry was in broadcasting house on this particular morning.

"Pity about *Thoughtless* being axed," drawled the younger man, with a sly smile. "Always thought it was a cracking idea."

In fact, you thought it was such a cracking idea you tried to steal it, Jer thought crossly. He frowned, realising Harry must have known *Thoughtless* had been axed before he himself had been told. What on earth was going on?

"And dear Stella is going to have a Halloween wedding – odd time to get married. But, then again, better an October bride than a December one, I suppose!"

He stared at Harry, trying to remember why he'd ever liked the man. Harry had been in his early twenties when they first met – fresh out of uni into the BBC on a trainee scheme, eyes bright as a fox. Now in his forties, his shock of red hair had faded to mouse and was shorn to a fuzz across his balding pate. He'd worked as a researcher with Jer when the latter was still a BBC staff producer. These days Harry's company was more profitable than Indigo but on a personal level he'd never matched Jer's success as an investigative journalist. Jer knew that rankled with the younger man and he felt a sudden disgust at the pettiness of it all.

"*Why don't you just piss off, Harry!*" he hissed, startling several young people who were queueing.

He marched to the counter and busied himself extracting his coffee from the machine but was forced to line up meekly for the check-out behind the young staffers, who looked warily at him. He was tempted to abandon his coffee and make a run for it, but wasn't prepared to leave the field to Harry, who seemed unnervingly cocky.

He paid for his coffee and hurried back downstairs.

In his distracted state he walked straight into Trix's office without knocking and was startled to see her sitting at her desk, face in hands. She lifted her head and gave him a furious look, making him wish he'd followed his impulse to leave the building.

"Sorry, I thought –"

"Come in. You might as well hear this from me."

He already knew his series was axed, so what further bad news could this be? He advanced into the room, holding his coffee, and stood uncertainly in the middle of the room. She didn't invite him to sit down.

"As Cliff already informed you, in his inimitable style, no more episodes of *Thoughtless* will be broadcast. Indigo will be paid for the episodes already in the pipeline, but there's no requirement to deliver them."

He set his coffee down on the meeting table, pulled out a chair and sat down. He felt nauseous. "I have people on the payroll . . ."

"Indigo will be paid for whatever we've commissioned to date, which should give you some breathing space to manage your staff situation."

He leaned his elbow on the table and rubbed the corners of his mouth. He felt the rawness of his stubble and thought of how sad and dishevelled he must have appeared to Harry.

"Presumably you've already sacked Rosie?" she said dispassionately.

"No, not yet."

She sucked a breath in through her teeth, as if he was beyond her help, such was his inefficiency.

"What's Harry doing here?" he said, his throat tight.

"Harry's here?" Her voice faltered.

He looked at her and couldn't remember a moment when he'd seen her so discomfited. "He's up in the canteen. What's going on, Trix?"

She looked away from him.

"They are making you Head of Television, aren't they?"

She gave a barely perceptible shake of the head.

"I'm really sorry," he began, but she raised her hand to silence him.

"They're restructuring."

"Never good news!"

"There's going to be an overall Head of Content, or some such ridiculous appointment. Can you imagine it? One person in charge of TV, radio and online. It's a crazy idea."

"But you stay as TV Commissioner?"

"They're creating a Commissioning Board, with input from the indie sector."

"What? You mean they're going to commission by committee? How on earth would that work?"

She opened her arms wide and then laid them on her desk, as if she lacked the energy to hold them aloft. "Cliff's idea – his parting gift, apparently."

"And your role?" he said, leaning towards her, feeling an urge to go and put his arms around her.

"Oh, they haven't quite worked out my role yet. They're arranging things so it'll be impossible for me to do my job, hoping I'll throw the head up and resign," she said, as if she had only now realised the import of what she'd been told, "but I'm not going to give up without a fight."

He nodded and sat back in his chair. "Good on you!" he said unconvincingly.

"Harry must be in line to be part of this new Commissioning Board," she muttered.

Jer felt as if the walls of the building had fallen away, and an icy wind was blowing through the room. "Poacher turned gamekeeper."

"One way to put it but, yes, I suppose so," she said and shrugged.

"Hang on a minute, I'm no lawyer, but surely there's a major conflict of interest here?"

"They know all that well enough, Jer. They'll create a legal firewall between Harry's BBC role and the commercial activities of his company. In fact, when I come to think of it, he posted an ad for a caretaker production manager yesterday." She stared over his head, finally realising that Cliff had been plotting against her for some time.

"I know it's selfish to be worried about my situation in the face of all this," he said, "but it looks like I'll never get another commission from the BBC. Harry will see to that."

"*No, he fucking won't!*" she said, through gritted teeth. "Send me a good proposal, and I'll use it as a test case. At the very least, I'll get them on the grounds of constructive dismissal."

His heart failed him. He was going to be used like a human cannonball.

"Come on, wow me with an idea – one I can fight for."

He swallowed and went for it. "I want to make a film about female power."

She put her elbows on her desk, made a fist with her left hand and covered it tightly with her right. She leaned her face forward, covering her mouth, breathing noisily through her nostrils. He could see the whites of her eyes as she stared over his head.

"It would be a film about witchcraft."

"*Perfect!*" She dropped her hands to the desk and made a disturbing scrabbling sound with her nails. "Send me a proposal asap and I'll bloody well force it through. And ask Carol to come in here." She stuck her neck out to peer at her computer screen, all business again, leaving him to exit the room without the benefit of her attention.

He stood for a moment outside her door, swaying slightly, then remembered he'd an order to carry out. He was tempted to ignore it but had a flicker of curiosity about how Carol would react to the summons since he suspected she'd been helping Cliff outmanoeuvre Trix. When she saw him approaching, she blew her nose to hide her distress and he felt a surge of compassion for the woman. Whatever side she was on, she was obviously deeply upset. They were both casualties of selfish, ambitious people.

"She wants to see you, Carol," he said gently.

"Have you ever, in the whole of your life, come across such an infernal witch?"

Chapter 21

Jer intoned one of his favourite lines from the Psalms, as he walked away from Broadcasting House: "*Let not mine enemies exult over me!*"

He thought about Trix's fatal underestimation of Cliff, who'd conceded defeat but left the battlefield booby-trapped. He couldn't bring himself to shed any tears for her predicament, reserving his sorrow for himself and Indigo. How he wished he could talk it over with Stella – she had great insight into the machinations of the BBC. Would she choose this moment of crisis to finally walk away from Indigo?

He was at the bottom of Ormeau Avenue before he registered he'd been on automatic pilot and had turned left instead of right on leaving the building. It was just like old times when he used to head for the river when he needed time out. Today he knew he must come to terms with what had happened before returning to the office to break the news that the series they'd all been slaving away on for months had been axed, and the production team would have to be disbanded. He crossed a busy intersection and entered the grounds of what had once been Belfast's Gasworks, remembering the foul smell of the town gas that had infected these streets when he was a child. The area was now a symbol of the city's regeneration, boasting stylish, glassy buildings and paved walkways. Drawn to the banks of the Lagan, where he used to walk at lunchtime during his years in the BBC, he leaned on the iron railing, careless of the beads of water threaded along its length. The ceiling of cloud over the city had thinned, allowing the sun's pale disc to cast a metallic sheen on the river. A seal appeared in the centre of the flow, turning its sleek head this way and that.

Why would you want to swim up here into the polluted waters of this godforsaken city, he mused. The seal disappeared, and he felt bereft, imagining its sinuous body negotiating a riverbed clogged with rusted metal and plastic detritus. High above, the cloud-membrane disintegrated, and the sun transfigured the grey water into splinters of light. The seal broke the surface again, yards from the shore, close enough for him to see its inky, filmed eyes. He was convinced the creature had seen him and come in for a closer inspection, and he felt consoled. We're all just animals after all, highly sophisticated animals, but animals just the same, competing for what we need.

It was probably all for the best that *Thoughtless* had ended. He was bored with it and itching to move on to a new project. He needed to write a cracking proposal and trust that Trix could swing a commission for him quickly. Maybe he wouldn't have to make anyone redundant. He stood up straight, drew in a lungful of fresh air and let it out slowly, feeling the tension leave his chest and shoulders. What he wanted now was the time and space to attend to the people he loved – Nora and Samuel.

The only way he could do that was to help Helena understand what had happened to Malachy and his benighted house. He tried to focus on Helena but found it impossible to fix her in his mind, realising she was a chameleon, presenting a different face to different people. Whether that was due to insecurity or simply a way of manipulating others he hadn't yet decided.

He walked towards the Albert Bridge, following the flow of the river, deep in thought. He would seek out Samuel and persuade him to leave the loom for half an hour to go and get a coffee with his little brother.

He was mildly put out when he failed to get his customary, radiant smile from Samuel's secretary. On this occasion she simply raised one eyebrow when he asked if Samuel was busy. He knocked on the mahogany door and, hearing no response, pushed it open and poked his head in. The smell of alcohol was unmistakable. It wasn't yet eleven in the morning, but Samuel was already into the whiskey, slumped in his large, leather chair. He barely looked up when Jer appeared and sat down on the other side of the desk, scanning its surface for any sign of a whiskey glass.

"You look as bad as I feel," said Samuel.

"Rough night?" Jer realised that the whiskey fumes were being sweated out of Samuel's pores rather than emanating from an active glass.

"How's Myra this morning?" Samuel mumbled, avoiding Jer's eye, obviously labouring under the misapprehension that Myra had stayed with him and Nora the night before.

It was tempting to cover up for Myra, to spare her blushes, but Jer decided Samuel would prefer honesty.

"Myra didn't stay at our house last night."

He straightened up in his chair and cocked his head. "Then where the hell is she?"

"I've no idea. She left our house around eight last night, just after she rang you."

"She didn't ring me." He looked over Jer's head. "What about Helena? Did she spend the night at your place?"

"Yes."

Samuel massaged his lower lip. "I have no idea what to do, Jer. I'm losing her."

Jer shifted uncomfortably in his chair. "The only thing you can do is hold steady and be prepared to forgive her, when this moment of . . . exploration passes, as I'm sure it will."

"Moment of exploration! Cute way to put it."

"I don't believe she's been unfaithful to you. She's just exploring some aspect of her own personality that has lain dormant up to now."

Samuel covered his eyes with his hand and rubbed it backwards and forwards, as if trying to erase mental images he found unbearable.

"People are complicated animals, Samuel. If you love someone, you've got to be able to accept the stuff you don't like as well as the stuff you do."

"I've never given you much credit for standing by Nora all these years. I'm sorry for that. I think you're a fucking hero. You took her back after her little adventure."

Jer winced at this description of Nora's betrayal which he'd found so deeply hurtful. He'd often wondered if he'd have found it easier if she'd taken off with a man, but in his more philosophical moments he accepted that emotional intimacy trumped sex every time. He decided Samuel wasn't yet ready for this kernel of wisdom.

"Now you're really freaking me out," he said. "I know you'll be back to calling me a blithering idiot any minute now, because hero I am not. I've just come from a ghastly meeting in the Beeb, where I've been completely wrong-footed, outmanoeuvred and dumped on! I don't have anything like the necessary ruthlessness to succeed in my chosen profession."

"Is this the stick-insect at her work again?"

"Absolutely," he said, relieved to have deflected Samuel's maudlin line of thought. "What we both need now is to mainline soda farls with bacon."

Twenty minutes later they were seated beside a wall of glass with a commanding view of the river and Jer wondered if his friendly seal was still somewhere under the slowly moving water.

"And what has old Auntie Beeb done to you now?" said Samuel, when they were both well through their soda farls, washed down with black coffee.

"For starters, they've axed my series!"

"Hardly a surprise. It was a bloody lightning rod for the BBC-bashers. I'd have been writing to them myself looking for a refund on my licence fee, if they'd let it continue."

"Gee, thanks for the solidarity!" Jer said with his mouth full.

"What else?" Samuel gave him a shrewd look. "There's something else bugging you."

"Trix has used the hue and cry around my series to unseat her boss, who's probably already on a plane back to London as we speak."

"Don't tell me – she's got his job."

"I only wish she had."

"Ah, again, I'm not surprised. I wouldn't promote her if I was her boss!"

Jer felt his usual flicker of irritation in the face of his brother's know-it-all attitude, while being reassured that Samuel was sounding more like his normal self.

"She's been chasing that Head of TV job for years, but it's destined to be restructured out of existence, while her role as Commissioner is being undercut by some class of a Commissioning Board."

"Nice one!" said Samuel, curling his lip. "I have to give it to those BBC management people, they know how to eviscerate people without shedding one drop of blood. How does all this affect you?"

"This is the bit that's really freaking me out. You remember my former friend Harry?"

"Foxy?"

"The very man! It looks like he's going to be on the Commissioning Board, so he'll stymie any chance of me getting a commission ever again."

Samuel frowned. "I thought he ran an independent company?"

"He does. When I questioned the appropriateness of this arrangement, she told me they're going to erect a legal firewall so there's no conflict of interest."

"*Mm*, tricky!" Samuel relapsed into silence while his legal brain whirred. "Don't worry too much. Same Harry will overreach sooner or later, and you can go in for the kill."

He tried and failed to imagine himself going in for the kill in any context. "I don't have the killer instinct."

"You sure? Our mutual friend Wright seems to think you do."

"Oh God, what's he plotting now?"

Samuel wiped his mouth with a large linen handkerchief. "I just got word this morning that the money that disappeared from Helena's account has been replaced."

"*What?* Do you know by who?"

"It seems to have been done by some entity in the Isle of Man. Very difficult to track the source."

"Does Wright know?"

"Well, no, I suppose he wouldn't."

"Can we please tell him, because he thinks I stole Helena's money."

"No time like the present."

"We can also tell him that I've now got proof that Malachy Murtagh's house in Islandmagee did exist and has indeed disappeared."

"Really? What kind of proof?" Samuel looked interested.

"You remember that series *Sky-High*, where a helicopter flew around Northern Ireland taking aerial footage? We've got hold of the stuff on Islandmagee, and the house that Helena described is there, on film."

"I really thought that woman was completely full of shit."

"I think we're looking at a murder here. Someone has gone to extreme lengths to wipe Malachy and his house off the face of the earth."

They walked around the corner, presented themselves at Musgrave Street Police Station and were shown to an interview room where they waited for Detective Wright.

"Let me do the talking," said Samuel somewhat unnecessarily since Jer was already wishing himself anywhere but in this oppressive building and had suddenly lost confidence in his scrap of film convincing anyone of anything.

Samuel had resorted to pacing up and down the small room by the time Wright made an appearance. The detective placed a fat file on the table and sat down facing the McCabe brothers.

"We have some new information for you in relation to the theft of money from my client Helena Santoro's account," declared Samuel.

"Oh?" said Wright, looking sceptical.

"I've just been notified this morning by her Building Society that the money's been restored to her account."

Wright looked hard at Jer. "And do we know where the money has come from?" he said, tapping his pen on the table.

"No, that's where we're hoping you can help. It's come via the Isle of Man, so hopefully your people can trace it."

"Well, Mr. McCabe, we're very short-staffed, and I can't see this being a priority. If the money is back in her account, whoever took it would just claim it was all a mistake."

"Aren't you even curious about who took the money and, indeed, why they've now put it back?" Jer said in frustration, earning an irritated look from Samuel.

"Perhaps it's something you could shed some light on?" said Wright.

"For heaven's sake, Wright, you're not still banging that old drum. Would I be here if I was guilty of anything?"

"You tell me."

Jer cast his eyes to heaven in exasperation, then glared at the detective. "Why did you tell Leo Greatrex's mother I'd given you information about him? You'd no right to do that! She turned up at my office, extremely angry and worried."

Wright leaned back and folded his arms.

"Have you tracked down Leo yet?" said Jer.

"Why are you so interested in this young man?"

He was about to respond when he felt Samuel's hand on his arm.

"We're interested in young Leo for the same reason as you are," said Samuel. "Because we think he's key to all of this. I find it hard to believe you haven't located him by now."

"Even if we had, I wouldn't be at liberty to share that information with you or your client."

"I've found proof that Malachy and Helena's house in Islandmagee did exist," said Jer, desperate to penetrate Wright's wall of cynicism.

"What kind of proof?"

"Video evidence," said Samuel before Jer had a chance to respond.

"And why haven't you passed this on to me?"

"Because you've taken possession of my laptop and mobile phone."

"We'll be handing over the video shortly," said Samuel, "but may I remind you, Detective, that my brother and I asked for this meeting for the purpose of keeping you informed of developments. And while we're exchanging information, how about you tell us the current status of the case. Do you still think it was an attempted murder-suicide?"

"Send us the video of the house and we will, in due course, review all the evidence. I'd say it's only a matter of time before his body washes up somewhere along the Antrim coast – perhaps on the beach where your wife likes to carry on her sexual cavorting."

Jer held his breath, afraid to look in Samuel's direction.

"Didn't your brother show you the little film he made? It looks like he wanted the world to see it before you did."

"*What the hell do you mean?*" growled Jer.

"That video you posted last night is taking on a life of its own on social media."

"I didn't post any video! You've leaked it," Jer said, appalled.

"That's a very serious accusation, very serious indeed, and one I suggest you think long and hard about before repeating."

"Come on, Jer, let's go," muttered Samuel, rising and heading for the door.

Jer felt like jumping on Wright and throttling the life out of him but instead followed his brother out of the police station.

Once out on the pavement, he began, "Samuel, I didn't – "

"Not here, he'll be watching us."

They turned and walked side by side back towards the river.

"I didn't post any video of Myra. I would never do such a thing."

"I know you didn't. He'll have leaked it to someone who has obliged. But what I can't forgive you for is filming it in the first place and, when you realised what you had, not deleting it. You need to tell me exactly what's on it."

"You'll be able to see it for yourself if it's online."

"No, I want you to tell me right now. Are Myra and Helena having sex?"

"God no, I told you, it's nothing like that. They're fully clothed. You've got to remember it's dark, the candles are flickering, and their hair is blowing around. There's just a glimpse of them . . . kissing," he said, subsiding into a miserable silence.

"On the mouth?"

He nodded. "And they sort of collapse in a heap and writhe around a bit . . ."

"Okay, I get the picture."

"But . . . it was all part of the ritual . . ." he added, his voice trailing off.

Chapter 22

Jer put off the moment of reckoning at Indigo when he'd have to announce that the *Thoughtless* series had been axed, by heading to the Sugarhouse for some liquid fortification. He was no sooner inside the door than he wished himself a thousand miles away. Harry was ensconced at a long table surrounded by a dozen production staff, holding forth about his elevation to the new Commissioning Board. He spotted Jer immediately and hailed him. Some of Harry's party, who were sitting with their backs to the door, turned around and, to Jer's dismay, he saw Rosie was among them. She rested her elbow on the back of her chair and gazed at him defiantly.

He approached the group and stood looking down at her.

"When did you get back?"

"Why don't you join us?" drawled Harry. "This is a momentous day for everybody in the indie sector!"

"Rosie, we need to talk," Jer muttered, ignoring Harry.

"She's working for me now and I won't have you giving her a hard time."

"And when, or should I say, what time did her employment with you start?" He stared at Harry. "It would be useful to know, from a legal point of view."

Harry's smile faded. "Isn't that typical of you, Jer? What are you going to do, get your big-guns barrister brother to sue her?"

"Not a bad idea. Thanks for the suggestion."

Rosie turned her back on Jer.

"Rosie, you don't just owe me an explanation, you owe one to your friends who are sitting in the Indigo office down the street. We all trusted you. Do you think your new colleagues here will do the same?"

There was an embarrassed silence around the table and Harry gave him a dirty look.

"Careful, Harry, the mask is slipping there."

Jer walked away towards the bar where he ordered his usual pint and pie, then seated himself on the far side of the room, with his back to Harry's gathering, picking up a stray newspaper to cover his isolation. He knew every mouthful was going to stick in his gullet, but that was preferable to running away. He'd been coming to the Sugarhouse for years and wasn't about to be forced out of it by Harry.

He rang Nora.

"Hi, love, everything alright at home?"

"Where are you?" came her usual refrain, "No, don't tell me, the Sugarhouse."

"Right first time. What are you and Helena up to?"

"I'm on my own. She's gone off with Myra."

"Oh right." He debated with himself whether or not to tell her that Myra hadn't gone home the night before but decided not to escalate the situation just yet. "Do you know where they've gone?"

"We were all talking about what could have happened to the house, and Myra suggested going to look for, what do you call it – a landfill site, that's it."

"I suppose there is a logic to that. Lorryloads of rubble must have been carted away from that hillside and ended up somewhere. You didn't fancy the expedition?"

"Myra doesn't really want me around, and I'm not sure if Helena does either."

"I'm sure Helena doesn't feel like that, Nora. After all, she did opt to stay with you and me last night."

"That's true. But it's weird, Jer – it's getting harder and harder to tell them apart, now that Helena's wearing Myra's clothes. And Myra's stopped wearing make-up!"

"That is weird," he agreed.

"To be honest, I'm getting fed up playing gooseberry. It might be better if she stayed with Myra for a bit."

He closed his eyes for a moment, thinking of his brother. "I'm not sure Samuel would be okay with having Helena in the house."

"He could have two for the price of one!"

Jer laughed despite himself. "*Ouch!* He doesn't deserve that! Listen, I was with him earlier and you'll never guess – Helena's money has been returned to her account."

"Really? Returned? It's back in her account?"

"Yes."

"How? Who did that?"

"They don't know yet."

"But it's good, isn't it? She could get a place of her own now, couldn't she?"

"She could indeed. Maybe that would be best all round. My

lunch has just arrived." He eyed a golden-topped pie which had been placed before him.

"Before you go, a young fella called here earlier, looking for her."

He stiffened. "What did he look like?"

"Small guy with bleached hair. Very tanned and good-looking."

"Did he give a name?"

"No, I should've asked, but he seemed very nervous, so I didn't like to."

"That's okay, Nora."

"You know who it was, don't you?"

"It sounds like Leo."

"Oh my God, you're not serious? What would a lovely young fella like him want with Helena? I mean, she's pleasant enough looking but a bit flea-bitten at this stage."

He laughed. "Nora, my love, I couldn't have put it better myself! To be fair, she did deny any love affair."

"I remember now, she said she was mentoring him or something. Should I mention it when she comes home?"

"I think you'd better, since he's likely to come back. Did he leave a number?"

"No, sorry, I should've asked – I'm hopeless about this stuff," she said, her voice betraying the beginnings of agitation.

"No, you're not. You're just sensitive to other people's feelings, which is lovely. He'll turn up again sooner or later, if he really wants to see her."

"What time will you be home?"

"Teatime, if not before. Just some stuff I've got to deal with at the office before I can clock off."

He realised she'd gone. He sighed and put his phone back in

his pocket, consoling himself by lifting his knife and stabbing the pastry crust. While he ate, he let his thoughts circle around Leo. If the young man was at loggerheads with his parents since giving up his university course, he was bound to be feeling very alone. It was hardly surprising he was seeking out Helena, who'd been his mentor during the summer. He wondered if Leo might be an obsessive who stalked people. Hadn't he followed him from Tyrella and, according to Aggie, been hanging around his parking spot? He didn't like the thought of Nora alone in the house with Leo prowling around and resolved to go home straight after he'd paid a visit to the office.

He was in the middle of a fulsome swallow of beer when Rosie slipped into the bench seat against the wall and faced him across the table. He set down his glass, glanced up at the mirror on the wall above her head and saw Harry staring in their direction.

"Your new boss doesn't like you being over here. He looks thoroughly pissed off."

"Technically, he's not my new boss yet."

"Do I take that to mean I'm still your boss, at this precise moment?"

"No, I'm an entirely free agent. I emailed you my resignation letter this morning."

He nodded and picked up his fork. His appetite had deserted him, but he was determined to appear nonchalant. "What happened in America? I thought you'd been offered a job there?"

"So did I. It turned out to be a little carrot dangled on a stick to get me over there."

"Did they even pay for your flight?"

Rosie dropped her eyes.

"I suppose the bank of Mum and Dad will cover all such eventualities," he said.

"They're furious with me. They say I owe you an apology – that you took me on when I had no experience and I – " She stalled.

"Look, Rosie, it's okay. You're very young and I hope you've learned something from all this. I'd just hate to see you turn into someone ruthless like – Trix. Do you know what her assistant called her this morning – an infernal witch!"

"You think I'm an infernal witch?" she said, shocked.

"No, of course not, but Rosie, your life's a blank canvas. You've put an ugly smudge on it, but you still have lots of time to paint over that. It's one thing to grab opportunities, but – "

"That's all I was trying to do – to take the wave because you didn't. I wanted you to, don't you remember?"

He laid down his knife and fork and wiped his mouth. "I took you on because you've lots of ambition, energy and guts. But . . ." He paused, searching for words that would be instructive rather than punitive. "At Indigo you were part of a team. This is a team sport and, in that interview, every sentence that came out of your mouth started with I."

"You're pissed off because I took credit for it all?" she said, sticking out her chin defiantly. "I could say, in my defence, that I was prepared to take the heat for it all too."

"There are two types of people in this game, Rosie: the ones who come up with original ideas and the ones who bring them to fruition. If the first crowd think that you'll claim credit for their ideas, they won't want to work with you."

"You think I'm just a fixer?"

"That isn't what I said. Practical go-getters like you are vital for people like me who get bored by the nitty-gritty, long before the great idea has reached the screen. But ideas are the currency."

"And you think I took the credit for yours?"

On the other side of the bar, Harry and Co were rising and putting on their coats. Harry called from across the room. "Rosie, we're leaving now!"

"Your master calls!"

"I thought you'd be more – forgiving," she said huffily.

"*Ach*, Rosie. Of course I forgive you. I just – miss you. We all do." Her eyes filled with tears.

"Go on, you'd better go. You don't want to piss him off on day one."

Her face crumpled, but she got up and left him staring at the congealing gravy at the bottom of his pie-dish. She hurried out of the bar, bringing up the rear of Harry's chattering disciples.

He trudged the short distance to the office, his heart like a stone inside his chest. He half hoped the place would be deserted but, to his consternation, he gate-crashed a little party to celebrate Stella's impending wedding. He felt like bolting, but they'd seen him come in and he resigned himself to putting a brave face on it. He walked over to the corner of the office where Stella, Hugh and Amy were seated at the coffee table which boasted an open bottle of champagne, a plate of crisps and some crumpled wrapping paper, indicating that gifts had been offered and opened.

"Maybe you'd rather I left you to it," he said gruffly.

Stella gave him a forced smile. "Of course not, Jer, don't be silly. Come and have a glass of champagne. I think there's a finger or two left in the bottle."

Hugh lifted a plastic wineglass and poured out the dregs of the champagne. "Sorry, we've made a big hole in it, I'm afraid," he said, with an embarrassed laugh.

"No problem. Here's to you, Stella!" Jer swallowed the thimbleful of champagne and coughed. "When's the big day?" he said, avoiding her eye.

"Friday," she said softly.

"So you won't be here on Friday then," he said, his voice sounding strange in his own ears.

She gave a little laugh. "Evidently not."

"And are you heading off somewhere on a . . ."

"They're going to that super hotel just across the border, the Slieve Gullion. It's supposed to be fantastic!" gushed Amy, trying to lighten the mood.

Stella began smoothing and folding the jumble of wrapping paper on the table.

Hugh got up. "Stella, if you don't mind, I'll be heading off now?"

"Of course, Hugh. It was good of you to call in."

"Can I have a word before you shoot off?" said Jer, feeling everything slipping away.

"Don't know that there's anything to say, Jer. I already emailed you my resignation."

He winced. "I'm sorry how everything has worked out. You've done a fantastic job on *Thoughtless*. I couldn't have done it without you, without any of you." He stretched out his hand and Hugh took it reluctantly. "With your going, that means there's two resignation letters in my inbox today."

Amy and Hugh looked at each other. "Who's the other one from?" said Amy, frowning.

"Rosie. I just bumped into her in the Sugarhouse, having lunch with her new boss Harry." They all looked shell-shocked, and Hugh sat down again as if he'd lost the power of his legs.

"She hasn't gone and – ?" said Stella.

"She has. According to Trix, Harry has advertised for a new Production Manager. You should throw your hat at that, Hugh. I'll give you a sparkling reference though, mind you, that might be more of a hindrance than a help."

"That's awful!" said Stella. "Harry's just using her to get back at you. He'll dump her in a heartbeat."

"She can't have gone to work for Harry. She hates him!" said Hugh, looking bewildered.

"Only what she deserves!" said Amy, getting up and starting to clear away the remains of the celebrations.

"Look, I know this isn't the ideal moment, but I'd rather you heard this from me than from the rumour mill. I was at the Beeb this morning. Cliff has been ousted. "

"You're kidding," said Stella, getting to her feet. "Trix has done for him then. She's quite something!"

"Yes, but, and there's a big but – she's not getting his job. There's a restructure under way."

"Ah, they really don't her want in that role then," she said sagely.

"Looks like it."

She put her hands her hands on her hips. "But she'll still be TV Commissioner, won't she?"

"They're creating a new Commissioning Board, and she's not sure what her role is."

She shook her head and picked up her presents.

"What do you think, Stella? Is she on her way out?" he said, trying to read her face.

"If it was anyone other than Trix, I'd say yes, but she's some operator. I really can't call it."

He nodded and watched her move towards her desk. "They're having someone from the indie sector on the new Commissioning Board."

She stopped and turned to face him. "Is it you?"

For a moment, he wished he could have answered in the affirmative, feeling that he might have regained a little of her respect.

"I wish! Or, actually, I don't wish."

She gave him a hard look and turned away again.

"What will this mean for *Thoughtless?*" said Amy, sounding worried.

"I'm afraid it's not good news there, Amy."

"They've axed it, haven't they?" contributed Hugh, from across the room.

"I'm afraid so, but Trix has assured me they'll honour the latest contract with us, although they don't want any more episodes."

Amy sat down again, looking gutted.

"Amy, please don't worry – I hope you'll stay with Indigo," he said quickly.

She nodded, still looking miserable. "I'm just sorry it's over. It's been such a fun gig to work on."

Hugh went over and stretched his hand out to her, pulled her to her feet and gave her a hug, then beat a hasty retreat from the office, leaving her looking bereft. Jer glanced towards Stella for support, but she was intent on packing her gifts into a large plastic bag.

Amy got up and busied herself clearing the table and carrying the litter into the kitchen, while Jer headed for his desk, needing to sit down. He had to write up his proposal right now and send it to Trix before Indigo sank without trace.

Chapter 23

Stella bustled out of the office with her bulging shopping bags shortly after Hugh, leaving Jer alone with Amy. The next time he saw Stella she'd be a married woman, he was thinking, trying and failing to imagine how they might relate to each other going forward. Anything would be better than the current chilliness which wounded and depressed him. He should probably suggest meeting her other half but was afraid he mightn't like the man, an outcome he suspected that would be only slightly more painful than the opposite. Then again, Stella had spent years working at his side, resenting Nora all the while – maybe he could do the same – but he doubted his own stamina for that kind of emotional war of attrition. Whatever about him and Stella, he needed to summon his creativity to save Indigo.

An hour later, he called out to Amy, "I've emailed you something! Would you read it and give me some feedback? Feel free to correct any typos."

"Sure. Is this something you're going to send Trix?"

"Yip. She told me this morning if I sent her a proposal asap she'll try and force it through quickly."

"A consolation prize for *Thoughtless* being axed?"

"Absolutely."

"That's decent of her. She can't be as bad as everyone says."

He considered telling Amy about Trix's intention to use his proposal as a test case, but decided to leave the positive note reverberating a little longer.

"What's your proposal about?"

"Female power!"

"Cool," she said, sounding intrigued.

While he was waiting for her to read the pitch, his desk phone rang.

"Jer, why don't you ever answer your mobile?"

"Trix, sorry, I thought I'd told you, the police have it. I need to give you my new number."

She paused. "Yeah, you probably did tell me. It's been a hell of a day! Have you still got the plait?"

"The plait? *Em*, yes, it's here somewhere."

"Well, put it in a safe place. I think I know who sent it. What about the package of poo?"

"That I dumped in a litterbin, on my way to see you this morning."

"Pity. I'd love to know whose it was."

He screwed up his nose. "What are you thinking?"

"I've just discovered Harry's girlfriend has long auburn hair."

He thought back to Harry's little party in the Sugarhouse but couldn't remember seeing a significant head of hair. "A little circumstantial surely?"

"I'm more and more convinced Cliff's been plotting with Harry for some time to unseat me. You need to take the plait to the police and tell them who you think sent it."

"Who *you* think sent it. I'm not sure the police would accept that the plait represents a threat to you or Indigo," he said, dreading the thought of bringing the complaint to Detective Wright.

"There's lots of foul stuff online about you, me and Indigo, and it all feeds into the narrative that we're being threatened," she insisted.

"While you're on the line, Trix, I'll be sending you the new proposal shortly."

"Good, all grist to the mill."

He felt like John Barleycorn being ground between two stones. Before he could say anything else, she rang off.

"I'd no idea there was a mass witchcraft trial here," said Amy, from the other side of the room.

"I know, it's a little-known fact. Eight women pilloried and put in prison for a year and a day for supposedly bringing about the demonic possession of a young woman."

"1711, a long time ago," she said, coming over to stand beside his desk.

"You think it's too ancient to be of interest?"

"No, I think the way you've combined it with the story of your friend Helena makes it very immediate. Have you got Helena's blessing for the idea? I mean, is she happy to be featured?"

He pressed his lips together.

"You haven't asked her," she guessed, screwing up her nose.

"It's a proposal, Amy. It has a long way to go before a single frame is broadcast, so time enough for that."

"What did Helena say when you showed her the aerial footage of her house?"

"She said it finally convinced her she wasn't going mad."

She nodded in satisfaction. "Poor woman. I was lying in bed last night trying to imagine what it'd be like to come out of hospital to find your house had disappeared. You would think you were going crazy."

"And that on top of losing her partner."

"You said the police think he took his own life."

"Sit down, Amy. I really need another brain to bounce this off."

She pulled over a chair and perched on it, all attention.

He cleared his throat. "Apparently Helena was found alone on the beach with a head wound, and a jacket of Malachy's was found nearby with a suicide note in the pocket. The police have been working on the assumption it was an attempted murder-suicide and that she survived where he didn't. Then, when Helena was discharged from hospital, it emerged that her account had been cleared out and a large amount of money stolen on the same day she was found on the beach and he disappeared: money that has now been returned."

"What? Her money's been returned?"

"Yes."

"Can't the police find who returned the money? I mean, it must be her partner, mustn't it? So he has to be still alive."

"It certainly looks that way but the police haven't been able to find him and they're pretty confident he hasn't left these shores. Whoever transferred the money seems to have covered their tracks very well."

"Where does the house fit into all this?"

"Good question. The police don't want to know about the missing house. They think Helena took me and Nora to an empty field on purpose so we'd have to take her home and look after her."

"Gosh, that seems a bit extreme. You'd think she'd be dying to go home to her own house." Amy looked him in the eye. "Do you believe she's telling the truth?"

"I didn't at first but now . . ."

"The idea of someone disposing of a house and being able to make it look as if it had never been there is pretty preposterous," she said, warming to her theme. "The thing is, why would anyone want to do that? I mean, your man Malachy's not going to destroy his own house, is he?"

"The only explanation is that someone hates Helena enough to want to leave her homeless and make her think she's lost her mind."

"There has to be someone else in this equation," said Amy thoughtfully.

"Helena's lover."

"Ah, well, now you're talking. What do you know about him?"

"His name is Leo Greatrex. He was studying architecture at Queen's but recently dropped out."

"He's a student? I thought –"

Jer raised his eyebrows. "He's years younger than Helena who must be in her forties."

"Blimey!"

"Young Leo is desperate to be an artist, but his parents are dead against it. Enter Helena who was encouraging his artistic endeavours."

"Do you think this guy Leo is capable of doing away with his rival and then disposing of his house?"

He shrugged. "There's a vulnerability about him, but you never do know with people."

"But, hang on, if he's in love with Helena he wouldn't have hit her over the head and left her for dead on a beach, would he?"

"There are personalities who'll destroy the love-object rather than give it up. Listen, Amy, if we can find out what happened to the house and to Malachy, we have one hell of a story on our hands."

"I think you should include a paragraph saying that, to whet Trix's appetite."

He nodded. "You're right."

"I've emailed it back to you with a few amendments."

"Great! And thanks for sticking around. I know I'm not always the easiest person to work with but –"

"Listen, Jer, you're never boring, and that comes tops with me! *Em . . .*"

"What?"

"I couldn't help overhearing something about a plait when you were talking to Trix just now. What was that about?"

"Ah, you know we've been getting threats from the God-squad about *Thoughtless*. I got some nasty stuff sent here through the post."

"A plait?"

"And faeces!"

"*Yuck!*"

"I know. I didn't tell you guys because it was so gross."

"Did you tell Stella?"

"No, maybe I should have."

"I'm sure it's not lost on you, Jer, but it is a bit witchy! I mean sending a lock of human hair."

"And there were pins and feathers with the faeces."

"Now that is really revolting," she said, sticking two fingers in her mouth for effect.

He laughed. "Have you ever met Trix?"

"No, but I've seen her. Remember you took me along to that

last commissioning round presentation. Oh my God, she has a wee plait at the back of her head!" Amy's hand flew to her mouth.

He raised his eyebrows.

"So it's really a threat against her," she said, eyes wide.

"She wants me to take the plait to the police and ask them to investigate."

"I think you should. It's seriously creepy. They could do a DNA test on it, and on the faeces come to think of it."

"I dumped the poo, I'm afraid," he said, imagining Detective Wright's face if he presented him with a bag of shit to analyse. "This is strictly between me and you, but Trix thinks it was Harry who sent the plait."

She frowned. "I know he's a prick, but do you really think he would be so petty? It seems more like something a female would do. Does that sound sexist?"

"A bit."

"Good that it was me who said it then," she said, grinning. "Where did you dump the turd? Is it in the bin out there?" She indicated the kitchen with her head.

"God, no – I stuck it in a litter bin on my way to the Beeb this morning."

"It might still be there."

"Are you seriously suggesting we go rummaging in a litter bin for a turd?"

"You do remember which one you dumped it in?"

"Yes, but – "

"Stella has a pair of plastic gloves in the kitchen."

Jer had to check his own sanity standing with Amy beside a litter bin in Waring Street, while office workers and shoppers hurried past. What if any of Harry's crowd were around? They would be sure to film him groping in the bin like a down-and-out. Amy pulled on the rubber gloves and slid her arm into the bin, feeling around.

"There doesn't seem to be too much in here," she said hopefully.

"Maybe it's been emptied," he said, willing the whole enterprise to be over. "Be careful, there might be broken glass or syringes in there."

"It's in a padded envelope, right?"

"Yes."

She lifted her arm out of the bin and, held delicately between thumb and forefinger, was the padded envelope, now stained red with what looked like tomato sauce. He held open a plastic shopping-bag and she dropped the envelope into it. She peeled off the rubber gloves and chucked them into the bag, then took it from him and tied a decisive knot with the handles.

"There we are. Where's the nearest police station?"

"Musgrave Park, but we don't have to do this right now. I mean, it's maybe not the ideal time to report something like this."

"Why not? Surely the police work 24/7? Come on, you don't want to be taking that home, do you?" She took his elbow and steered him away from the bin.

In the event, they were told to come back next morning when someone would take a statement from them. They crossed the road to a small, fuggy Mexican restaurant where they ate fajitas, trying not to think about the contents of the plastic bag under the table.

"Would you like to meet Helena?" he suggested, after Amy had bombarded him with questions about his houseguest.

"I thought you'd never ask," she said, her eyes sparkling.

He smiled and relaxed. "There's some other stuff I should maybe fill you in on, if you're coming home with me."

Night had fallen by the time they reached the house. On the way, he'd given Amy a summary of the state of Samuel and Myra's marriage, Myra's current obsession with Helena, and Nora's antipathy to her sister-in-law. No sooner had he shared these details of his personal life than he wished he'd kept it all to himself. He sought her assurance that she'd treat what he'd told her as confidential, knowing that, despite her best intentions, the intricate web of knowledge he'd revealed to her would inevitably inform everything she thought and said about the situation from here on.

Getting out of the car, they could see Helena and Myra sitting at the kitchen table by candlelight. The rest of the house was in darkness. He felt a flicker of unease for Nora.

"Are they having a séance?"

"Are you sure you're up for this? I'm happy to drive you home if you'd rather not get involved."

"No, bring it on! I'm really curious to meet Helena."

Alerted by the car headlights, Myra got up and switched on the light above the table.

Jer brought Amy round to the front door and walked into a hall that was dark, save for a line of light showing under the kitchen door. He groped for the light-switch and smiled reassuringly at Amy who blinked.

Myra had resumed her seat at the table facing Helena when they entered the kitchen, and he did a double take. She had her long hair loose around her shoulders and was wearing a voluminous, black garment while Helena had contained her hair in a French roll and sported a cast-off, coral, cashmere twinset of Myra's which gave her skin a peachy tinge in the candlelight. He had the disturbing sense that there'd been an exchange of more than clothes between the two women.

He wondered what his young colleague would make of them and introduced her. "Amy was the one who found the footage of your house, Helena."

She stood up and offered Amy her hand with a smile. "Thank you very much, Amy. I can't tell you what it means to me to have that film of the house."

"You're welcome. Glad to help." Amy glanced at Myra, who was sitting, still facing Helena's now empty chair.

Myra gave Amy an appraising glance but didn't seem to think a greeting was merited.

"Won't you join us for a chat?" said Helena. "We've been driving around all day."

"Jer said you went to look at some landfill sites. Any joy?" Amy said pleasantly, sitting down beside her.

"No," said Myra flatly.

"Would you like some tea, Amy?" said Jer, to cover Myra's rudeness.

"Thanks, that would be great."

"Helena, Myra?"

"Thanks, I'd love some," said Helena.

There was silence from Myra.

"I think Myra's okay," Helena said softly.

Jer ground his teeth with annoyance. This was his house. If Myra wanted to spend time here, she might at least be civil to him.

"Where's Nora?" he said, trying not to sound accusatory.

"She wasn't here when we got back," said Myra, without looking him.

He filled the kettle, turned it on, then left the room to ring Nora.

"Where are you?" he asked wearily when she answered her phone.

"That's my line," she said with a smile in her voice.

"Golf Club?" he guessed.

"Right first time. Have the witches returned?" she said with a little giggle.

He stepped into the living room, which was lit only by the streetlamps outside, and stared out into the night. "Nora, don't! You started all this, remember?"

"I know – *mea culpa, mea culpa*. Did they find anything in the landfill sites?"

"No, seems not."

"Don't forget to tell Helena that the money's back in her account. That might make her decide to move on."

"Yeah, right. I'd forgotten about that."

She ended the call, and he stood thinking about the proposal he'd just sent to Trix, which depended on Helena's cooperation. He didn't want to cut her loose just yet. But then there was Myra who was becoming an unwelcome fixture in his house. How on earth was he going to break it to her that the footage of her and Helena was circulating online?

Chapter 24

He turned on a table-lamp, pulled the curtains, and sat down in his favourite armchair to draw breath, thinking of his brother Samuel coming home to an empty house. He rang his number which went to answer-phone.

"Samuel, it's me. I just wanted to let you know that Myra is here. It sounds like they had a disappointing day searching landfill sites. Anyway, didn't want you to worry." He put his phone back in his pocket and breathed out. He debated with himself whether this was the moment to tell Myra about the online footage and decided to play it by ear.

When he re-entered the kitchen, he saw with approval that Helena was making tea. She seemed different this evening, more present. He sat at the end of the table, rather than take the seat beside Myra, who was responding grudgingly to Amy's questions about which landfill sites they'd visited.

"Have you thought of talking to your postman, Helena?" said Amy brightly. "He might have seen lorries coming and going. Could your house be seen from the road?"

"I'm afraid not. One of its charms was its seclusion," Helena said, setting two mugs of tea on the table.

"I think we should follow up the postman idea tomorrow. What do you think?" Jer said, taking a slurp of tea.

"That would be fantastic!" Helena shot a glance at her friend. "What do you think, Myra?"

Myra gave a deep sigh. "It's worth a try."

"Someone removed the post box from the end of the lane," Jer said to Amy.

"Seriously? That's really random! There must be post piling up for you somewhere." Amy cocked her head. "I think your phone's ringing, Jer."

Still unused to its synthesised summons, he hadn't recognised it as his own. He scrambled for the phone. "Samuel, I – "

"The clip of Myra and Helena has just been shown on the local news!"

"*What?* Oh my God, how did that happen?"

"That's what I want you to tell me. You stupid bastard, how could you?" Samuel groaned, as if in physical pain.

"Hang on a second," he said, getting up from the table.

He looked in Myra's direction and saw she was staring at him. She shook her head, indicating that she either didn't want her husband to know she was there, or didn't want to talk to him. He took refuge in his study.

"What way did they – I mean, what's the story?" He closed the door. "How can it possibly be newsworthy?"

Samuel made a derisive sound. "They linked it to your series, saying the production team had received threats which had overtones of witchcraft. Have you been threatened?"

"Only Trix knew about those threats. She must have done this!" he said, appalled.

"Did you give her that video?"

Jer swallowed. He'd put a link to the video clip into the proposal he'd sent her. "She'd have been aware of it. She rang me earlier, asking me to take a plait of hair and some faeces I was sent through the post to the police."

"Dear God! But who made the connection between that and the clip of my wife behaving like a bloody dervish on a beach in the middle of the night? That had to be you!"

"She's capable of making that kind of connection all on her own. She's very unscrupulous and will use anything to get one over on her enemies."

"And you're one of her enemies, it seems? The report said there'd been other instances of witchcraft here recently."

"I didn't know that. Did they mention Malachy's disappearance?"

"Oh yes, that was the punchline – the fact that the beach where they were cavorting was where Malachy Murtagh had purportedly taken his own life."

"I'm sorry, Samuel, I don't know what to say."

He could hear Samuel breathing heavily. "Is Myra there?"

"Yes, she's in the kitchen."

"With that bloody witch?"

"Yes, but I – "

"Have you told her about the video being online?"

"Not yet. I don't think she even knows of its existence."

"Listen, Jer, I don't know how she'll react when she finds out that not only is it circulating online but it's been on the fucking News. You know how much store she sets by her – image, her place in society."

"What do you want me to do?" His heart sank. He dreaded the idea of telling Myra what had happened.

"I'm coming over. Can you make sure she doesn't leave till I get there?"

"I'll do my best. She does know it's you on the phone."

"Don't tell her I'm coming in case she takes off. I need to talk to her. If she wants to know what I've said, tell her I want her to ring me when she feels ready."

After the call, Jer sat holding his phone in both hands. He was tempted to ring Trix, but knew she'd only deny planting the story. Was this some plot of hers to discredit Harry? If it was, she'd really crossed a line.

The door opened and he tensed when he saw it was Myra. She closed it behind her and sat on the piano stool. He gazed at his sister-in-law as if he'd never really seen her before. Nora was right, Myra wasn't wearing make-up or jewellery. She looked older, despite the long, thick, auburn hair framing her face. She was wearing some kind of leggings under the flowing black top and her feet were bare. It was the naked feet that broke his heart for he'd never seen Myra without high heels, even in her own kitchen.

"That was Samuel?" she said, trying and failing to meet his eye.

"I'd left him a message saying you're here safe and sound. That was him ringing back. He said for you to ring him when you feel ready."

"Would it be okay if I stayed here tonight?" she said, lowering her eyes, as if having to ask for a bed for the night was beyond humiliating.

"Of course, Myra, if that's what you need to do," he said, chewing his lower lip. He couldn't bear the thought that his brother's marriage might be over. Samuel wasn't the kind of man who'd be able to make a new start with someone else. He thought of the film clip out there in the world, making her a laughing stock, and felt ashamed of his part in creating it. If Myra was miserable now, what state would she be in when she discovered how she'd been outed on the News?

"How have you managed to stay with Nora all these years?" Her voice was anguished.

"I'll be honest, there've been times when I've come close to leaving but – I care about her too much to leave."

She nodded.

"You're the strong one, you do realise that," he said, leaning towards her. "I know Samuel seems indomitable but, if you leave him, he'll not survive it."

"He's on his way over here, isn't he?" she said.

He hesitated.

"Don't worry, I'm not going to run away." She sounded close to despair. "Where would I go?"

They sat in an uncomfortable silence for a few moments. Afraid he was about to confess what he'd filmed, he tried to change the subject.

"Tell me about how Helena was today. She seems different."

"I think it's because she's no longer taking her medication," she said with a hint of regret.

He nodded, all too familiar with that feeling. "I hope Nora doesn't follow suit!"

She gave him a sympathetic look and he had the sudden thought that, after decades of permafrost, his relationship with Myra might actually be thawing.

"Is her memory coming back? I mean, can she remember anything about the morning she was found on the beach?"

"Did you know that she'd suffered a head injury? She showed me the scar down the back of her head." She rubbed her fingers up and down the nape of her own neck.

"She probably had concussion when she went into hospital. Did she talk about anything else today, her past for instance?"

She looked away. "Anything she said was in confidence."

"Myra, I'm only trying to help."

They relapsed into silence, and he became aware of the tick of the clock. He tried a different tack. "Nora told me that young man Leo called here today looking for Helena."

She licked her lips.

"Did she mention him at all?"

"No," she said, looking away again, "she just talks endlessly about Malachy. She still hasn't accepted that he's dead." She dropped her head, letting her hair covered her face. "Jer, please, could you give me some time alone? I need to gather my thoughts before Samuel gets here."

He hoped she wasn't about to make a run for it, but she'd assured him she wouldn't. In any case, there was only so much he could do. Samuel and Myra had to untangle their own marriage.

When he rejoined Amy and Helena in the kitchen, he found they were getting on like a house on fire. He sat down again at the end of the table and took a sip of his tea, which was now stone cold.

"Amy's the age my Isabella would be, if she'd lived," Helena said to him.

"It's a beautiful name," said Amy gently. "Did you call her after someone?"

"My mother's name was Isabel. She died when I was twelve."

"That must have been awful!" she said.

"And you preferred the Italian version of the name?" said Jer.

"I was living in Italy at the time so . . ." Helena's face stilled.

He leaned forward, keen to keep her talking, now she'd opened up. "Was Isabella's father Italian?"

She nodded. "He was a lot older than me and married. I was punished for my sin, but Isabella shouldn't have been. She was totally innocent. I stopped believing in God the moment the nurse put her in my arms."

"Did you have some time with her before . . ." said Amy, her young face stricken.

Helena crossed her arms, gripping her forearms, as if she could still feel the weight of the baby in her embrace. "She had a lot of dark hair, but I couldn't see her eyes. She never even got to see me. She was cold, so cold." She turned to Amy. "I'm sorry, you don't want to hear all this. Looking at a beautiful young woman like you just makes me wonder what she would've been like. You and Nora must do the same when you see a young man the age that Liam would have been."

He nodded and Amy looked at him, startled.

"Leo came here today looking for you, Helena. He spoke to Nora."

"Leo?" She was taken aback. "It would be – strange to see him again now. It's as if he belongs to another life. Is he okay?" Her voice was faint.

"He seems terribly upset about Malachy."

"Did Nora say that?"

He realised he was going to have to come clean about his trip to Tyrella. "No. I met him on Saturday."

"On Saturday? But I was . . ." she began, looking confused.

"I went looking for Malachy's swimming friends and Leo was there with them, at Tyrella Beach."

She looked terribly taken aback.

"Maybe I should have told you, but you were very fragile, and I was afraid of upsetting you." He took another sip of cold tea to hide his embarrassment.

"But Leo came here today? You told him I was here?"

"I told him you were staying with us, but not where I lived. He obviously found that out for himself."

"Are you afraid of him?" said Amy.

"Leo? Oh no. We're soulmates."

Jer and Amy exchanged a look. "Helena mentored him during the summer," he said to Amy.

"I don't know if you could call it mentoring, Jer. I just encouraged him to draw and paint. He has such talent, Amy – the kind of talent I could only dream of. He wants to be an artist, but his parents are horrified at the idea."

"Have you ever met them?" she asked.

"No. Leo didn't want me to meet them. He felt he had to keep his artwork secret from them, which is so sad."

"His mother Babs thinks you're a bad influence on him," said Jer.

Helena stared at him. "You've met his mother?"

"She was at Tyrella on Saturday. She's one of Malachy's swimming friends – didn't you know?"

"Yes, yes, I think – I did know that." Helena looked troubled, as if she was struggling to fit all the pieces of a jigsaw together. "She thinks I'm bad for her son?"

"She turned up at my office yesterday evening looking for him. She seems to be at her wits' end about him."

"And she blames me?"

"Apparently he's dropped out of university, so maybe it's understandable that his parents would be worried."

She picked up the note of antagonism in his tone and a wariness entered her expression. "They need to sit down and listen to him. He hates, hated the course he was doing. He told me all he's ever wanted is to be allowed to draw and paint, but his mother always discouraged it."

"How did Malachy feel about Leo hanging around?" he said, watching Helena intently.

"You asked me about this before, Jer. I honestly can't remember." She rested her elbows on the table and massaged her forehead with the tips of her fingers.

Amy looked questioningly at him.

"I thought your memory was returning now you've stopped taking your medication."

Helena dropped her hands and gave him an anguished look. "Yes, and I can feel the anxiety taking me over again, but I don't want to give in to it. I need to get back some clarity of thought. The tablets drop a veil over everything. I want to remember what happened." She closed her fists.

"There's been another development today," he said.

She opened her mouth in surprise, and looked at him questioningly.

"Apparently the money has been returned to your account."

She sat back in the chair. "Do they know now who took it?"

"No. Samuel has asked the police to look into it, of course, but I'm not sure it's now a priority for them."

She rubbed her hand across her face as if trying to clear it of cobwebs. "And the police, are they still saying Malachy took his own life?"

"They've been switiching from one theory to another! Unless his body is found, it's likely to be an open verdict."

"So I may never know. That would be impossible to live with."

Chapter 25

Samuel's car swept into the drive, his headlights raking the kitchen like a searchlight. Jer opened the patio door and raised his hand in greeting, letting in a gust of cold, damp air. Watching his brother exit the car and take the two steps up onto the patio, he was struck by how much he seemed to have aged in the past few days. Even before he stepped through the glass door, Jer could see his eyes searching the room beyond and not finding Myra. He attempted to pull him into a hug at the door, but Samuel pushed past him, a man on a mission. He looked haggard in the harsh light of the kitchen and Jer willed him to find the words to save his marriage. He nodded in Helena's direction in response to her greeting.

"Jer told me the money has been returned to my account?" she said, gazing up at him.

"Yes, your bank contacted me today asking me to pass on that information to you."

"Thank you for all you've done," she said warmly and was rewarded by a curl of his lip. Undeterred by his coldness, she went on. "And they still have no idea who took it?"

"I'm afraid that's one for the police, if they choose to pursue it," he said, glancing suspiciously at Amy.

"I'm Amy," she said quickly. "I work with Jer." She rose and stretched out her hand.

Samuel hesitated then gave her slender hand a cursory shake.

"It was Amy who found the film of our house," said Helena.

His face darkened. "Where's Myra?" he muttered to Jer.

"She's waiting for you in my study."

Samuel set his jaw and headed for the kitchen door.

"Anyone for another cup of tea?" said Jer, trying to keep his voice light.

Amy had pulled out her phone. "I really should be going."

"If you can hang on a wee bit longer, I'll run you home. I just don't feel I can bail out right now."

"No worries, I'll call a taxi."

"That'll be on me," he said, questioning his own wisdom in bringing Amy home with him in the first place, though he had to admit she'd managed to elicit some new information from Helena.

"More tea, Helena?"

"No, thanks," she whispered, her face displaying the strain she was feeling.

He filled and switched on the kettle, grateful that the sibilant sigh of the heating water masked the raised voices in the study. They heard a door being wrenched open. He held his breath before Myra burst into the kitchen, her eyes wild. She went straight up to him and slapped him hard in the face.

"*You stupid, stupid, selfish bastard!*" she screamed, delivering a punch to his chest with every adjective.

He raised his arms to shield himself but didn't attempt to restrain her.

"*Myra, stop, please stop!*" cried Helena in a shocked voice.

Myra stalled, panting and turned to Helena who was now beside her. "Do you know what he did? This stupid – " she groaned, beginning to weep.

Helena put her arms around her.

Jer felt the heat of the steaming kettle at his back, and took advantage of Helena's intervention to slide himself out of the corner, away from Myra, only to find himself face to face with Samuel.

Jer immediately understood that he was being used as a deflection by Samuel and Myra. So be it, he thought, if it means they don't split up. He wiped his nose with the back of his hand and saw a smear of blood. Myra was sobbing on Helena's shoulder. He'd never seen his buttoned-up-tight sister-in-law betray this kind of emotion. The power of it singed the air in the room like an electric charge.

He glanced at Amy who was still sitting at the table, her young face full of distress. She gasped and jumped when a pale face appeared at the patio door. His heart sank. Nora would choose this moment of high drama to appear. He slid open the patio door.

"Hi, Nora," he said, feeling like a child who's broken his mother's best china while she was out.

"You're bleeding!"

"I'm fine," he said, wiping his nose on his sleeve.

She stumbled over the threshold, and he put a steadying arm around her shoulders. "What's going on?" she said in a slurred voice.

"Your bastard of a husband filmed me and Helena on the beach, and now it's online for everyone to see!" said Myra.

She shrugged. "It's what he does, Myra. What did you expect? Jer, I don't feel very well. I want to go to bed."

"Good idea," he said, grateful for an excuse to leave the room, but aware he was abandoning Amy to this middle-aged, marital crisis. He steered Nora upstairs and into the bedroom where she disappeared under the duvet fully clothed before he'd even turned on the light. He sat beside her in the dark, listening to angry voices downstairs.

"Now the shit's really hit the floor!" she murmured.

"You mean the fan?"

"Do I? Whatever. Who's the wee girl?"

"That's Amy. I shouldn't have brought her home with me. She must think this is a madhouse." The words were out of his mouth before he could stop himself. He bit his lip and tasted blood.

"I wish they'd all just go away," she whispered, and slid into sleep.

He sat for a while listening to her breathe, until the sound of the front gate opening then clanging shut roused him and he went over to the window. He couldn't see anyone but heard a car engine start up somewhere nearby. He drew the curtains and left Nora to sleep, closing the door, then went to the bathroom to clean up his face.

A draft of chilly air met him on the stairs, and he guessed the patio door was open. Downstairs, he found the kitchen cold and empty, and stepped outside to see that both Myra's and Samuel's cars were gone. Helena must have left with Myra, he supposed, and wasn't sure whether he felt disappointed or relieved. He went back inside and locked the patio door. He assumed Amy had also made herself scare, but couldn't face ringing her, so texted instead: **Sorry about all that Amy! Hope u r ok. J.**

He got a glass, and left the kitchen, turning off the light behind him. Once safely in his study, he pulled his secret bottle of Bushmills from behind some books and poured himself a generous measure, then put on his headphones and played an album of bagpipe music at high volume, letting the deluge of sound wash away all his guilty thoughts.

He woke sometime later, in a dead silence, still wearing the headphones. He lifted them off his aching ears and reached for his whiskey glass, disappointed to find it empty. He contemplated another drink but decided sleep in a horizontal state was preferable to waking stiff and cold in his chair in the early hours. He padded into the kitchen and turned on the light to get a glass of water to take upstairs, almost dropping the glass in shock when a face appeared just outside the window above the sink. It was Helena, looking frightful.

He hurried over to unlock the patio door.

"Helena, I'm so sorry. I didn't mean to lock you out. I thought you'd gone with Myra."

She was shaking with cold.

"You haven't been out there all this time, have you? Why didn't you ring the doorbell?"

"No, no, I was with Myra for a while, but I asked her to bring me back here. Then I thought you must have gone to bed, and I didn't want to disturb you."

"You need a hot drink. What about some chocolate?"

"I think I'll just go to bed, but thank you, Jer. I don't know why you're being so kind to me. I've brought nothing but trouble on you and your family."

"Nora's no better or worse than she ever is and, the Myra thing, well, I'm beginning to think that was an accident waiting to happen. I'll put the kettle on so you can fill a hot-water bottle. You must be foundered!"

"Foundered," she said with a sad smile. "Malachy says – used to say that."

He hoped Helena was no longer clinging to her delusion that the late Malachy's spirit had taken refuge in his head. He switched on the kettle and rummaged in a cupboard for a hot-water bottle, pulling out Nora's favourite which sported an Aran-knit cover. He and Helena stood looking at each other uneasily, waiting for the water to heat.

"Where's Myra now?" he ventured, for something to say.

She went over to the table and sat down heavily. "I tried to persuade her to go home but I don't know if she – can."

He folded his arms and dropped his head onto his chest.

"If she could be content with us being friends, sisters, it would be wonderful. When we're together it feels like we're two parts of a whole person."

"You complete each other."

"Yes, exactly."

"But she wants more than that?"

"I've tried to explain that I don't feel any physical desire for her. It's the otherness of men that attracts me sexually."

He turned away to switch off the kettle before it came to the boil, glad of the distraction. He busied himself filling the jar.

"You filmed us kissing on the beach," she said to his back.

He screwed the top into the hot-water bottle and turned around, feeling idiotic with it hanging from his thumb and forefinger.

"I'm sorry. I had no right to do that. I was just taken by the circle of candlelight in the darkness, and your wild shapes flitting around. Visually, it was beautiful."

"That I can understand, but you put it online? Surely you knew that Myra wouldn't want to be seen in that – state of abandon?"

"I didn't put it online. I wouldn't even know how to do that. I'd totally forgotten about the clip, which was on my mobile. You remember the police took my phone and laptop because they suspected I'd something to do with the disappearance of your money. I think Detective Wright leaked that footage to embarrass Samuel. He's had run-ins with him before on various cases." He carried the hot-water bottle over and laid it on her lap.

She placed her hands on the woolly covering, tracing the knitted shapes with her fingers.

"They used to identify drowned fishermen by the pattern of their Aran jumpers," she said, looking down at the intricate weave of the stitches.

"Each family had their own pattern," he agreed, watching her, thinking of the nurse placing the stillborn baby in her arms. How does a teenager, far from home, recover from such an experience? It was no wonder she struggled to find a firm footing in the world. Whoever had erased her house had been aware of her vulnerability. "Did you ever see Isabella's father again?"

"What?"

"You were working as an au pair, so was he the husband of – ?"

"I don't want to think about all that, Jer. Please . . ."

"I know, Helena, but someone means you harm, and I'm determined to find out who it is. I mean, could it be this older man you had the affair with?"

She shook her head wearily. "He died years ago."

His shoulders sagged.

"It wasn't really an affair," she added, closing her eyes.

He froze. "Was it – were you . . ." he began, failing to find the words to voice his intuition.

"He was an artist – a very fine artist and he asked me to model for him. Everyone trusted him. I trusted him."

"He took advantage of you?"

"If only it was that simple. I went there, to his studio, every day for weeks. I didn't have to go. I could have said no – run out of there."

She was speaking so softly he could barely hear her.

"It sounds like you were being groomed," he said gently.

"You're not the first person to say that. The thing is, you need to understand that those times with him were the most intense sexual experiences of my life. I would lie there naked in that sun-filled studio for hours while his eyes roamed all over my body. I often fell asleep. I've never been able to reclaim my sleep. He's always there watching me."

Jer was ashamed to feel himself becoming aroused. He went and sat down at the table to hide his discomfort. She glanced in his direction, then dropped her eyes, as if she understood exactly what was agitating him.

"Did you try to relive that experience with Leo in your own studio?"

She looked appalled. "How could you think that? I thought you were someone who might understand."

Stung, he decided he had to press on. "That nude drawing that Derek showed me – you were modelling for Leo, weren't you?" he finished, his chest tight.

She hugged the hot-water bottle to her breast and rocked herself. When she spoke, he realised she was crying. "Leo didn't draw that. I did. It's a self-portrait. You shouldn't listen to Derek. He's full of – "

"Shit!" he said grimly.

"Yes." She wiped her tears away.

"I'm sorry, Helena, please don't cry. I'm just trying to make sense of all this." He tore off a piece of kitchen-roll and handed it to her.

"I would never do anything to harm Leo."

"Okay, I believe you. Really, I do."

"I'm going to bed now. Tomorrow, I think I should look for somewhere else to stay."

Nora was snoring when he went to bed, and he spent a long time lying on his back, staring into the darkness, trying to still his mind. When he finally sank into unconsciousness, his sleep was disturbed by strange dreams. He'd given Helena a baby and was afraid she was too distracted to look after it. The baby was lying on her lap, and he wanted to shout at her to put her arms around it so it wouldn't roll onto the ground. Then it came to him that the baby had been dead for some time, and was nothing more than a bag of skin, filled with putrefied liquid. Then he himself was the infant, drowning in amniotic fluid in the womb.

He woke with a sense of horror, to find Nora's clothed body wrapped around his, her sour breath in his face. He disentangled himself and threw off the duvet, letting his body cool, until a shiver rippled across his skin. He got up and put on his bathrobe and walked stealthily past Helena's closed door and took a long, noisy leak, before standing for a while at the landing window, watching the dawn break, listening to a solitary bird calling out in the garden. He could still stop Stella going through with her marriage. It was completely in his power; he had no doubt about that. But if he did, he could control none of the consequences. He knew he had to let her go. He leaned his forehead against the glass and felt a warm tear fall onto the cold flesh of his foot.

Thursday 30th October

Chapter 26

He was woken at ten in the morning by the house-phone, dully aware it had been ringing for a long time. A minute later, Nora came into the bedroom in her dressing gown, looking agitated.

"Jer, do something. These people keep ringing and ringing," she said in a shaky voice, handing him the phone and beating a hasty retreat.

"Who is this?" he barked, sitting up in the bed.

"Hi, Jer, this is Ricky from the BBC Newsroom."

"How the hell did you get this number?"

"I did try your office a few times but got no answer. Sorry to bother you at home but – "

"You're not a bit sorry, so don't give me that guff!" He swung his legs out of the bed and tried to get his brain in gear.

"Come on, Jer, you know how this goes. We're working on a follow-up to last night's witchcraft story. We understand Helena Santoro is staying with you and we'd love an interview with her. Do you think that's possible?"

He remembered what Helena had said the night before about

finding somewhere else to stay. Maybe she'd already gone. "Look, you have to understand she's in a very vulnerable state. I mean she recently lost her partner – "

"And she's just out of a psychiatric hospital, isn't she?"

"Who told you that?" He felt dizzy. He'd forgotten how quickly a news story gathered momentum.

"And your company has received threats, isn't that right?"

"I can't believe Trix told you that!"

"You mean Trix Maidstone?" said the reporter. "She hasn't told us anything. Sounds like she might have something to contribute though – what does she know?"

"Then who told you Indigo received threats?"

"It's all online. Would you be willing to talk to us about the threats and your series being axed?"

"But that has nothing to do with Helena and – "

"You get human hair and shit through the post when this woman who practises witchcraft is staying with you?"

"You're not suggesting she sent that stuff?"

"No, but it can't be a coincidence."

"Ricky, once witchcraft is mentioned, people jump to all sorts of conclusions."

"Couldn't agree more which is why it'd be great if we could talk to you and set the record straight."

He had a moment of clarity. The reporters would keep coming, even if he refused to cooperate. It was a high-risk strategy, but he could use the news story as an accelerant. Reporters sniffing around might turn up interesting angles on Malachy and Helena, while the hue and cry about witchcraft would increase the chances of his proposal being commissioned.

"Okay, but not this morning. I have to go up the Antrim coast shortly. I could do something around three o'clock."

"*Mm*, cutting it a bit fine for the six o'clock bulletin. I tell you what, since you'll be up around the north coast, we can do it at Cladrach Beach. I take it your friend Helena will be with you?"

"I'll talk to her and see how she feels about giving an interview," he said, hoping she was still in the house. "It's her call obviously."

"Of course, of course. Has she agreed to give an interview to any other outlets?"

"No, Ricky, you've got your scoop."

They exchanged mobile numbers before ending the call. He shivered and looked around for his towelling robe which was nowhere to be seen. He heard the front door being opened and listened intently. Nora was still in her dressing gown so she couldn't be heading out. He heard female voices in the hall and hoped it didn't mean Helena was leaving? He pulled on some clothes and exited the bedroom. Helena's bedroom door was tightly shut. Descending the stairs silently in his bare feet, he was relieved to hear Amy's bright young voice in conversation with Nora in the kitchen.

"Morning, Amy, do we have something arranged?" he said, wondering why she was there.

She grinned at him, "We're going to find Helena's postman in Islandmagee, aren't we?"

"Of course, sorry, yes. I slept very badly last night, hence the – "

"No problem. I've brought the camera. Thought we could film the encounter," she said, looking meaningfully at him.

"Good idea." He avoided Nora's eye.

"If we're off to Islandmagee, I'd better wake her up," said Nora.

"She's definitely still here then?" he said.

"Why wouldn't she be, Jer? What did you do to her last night?"

"I didn't *do* anything to her, Nora. I just talked to her."

"Interrogated her?"

"She was really lucid last night, and I thought I could get more information from her while the going was good."

"And you've offended her, no doubt," she said, walking out of the kitchen.

He made the face of a guilty schoolboy and Amy dropped her eyes in embarrassment.

It was midday by the time they set off for Islandmagee. Helena had emerged from her bedroom, dressed in a black polo-neck cashmere jumper and wool slacks, courtesy of Myra. She looked hollow-eyed from lack of sleep. Her hair was coiled into a loose bun at the back of her head, and she was wearing the single sea-horse earring he'd seen in her bag. Nora insisted that Helena sit in the front seat beside him, since it was assumed she knew the way to Ballystrudder Post Office. Helena was very quiet, and he wondered if she was still angry with him about what he'd said about her corrupting Leo. He wanted to tackle the subject of the interview but was reluctant to do it in front of Nora. The lack of conversation in the front of the car was more than made up for by the chatter from the backseat, where Nora and Amy were getting acquainted.

"How is dear Stella these days?" Nora asked her, making him tighten his grip on the steering-wheel.

"Great. She's getting married tomorrow." The words were no sooner out of Amy's mouth than she realised her faux pas.

"You didn't tell me that, Jer!" said Nora in astonishment.

He took a deep breath and was aware of Helena turning to look at him. "I only just found out myself."

"I find that very hard to believe," Nora said icily.

"He really didn't know, Nora. Sorry, I've got a big mouth. Shit!"

"Don't worry about it, Amy," he said.

"She can't be getting married tomorrow," said Nora, her mood swerving towards derision. "Who in the name of God ever heard of getting married at Halloween?"

"Tomorrow is Samhain?" said Helena, in an awed voice. "I'd completely lost track. We have to contact Malachy tomorrow. It's our best chance."

"Will you be doing one of your rituals?" Nora sounded perturbed.

Helena reached back and touched her. "I know you don't like these things but, if you could only trust me and come into the circle, you could do amazing things."

"Hang on a second, Helena – I won't stand for you trying to talk Nora into this kind of – "

"Please don't worry, Jer, I only encourage her because I truly believe she would find great comfort if she could allow herself to have intercourse with the spirit world."

"Nora's problem is she's already too much in the spirit world. What you're suggesting is the last thing she needs!" he insisted, thumping the steering-wheel for emphasis.

"I'm convinced she has second sight. If she could just open herself to the other side, instead of fearing it, she would find healing."

"*Are you out of your mind?*" He considered pulling over the car, such was his anger.

"*I am here, you know. I can hear you!*" cried Nora. "Please don't discuss me as if I'm a child. This is what happens when you suffer from mental illness, Amy – people treat you as if you're no longer a person with rights."

Jer caught Amy's eye in the rear-view mirror and was relieved to see she looked fascinated rather than alarmed by the turn the conversation had taken.

"Anyway, I think you should use Myra again for your spell-making. She's gagging for it!" said Nora crossly.

Helena turned away from them all to gaze out the window.

"What happened with her and Samuel last night?" continued Nora, her voice taking on a spiteful edge. "I think their marriage is on the rocks!"

There was a charged silence in the car, and he turned on the one o'clock radio news, hoping to lower the temperature. What he hadn't bargained for was the witchcraft story being discussed by a local church leader who was bewailing an apparent increase in satanic practices.

"My God, are they talking about you and Myra?" said Nora.

"Yes," Helena said in a small voice.

"Did you do this, Jer?" Nora sounded horrified.

"No, of course not!"

"No 'of course' about it! It's just the sort of thing you'd do to set the cat among the pigeons."

"Well, not guilty, in this case."

"Was it him, Amy?"

"No, no, it wasn't. We think it was Trix."

"Ah, the infamous Trix!" she said, in an all-knowing voice.

"Who's Trix?" Helena asked timorously.

"She's – " said Jer and Amy simultaneously.

"Go on, Amy," said Jer. "You could probably describe her more objectively than me."

Amy cleared her throat self-consciously. "She's Head of Commissioning at the BBC here in Belfast. I don't really know her, but everybody says she very ambitious and ruthless, but great at her job."

"He calls her his *bête noire*," contributed Nora.

"I thought you said it was some police detective who'd leaked the film. So, which is true?" Helena asked him, in a tone he hadn't heard her use before.

"Actually, I think Detective Wright or someone close to him put the film online, Amy, and it's possible that Trix brought it to the attention of News. If it was Trix, I don't think I'm the target. She might be plotting against another independent producer who's becoming too powerful."

"But surely she knew this would hurt you and your family?" said Helena.

"She wouldn't give a damn about that. I'm just collateral damage."

"Charming!" chimed Nora.

"Okay, this is Ballystrudder," said Amy suddenly.

"Oh my, I blinked. Have I missed it?" said Nora and laughed.

He pulled the car in tight to the hedge, just before the village petered out.

"We won't be able to get out!" Nora cried.

"Okay, okay," he said, putting his foot down and accelerating into a U-turn, earning a furious horn-blare from a passing motorist who missed them by inches.

"*Steady on!*" Amy shouted. "*I'd like to live to grow old!*"

"Sorry about that. I definitely need less of the backseat driving!" he said through gritted teeth, edging into a parking spot outside the post office with exaggerated care.

"Oh, my fault, as usual!" said Nora in an infuriating sing-song voice.

"I think it might be better if Helena and I make enquiries in the post office on our own," said Amy.

"I couldn't agree more," said Nora. "If he starts interrogating them, they'll completely clam up."

Amy and Helena disappeared into the tiny post office, and he got out of the car and lit a cigarette. Ballystrudder village had closed ranks along one side of the road, to face empty fields on the other. He sucked hard on his cigarette and tried to relax. He needed to keep a clear head for what lay ahead and reminded himself not to let Nora wind him up. He wondered if she'd taken her medication that morning, but didn't dare ask, since it would only trigger another flash of anger. He leaned his forearm on the roof of the car and looked north along the road. Would Helena want to visit the house-site again? Probably. Maybe no harm, he thought. It would give Amy the chance to do some filming in the area.

A man, wearing a fluorescent orange jacket with Royal Mail emblazoned on the back, exited the supermarket next door to the post office, carrying a paper bag and a takeaway drink, and got into a post-office van.

Jer threw his cigarette away and hailed him. The man rolled down his window.

"Sorry to bother you. I'm making enquiries about a house you used to deliver to: a place called Carraig na Rón?"

"Oh yeah, I know where you mean. It's that guy Murtagh, isn't it, the one who's gone and drowned himself? I saw it on the news. Desperate that."

"You know the house?"

"No, they used to have a post box at the end of the lane."

The man drew a bulging half-baguette from the paper bag on his lap and took a bite.

"Sorry to interrupt your lunch, but this is very helpful. You said there used to be a post box at the end of the lane?"

"Yeah, but it's gone now. Pain in the ass!" he said, his words muffled by his mouthful of bread.

"Have you delivered letters there since the post box was removed?"

He chewed thoughtfully for a few moments, and then shook his head and took a slurp from the hot drink he had placed in the holder. "I was seriously pissed off when I saw the post box was gone. I had to drive up that bloody lane."

Jer felt a frisson of excitement. "Was there a locked gate at the end of it?"

The man frowned in concentration. "No, I remember now, I met a fucking big lorry coming the other way, and had to reverse back to the road."

Jer felt a surge of adrenaline. "Did you go on up to the house after the lorry had gone?"

"No, I don't have time for that sort of lark. They don't give you enough time to do the deliveries in areas like this," he said, taking another big bite of his baguette.

"What about the next time you had a letter for Mr. Murtagh, did you go up the lane to the house?"

The man wiped his mouth on the back of his hand and shook his head. "I saw on the news that the poor bastard was drowned, so any post for him would be filed as undeliverable until somebody comes to claim it."

Jer nodded, disappointed. The man set his sandwich on the seat beside him and started his engine.

"Before you go, do you remember anything about the lorry that came down the lane that day?"

"A big fucker, I remember that okay. I wasn't going to argue with it. It was making a real mess of the lane."

"Was it carrying rubble?"

"*Em*, no, it was one of those low-loaders."

"Are you saying there was another machine on the back?"

"Yeah, a JCB or something."

"Can you remember when this was?"

"Let me see, must have been a couple of weeks after I saw the news story."

"Do you think you could identify the driver?"

"Not sure. I was kinda busy steering my car. I got the feeling the bastard was going to drive over me if I stalled. It was an older fella – bald, I remember that. I got a look at him at the bottom of the lane. I reversed out to the left, and he was pissed off. I think he wanted to turn that way, but I was still in his way."

"I don't suppose you'd remember the colour of the lorry?"

"Blue, I think – at least the cab was blue. There was this logo on the front, like one of those Masonic things. A triangle with an eye in the middle. All I could see was that fucking eye coming at me."

"Thanks, thanks very much. You've been a great help. Sorry, what was your name again?"

"Des. Did they ever find your man?"

"Not yet."

"Poor bugger."

Des reversed his car neatly out into the road and roared away northwards, leaving a trail of blue exhaust fumes in his wake.

Jer reached his own car at the moment Helena and Amy walked out of the Post Office looking deflated.

"Well, that wasn't much use," said Amy. "We got a 'more than me job's worth' brush-off in there. She did say there's two postmen doing deliveries round here, one called Grant and the other called Des."

"It's okay, I bumped into Des out here. He was coming out of the supermarket with his sandwich," he said, trying not to smile.

"What? You're kidding?" she said, giving him a thump on the chest.

"Hey, hey, I am still your boss!" he said, laughing.

Nora opened the car door behind him and clambered out. "What'd he say?"

"He remembers delivering letters to Malachy at your address, Helena. Talked about the post box at the end of the lane and how it was removed."

"Did he go up to the house?" she asked, her face alive with hope.

"No, he attempted to on one occasion after the post box disappeared but, wait for it, he met a big blue lorry coming down the lane."

"Carrying the remains of our house!" she said, with a gasp.

"He said it was a low-loader with a JCB on the back."

"Did he see who was driving?" asked Amy.

"An older, bald man. He might be able to identify him if we can find a likely suspect. The key thing is, there was a logo on the front of the lorry, a triangle with an eye in the centre. Interestingly he associated it with the Masons."

Helena nodded. "The square and compass, and the all-seeing eye."

"Helena, sit in the back there with Amy and do a search of local construction and haulage companies, and see if you can spot that symbol on their vehicles. In the meantime, Nora and I will get coffee and sandwiches for everybody."

Chapter 27

"We've found it!" Helena's voice was taut with excitement.

"Let me see?" Jer reached for Amy's phone and enlarged the photo of a blue lorry. There it was – a modern version of the ancient Masonic square and compass, with an eye staring back at him balefully.

"The Eye of God!" said Helena.

"It looks kinda female!" said Amy.

She laughed, "It does, doesn't it!"

"I always knew God was a woman!" declared Nora.

"Where's this company based?" Jer handed back the phone.

"Near Ballymoney," Amy said. "It's called Palliate Construction."

"Great! Are we all game to pay a visit to Palliate Construction?"

On the way, they argued about who would ask the questions, with Jer insisting that he and Amy should go in, wearing a hidden camera. She pointed out that only Helena could give legitimacy to what they were doing, since it was her partner's property at issue. Once they'd decided that Helena needed to accompany them, Nora was adamant she wasn't going to be left behind in the car.

When Amy's phone announced they'd arrived at their destination, Jer drove past the front gates of the construction yard and parked nearby.

Walking into the premises, he couldn't help feeling they made an unlikely quartet. Amy lingered a moment in the yard, turning this way and that, making sure her concealed camera took in the large earth-moving vehicles parked there, all sporting the logo the postman had described. Jer led his little posse to the door of a squat, brick building announcing itself as the Office.

"Let me do the talking," he whispered, pushing open the door.

They filed into the building and found themselves in a large, square room about the size of a classroom, though here there were only four desks, one in each corner and several filing cabinets lined up against the wall facing the door. The room was overheated and the daylight coming through the dirty windows was diffused by a layer of dust. Every horizontal surface was piled with paperwork, and several dead, potted plants added to the air of neglect. The only occupants of the office were two obese women seated at the desks at the far corners of the room. The older of the two took off her glasses and squinted at them while the younger woman popped something into her mouth and chewed vigorously. They both had wavy, frizzy hair with one grey and the other an unnatural shade of red.

"Good afternoon," Jer croaked, then cleared his throat. Indicating Helena with his head, he said, "My friend here wants to enquire about the demolition of a house on her property."

"Righty-o," said the older woman, looking from face to face in a puzzled way. "What kind of house is it you want knocked down? Two storeys, bungalow, how many square feet?"

"The house has already been knocked down, that's the problem," piped up Nora, making Jer clench his teeth. Helena laid a restraining hand on her arm.

The younger woman swallowed whatever she'd been masticating, pushed herself out of her chair, waddled over and stood by the older woman's side. He thought they might be mother and daughter. He was tempted to ask to see the boss but knew that would be unforgivably sexist.

"Are you the boss?" he asked the older one.

"It's a family firm, Mr. – ?" said the younger one, adjusting a loose-fitting flowery garment over her considerable stomach.

"McCabe."

"Are you saying there's a problem with a demolition? If you could tell me where this job is, maybe I could ..." she said, staring at them.

"The address of the property is Carraig na Rón, Mullaghboy, Islandmagee," said Helena.

Jer saw a flicker of recognition in the young woman's face. She leaned down and whispered something in the other woman's ear.

"Give him a call," said the older one, under her breath.

He glanced over at Amy, who'd positioned herself a little distance away from the group. He hoped she was getting all this on camera.

The younger woman shuffled back to her desk, lifted a mobile and left the room. Watching her departure, he gestured with his head for Amy to follow her while he, Helena and Nora were left staring at the older woman who looked deeply uncomfortable.

"Is that your daughter?" he said in a chatty way. She nodded. He smiled encouragingly and lifted a small, desk calendar. "*Morgane and Sons*," he read. "Should be '*Morgane Sons and Daughters*', shouldn't it?"

The woman looked confused.

"Who's your daughter calling?"

She frowned and looked round the room as if searching for someone to help her.

"Your husband?"

"What is it you people want?" she said, her cheeks flushing.

"Please don't be upset." Helena moved nearer the desk. "We don't mean anyone any harm. We just need to understand what happened to my house."

"Can you ask your husband?" suggested Nora, moving around the side of the desk, and making the woman recoil.

"My husband isn't here, he died a year ago," she said, and tears filled her eyes.

"I'm so sorry," said Helena. "You poor thing!"

"Then who's your daughter ringing?" insisted Nora.

The woman looked desperately towards the door. "I want you to leave," she gasped, at the very moment her daughter re-entered the room, closely followed by Amy.

She took one look at her mother's agitated face and glared at the intruders. "What have you said to my mother? You people need to leave *right now*." She hurried over and put her hands on her mother's shoulders.

"What did he have to say, Miss Morgane?" Jer asked her.

"I didn't say anything, Susan, honestly!" the mother said, looking up at her daughter in alarm.

"I'll deal with this, Mum." She looked Jer in the eye. "If you've a complaint to make about this firm and any job we've done, you need to send us the details in writing, and we'll look into it."

"It will all come out, you know, if you've aided and abetted a crime," he said quietly.

"What's he talking about, Susan? We should call the police."

He noticed the woman wince in response to the tightening of her daughter's hands on her plump shoulders.

"I think you should contact the police, Mrs. Morgane, for this isn't just about a house being illegally demolished – a man is dead," he announced solemnly.

"Who's dead? What's he talking about, Susan?"

"What kind of people are you, coming in here and frightening my poor mother and her only recently widowed. You should be ashamed!"

"Jer, let's go." Helena turned to the two women. "Please don't be upset, we just want to understand what happened. You're not in any trouble."

"For heaven's sake, Helena," said Nora, "they'll be in all sorts of trouble if they've allowed their machinery to be used to demolish your house while you were in hospital."

"The police are already involved, Mrs. Morgane," Jer said. "I suggest you ring Detective Inspector Wright at Musgrave Park Police Station right now and tell him what you know." The mother's high complexion had taken on a bluish tinge and Helena put her hand on his arm.

"Jer, this is about Malachy's house, and he wouldn't want this. All will be revealed tomorrow when the dead walk."

Back in the car, Jer noticed Helena's hands were shaking.

"Helena, why did you do that?" wailed Nora. "She was just about to crack!"

"I know she was, Nora, but I don't want anyone broken on my account. I don't think that poor woman knows anything about the house and I was afraid if we kept on pressurising her she'd have a heart attack. The truth will out, no matter how hard people try to hide it."

"The daughter definitely knows something," said Amy grimly.

"I think you're right," he agreed, "but she's a tougher cookie than her mother. I doubt if we were going to get any more out of her. But what about that phone call she made? Did you hear any of what she said?"

"I'm afraid not. She disappeared into that shed there to make her call."

"What now?" Nora sounded fed up.

He took a deep breath. "I'm going to suggest something which you may not like but could blow this thing wide open."

"Great, spit it out!" said Nora.

"This morning I was contacted by a BBC News reporter, asking if I'd be willing to do an interview about the story they ran last night."

"About me and Myra?" said Helena.

"Think about it," he said. "The main thrust of the piece was the increase in interest in witchcraft locally, but they tied in Malachy's disappearance, your ritual on the beach, and the threats to my company."

"I didn't know Indigo had been threatened," said Nora crossly. "Why didn't you tell me?"

"It was unpleasant, but I didn't attach much importance to it, Nora."

"But I don't understand what that has to do with witchcraft," said Helena.

"I received some weird stuff through the post."

"A little plait of hair, and faeces mixed with pins and feathers," said Amy.

Nora made a gagging sound.

"Ah, I see," said Helena.

"What do you think they mean?" Amy asked her eagerly.

"That depends. Do you have any idea who the hair belongs to, or who it's associated with?"

"Yes, we do. It's Trix Maidstone, a BBC exec," she said.

"Right. Hair is generally used to create a spell to make the target fall in love. Is that relevant here?"

"Definitely not," he said. "Helena, I've agreed to do an interview for them this afternoon, to talk about the threats and my series being axed. But they would love to interview you too."

"Me?" Helena was plainly horrified. "I couldn't possibly go on television!"

"Please listen to me for a moment," he pleaded. "You said yourself, if we're ever going to find Malachy, it'll be tomorrow. We can use this media moment to provoke a reaction from whoever is responsible for all this. The police will have to take notice then. Do it for Malachy ... and for Myra," he finished, afraid he'd over-egged it.

"Why Myra?" Nora said huffily.

"You can explain that you and Myra were simply carrying out a ritual, playing roles," he urged. "You can say she was helping you to find your missing partner."

"That's what she *was* doing," she said, relenting a little. "If you think it – "

"Helena, don't let him bamboozle you into this," said Nora. "He'll make a holy show of you if you let him!"

"I think he's right, Helena," said Amy. "This is our one chance to get everyone's attention, to get the public on your side. Someone must know what happened to your house!"

"And to Malachy – I'll do it," Helena said resolutely.

"Good on you," said Amy, beaming.

Before she might change her mind, Jer started the engine and did a quick, three-point turn in the narrow road before heading north.

Peace reigned in the car for a few miles. Nora had subsided into a huff in the backseat and Amy was busy texting. It was a while before Helena realised they were heading away from Belfast.

"Where are we going to do the interview? I thought it would be in your house?"

"No, the reporter wants to meet us at Cladrach Beach."

"What did I tell you!" said Nora, triumphantly. "They're going to sensationalise your tragedy. They always do."

"It's TV, it's all about the pictures," said Amy. "Filming on the beach will make it more visually powerful."

"Amy's right, Helena," said Jer. "And I was thinking, being there might trigger some more memories of that night now your head's a bit clearer."

"And I'm off my medication," she said, nodding.

"Amy, would you mind giving the reporter a bell and tell him it'll be more like half three by the time we get there?" he said, handing his mobile back to her. "He's listed as Ricky."

Arriving at Cladrach Beach, they found it deserted. A restless wind was blowing the clouds about, with sunshine intermittently splashing colour on the scene. In daylight, it all looked very benign.

"I wish I'd known we were coming here," said Nora. "I'd have dressed more warmly."

"Why don't you stay in the car, love, there's no need – "

"I wouldn't miss this for the world!" she insisted. "Don't you think you should let Samuel and Myra know you're going to be on the News tonight talking about her?"

There was an uncomfortable silence in the car.

"What do you think, Helena? Should I contact Myra?"

"If she freaks out and says no, we're fucked," said Amy quickly. "Sorry!"

Helena turned to him. "Samuel is your brother. If you think doing this will damage your relationship with him, then maybe we should think again."

He looked out of the windscreen at the rushes bending before the wind. "Once a story is out there, it takes on a life of its own. If we don't try to control it by feeding in more information, the journalists will – "

"Make it up," said Nora.

"They'll grasp at straws and go off in all sorts of unlikely directions. It's like being in a car when the brakes have failed. All we can do is point the car in a particular direction and hope for the best."

Helena nodded. "For the first time since Malachy disappeared, I feel as if I'm taking back some control."

Chapter 28

When Ricky arrived, they all trooped down onto the beach, quickly finding themselves up to their ankles in rotting seaweed. Wading through the black, slippery mess, Jer had a sudden, sickening fear they might stumble upon Malachy's swollen corpse. He was glad to reach the edge of the surf where the pebbles were rinsed clean and rasped underfoot.

Ricky had been engaging Helena in conversation on the way from the cars and was now explaining that he wanted to start by doing a few establishing shots. He set his camera on a tripod and asked her to walk a hundred yards along the beach, turn and walk back towards him.

Jer nodded to Amy who stood a few yards to Ricky's left, wielding a small, hand-held camera.

"Come and stand here with me, love, if you don't want to be in shot," he said to Nora, who then joined him behind Ricky.

"Should I look towards the lens?" Helena asked the reporter nervously.

"Best not, if you don't mind. Just walk along the beach, taking the odd look out to sea. Easy-peasy!"

She nodded, folded her arms, and walked away from them, her gait self-conscious and stiff. She stopped and turned a couple of times only to be waved on by Ricky. The third time she hesitated and turned, he gave her a thumbs-up. She unfolded her arms and walked slowly back towards them, looking down at the shingle and occasionally turning her head to look seaward. Instead of stopping when she reached the camera, she walked on past, without once glancing in their direction.

"*Fantastic, Helena! You're a natural!*" Ricky shouted.

She halted and stood with her back to them, staring at the rocks at the end of the beach.

Ricky scrambled over to see what was attracting her attention, closely followed by Jer.

"Are those the rocks where Malachy Murtagh's jacket was found?" he was asking when Jer caught up with them.

"Yes, I believe so," she agreed.

"Stand there with your back to me till I get a shot of you and the rocks."

He hurried back to the camera to refocus, then asked her to turn towards him, to get a shot with the outcrop of rock behind her.

"Just come a bit nearer now," he instructed. "It's too windy for radio mics so I'm going to use the hand-held."

She nodded like someone who'd been interviewed many times.

Positioning himself beside her, he did a brief introduction directly to camera.

"I'm joined here on Cladrach Beach by Helena Santoro, whose partner Malachy Murtagh disappeared from this very place back in August and Helena herself was found here, injured." He turned to her. "Helena, we all appreciate how difficult it must be for you to return here. What do you remember about that night?"

She swallowed, her eyes darting between Ricky and the camera-lens. "As you maybe know I've been very ill since then but, little by little, my memory is returning." She looked towards the bank of glistening seaweed. "I was found buried under the seaweed there. The first thing I remember was a dog licking my face."

Jer pricked up his ears – of course – she had been found by a dog-walker.

"I was very, very cold. I'd obviously been in the sea because my clothes were wet."

"Do you remember regaining consciousness?"

Her eyes slid away from the reporter's while she searched her memory. "I felt this breath on my face and then a tongue licking me."

"That must have been terrifying! Did you scream or cry out?"

"No, I couldn't move or make a sound. I thought I was dead, you see. I was covered in this wet, slimy stuff and I couldn't see anything. Then I heard a faint whistle. There was a scrabbling sound on the stones, and it was only then I realised it was a dog."

"And presumably it was the owner of the dog who found you?"

"Yes, a man. I don't remember everything clearly because I must have been still slipping in and out of consciousness. That man phoned the emergency services, and I'm very grateful to him for that."

Jer realised Nora was shivering and he took her hand and tucked it into his pocket. She leaned into his arm, and he wondered if she was as struck by Helena's transformation as he was. It'd only been a matter of days since they'd witnessed her panic in Islandmagee, while now that anxiety and self-doubt seemed to have been replaced by a quiet sense of purpose. Had everything that had passed between them over the last week been leading up to this moment?

"It was reported, at the time, that your partner Malachy's jacket was found on those rocks behind you," said Ricky carefully. "Do you remember what happened to him here?"

She looked over her shoulder at the rocks and then faced him once more

"I'm afraid not. I was injured, you see."

"What was the nature of your injury?"

"There was a wound on the back of my head," she said, "but I've no idea how I came to have that."

"Is it possible you fell on the rocks?"

She looked momentarily disconcerted. "I suppose it's possible."

The reporter was nodding vigorously, encouraging her to continue and when she didn't he said, "I'm sure you're aware there's a video clip being shared on social media, of you and your friend on this beach a few nights ago. It's been suggested you were practising witchcraft. Would you like to confirm or deny that?"

She crossed her arms protectively over her breasts and massaged her left shoulder. "When someone dies, it isn't an absolute. I believe Malachy's spirit is in a transitional state. He's somewhere close and I long to find a way to commune with him. That's what my friend was helping me do."

Her eyes were bright and there was an intensity to her voice that Jer found arresting. She was leaning towards the camera as if willing the viewers to become believers.

"The word 'spell' has been used to describe what you and your friend were doing. Is that a word you would use?"

She relaxed her arms and clasped her hands. "All religions use rituals to focus human concentration for a given purpose. I would describe this use of positive energy to influence things as a 'blessing'."

Jer smiled to himself. If Ricky thought he was going to use Helena to sensationalise the witchcraft story, he was being elegantly frustrated.

"This is a difficult thing to ask," Ricky went on, "but some people online have suggested that your partner Malachy tried to kill you and then took his own life. Is that what you think happened?"

She shook her head decisively. "Absolutely not. Malachy was the best of men. Even at my most confused I knew it wasn't Malachy who hurt me. Now that I'm clearer in my mind, I'm convinced there was some other evil force at work here. When I was discharged from hospital a week ago, some good friends drove me home to Islandmagee, only to find the house that Malachy and I shared had disappeared."

Ricky turned and looked at Jer with raised eyebrows, unwilling to enter unknown territory. They were all trained to know, as far as possible, what their interviewee was going to say, and to formulate questions accordingly. It was all about guiding a known narrative. Jer shrugged in response and Nora pulled her hand out of his pocket.

Ricky had turned back to Helena.

"Just to clarify, you're claiming that the house you and Malachy shared disappeared while you were in hospital recovering from your injuries?"

"Yes, that's exactly what I'm saying. I think someone is trying to make me think I'm going mad."

Jer imagined the TV audience concluding that this woman was

definitely off her rocker, especially if they played the clip of her behaving like a lunatic on a dark beach with another wild-haired female. There was a sudden crunch of shingle, and Ricky spun round in exasperation to see Nora marching away from them up the beach, in the direction of the car.

"Sorry," Jer mouthed to the reporter who waited till the sound of Nora's footsteps had receded, before resuming the interview.

"Our viewers at home will be thinking that the idea of a house simply disappearing is pretty unlikely."

"Yes, of course they will. Whoever got rid of the house has done a very good job. There's really nothing left to suggest that a house once stood there. I did doubt my own sanity for a while, but now we've found proof: number one, that it did exist, and number two, the company that demolished it."

Ricky looked at Jer and the latter ran his index finger across his throat. Ricky turned off the camera.

"You can't name the company, Helena," said Jer, going over to her. "We need to be very sure of our ground before we make public allegations about a company or an individual. We could be sued."

"But we have a witness. You said the postman –"

"Yes, and I'm sure that will all contribute to that company being charged in due course *if* they did it – but, in any case, we can't name them publicly at this stage."

Her face fell, and she walked away from him towards the rocks.

"What the hell, Jer? I'm not sure I can use any of this." Ricky looked tense.

Amy joined them. "Ricky, we have a clip from the '*Sky High*' series, that Helena claims shows the house," she said. "I can send it to you if you want."

"How clear is it?"

"There's a bit of camera flare at the crucial moment," Jer said reluctantly.

"For God's sake, I'm never going to clear this for half-six!" He looked along the beach at Helena who was now clambering onto the rocks and he quickly reactivated his camera to get a shot of her on all fours.

"I'd better go and see if Nora's okay," said Jer.

"Hang on, Jer. I need something from you and then I'm outta here."

"I'll go and make sure she's alright," Amy offered, leaving them to it.

"Nora's not to be mentioned, Ricky!" said Jer.

Ricky swung the camera round and focused it on Jer, then stood beside the tripod with the camera at his shoulder. "Jer McCabe is Chief Executive of Indigo Productions which has been in the News this week, accused of bringing Northern Ireland into disrepute."

He paused for breath while Jer tried and failed to keep his expression neutral.

"Your *Thoughtless* series has attracted a lot of adverse reaction recently and has now been axed. Where to now for Indigo Productions?"

"You win some, you lose some." Jer hoped he had a twinkle in his eye. "Satire is always tricky and I'm afraid we strayed into bad taste which is unforgiveable. The earlier episodes were a lot of fun, so I hope some of the audience will find those online and enjoy them in retrospect."

"I understand your company has received threats?"

"There's no escaping the online trolling but we also got some pretty nasty stuff sent through the post."

"What sort of stuff?"

"Human hair and faeces mixed with feathers and pins."

Ricky's face registered astonishment. "And do you think this is related to the growth of interest in witchcraft and satanism locally?"

Jer was tempted to say that it was more likely to be related to good old peer jealousy but, with his witchcraft proposal for Trix in mind, he took advantage of the moment to stir the cauldron. "It does seem to point that way!"

"As a close friend of Helena Santoro, can you shed any light on what happened to her partner Malachy Murtagh?"

"I only met Helena a week ago and have never met Malachy Murtagh, so I'm afraid I'm as much in the dark as everyone else on that subject."

Ricky looked disappointed. He tried again. "I understand it was you who drove Helena home when she was discharged from hospital. Do you believe her house has been made to disappear?"

Jer looked directly into the camera. "I honestly don't know what to believe, but I'm determined to help her get to the bottom of it."

"Your sister-in-law has been participating in Ms. Santoro's witchcraft. Is that something you're also involved in?"

"My sister-in-law has been a good friend to Helena this week – something we all appreciate."

"You didn't answer my question."

"I think we could all do with a little magic in our lives, don't you think?"

Ricky grinned in defeat and switched off his camera. "You missed your calling as a politician!"

"What are you thinking, Ricky? Is she mad or bad?"

"Or both? That yarn about the house? You should've given me a heads-up. I didn't see that coming."

"Yeah, sorry, I guess I should have."

"Be honest with me, Jer, is this bit of video going to convince the viewers that this house existed?"

Jer grimaced.

"Right!" said the reporter. "Have you ever actually seen the house?"

Jer shook his head.

Ricky laughed. "Are you sleeping with her or what?"

"No, of course not!"

"I hear Stella's getting married tomorrow."

"What's that got to do with anything?" said Jer, folding his arms defensively.

"You tell me, Jer."

"For heaven's sake! Look, I talked to the postman who used to deliver to their house in Islandmagee, and he was nearly run down by a bloody great lorry, carrying a JCB coming down their lane."

Ricky rocked back on his heels. "Did he actually see the house being demolished?"

"No, he didn't see the house."

"Ever?" guessed Ricky, with a grim smile.

Jer shook his head, "But someone removed the post box from the end of the lane."

"I tell you what, Jer, I've no intention of building a story on a disappearing post box. That's Enid Blyton territory!"

"I think this poor bugger Malachy Murtagh has been murdered."

"And what do the good old PSNI have to say about it?"

"A Detective Wright is on the case."

"Yeah, I know him."

"At first he was convinced it was a murder-suicide but now,

hopefully, he's got a more open mind. Between you and me, I'm pretty sure he was the one who leaked the footage of Helena and my sister-in-law casting spells on the beach."

Ricky's eyebrows shot up under his fringe and didn't descend. "And why on earth would he do that?"

"Because he has a vendetta going on against me and my brother."

Ricky gave him a hard look and turned away.

Jer left the reporter doing his "noddies" – getting shots of himself asking a few of the questions he'd already posed and nodding in response to the answers they'd given, which he would later edit together.

Jer trudged through the shingle after Helena, who was sitting on the rocky promontory, looking out to sea. She inclined her head to watch him approach and clamber over to where she was posed. He was eventually reduced to moving on all fours, finding it impossible to keep his balance on the slippery ridges of rock. He hoped Ricky wasn't filming his progress.

"If you were going to kill yourself, do you think you would crawl up here to take off your jacket?" she commented, when he was within earshot.

He carefully raised himself to a standing position beside her. "Definitely not. It's more likely someone put the jacket here to make sure it wouldn't be washed away by the tide."

He looked at the sea, which had turned a sullen grey. Choppy waves flecked with white were worrying the rocks below them.

"That reporter thinks I'm mad, doesn't he?" she said.

"I doubt if he'll get your interview on this evening but tomorrow is Halloween, so they'll try to legal it in time for tomorrow's evening news."

"How do you mean, 'legal' it?"

"They'll have to get the content of what we said checked by a BBC lawyer to be sure they're not making themselves liable to be sued for defamation. Par for the course."

"Maybe Nora was right, and I shouldn't have done it. I'm just going to be pilloried as a witch."

He knew she was right but tried to find some words of consolation. "It was brave of you to do the interview and I hope they broadcast it because it'll strike a chord with people and who knows what memory it might spark in a witness? And if Malachy has been – murdered, then his killer is bound to feel under pressure. Maybe he'll panic and make a mistake."

She looked desolate.

"You look frozen," he said. "Let's go and find Nora and Amy."

They reached the car in time to see Ricky drive off at speed. Helena got into the backseat of Jer's car beside Nora. Jer took out a cigarette and longed to light it, but the wind whipping the heads of the rushes made that impossible. Amy was busy stowing the camera in the boot which she closed as he approached.

"How do you think that went?" she asked doubtfully.

"Did Ricky say anything to you?"

She gestured to him to move away from the car. Once in the shelter of the dunes, he crouched down to light his cigarette, then sat down heavily on the sand and stretched out his legs.

"You'll get a damp bum!" she warned him, remaining on her feet.

"Nothing new there then!" he said, earning a throaty laugh from Amy who squatted beside him.

"He thinks she's a nutcase!" she said.

"Ah, I was afraid of that!"

"Do you think they'll broadcast it tonight?"

"I doubt it. If he thinks Helena is flaky, at the very least he'll need to get another interviewee, to get some balance. He may go looking for a comment from Detective Wright."

"Will he get it?"

"Probably not but, then again, Wright likes stirring things so who knows?" He took a pull on his cigarette. "Has she been playing me the whole time, Amy?"

"Who?"

"Helena."

She looked troubled and stood up. The wind caught her hair and blew it across her face. She gathered it with both hands, twisted it and shoved it into the collar of her coat, then folded her arms and looked down at him thoughtfully.

"I don't blame Ricky for being sceptical about the house. I was too when you first told me about it, but now there's a lot of – circumstantial evidence. The video for a start!"

"And the neighbour Samuel Ewart said he'd never been allowed to go near the place," he said.

"That woman at Palliate Constructions definitely knew something about the house and I'd like to know who she rang."

He nodded. "You're right. Thanks for that, Amy. Let's drop Nora and Helena off at home, and you and I will go to the office and view what you shot today."

Chapter 29

Driving along the quays, starlings were eddying over the river like a host of spellbound souls, heralding twilight in the city, and he wondered if Liam's little soul was among them, moving in the darkening air. He had a sense of the present being inverted as he and Amy swam against the tide of humanity streaming out of the city centre. Passing Samuel's chambers, he noticed a light at the window and resolved to ring his brother before the evening was out.

The glacial air in the office bore testament to Stella's absence that day and he silently admonished himself for feeling irked by her dereliction of duty on the eve of her wedding. He boiled the kettle while Amy uploaded the camera-footage to her laptop and ordered pizzas. Opening up his own PC, he saw that his tally of unread emails had now reached four figures, making him feel he'd lost all control over his working life.

He scanned that day's crop and saw one from Trix which he opened and read with trepidation. She began by asking him if he'd given the plait and faeces to the police, making him break out in a light sweat.

"Amy, we mustn't forget to take the plait and whatever round to Musgrave Park!"

"I did it this morning before I came over to your place," she said, looking up from her laptop.

"You're a star!" he said with relief. "Did you get to speak to Detective Wright?"

"No, but I said the package was for him when I handed it in."

He wondered what Wright would make of the loathsome contents and decided he'd better get Samuel to contact the detective to explain their significance before they ended up in the bin, if indeed they hadn't already suffered that fate.

Samuel answered after one ring.

"Is Myra with you?" Samuel said without preamble.

"No, sorry, I'm at the office. I've no idea where she is."

"She did stay at your place last night, didn't she?"

He hesitated. It seemed an age since Samuel and Myra had been in his house the evening before. "No," he began carefully. "You remember I took Nora upstairs and, when I came back down, you'd both gone." His voice faltered. There was silence at the other end of the line. "Where are you now?"

"I just got home. I hoped she might be here, but she isn't." He sounded defeated. "Has she been in touch with Helena today?"

"Not that I'm aware of. Stupid question, but I take it she's not answering her phone?"

"Stupid question!"

Jer bit his lip. "I presume you've rung round her friends?"

"No, I haven't. I don't think she'd want me to, now that clip is out there," he said bitterly.

Jer decided distraction might be the best medicine. "She

definitely wasn't with Helena earlier today because I took her and Nora to Islandmagee to speak to a postman at Ballystrudder. He remembered delivering letters to Malachy Murtagh and, apparently, when he found the post-box was gone, he attempted to drive up the lane to the house and met a low-loader coming the other way carrying a JCB. You could make short work of a house with a monster machine like that!" He paused for effect then continued, "The lorry had a distinctive logo which we were able to trace to a company near Ballymoney and we paid them a visit." He took a breath, hoping for a response from Samuel, but when none was forthcoming, he added lamely, "Definitely something fishy there!"

"Fishy won't cut it! Have you any actual evidence that this house ever existed, apart from a brief shot of it from outer space? And the alleged owner, this guy Malachy – have his remains washed up anywhere yet?"

Jer knew there was no point in continuing the discussion with Samuel in his present mood. "Look, when I finish up here, I'll come over to your place," he offered, but Samuel had already rung off.

He sat down beside Amy. "Thanks for leaving that stuff at Musgrave Park. Trix was asking about it in an email."

Amy turned to him eagerly. "Did she mention the proposal?"

"She's taking a raincheck on it until she sees whether or not Current Affairs team are going to tackle the story."

"They will, won't they? All that stuff Ricky shot today would be perfect for an in-depth exposé. We really need to keep Helena on-side."

He nodded. "She also asked if I'd be interested in applying to join the new Commissioning Board."

"What? Way to go! That'd put the brave Harry back in his box."

Their pizzas arrived and while they ate they settled themselves to view the footage Amy had filmed at the beach.

"Hang on, there's loads more here than I shot today," she said, frowning, "but we can spin on through it."

"No wait, that's stuff I filmed last week in Islandmagee."

"Happy days! I've got to see this famous, invisible house."

They sat chewing, watching Helena wandering around the patch of muddy ground where she claimed Malachy's house should be.

"It really is a beautiful location," murmured Amy, leaning closer to the screen. "But what on earth is she doing?"

He waved a slice of pizza at the screen. "Watch what happens next!"

"She's going to fall into those bushes. *Aaah! And there she goes!*"

The image on the screen tipped and blurred at the moment when he'd thrust the camera into Nora's hands and dashed over to rescue Helena. All they could now see was brown brambles and withered blackberries, but they could hear Helena's cries and his voice trying to reassure her.

"Oh dear, poor Helena!" Amy made a face, "She does look a bit mad, Jer."

"I know, that's what I thought at the time. There's a bit more coming up, after I took the camera back from Nora."

They watched his panning shot, which swept the whole area from left to right. Then the eye of the camera settled, allowing the ancient trees to frame the empty site.

"*Wow!*"

"What do you see?" he said, his mouth full.

"I remember you saying something about the trees pointing at the space where the house stood. They kinda do, don't they?" She shook her shoulders. "It's seriously creepy!"

Helena came into shot, bending down repeatedly to the muddy ground. "What's she up to now?"

"She kept picking up bits and pieces she claimed were from the house."

"Like what?

"A piece of pottery and a little metal bird, which she said had been part of a windchime hanging outside her studio. Oh yeah, and she showed me a chunk of masonry with one side painted olive green. I was struck by that since she'd already told me the house was green. There was something else that I haven't given a lot of thought to since but did intrigue me."

She was hanging on his every word.

"Have you ever heard of a desire line?"

She shook her head.

"You know how people are inclined to take a shortcut across grass to wherever they want to go. They'll often deviate from a nice, paved path that's been provided by the planners and insist on taking the more direct route."

"A right of way?"

"I suppose if a track like that exists for long enough, it can become a right of way. Helena showed me a desire line through the grass which she said was a shortcut she and Malachy would take when they were on foot. It did ring true for me. The first time we brought her there, she'd followed exactly the same route over the hill and through the trees." He looked at her. "You're not convinced?"

She screwed up her nose. "It's not going to convince the authorities, is it? If we'd some paperwork, bills or something? You said Malachy had his own wind-turbine, so there wouldn't even be a record of electricity payments." She moved on to the footage from that afternoon on the beach. "She's a real natural in front of the camera!"

"I know, I was surprised," he said, wondering and not for the first time if Helena had been putting on a performance all along. "She seemed really nervous at the start but then the chance to tell your story is empowering."

"*Mm.*" She looked sceptical. "What do you think she's planning to do tomorrow in Islandmagee?"

"Cast some class of a spell, no doubt."

"Then she's bound to be disappointed because Malachy is not going to rise from the dead, or show up if he's done a runner, now is he?" she said sagely. "How will she deal with that?"

"Sooner or later, she'll have to accept that he's gone," he said, keen to close down the conversation, all too aware of Nora's refusal to accept Liam's death and the toll that denial had taken on her and their family.

"Time will work its magic," she said blithely.

She's too young to understand what grief can do to people, he thought, and made a silent wish that she might remain in that state of bliss for many years to come.

"Look, it's nearly half-six. Let's watch the local news and see if Ricky got his piece on!" she said enthusiastically.

The remainder of their pizzas lay cooling and congealing in their boxes while they watched Ricky taking ownership of Helena's story. Amy's right, he was thinking, I need to keep Helena close, or she'll end up making a documentary with someone else. Predictably, Ricky was playing up the witchcraft angle and opened his piece with the clip of Helena and Myra in their ghostly, candle-lit circle. This was followed by an interview with the female author of a book about the Wicca Religion who explained how Wicca followers worship a horned God of Fertility, and a Mother Goddess. He ran the shots of Helena walking along the beach while the professor described the Wiccan belief that the Mother Goddess embodies self-transformation and is a force for change for those who open themselves to her. Jer couldn't help thinking of Helena's effect on Myra.

"She's really photogenic," said Amy, watching Helena walk towards camera and look wistfully seaward.

Ricky summarised the mystery surrounding Malachy's disappearance and set up Helena to describe the moment she regained consciousness on the beach. When she mentioned the dog-walker, he cut to Detective Wright who managed to be even more pompous on screen than he was face to face. The detective gave a knowing smile and informed the viewers that the police believed they were dealing with an attempted murder-suicide.

"Is that what you think, Jer?"

"I suppose he could have attacked her then driven her to that remote beach and walked into the sea. His jeep was found there at Cladrach."

"Okay. That doesn't look good. I mean if he didn't walk into the sea, how would he have got away?" Amy chewed her bottom lip, thinking hard.

"He'd have needed an accomplice," said Jer.

"Why was she under the seaweed? It's like someone was trying to hide her."

"Interesting thought!" he said, looking at her approvingly.

The report ended with a shot of Helena standing on the rocks, looking out to sea.

"What about this young guy Leo, who we think might be

Helena's lover?" she said. "He could have got rid of Malachy but couldn't bring himself to kill his beloved Helena?"

"But then, why demolish the house and make Helena think she's going mad? And there's the money that was taken and then returned. It does suggest someone has a guilty conscience."

"Or is afraid of getting caught," said Amy. "Think about it, if you and Nora hadn't taken Helena in, imagine the state she'd have been in when she found her home was gone. She'd probably have had another breakdown."

"And what if she is mad as a hatter and is leading us all a merry dance?"

They sat in silence for a few moments, then Amy closed the lid of her pizza box and stood up.

"I really need to go. What time are you going to Islandmagee tomorrow? I won't see you until then. I'm thinking she'll want it to be dark."

He was momentarily disconcerted. The following day was a Friday, or had he completely lost track? "Won't you be in the office tomorrow?"

She moistened her lips. "I'll be at Stella's wedding."

He closed his eyes for a moment. "Of course you will. Sorry, I …"

"But it's in the morning," she said quickly, "and I don't think the après-wedding thing is going to be major, so let me know what's happening. I'd hate to miss Helena casting her spell. I've a feeling something really weird is going to happen."

"I know, that's what I'm afraid of," he said, thinking of Nora.

It was after midnight by the time he left Samuel's house and took a taxi home, leaving his brother snoring on the sofa in the family room Myra had designed and decorated with such care. He'd drunk his fair share of Laphroig, mainly to stop Samuel emptying the bottle single-handedly. He was frustrated at having to leave his car in Samuel's drive but reasoned that he could use Nora's to go to Islandmagee next day.

He half-expected to see Myra's white BMW in the driveway when he got home and felt relieved for himself but disappointed for Samuel's sake when it was nowhere to be seen. Maybe she'd checked into a hotel.

There were lights on in the house and he let himself in and stood in the hall for a few moments, listening for voices, but it was deathly quiet. The living room and kitchen doors were ajar, casting shafts of light into the shadowy hall, but when he checked them he found both rooms empty. In the living room angry faces flickered across the muted television. He turned off the switch at the wall, and went round extinguishing lights, before heading upstairs.

He was worried about Nora's state of mind for she was normally compulsive about turning off lights and appliances before going to bed. The door to Helena's bedroom was closed and he presumed she was in there asleep. Opening the door of the master-bedroom, he stood rigid with shock. There were two people in the bed. It reminded him of the years after the accident, when he'd come to bed to find Rory had got there first, and was wrapped around his mother, afraid she might be snatched away while he slept. He pushed the door wider to allow more light into the room, before approaching the bed and bending over the two shapes. One was definitely Nora. He moved around to his own side of the king-sized bed and lifted the duvet, taking a moment to work out that Nora had placed two pillows behind her. His shoulders sagged with relief and a wave of tiredness washed over him. He clicked the door shut, undressed and climbed into bed, leaving the pillows between himself and Nora.

Lying awake in the darkness, the thought he'd been avoiding all day was no longer possible to ignore. Stella was getting married tomorrow. His face was wet with whiskey-induced tears, wondering if she'd spare a thought for him on this, her last night as a single woman. Then he chided himself. Her thoughts would be full of her bridegroom. He wished now that he'd suggested meeting her fiancé to give him the once-over, appalled at the possibility that Stella might marry a man who would treat her badly. He realised he'd no idea what kind of man Stella might have chosen. Would he be a Jer Mark Two – a notion Jer Mark One found disturbing? He had to accept that Stella's marriage was best for all concerned. When they next met, she'd be a married woman and their working relationship would have to morph into something more formal and professional, though how that was to be accomplished he had no idea.

Nora began to snore, and he reached across the bulwark of pillows and nudged her gently until she turned over crossly. It seemed to him that Nora routinely slept in a state of anger, while his default emotion seemed to be regret. What if he'd never met and married Nora, he reflected, but quailed at the task of constructing even an imaginary life without her. They'd got married in the dead of winter – it not being deemed possible to wait for spring according to the matriarchs on both sides, due to Nora's pregnancy. Both barely twenty, they'd been catapulted to the altar rails by familial choruses of dismay and their own panic, and when he arrived at the church that grey, freezing morning, it was all he could do not to run for the hills.

Nora had been five months gone when he watched her walk up the aisle, on the arm of her alcoholic father, her slender body only beginning to show the life within. Her long, strawberry-blonde hair had been loose and threaded with flowers she'd later informed him were artificial. She held one, long-stemmed white rose instead of a bouquet and he thought she was like a girl in a painting, in the high-necked, ivory wedding dress she'd bought in a Laura Ashley sale. She stepped lightly through the shadowy church, a nervous smile playing about her mouth, and she met no-one's eye but his when they stood and made their world-without-end promise to each other.

Friday 31st October: Halloween

Chapter 30

He could still stop her! It was the first thought in his head when he woke on Halloween morning. He had a sudden vision of himself bursting through the doors of some solid Presbyterian church and bawling words of love. Would Stella even turn around? Of course she would, but he wasn't at all sure she'd walk away from her intended and flee the scene with him. And where would Nora be during this romantic scene, because he'd have to follow through? He couldn't drag Stella from the altar-rails and then consign her to the role of mistress for eternity.

Too restless to lie any longer, he slid his legs from under the duvet and sat on the edge of the bed with his head bowed. What would Stella be doing now, he wondered. He couldn't imagine her sitting under a hair-drier or indulging in any of the rituals modern brides seemed to find mandatory. She'd keep it simple. He rubbed his face, trying to banish the unwelcome images. His mobile was telling him it was a quarter past ten, but it felt earlier – there was so little light coming through the curtains.

He desperately needed distraction and forced himself to focus on Helena and her plight. She'd said something about Halloween being her last chance to make contact with Malachy. When that failed to happen, she'd feel newly bereft. Above all, he needed to make sure all this dabbling in the occult didn't upset Nora's fragile equilibrium. He heard female voices downstairs and headed for the shower, keen to have his emotions firmly in check before facing Nora this morning. While in the shower, he thought he heard knocking at the bathroom door.

For God's sake, can't they hear the shower running? he thought.

The knocking became a pounding, and suds coursed down his face, stinging his eyes.

"*Okay, okay, I'm coming!*" he shouted.

He stumbled out of the shower, wrapped a towel around his midriff and opened the door to see Helena and a person who looked like Myra. He reached for a hand-towel to wipe the soap out of his streaming eyes. It was Myra, but she'd cropped her lovely auburn hair. She hadn't a trace of make-up on her face and was wearing what looked like a man's cast-off clothing.

"Myra?" he spluttered.

"We think Nora's heading for Stella's wedding," said Helena, her face pale.

He froze. "Oh dear God! How do you know?"

"She was talking about it endlessly last night, but I never thought for a moment —"

"Has she taken her car?"

"Yes."

"I hope yours is handy, Myra, because I had to leave mine over at your place last night."

"It's parked round the corner," she said, dropping her eyes.

He didn't have time to wonder where she'd spent the night and pushed past the two women, hurrying to the bedroom to throw on his clothes. Ten minutes later he joined them in the hall.

"Do we even know where the wedding is?" he asked breathlessly.

"Yes, Amy told us, but it'll take a good hour to get there, so hurry up," said Myra.

Relegated to the back seat, he studied her profile, trying to reconcile this radically different version of his sister-in-law with the one Samuel had married. He shuddered to think what Samuel would make of her transformation.

"I'll ring Amy and get her to look out for Nora," he suggested.

"Good idea!" Helena sounded relieved.

Amy answered immediately. "Jer?"

"Hi, Amy. Look, we think Nora is heading for the wedding and – well, we don't want her to upset Stella on her big day."

"Nora is coming! *Shit!*"

"It hasn't happened yet, and we're going to do our best to make sure it doesn't," he said with feeling.

"You're not on your way too, are you?"

"Yes, but we're still up to an hour away."

"You definitely should not show up at Stella's wedding."

"Believe me, it's the last place I want to be. Helena and Myra are with me and hopefully they can intervene. I'm only here as back-up."

"What will I do if I see Nora outside the church? I mean, will she even listen to me if I try to head her off?"

"You might have to hit her over the head and drag her into the bushes!"

"That's not funny!"

"Sorry. Improvise, Amy, improvise."

"Hugh's here with me – we'll try and think of some diversionary tactic."

"Thanks. You're a – "

"Star! I know," she said wryly, and rang off.

"Maybe I shouldn't have come," he said. "It'd be ghastly if Stella saw me," he said, his skin crawling.

"Are you okay?" Helena turned to look at him.

"No, not really. What about you?"

"It's one of those days that has to be faced, don't you think?" she said firmly.

He leaned back in the seat and gazed out the window. He'd been so startled by Myra's metamorphosis, he'd failed to notice that Helena had reverted to her own dress-style and was wearing the long, pale-green linen skirt and gossamer cardigan she'd had on when she was discharged from hospital.

"I see you're wearing your own clothes again."

"Yes, it's important I connect with the person I was with Malachy."

He digested this for a moment, uncomfortable with the idea that Helena had multiple personas. "Those clothes – are they the ones you were wearing the day you were found on the beach?"

"When I try to remember anything about that day, there's a blankness I can't seem to get past."

"Are they definitely your clothes?" asked Myra. "I mean, you had them before you went into hospital – before all this happened?"

"Oh yes, definitely. I bought this skirt at the Skye Folk Festival years ago. The day I was discharged, they brought them to my room. The nurse told me the police had been holding on to them for forensic checks but had now finished with them. It made me think they'd closed the case. But I was glad to have my things. It felt like I was getting something of my life back – that is until we got to Islandmagee."

"What did you wear while you were in hospital?" Myra asked her, in a business-like tone.

"Oh, they gave me leggings and sweat-shirts to wear."

"Had you any visitors when you were in there?" Jer asked her.

She seemed bemused by the question. "Not that I remember, but I was sedated for a good while at the beginning."

From a long way off they spotted the whitewashed walls of Killnagee Church standing sentinel on an exposed foreshore.

"Killnagee – Church of the Winds," he said. "It's well named."

Approaching the coast, Myra suddenly braked and pulled into the gateway of a caravan-site. "Jer, I think you should get out here. We can ring if we need you."

He climbed out and watched them glide down the slope and park behind a row of cars lining the narrow road leading to the church gate. He glanced behind him and realised he needed to find some cover before anyone drove past and recognised him.

He slipped into the deserted caravan park and worked his way towards the perimeter wall, using the empty caravans to shield him from the road. He cupped his hands and looked in the windows of several, and it came to him that each caravan was like a chest of memorabilia from a family's life – bric-a-brac from tourist shops, worn toys and faded photographs. He and Nora had amassed a house-full of artefacts like these too, only to him the chest containing their family life felt like a coffin. Maybe they should have divorced when Eimear and Rory grew up and left home. He tried to imagine what would have become of Nora without him. Stella had waited all those years, hoping one day he'd belong to her, although he'd been careful never to make any promises. She had a chance now to create something of her own with another man and he knew he mustn't let anything stand in the way of her happiness – he owed her that.

A gust of cold, salty wind carried the smell of fetid seaweed to him from the shore, and he sought shelter behind the rough stone wall marking the boundary of the park. He lit a cigarette and leaned on a flat stone, from where he had an unimpeded view of the church. There was a knot of people outside the door, and he wondered if Stella was among them. He spotted Helena's tall figure walking towards the church in her pale clothes, every inch the white witch, he thought. At least Stella didn't know her, whereas she might recognise Myra but, then again, she looked different from her old self. He scanned the cars parked along the road. There was one that looked like Nora's but, at this remove, he couldn't be sure. What if she was already sitting in the church, growing ever more agitated. Would she cause a scene? He texted Amy: **Any sign of Nora?** He set the phone on top of the stone, hungry for any communication.

A large, black car swept down the road, nosed past the parked cars, and entered the church gates, coming to a halt beside the door. He straightened up. This had to be Stella. He wished he was closer so he could see her more clearly. All he got was a glimpse of an older woman being helped out by a woman dressed in a pale suit and wide-brimmed hat, whom he decided must be Stella. A wheelchair was produced from the boot of the car and then Stella and her mother were swallowed by the church. His phone vibrated on the stone, and he grabbed it eagerly and read: **No N so far!**

Maybe Nora had chickened out or, more likely, got lost. He threw away his cigarette and jogged back to the gate of the caravan park. If she was on her way, she'd have to come along this road, and he was determined to stop her. The gateway was too near the corner for safety, and he started walking down the road, intending to take up a position from where he could command a stretch of road. He heard the purr of an engine and turned to see Nora's car coming around the corner. He stepped into the middle of the road waving his arms and saw her shocked face. Instead of slowing down, it seemed to him, in that instant, she accelerated. He jumped aside just in time, and she slammed on the brakes coming to a screeching halt, slewed sideways across the road. He picked himself out of the ditch, cursing the brambles which had scratched his face and hands.

Myra came running up the road and reached Nora's car before he did and wrenched open the driver's door.

He could hear Nora shouting. *"What's he doing here? I nearly killed him. Stupid, stupid bastard!"*

He got to the car door at the moment she turned to stare up at Myra and was so shocked by her sister-in-law's changed appearance that she stopped shouting and said *"Myra?* What on earth have you done to yourself?"

Myra recoiled and backed away from the car while he glanced towards the church and saw Helena emerge and come hurrying in their direction.

Nora was now out of the car and stood glowering at him.

"Why are you here?" she snarled at him.

"You put your foot down when you saw me!" he said in a choked voice.

"I should have bloody well put my foot down years ago!" she shot back.

They glared at each other.

He gritted his teeth, and for Stella's sake decided not to contest the matter. "Okay, point taken. Now you've put your foot down, can we please get the hell out of here and let Stella get married in peace?"

Helena joined them at the car door. "Nora, are you okay?"

"She definitely is in there getting married, is she?" she said grimly.

"Definitely!" said Helena. "The knot will be tied any minute now," and Jer had to resist the temptation to bolt towards the church.

"Nora, please come with me to Islandmagee," Helena said softly, putting a hand on Nora's cheek. "You've found some closure here today – can you help me accept that my lovely Malachy is gone?"

Nora leaned her head into Helena's hand for a second, then straightened up and addressed her husband in a huffy voice.

"Jer, you'll have to turn this car around. I'm completely stuck!"

He drove Nora's car away from the church, afraid to speak in case he started to weep, while Nora sat beside him, picking at her nails. Myra and Helena were following.

"If I hadn't nearly run you over, would you've gone in there and stopped her getting married?" she said eventually in a small, scared voice.

"I wouldn't have even been here if you hadn't decided to attend the wedding."

"Really?" she said, turning to him.

"I've told you before, the thing between me and Stella petered out a long time ago."

"And what about us? Have we petered out too?"

"I'm here, aren't I?"

"Here in body!" she said, turning her face away.

"Talking of spirits, what I need is a hot whiskey!" he said, spotting a likely looking hostelry up ahead.

"Purely for medicinal purposes," said Nora in a conciliatory tone.

"Of course. And a wee hot port for you?"

"Any port in a storm," she said wryly, making him smile despite himself.

After the shot of alcohol and something to eat, they were all in a more positive state of mind and Nora opted to go in the car with Myra and Helena, commenting to him in a theatrical whisper that she much preferred this new Myra to the old one.

"I'm not sure Samuel will," he said under his breath.

"Samuel will what?" said Myra, looking hard at him.

"Would you give him a ring or just text to stop him worrying?"

"I'm not sure I can cope with that just yet," she said, more honestly than he expected.

"Where were you last night?"

"In your spare room."

"*What?*"

"I didn't park in your drive because I didn't want Samuel to know where I was. I just need some space, to sort out my feelings."

When she turned away, he texted Samuel to reassure him that Myra was okay.

The glory had already gone from the day when they exited the pub and thick clouds were piling in from the west, stealing the light. Over lunch they'd agreed to Helena's plan to pay one more visit to the house site in Islandmagee and he felt as if he was going to a funeral which suited his mood.

Turning into Malachy and Helena's lane once again, with Myra's car on his tail, he could hardly believe only a week had passed since he'd first driven Helena here, thinking he was simply going to drop off this new acquaintance. When he got to the gate which had barred their progress before, he was surprised to see it lying open. He edged the car through the opening and parked in the field beyond. Myra drew up behind and Helena got out, pulling on his old anorak, and went to examine the metal chain and padlock which were hanging loose from the bolt.

"It looks as if someone's cut the chain," she said when he joined her at the gate.

"What are you planning to do here?" he asked her.

She looked down at the sheared-off edge of the chain, which she was rubbing against the palm of her hand. "I don't really have a clear intention, Jer. I'm just going on instinct."

"Are you going to carry out a – a ritual or – ?"

"I'd like to light a fire, where our hearth-fire used to be." She looked away from him towards the trees and her face suddenly went rigid with shock. He followed her gaze to see a thin trail of blue smoke rising from the little wood.

"It looks as if someone's got here before you."

Myra and Nora joined them, and he pointed out the smoke, adding that they needed to be careful.

"*Yes, I see it!*" cried Nora.

Helena strode away from them along the little track through the grass – the desire line – closely followed by Myra.

He scanned the area beyond the gate, thinking that someone must have cut the chain to get a vehicle in.

"Look there's tyre marks in the mud. Someone has driven a vehicle in that way,' he said, pointing towards the back of the trees.

"Maybe it's Malachy," Nora whispered to him, her eyes wide. "Come on!" she urged, excited.

He grabbed his jacket from the backseat of the car and hurried along the desire line, after Nora.

Helena and Myra paused at the edge of the trees, giving him and Nora time to catch up. Jer was acutely aware of being the only male present and hoped he wouldn't be called upon to take on any aggressor, physical combat not being his forte.

"Take it easy, Helena, we've no idea who might be here," he warned, breathing heavily.

"There's a tent in there," she said in a low voice. "Do you see?"

"Yes, yes, I do," said Nora.

Myra shushed them crossly. "Whoever it is, we want to take them by surprise."

Do we, he thought?

Helena caught up her skirt and, wrapping it around her thighs, plunged into the thicket, weaving her way through the trees like an angry fairy queen. The other three followed more cautiously.

A small, white tent had been pitched in a clearing, but the only sign of life was a feeble campfire which continued to emit its silent signal. A pair of walking boots lay near the fire along with a small saucepan and a few empty tins.

She halted a few yards from the tent and called out in a voice full of longing, "*Malachy, are you there?*"

There was a scuffling sound from inside, and a person wearing a black woolly hat and navy duffle coat crawled out.

"*Leo?*" she gasped, stepping backwards, and was only prevented from falling by a steadying hand from Jer.

Leo got to his feet. "Helena, I'm so sorry – it's me, not Malachy."

They stumbled towards each other, and half fell into an embrace, rocking from side to side.

"You startled me, that's all. Darling Leo!" she sobbed, while the young man buried his face in her neck.

"He was the one who came to the house," Nora whispered to Jer.

Drawing apart at last, Leo gazed at Helena. "What happened to your house? It was here, wasn't it?"

She stroked his cheek, then turned to the others and smiled. "This is Leo, my beautiful young friend, who's one of the most talented artists I've ever met."

He pulled off his hat, revealing his bleached hair and advanced shyly to shake hands with Myra and Nora. Reaching Jer he stalled, and his engaging smile was replaced by a guarded look. Jer extended his hand and Leo took it, gratefully.

Chapter 31

Leo dived back into his tent and re-emerged carrying a sleeping bag and a pile of clothing which he arranged around the fire, then busied himself trying to tease a flame from some twigs he piled on the embers. Helena sat cross-legged on the sleeping-bag and extended a hand towards Myra, who sat beside her, struggling to accommodate her long legs. Jer took Nora's hand and they made themselves comfortable on an assortment of Leo's clothes. Nora slipped her arm under Jer's and curled herself close to him while he hugged his knees and watched Leo dance attention on Helena, and finally sit beside her. Helena took the long stick he'd been using to poke the fire, slid it under the pile of twigs and gently lifted them, allowing the fire to breathe. The flame when it appeared seemed unnaturally vivid to Jer – a tiny miracle of light and warmth amidst the dank, dripping trees.

"I knew I'd find consolation here today," she said, smiling at Leo.

"How long have you been here?" Jer asked him.

Leo's eyes darted to Jer. He looked scared. "A few days."

"Where's your car?"

"It's round the back of the wood near the well."

"The well?"

"There's an old holy well back there. You showed it to me, Helena."

"Yes, of course I did," she said wonderingly, as if the memory he'd elicited had brought with it a host of other happy memories.

"I didn't realise it was possible to drive round there," said Jer thoughtfully. He scrutinised the young man. "Your mum's worried about you. Have you contacted her to tell her you're okay?"

Leo shifted uneasily and shook his head.

"Don't you think you should? If one of my kids disappeared without a word, I'd be doing my nut."

Leo turned to Helena. "What do you think?"

"Ring her. She must be terribly anxious."

He took out his phone and looked at it uncertainly before turning it on.

"Mum? It's me." They all watched as he listened, his face filling with tension. "I'm fine. I'm camping for a few days, that's all." His face crumpled and he held the phone towards Helena. "She wants to know if I'm with you."

Helena looked puzzled and took the mobile from him. "Hello?"

Even though the rest of them couldn't make out what Babs was saying, they could hear the manic tone.

"Leo's fine. He's here with me in Islandmagee."

Leo snatched back the phone and switched it off again. "You shouldn't have told her where we are." He sounded panicky.

"Has Babs ever been here to your house?" said Jer.

Helena looked at Leo and shook her head. "No! I've never even met her."

"Why are you hiding out here, Leo?" Jer asked.

"I'm not hiding. I just need time to sort myself out before I tell Mum I've left uni."

"You've given up your course," said Helena, nodding.

"She'll go crazy when she finds out," he said miserably, hunching his shoulders.

Jer was tempted to tell him that Babs already knew but thought better of it. Leo was already wound tight as a fiddle-string. He didn't want him to cut and run.

"Did you come here in the weeks after . . . Malachy disappeared?" Jer asked him.

He shook his head. "Mum insisted I go to Boston to stay with my uncle. They said it would help me get over it all."

"And did it?" said Nora.

Leo looked at her for a moment and then shrugged. "No."

"Of course it didn't," she said, as if confirming something to herself.

"Helena, I'm really sorry about Malachy," he blurted out. "Mum said he – did what he did because of you and me." He covered his face with his hands.

Shocked, she got onto her knees and drew Leo's hands away from his face. "Leo, dearest Leo, listen to me. We still don't know what happened to Malachy, and I can't believe he took his own life. What I do know is that he had no problem with you and me being close."

Leo looked at her, as if afraid to hope. "Then why did you destroy the house?"

She sat back on her heels. "I didn't. I loved the house, my studio, everything about it. Someone else destroyed it while I was in hospital."

His face drained of blood.

A thought struck Jer. "I think you know who it was, don't you, Leo?"

Leo looked around wildly and scrambled to his feet. Helena was trying to get to her feet too but was impeded by her long skirt. Leo backed away from the fire, then turned and ran away from them through the trees.

"*Leo!*" she shouted. "*Please come back!*"

Jer was on his feet now too. He pulled out his mobile and walked away from the fire.

"Detective Wright, Jer McCabe here. I now have a witness who visited Malachy Murtagh's house on multiple occasions, and I think the person who demolished the house illegally was Ed Cromey, who either part-owns or works for Palliate Construction."

"Who's your witness?"

"Ed Cromey's stepson Leo Greatrex."

"Where are you now?"

"I'm at the house site in Islandmagee."

"And is Leo Greatrex with you?"

"Yes."

"I suggest you exercise some caution in dealing with him."

"Why?"

"His mother says she's afraid he's psychotic."

He looked back towards the fire and realised with concern that Nora, Helena and Myra had followed Leo. "I have to go!"

He set off through the trees, his heart thumping. His phone rang. Thinking it was Wright, he paused to answer it.

"Hi, Jer – how's it going there?"

"Amy! A bit intense, to be honest."

"We've already bailed out. There wasn't a drop of booze to be seen at the wedding and it was all running out of steam by the time we left."

"Blimey!"

"I know, poor Stella. Can we come and join the party there?"

"Course you can. It's shaping up to be the Halloween party to end all!"

"Jer, Rosie's with us."

"Good on Stella," he said with a lump in his throat. "Nice of her to invite Rosie despite everything."

"I know. She's the best." There was an awkward pause. "Rosie's parted company from Harry."

"Already? That was quick."

She dropped her voice. "She's not in a good place."

"She's welcome if she wants to come, Amy. Have any of you got a camera with you by any chance? I had to leave my car at Samuel's last night, so I've only got my phone."

"Yeah, sure, Hugh was filming the ceremony. See you shortly!"

He put the phone in his pocket and then jumped. "Christ, Nora, you nearly gave me a heart attack. Don't creep up on me like that."

"What was she saying about the wedding?"

"It's dry, so Amy & Co have bailed out and are on their way here with a camera. Nothing like the All-seeing Eye to keep people's behaviour civilised."

"Not even champagne?" she said with a wicked grin.

"Stella met her – her . . ."

"Husband!"

"Thanks – husband, at her church. I'm guessing he's very religious."

"So, she's been saved, in more ways than one!"

"Looks like it," he said sheepishly. "Where are the others?"

"They're down there where the house was," she said. "I came back to get you."

They came out of the trees to find Helena at the centre of the flat area setting out stones in a large circle, stones which Leo and Myra were gathering.

"She's very good at getting people to do things for her," Nora muttered.

"She is, isn't she? Leo seems to have calmed down."

"He's obviously terrified of his mother," she said sadly.

They stood watching the stone circle taking shape.

"I don't think a few wee stones are going to be any protection from his mother's wrath if she thinks Helena is trying to steal him away."

Jer looked at his wife. Nora's moments of clarity were often more unsettling than her habitual confusion.

"What do you make of him?"

"He's besotted with her."

"You think they're lovers then?"

"No, more puppy love, I'd say."

"Do you think he's capable of murder?"

"We're all capable of that!"

Helena had spotted them and gestured enthusiastically for them to come over. When they were close enough to hear, she called out, "I think we've nearly enough stones now, but we need kindling for the fire!" Her face was glowing from the physical exertion and the cold air.

"Amy and her friends are going to be here shortly, Helena. Would it be okay for us to film what you're doing?"

She spread her arms wide and smiled. "Of course it is. I have a very good feeling about this!"

Jer wished he felt the same.

"I'm not a bloody Girl Guide," Nora said under her breath. "There's no way I'm crawling around looking for kindling!"

"You might as well. At least it'll keep us warm."

"You suit yourself," she said, folding her arms.

He watched her walk away stiffly in her high-heeled boots. He wondered how Stella was feeling after her low-key wedding reception. He lit a cigarette and, to distract himself, tried to picture Malachy's house as it had been, with its glass gable looking towards the sea. Myra and Leo were moving about the site like two ants, busily collecting wood for the fire, each keeping their distance from each other but seemingly attached to Helena by an invisible bond. The air was still and pungent with the smell of damp earth.

He wandered away from Helena's nascent stone circle down the slope towards the bank of gorse and brambles which formed a barrier between the house-site and the cliffs. A few yellow flowers, blooming out of season, spurted like flames from the bushes. He imagined the gorse as a golden shield come spring. He walked along the edge of the brushwood, remembering how Helena had thrown herself into brambles, eyes tightly closed, following some instinctual summons. He nipped his glowing cigarette butt between his thumb and middle finger and flicked it deep into the dark tangle of thorns, then bent to gather some twigs, cursing under his breath when they pricked his cold flesh.

By the time he walked back to deposit his offering in the centre of the circle, he was relieved to see Amy, Hugh and Rosie with Nora stumbling along beside them, trying to keep up. Amy and Hugh had come prepared and were dressed in anoraks and stout boots while Rosie was shivering in a short purple fun-fur and sequinned mini-skirt. Her legs were bare, and she was trudging along in wellies that were obviously too big for her.

"*Thanks for coming, guys!*" he called out, going over to meet them.

"*It was a pretty crap wedding apparently!*" shouted Nora.

Amy winced. "It was dead on," she said quickly. "Each to his own and all that!

Rosie faltered at his approach, but he strode up to her and gave her a bear hug. When he loosened his embrace and looked into her face, he saw her mascara was smudged as if she had been crying.

"Sorry," she managed.

"It's fine, Rosie. We're fine. I'm glad you're here."

"She's well and truly married then, is she?" interrupted Nora.

Rosie nodded, looking at Jer sympathetically.

"She seemed really happy," said Hugh, sounding choked up.

"Good," said Jer, trying to keep his voice upbeat.

"What's the husband like?" said Nora, unwilling to let the hare sit.

"Nice," Amy said firmly.

"Nice?" Nora gave a snort. "God preserve me from *nice!*"

Helena came over and gave Amy a hug and was introduced to Hugh and Rosie.

"What's the plan?" Amy asked her.

"We're building a fire where our hearth used to be. If Malachy's spirit is nearby, he'll be drawn to it."

"Is it okay with you if we film?"

"Yes, of course, Jer already asked." She turned and suddenly gasped. "Goodness, look at that!" she exclaimed. "It's a full moon!"

They all looked towards the sea, where the mass of thick, grey cloud, that had weighed on them all afternoon, had rolled back to reveal a clear, violet sky. A pale, perfect moon was rising, insubstantial as a ghost, making Jer all too aware that the world was tipping towards night.

"I can see the man in the moon," said Nora.

"The hare in the moon!" laughed Helena. "The Chinese see a hare, where we see a human face."

She co-opted Amy and Rosie to help gather wood to add to the growing pile in the centre of the circle while Nora wandered away.

Jer drew Hugh aside.

"Thanks for coming," he said, and was rewarded by a nod. "Can you get some shots of the whole scene – the fire being built and the rising moon?"

"I presume she's going to wait till it's dark before lighting it?" said Hugh, his brow furrowed.

"Are you planning to wait until it's dark?" Jer called out to Helena.

"No, the light's already fading. The twilight is perfect – the time when day and night are in balance."

When Helena was satisfied enough wood had been gathered, she positioned herself beside the pyre and called everyone together, putting her arm through Leo's, with Myra standing to attention beside her.

"Thank you for being here with me this evening. In a moment we'll light the fire, to serve as a guide to Malachy, wherever he is in the darkness."

Jer licked his lips and went over to Nora who seemed transfixed.

Helena's face was radiant. "There's nothing to be afraid of. We're simply going to focus our collective, mental energy on one intention."

"What intention?" asked Rosie, looking intrigued.

"I lost my partner Malachy recently and I just want him to know that I'm missing him and long for a sign from him."

Jer whispered to Nora. "Are you okay with this, love?"

"I'm fine. We should do something like this for Liam." She stepped away from him and entered the circle.

He felt a wave of desolation, convinced that Liam's baby soul was a spark too tiny, too fleeting to ever be located in the vastness of time and space.

Helena took off the black anorak she was wearing and threw it outside the circle. She loosened her hair, running her fingers through it, then stretched out her arms to Amy and Rosie.

"I'd love you girls to come into the circle with us. You're full of youthful, positive energy like Leo. Nothing bad can befall us while you're here."

Rosie didn't hesitate while Amy glanced questioningly at Jer, then stepped over the stones and stood self-consciously near Helena.

"Aren't you going to join us?" Helena asked Jer and Hugh.

"I'll stay out here, if you don't mind," said Hugh, indicating the camera on his shoulder.

"Jer, you can do the honours and light the fire."

"Me?" he said, surprised.

"You're the only smoker here, my love," said Nora wryly.

"And can you all form a circle? That's it." Helena stretched out her arms. "Space yourselves out."

Jer groped in his trouser pocket for his lighter, stepped into the ring of stones and crouched at the base of the bonfire. He looked at Helena for a signal that she was ready, and she gave him a decisive nod. His hand was cold, and it took him a couple of clicks to produce a tiny flame which caught the edge of a brown leaf, flared and died, leaving a red, molten crescent across the parched membrane. He cupped his left hand as a windbreak and flicked the lighter several more times, trying and failing to maintain a steady flame. Frustrated, he stood up to stretch his legs, but before he could bend down to try again, a breath seemed to rise through the earth and shift the pyramid of mouldering detritus, sending a whorl of sparks funnelling along the ground, igniting slivers of dead matter. The fire found its voice and began to whisper.

He stepped back, making to exit the circle.

"Oh Jer, aren't you going to stay with us in the circle?" cried Helena, stretching a hand towards him.

"I'd rather observe."

He looked around for Hugh who'd positioned himself a few yards away and was already filming. Jer could hear the fire fussing behind him as he moved away. When he drew level with Hugh, he turned to see the six remaining inside the stones had started to walk slowly around the circle, in jerky, ungainly steps, as if jostled by the flickering shadows. Helena's eyes were fixed on the fire, and she began to hum. The others were all watching her, trying to match their steps to hers and stay in formation. Small bursts of flame were now sprouting from the twigs and branches at ground level and the fire began to hiss and spit. He looked away from the fire for a moment, aware that the increasing intensity of light from the flames was seeing off the remains of the daylight on the hillside, while above the horizon the moon was claiming dominion over sea and sky with a cold intensity.

"Watch my back," Hugh said to him, and started to orbit the fire in the opposite direction to the six within the circle.

Jer held the younger man's upper arms from behind, steadying him while they moved together across the pitted earth. There was a greedy urgency to the flames now and cracks like pistol-shots could be heard as the dead wood expanded and split.

The other women had now joined in Helena's humming and were staring into the fire, while Leo never took his eyes off Helena who'd been transformed by the firelight into a luminous, angelic figure, with her upstretched arms and pale, fluttering clothes.

Chapter 32

The fire roared, consuming the dead wood like a ravenous animal, creating a beacon that could be seen for miles. The shadows of the moving figures danced at their own feet as if their spirits had become detached from their bodies. Without warning, Helena sent Malachy's name shrieking into the air like a crazed bird, shocking them all. Myra quickly added her contralto to the incantation and Jer realised, with a shudder, that Nora had started to scream – but it was Liam's name she was offering up in anguish to the night sky.

Jer gripped Hugh's shoulders hard and froze. A cold, dark wind seemed to be gathering itself, moving across the naked soil, rushing towards the cliff-edge. It circled the fire, urging the flames higher. They cringed as a shower of sparks flew over their heads and dropped through the tangle of briars near them – each point of light pulsing its message, before being extinguished on the damp soil. An acrid smell, with some putrid sweetness at its core assailed them. Jer coughed and doubled over, retching, his hands sinking into the soft earth, to stop himself falling forward.

Hugh lowered the camera and put a hand under Jer's arm to

steady him. "What is it?" He sounded scared.

A cloud of smoke enveloped them, making Jer's eyes sting and water, and Hugh pulled him further from the fire. When his vision cleared, he noticed a movement in the dark between the fire and the trees.

"There's someone over there," he said. "Keep it running but move away from the fire a bit till we get a look at them." He guided Hugh by the elbow.

Two figures were now distinguishable, one a few yards in front of the other, moving stealthily towards the fire. When they were near enough for the firelight to light up their faces, he recognised them.

"It's Leo's parents," he whispered into Hugh's ear.

Babs Cromey faltered, then stopped dead. "*Leo!*" she called out in an agonised appeal.

There were frightened gasps inside the circle and Helena and the others stilled and fell silent, staring in the direction of the strange voice. Leo moved closer to Helena. At that moment the fire collapsed in upon itself with an inhuman sigh, sending a column of smoke and flame heavenward, and the darkness seemed to close in on the circle.

Ed Cromey caught up with his wife and touched her arm. He was breathing heavily, his face a mask of distress. She shook him off.

"*You can't be with that woman, Leo!*" Babs shouted furiously.

Leo gazed out at his parents, as if protected by the ring of stones at his feet.

"*Why won't you listen to me? You know how much I love you – how I only want what's best for you, yet you do this!*" Anger was threading through her voice like smoke.

Helena stepped in front of Leo.

"I know you," she said ominously. "I know your voice."

"No, you don't," said Babs. "I've never met you before in my life!"

"Come away, Babs. We shouldn't be here," said Ed Cromey.

"*It was you!*" Helena's voice was ragged with shock. "You're the one who brought Isabella to me!"

Babs' face went rigid, then she advanced on Helena, craning her neck to see Leo who was cowering behind her.

"You can't be with her, my darling boy – you just can't be." Her tone had become wheedling. "You have to trust me on this. Please come here to me. Come home with me and your dad!"

Helena turned her back on Babs and took Leo's face in her hands, as if seeing him for the first time. She ran her thumbs along his eyebrows and touched his mouth with the tips of her fingers.

"How did I not see it before? You're so like him – so like your father." Her face was transfigured with joy. "You're my son!"

Babs howled like an animal in pain and attacked Helena, toppling her over. Helena rolled towards the fire, sending up a shower of sparks. Babs made a grab at Helena but Leo pushed her aside and she fell heavily, then he caught Helena's arm and pulled her away from the fire and into a sitting position.

Helena gasped and tears began to stream down her face. Leo wiped them away tenderly, leaving the tracks of his fingers on her face which was dusted with ash.

Babs Cromey was on her knees, watching them from a few feet away, immobilised by her husband who had pinned her arms to her sides from behind in a bear hug.

"What the hell is going on here?" came an authoritative voice out of the darkness and a beam of strong, white light swept across the hillside.

"*Is that you, Wright?*" Jer shouted back. "*We need help here!*" He lifted his arm to shade his eyes from the torchlight. He heard the crackle of a police radio and a female voice calling for back-up and breathed a sigh of relief. "Help is coming," he said.

The detective loomed out of the darkness with Constable Matthews on his heels, raking the group with his torchlight. Ed Cromey hauled Babs to her feet and was whispering to her, but she struggled out of his grasp.

"*That woman is a witch!*" Babs shouted, pointing at Helena. "*She has bewitched and corrupted my son!*"

"He's not your son. You stole him from me!" Helena cried.

"Is it true, Babs? Is she Leo's mother?" said Ed Cromey, his voice webbed with hurt.

"She should be burned as a witch. She's not fit to walk this earth, slut that she is, fornicating with that artist old enough to be her grandfather!" Babs' mouth was flecked with spittle, as she spat out her imprecations.

Ed Cromey released his wife and backed away from her. "All these years, you were lying to me." He sounded breathless. "You told me he was yours."

She turned to confront him. "He *is* mine. She doesn't deserve him. A stupid, selfish creature like her. She couldn't have looked after him." She turned back and stared down at Helena. "She was delighted when I put that dead baby in her arms. Solved all her problems."

There was a horrified silence then Nora's voice cut through the air.

"*That was my baby!*" she screamed. "*You killed my baby!*"

Jer hurried over and put his arms around her.

"No, no, Nora, it was some other woman's baby – some poor Italian mother whose baby girl had died in childbirth. Not yours. Not our wee Liam."

Nora pushed him away.

"We'll look after her, Jer, don't worry," said Rosie, taking one of Nora's arms while Amy hurried over to take the other. They led her away from the fire, Rosie speaking softly to her all the while.

Babs had used the moment of distraction to move closer to Helena. Leo got to his feet and faced the woman he had thought of as his mother, his face ashen.

"Leo, we're going home now," said Babs, in a tone that brooked no argument. "Come with me this very minute!"

"He's not going to come with you, Babs," said Ed Cromey, his voice breaking. "You won't ever see him again and neither will I."

Jer saw the moment of weakness and challenged her. "What about Malachy? What did you do to him, Babs?"

Her head swivelled like an animal sensing danger. "He wouldn't listen!" she growled.

"Don't, Babs," pleaded Ed Cromey, but she ignored him and stared Jer down.

"I told him what she was like, but he wouldn't listen. He laughed in my face."

"So, you killed him to wipe the smile off his face, did you?"

"Shut your mouth now," said her husband, in a panic.

"*Don't you dare tell me to shut my mouth!*" she roared at him. She looked around in panic.

Wright came and stood shoulder to shoulder with Jer and shone his torch directly into her face. "Did you kill Malachy Murtagh?"

Her teeth were bared, her eyes wild. "He drowned himself because of her. You'll never find him. He's out there in the ocean, lost forever, like his house of shame."

"No, I think he's right here," said Jer.

Babs blinked and squinted into the light, trying to see the face of her tormentor.

"He's under the brambles, isn't he?" said Jer.

Her change of expression told its own story. She turned and glared at her husband.

"*You stupid, stupid little man! What did you tell him?*"

Ed Cromey took a step backwards, shaking his head.

She raised her arm against the harsh beam of light, breathing hard. "Thorns stop the dead rising from the grave, that's what my mother always said."

"And protect them from evil spirits like you," said Helena, struggling to her feet with Leo's help.

"Babs Cromey, I'm arresting you on suspicion of the murder of Malachy Murtagh," said Wright. "Matthews, cuff her and read her her rights."

The reality of the situation suddenly hit Babs and she made a pathetic attempt at escape and had to be restrained by Wright and Constable Matthews.

Ed Cromey watched her being led away flanked by the two police officers then sank to his knees. Jer made a sign to Hugh to carry on filming and crouched beside Ed.

"I know it was all her idea, Ed, but you helped her dispose of the body, didn't you?"

"I didn't kill anyone," he said, breaking down. "I shouldn't have helped clean up her mess. I only did it to protect you, Leo," he pleaded, looking up at the young man "I'm sorry," he sobbed, "sorry for it all." He wiped his cheeks with the heel of his hand.

Jer understood the man would be reassessing everything his wife had done in the previous months, in the light of what had just been revealed about Leo's origins.

"Did she come here intending to kill Helena?" he said quietly.

Cromey looked away into the darkness, as if trying the fathom his wife's soul. "She was in a terrible state. She'd just found out Leo was – was seeing her," he said, looking at Helena.

"She thought they were lovers?" said Jer, and Cromey nodded miserably.

"She found sketches of her in Leo's room. Now I understand why she was so horrified."

"But coming here was a huge risk." Jer shook his head. "She must have known Helena might recognise her and that would've been game over."

Cromey looked at him in despair. "She was beside herself. She wasn't thinking straight."

"What happened when you arrived at the house that day, Ed?" said Jer, standing up.

"The jeep was outside and the front door was lying open, so we went inside, looking for Leo, but the house was empty."

"Where was Malachy?"

"When we went into the studio at the other end of the house, we saw him through the window. He was working in the garden."

"Didn't he see you drive up?"

"No, we parked the car behind the trees, same as tonight."

"Did Malachy come in and find you in the house?"

He shook his head. "There was a big painting of her – naked," he said, looking towards Helena. Babs lost it when she saw that. She ran out of the house and went down to Malachy."

"Did you go after her?"

He shook his head. "I only wish I had." He looked at the semicircle of faces around him in supplication. "There was this wall of glass. I could see her talking to him. I knew no good could come of it. "

"How did she do it?" said Jer softly. "She's a small woman."

Ed Cromey clasped his hands to stop them shaking. "He was down on his knees weeding. They talked a bit, and he went back to his weeding." Cromey's face creased in pain. "She pulled the spade out of the ground, and I knew what she was going to do." He looked at Leo. "I shouted but she couldn't hear me through the glass. She hit him over the head."

Helena gave a strangled cry and covered her mouth with both hands.

"I ran outside then. I still thought I could stop her," Ed said quickly.

Helena threw her arms wide. "Why didn't you call an ambulance?" she cried out in an anguished voice.

Cromey hung his head. "There wasn't any point. He was dead."

She began to cry, and Leo put his arms around her.

Jer swallowed. He didn't want to further upset Helena, but he knew he needed to press on before the cavalry arrived to whisk Cromey away. Once he was in custody, he would likely be advised by a lawyer to stay silent. He glanced in Hugh's direction to satisfy himself that he was still filming.

Jer crouched down beside Cromey again. "What did you do with Malachy's body, Ed?" he said gently.

Cromey turned to him gratefully. "Babs said we needed to – get rid of him before she came back." He looked over at Helena and Leo. "I was afraid you'd be with her, Leo," he said despairingly. "I didn't want you finding your mother like that."

"It must have taken quite a while to bury him?" said Jer, trying to keep him focused.

Cromey didn't answer but turned to gaze towards the sea, making Jer wonder if they'd simply thrown Malachy's body over the cliff.

The fire was now reduced to a mound of glowing embers which were casting a coppery sheen over the faces of those present. The air temperature was plummeting. Leo took off his jacket and put it around Helena's shoulders.

"You were there when I got home," Helena said faintly. "I sensed something was wrong."

"What happened when she showed up, Ed?" said Jer.

Cromey blinked. "We heard her car arrive. To tell you the truth, I was kind of relieved, for the waiting was desperate. I kept begging Babs to leave but she'd come up with the idea of making it look like a murder-suicide. She watches all those crime dramas," he said sadly, as if that in some way excused his wife's calculation. "She came up with it all while I was out in the garden burying him. She found his laptop open and wrote the suicide note on it."

"Did she show it to you?"

He gave a hollow laugh. "Yes. I got her to delete all but a few lines of it. The rest was all horrible stuff about her," he said, nodding at Helena. "I told her the shorter the better."

"Can you remember what those few lines were?"

Cromey shook his head and looked down at the earth.

Then Helena spoke out clearly. "*God sees everything. God understands everything. My only crime was loving you too much.*"

There was a shocked silence.

"I knew Malachy hadn't written that," she said emphatically. "He didn't believe in God. I told the police it was nonsense."

Cromey lifted his head and looked at her coldly, obviously repelled by the idea of Malachy's agnosticism.

Jer stood up again, repelled in turn by Cromey. "She spent quite a while on his laptop then," he said. "Is that when she stole the money?"

"I only found out about that a few days ago," said Cromey, glancing up at Jer. "I couldn't believe she'd been so stupid."

"Or so greedy!"

"It was for you, Leo. She said it was your right. I didn't understand why she said that at the time, but now . . ."

"You got her to give it back," Jer prompted him.

Cromey nodded. "I knew they'd track it down sooner or later even though she thought she'd done it really cleverly."

"You were waiting for me when I got home that day," said Helena, who was staring at Cromey in horror. "It was you who hit me when I came through the door. I remember now. I saw your reflection in the hall mirror for a split second before . . ."

"I had to or she'd have killed you. I didn't hit you too hard."

Leo gave a heartbroken sob and Cromey looked at him beseechingly.

"I saved her, Leo. Babs wanted her dead."

"What did you use to hit her?" asked Jer.

"A hammer."

"A hammer!" echoed Leo, appalled.

"But I only wanted to knock her out. I knew Babs was waiting for her in the kitchen with a knife. If I hadn't got there first she'd be dead."

"Did Babs think you'd killed her?"

"She came out of the kitchen when she heard her hit the floor. But I don't think she could bear to look at her. She told me to put her in your man's jeep and cover her with something. Mind you, she still had the presence of mind to throw her bag in with her," he said bitterly.

"Then what?" said Jer.

"She was desperate to get away from the house then in case you turned up, Leo. She had it all worked out. She'd printed out the suicide note and put it in a jacket of his. She wanted to burn the house but I talked her out of it. I said it would attract too much attention. She cursed me for that later that night."

"And you went back later and cleared it off the face of the earth," said Helena.

"How long after?" said Jer, keen to get detail.

"About two weeks. She wouldn't let it rest. I knew I wouldn't get a moment's peace till I'd got rid of it. It was crazy. She was crazy."

"What happened when she found out Helena had survived? She must have been furious with you," said Jer sympathetically.

"You've no idea," said Cromey. "I told her the cold water must have brought her round and she'd managed to swim to the shore but she blamed me – called me all the names of the day. That was when she packed you off to the States," he said, looking at Leo.

Helena moved nearer to Cromey and knelt down in front of him.

He looked at her, wide-eyed with fear.

"At the beach. You tried to drown me," she said in a low voice.

"No, you don't understand. I had to take you into the water. She was standing there watching. When I pushed you under, she ran away so I pulled your head up again. The cold water had brought you round and you were choking and . . ."

"You took me out of the sea?"

"Once Babs was gone, I pulled you out and hid you under the seaweed. You were conscious for only a minute or two."

"You whispered something to me."

"I told you to be quiet."

"That's what he would say," she whispered.

"Who, Helena?" said Jer, moving closer to her.

"He would say that to me in the studio. *Silenzio!*"

Jer looked over his shoulder towards Leo, sad to think there was more ugliness this young man would have to hear about.

The sound of a distant siren reached them, and Cromey struggled to his feet, looking panicky.

"Please forgive me, Leo. Everything I did was to protect you. I couldn't bear for you to know your mother could . . ."

"You let me think it was my fault Malachy had taken his own life," said Leo in a choked voice. "How could you do that to me? You knew I was haunted by the idea of him swimming out into the sea in the dark."

"I said all that to your – to Babs, but she was convinced that sending you away to the US would make you forget all about it."

Leo made a derisive sound.

Afraid that Cromey was about to take off, Jer said, "Who drove Malachy's jeep, Ed?"

"I did. She drove behind me all the way to Cladrach so I couldn't' stop and let you out." He looked down at Helena who was still kneeling at his feet.,

"You left me there for dead," said Helena in a flat tone.

"You wouldn't be alive now if it wasn't for me," insisted Cromey, taking a step back.

"I might never have been found under the seaweed and the tide could have come in over me when I was unconscious."

"I prayed all the way home that someone would find you and God answered my prayer. I mean, if that man hadn't had a dog with him, he wouldn't have found you, but the dog did. God bless it!"

The siren which had been steadily approaching stopped suddenly and Cromey looked at the silent, accusing faces around him. Blue light flickered in the air like cold lightning.

Chapter 33

Cromey stared up the hillside where a string of torchlights was approaching, then backed away from the stone circle and took to his heels, scuttling in the direction of the trees.

"*For God's sake, stand your ground, you snivelling coward!*" Myra shouted after him. "*Jer, do something, he's getting away!*"

Jer folded his arms and watched several of the torchlights detach themselves from the line and move off to the right, their beams picking out Cromey's shambling figure. They all watched him stop and double over as the lights closed in on him. Other lights were moving in their direction.

Jer went over to Hugh and said quietly, "That detective will be here in a minute and will demand the footage. Would you mind making yourself scarce and copying it before we have to hand it over?"

"Good idea!" he agreed, lowering the camera.

"And Hugh, thanks," he said, putting a hand on his shoulder.

"No problem. That's quite a story we have in the can! What do you plan to do with it?"

"I don't know, Hugh, but we have the truth there and that's what matters."

Jer made to turn away, but Hugh stopped him.

"What about the girls?"

"I'll be over there shortly to look after Nora," Jer reassured him.

A couple of paramedics had arrived with two constables and Myra asked them to look after Helena. There was no sign of Wright and Jer surmised he must be among the officers taking Ed Cromey into custody. The paramedics had wrapped Helena in a survival blanket and made to lead her away but she turned back, went over to Jer and put her arms around him.

"Thank you," she whispered in his ear.

Too full of emotion to speak, he watched her being escorted from the scene with Leo at her side. Myra stood staring after them, looking bereft. He pulled out his phone and texted Samuel, explaining the gist of what had happened and giving him directions to where they were. Then he approached his sister-in-law.

"It worked!" she said under her breath.

"What?"

"Helena's spell or whatever it was. She got her son back. There has to have been some supernatural intervention, don't you think?"

This was a conversation he was too tired to have with Myra and changed the subject. "We need to check on Nora."

"She's with Amy and her friend," said Myra, frowning.

"But I told Hugh to take off, and they'll want to go with him."

Myra gave him a searching look. "Ah, of course, your precious film! You don't want the police commandeering that, now do you?" she said bitterly, walking away from him up the hill.

He was about to follow her when Detective Wright hailed him.

"What was all that about babies?"

He swallowed his annoyance. "Helena worked as an au pair in Italy when she was very young. She was sexually abused by the father of the family she was working for and gave birth in some sort of private clinic there. I'm guessing the father of her baby arranged to have the child adopted."

"And your woman Cromey worked there?"

"Yes, Looks like that. She took Helena's baby, a boy, and convinced her that her baby had died. She put a dead baby girl into her arms."

"Devilish! And this happened in Italy, you say? A Catholic clinic then!"

Jer sighed. "Very possibly."

Wright's lips curled with distaste.

"I take it you'll start digging tomorrow?" Jer asked him.

"Digging?"

"To find Malachy's body."

"Did they bury him?" asked Wright, looking sceptical. "I heard her say he was lost at sea like his – what did she call it?"

"His house of shame. But then she all but admitted he's buried under the brambles."

Wright turned to survey the scene. "Hell of a big area to dig up."

"I was filming here during the week and, when I was viewing the footage, I noticed there was a patch of brambles where the blackberries were brown whereas all the rest were nice and plump."

Wright frowned. "You'll have to hand over all that footage."

"Of course."

"Where's that young fella who was filming?"

"He's gone home. I'll get one of my team to send everything to you tomorrow."

"You do that. We'll need statements from all of you tomorrow," said Wright and turned on his heel.

Jer trudged up the slope, pausing at the top to look back at the scene below. Arc lights had been set up transforming the crusted mud into a moonscape, and official figures, bundled up against the cold, criss-crossed the space where Malachy's house had once stood. The police had now squared off Helena's stone circle with tape, and all that remained of the fire was a mound of cinders emitting an occasional tongue of blue flame, in response to the eddies of icy air moving around the hillside. He suddenly felt overwhelmed with exhaustion.

Approaching the gate, he saw a cluster of official vehicles, some with their headlights on. Myra was talking to a female officer and hurried up to him.

"Nora's gone!"

"What? Did she not go with Hugh and the others?"

"No."

"Oh God!" Jer looked into the darkness. "You've checked the car?" he said, trying the keep the agitation out of his voice.

"I'm surprised she'd go wandering off in the dark on her own," said Myra. "Maybe the policewoman there will lend us a torch," and she made a beeline for the officer who opened the boot of one of the squad cars and handed her a large flashlight. She ran to catch up with Jer who had already set off up the slope again, calling Nora's name into the night. He stopped when he realised Myra was on his heels.

"Myra, there's no need for you to come with me. I'll – "

"I'm going to help you find Nora," she said firmly.

"Thanks," he said, sounding anything but grateful.

When they reached the top of the hill, he looked towards the sea. The full moon was now higher in the sky, lighting a seductive path onto the dark water. The outline of the bank of gorse along the clifftop was stark against the sea-glitter.

"There's no way she could get to the cliff from here, is there?" he said anxiously.

"She wouldn't do that, would she?" said Myra, reading his thoughts.

"I think we might be better off without the torch," he said irritably. "That way our eyes will adjust, and we'll see more."

She clicked off the flash-light and they stood side by side in the darkness.

"I'm going to check down there near the cliffs," he muttered. "Why don't you see if she's over there near the – "

"I'm coming with you!"

They made their way down the hill together through the long, wet grass, giving the house-site a wide berth until their way was blocked by the gorse. He shouted Nora's name a few times and listened for a response but heard only the sea rumbling on the rocks far below and distant shouts of the police officers calling out to each other.

"She couldn't have got through this," said Myra. "Let's check further down."

With their backs to the spill of light from the crime scene, they moved along the edge of the bushes, eventually coming upon an area clear of grass.

"Hang on," he said, squatting to feel rock, cold under his hand. He looked to his right and saw the gleam of the sea through the lower branches of the gorse bushes, which were bare close to the ground. "There's a way through here," he said and started to crawl through a narrow gap between the bushes.

"She'd never have gone in there, surely?"

Swearing as tiny thorns pierced his hands and knees, he pulled the sleeves of his jacket over his hands and padded on like an animal, weaving between the twisted branches. Emerging on the far side of the gorse, he felt the updraft from the sea. He looked left and right along the cliff-top and saw no-one. Lying flat on his stomach, he inched his way to the edge and looked over, immediately gripped by the sensation that he was being pulled into the void. He closed his eyes and fought the vertigo, trying to steady his breathing.

"Are you okay?" Myra called to him, sounding worried.

He swallowed. "I'm fine."

"Is there any sign of her?"

He took a deep breath, opened his eyes and looked down. In the moonlight he could see that a heavy swell was pushing large waves towards the base of the cliffs, with shreds of white spray, moving and shifting on the water.

Then he heard voices calling his name.

"*Jer, come back please! She's been found! Nora's okay!*"

He leaned his forehead on his hands for a moment in relief and felt like weeping. "I'm coming," he answered and made the painful journey back through the gorse.

The female officer from whom they'd borrowed the flashlight had joined Myra and helped him to his feet when he emerged from under the bushes.

"She's curled up in Leo's tent and won't budge," said Myra.

He sighed. "Thank God!"

"She needs to go home," she said, stating the obvious.

He gritted his teeth. "I know, but will she let me take her home? That's the problem!"

Myra was looking at her phone.

Jer cleared his throat. "I messaged Samuel a while ago and he's on his way."

"He's already here," she snapped. "The police have stopped him at the entrance to the lane."

"Why don't you go on home with him?"

"Will you and Nora be alright?" she said, making him feel guilty for being irritable with her.

"We'll be fine. What Nora needs is quiet."

They walked back up the hill with the officer and he headed for the wood alone. Stumbling through the trees in the dark, he began to wish he'd asked the officer for the use of her torch. He activated the light on his phone again and managed to pick his way to Leo's little campsite. The white tent was reflecting the moonlight.

"*Nora?*" he called, getting no response.

He gathered the clothes and sleeping bag strewn around the ashes of the campfire and made himself a nest at the entrance to the tent, which remained stubbornly zipped up. He lit a cigarette.

"I'm just having a ciggie, then I'm coming inside, cos I'm freezing my bollocks off out here!"

There was still no sign of life from within. He sat and smoked, gazing back at the moon's pale face, which was visible through the bare branches. The wind had died, and he became aware of the dew chilling the top of his head and shoulders. He heard a car engine start up and then recede. He was glad there were still some police officers on-site for he felt assailed by the shadows of the night. Here in this ancient woodland on Halloween, it was easy to believe there were spirits abroad – restless, unhappy souls who envied the living. His cigarette done, he flicked the glowing butt into the remains of the campfire.

"I'm coming in now, Nora. I have a sleeping-bag here, so we can make ourselves cosy."

He struggled with the tent-zip and eventually managed to open it enough to crawl into the small tent and zip it closed behind him. He used the light of his phone to orientate himself and by its glow saw Nora lying curled up in the foetal position. He could hear her breathing and sensed she was awake.

"Are you cold?" he whispered. She opened her eyes, and his phone went dark again. "I've got some clothes and a sleeping-bag here so let's make ourselves comfortable or we'll catch our death before the night's through."

"I feel close to him here, Jer," she whispered. "Do you feel his presence too?"

"Yes, love, I do. Here put this under your head and snuggle in close to me and we can both get under the sleeping-bag."

She moved nearer to him, and he lay down and gathered her in his arms.

Saturday 1ˢᵗ November: All Souls Day

Chapter 34

Jer slept fitfully in the tent, dreaming that he and Nora were adrift on the open sea. By dawn it seemed to him they'd travelled a huge distance across a fathomless ocean. He lay still, unwilling to wake her, but as the canvas above him began to admit light and with it, texture and shape, he stretched his cramped legs.

She stirred and rolled onto her back, her eyes wide open.

"How do you think Stella will feel when she wakes up this morning?"

"Happy, I hope," he said, trying to keep his voice steady.

"Sure about that?"

"You think her marriage is doomed from the start?"

"Well, yes, it's bound to be, isn't it? She's loved you for years, and she's loyal to a fault. I don't think she could stop loving you, even if she tried. She's trying, I'll give her that!"

"You make love sound very black and white, Nora – all or nothing."

"But it is!"

"I feel it more like an ebb and flow."

"How convenient!"

"Okay then, more like the moon. It's always there but there are periods when part of it is in shadow." When she didn't reply, he went on, "To be honest, the overwhelming feeling I have about Stella right now is relief."

"You're relieved she's off your hands?"

He closed his eyes.

"Do you think there's any food in here?" she said. "I'd kill for a cup of tea."

"Maybe the police people have supplies? What do you think?"

"Are they still here?" She sat up.

"I hope so! I told Wright Malachy is buried here somewhere."

She shivered. "I need to pee."

She struggled out of the tent, while he groped among Leo's belongings and found a packet of biscuits in a rucksack. When she crawled back in, he encouraged her to put one of Leo's jackets on over her own.

"Come on, let's take the biscuits with us, and see if we can beg a cup of tea down there."

They picked their way through the woodland, the moss underfoot spongy with moisture, and stood at the edge of the trees looking down on the scene of the previous night's drama. Police-tape still delineated a large square, with the remains of Helena's stone circle and a pile of grey ash at its centre.

"It's like they've marked out where the house was," Nora remarked.

He raised his eyes to the horizon. The sky looked like a baby's eyelid with a blush of pink at the rim.

"They're going to have to dig up this whole place to find him, aren't they?" she said, hugging herself.

"I should take you home, love."

"No, you will not!"

They were sharing a cuppa with a female officer when a truck arrived carrying a small digger. It trundled over the hill and parked in the long grass. Wright was in a car directly behind. They watched the digger being reversed down a ramp. Once its engine had coughed into life, it lumbered away from them.

"*Morning!*" Jer called out to Wright, as the detective exited the squad car.

"You two been here all night?"

Jer shrugged.

"Have you charged that horrible woman and her husband?" said Nora.

Wright frowned with irritation. "I'm afraid I can't share any details about that at the moment."

"Oh, for God's sake," she muttered.

"Leave it, Nora," said Jer. "Your car's over there. Let's get in and thaw out."

"Don't you think you should take her home out of this, McCabe?"

"I'm standing right here!" said Nora. "Don't you dare speak about me as if I'm a child."

"There really is no point in you hanging around. This is going to take all day!" said Wright, ignoring her.

"What a prick!" she said loudly to his retreating back.

Jer shook his head and they headed for the car. He started the engine and let it idle for a while before turning on the heater.

"Can you imagine it, Jer? That dreadful woman put a dead baby in her arms. How could she do such a thing, knowing that Helena's baby was alive and well? And where was the father? He should have protected them both."

He rolled the cardboard cup between his palms, warming his hands. "I'm guessing he was steering well clear for the sake of his marriage and reputation. I bet he wanted Helena to have the baby adopted."

"And what do you bet she refused?"

He looked at her and nodded. "And that set this whole thing in motion. The father, whoever he was, wouldn't have wanted that baby around, so probably struck a deal with the clinic or maybe even with Babs herself to have it spirited away."

"They probably told her the baby was dead assuming she wouldn't insist on seeing it. God help her, she was only sixteen."

"But she did – insist on seeing it, that is," he said thoughtfully, "and giving her a baby girl to hold would've thrown her off the scent entirely."

"How could one woman could do that to another? You know, I'm beginning to believe Helena's theory about the power of three. All the evil that woman Babs did is coming back on her now. Just think of it, all these years later to find that her son is involved with his birth mother!"

He turned on the radio to hear the eight o'clock news. "*A man and woman have been charged with murder, after an all-night police operation in Islandmagee,*" said the announcer.

"It's on the flipping News and he couldn't tell us. What a prick!"

"Nora, every reporter in the country will be here shortly. I need to get out there and see what's going on."

"Go for it," she said. "I'm going to stay here in the warm for a while and have a snooze."

He stood in the shelter of the trees, watching the digger gouging out barrowloads of earth and heard a dull clang as metal hit stone.

The foundations of the house, he thought to himself. They were digging in completely the wrong place.

Wright saw him striding down towards them and detached himself from the group of officers to intercept him.

"I thought I told you to go home?"

"There's absolutely no point digging there." He pointed. "That's where the house would've been."

"How the hell do you know? Did you ever actually see this house?"

"No, but you heard what Babs said about the brambles stopping the dead from rising."

"I heard her say he was in the sea," said Wright, rounding on him. "We're all going to look pretty silly if we can't find this body. No body, no case."

"But she admitted it all on camera last night!"

"Oh, some fancy barrister will get that thrown out. She's obviously a nutter and was just messing with your heads. A murder charge will never stick without a body."

He felt surge of anger. "You need to find the patch where the blackberries are withered."

Wright gave a dry laugh. "I tell you what, McCabe, go away down there and have a look yourself. All those bloody blackberries are past their best." With that, he marched back to the digger, which repositioned itself slightly and started digging again.

Jer approached the tangle of briars beyond where the digger was at work and, to his dismay, saw the blackberries that a week before had been plump and glossy had since been picked over by the birds or were shrivelling. He skirted the thicket to the point where the gorse triumphed over the brambles, trying to quell his growing unease. Maybe he had this completely wrong? A salty, inshore breeze was combing through the moist undergrowth, and he looked towards the sea for inspiration. Dark clouds were heaped on the horizon like discarded clothes, as if trying to bury the dawn. He watched and waited until the sun raised its head above the murk, lighting up the dewdrops. What had been invisible a moment before was now revealed, and he saw that the gorse was wreathed in layer upon layer of cobwebs. He closed his eyes and felt the November sun like a fingertip on each eyelid. He breathed in the sea air, opened his eyes and walked back the way he'd come, searching for a patch where the weave of gossamer had been disturbed. The odour of earth and vegetation rose all around him. There was another bitter-sweet smell mixed in with it, which he struggled to place.

"*It's here, he's here!*" he shouted.

Wright turned to stare in his direction, and Jer watched him deciding.

Then the detective walked slowly down to where he was standing. "Okay, why are you so sure he's here?"

He swallowed. The sun was obscured once more, and the shining webs had become invisible. "Can you smell that?"

Wright frowned, tilted back his head and sniffed. "What is that?"

"Thyme. I think we're standing in what was Malachy's herb garden, the place where he was killed and buried."

Wright blew out his cheeks. "He could've buried him very deep with a JCB."

"Yes, he could, but I don't think Ed Cromey will have been keen to see that body again. He's more likely to have shifted some bushes to cover up the grave."

"Maybe they just threw the body into the sea."

"Possibly. But they wouldn't have wanted him being washed up anywhere. Not with a split skull."

Wright redirected the digger, and Jer watched it clearing away the brambles, willing them to find Malachy, all the while dreading the moment the metal teeth would fasten on flesh. Finding the suspense unbearable, he wandered away, thinking about Malachy and Helena living in this beautiful place. Helena had talked about how they loved to watch the sunrise from the cliffs, yet he couldn't see any access to the cliff-edge. Had Ed Cromey created this barrier of gorse to keep the curious away?

Jer reached the spot he and Myra had found the night before. Now, in the daylight, he saw that strips of grass had been scraped off the bedrock. He got down on his hands and knees and retraced his painful journey between the lower branches of the gorse. Emerging, he grasped two tufts of grass and wriggled forward until his head was clear of the cliff edge. He felt dizzy and closed his eyes, taking a deep breath and letting it out slowly. When the wave of nausea had passed, he stared down, trying to make sense of what he was seeing. A shiver ran across his shoulders.

The tide had gone out during the hours he'd been asleep and now, scattered on the black rocks he could see a tangle of shapes and shades that didn't fit and knew he was looking at the remains of Malachy's house. He let go his hold on the grass and rolled onto his side so he could pull out his phone, then stretched his arms out over the void and took a few pictures. At that moment he heard the throb of a helicopter. He guessed it was a news-outfit, keen to get footage of the search for Malachy's body. Would they spot the rubble at the bottom of the cliff?

He crawled back out of the gorse and dusted himself down, his trousers dirty and shredded at the knees. He scanned the surrounding countryside and spotted a camera crew approaching from the direction of Ewart's farm, flanked by the unmistakable, burly figure of Samuel Ewart. The helicopter was now hovering directly above Jer, the tattoo of its engines reverberating around the hillside. He saw with relief that the police were hurriedly erecting a white awning to shield the murder-scene from the helicopter's baleful eye. So they'd found the body.

He waited till he saw Wright come out of the tent, talking on his phone, and approached him.

"Detective?"

Wright held his hand up, to fend him off. "*Is this your doing?*" He pointed upwards, shouting over the noise of the helicopter.

He shook his head. "*Have you found him?*"

Wright nodded. "*Time you went home, McCabe, and let us do our job!*"

He moved closer and shouted into his ear. "*Malachy's house is lying at the bottom of that cliff in a million pieces!*" He took out his phone and showed Wright the images.

Wright exhaled. "*Send me those!*" he shouted. "*And then bugger off home!*"

Jer gave a grim smile and walked away.

Back at the car, he found Nora had nodded off. The sound of the car door woke her.

"I found the house."

"You're kidding!"

"It's at the bottom of the cliff. Cromey must have demolished it and shoved it over the edge."

"Babs said that last night!"

"Did she?"

"She said Malachy was lost in the sea like his house of shame."

"Of course she did. Clever you!"

"Have you told them?" she said, indicating the police vehicles beside them.

"Yip!"

"And was that detective pissed off?"

"Totally! He told me to bugger off home and let them do their job."

"Priceless!" Her eyes gleamed.

He hesitated. "Nora, they've found Malachy's body," he whispered.

She made a sharp intake of breath, her eyes filling with tears. "That poor, poor man. At least now Helena will know where he is and find some closure."

"Do you think we could find closure too, love, for Liam?"

She met his gaze, her eyes wide. "Don't ask me to let him go, Jer. I can't do that."

He nodded, not trusting himself to speak.

"You're not going to leave us, are you?" she asked.

He took her hand and held it to his lips.

The End